The Cleansing

Also by Sam Kates

Pond Life and Other Stories

The Village of Lost Souls

That Elusive Something

The Beacon (Earth Haven: Book Two)

The Reckoning (Earth Haven: Book Three)

Strange Shores and Other Stories

Ghosts of Christmas Past & Other Dark Festive Tales

The Elevator: Book One

Jack's Tale (The Elevator: Book 2)

The Lord of the Dance (The Elevator: Book 3)

The Cleansing

Earth Haven: Book 1

Sam Kates

This is a work of fiction.
All characters appearing in this work
are products of the author's imagination.
Any resemblance to real persons,
living or dead, is purely coincidental.

First edition published December 2013
by Smithcraft Press
Second edition, March 2018
This paperback edition, June 2018

ISBN 978-1-912718-04-7

www.samkates.co.uk

To Joanne,
for putting up with a husband
often lost in imaginary worlds

Contents

Part 1: Santa Claus is Coming to Town

Chapter One

The message washed over her like a cold wave. She gasped and sank back into the armchair, which groaned beneath her bulk. She closed her eyes and saw the images, still so familiar to her after all this time: ebony spires and minarets and monoliths, great glass domes peering from the constantly shifting dunes, pyramids and ziggurats, obelisks and amphitheatres, and endless deserts of dark sands gleaming faintly in the baleful light of a dying sun.

She gasped again when she saw the craft: vaster than a mountain range, blacker than night, sleeker than an otter's hide. It was emerging from the desert floor, the sands boiling and parting; she could almost hear the slithering sound the sand made as it cascaded off the smooth sides of the craft.

Her jaw set into a determined line and she opened her eyes. At last, they were coming.

It was time for her to send a message of her own.

The armchair creaked and complained, then sighed as she pulled herself upright. From habit—there was nobody before whom she had to make herself presentable—she smoothed down her housecoat and walked in a rolling gait across the apartment to the work station upon which stood her computer.

She eased herself into the chair that she'd had custom made; it supported her weight without so much as a creak. The work station stood before a picture window that looked out over Central Park. While she waited for the computer to boot up, she stared down at the people braving the December cold. Couples strolled beneath the weak morning sun, muffled and gloved and hooded against the biting winter breeze. Long-coated businessmen strode purposefully, clutching briefcases or portfolios, intent on reaching the cosy sanctuaries of their plush offices on Fifth or Madison. The occasional fitness enthusiast in jogging bottoms and sweat shirt bounded by. A chattering kindergarten class snaked along the paths, the children in woolly hats and gloves, the cold failing to douse their excitement at the field trip.

She watched this snapshot of humanity and for a moment, only a moment, felt a pang of sorrow. Her broad brow wrinkled into a frown and she shook her head to clear it. This was no time for regrets.

Returning her attention to the computer, she opened her e-mail application. The message had already been written. It had sat in her drafts folder for years, since she had first decided that e-mail would be a far simpler, relatively effortless way to spread the word. Of course, not every intended recipient of the message would have e-mail access. Even with today's blanket coverage, some remote corners of the globe were out of reach or were blocked from communication with the outside world by isolationist governments. She had another method of reaching them; a method that would cost her a great deal of mental energy, but she was prepared. She had been prepared for many years.

She opened the message from the drafts folder. It was simple, only four short sentences: *They are coming. Begin immediately. Mercy is not an option. Acknowledge.*

The e-mail was set up to be sent to almost five thousand addresses, addresses that she had painstakingly kept up to date.

Her right hand clutched the mouse, moving the cursor over the send button. Her index finger hovered over the left-click button of the mouse while she hesitated.

She allowed herself one more glance out of the window, at the people moving through the Park, and was powerless to prevent a profound look of sadness from moving across her face like a dark shadow.

Again she shook herself and her features hardened. Looking back at the computer screen, she pressed the send button.

Mankind's fate was thus sealed by the click of a mouse.

Three thousand miles or so across the Atlantic Ocean, Tom Evans glanced up at the clock on the classroom wall. Ten past three.

He rose to his feet and stepped around the desk. Leaning back against it, he clapped his hands.

"Everybody! Pay attention, please!"

Twenty pairs of eyes turned towards him, two of them belonging to his teaching assistants. That was the beauty of teaching in a village school: manageable class sizes.

"Right, then," said Tom. "As you know, children, from all the chocolates you've been eating every morning from your Advent calendars before coming to school, we're well into December." One or two children giggled and Tom smiled. "There are only two weeks left in school before we break up for the Christmas holidays. So, on Monday, we'll be starting rehearsals for the Nativity."

A murmur rippled through the class as children turned to each other and grinned or whispered excitedly.

Tom clapped his hands once more and the children all stared up at him raptly.

"Miss Jones and Mr Davies—" Tom nodded towards his teaching assistants "—will be helping me decide which parts you'll all be playing. There's Mary and Joseph, and the kings and shepherds, and angels, even the star."

"Mr Evans… sir?"

"Yes, James?"

"Sir, can I be the baby Jesus? Sir, please?"

Hands shot into the air as other children vied to stake their claims.

"Sorry, James, but the baby Jesus is the one part that nobody will have." Tom grinned wryly at his teaching assistants, recalling last year's Nativity. The way that Mary had swung the baby Jesus by the legs, clonking His head on the manger, even dropping Him once or twice, had ensured that the part of the holy babe would always have to be played by a doll. "Hands down, everybody. You'll all get a part, I promise."

Tom glanced again at the clock.

"Your mums and dads will be outside waiting to take you home so pack away quietly. Miss Jones and Mr Davies will help to make sure all your things go away into your trays. Oh, and one last thing. Shush for one second, please…" He held up a hand and the bustling ceased. "A few of you have been away from school with coughs and colds and flu, but I want you all fit and healthy to make this year's Nativity the best one yet. So, no playing outside this weekend unless you're wrapped up warmly. I don't want anybody catching chills and falling ill, okay?"

"Yes, Mr Evans," the class chorused.

"Good! See you all on Monday, bright and breezy."

On the other side of the world, darkness had long fallen in Sydney. The heat of the day had faded with the light, but the night breeze was balmy.

Troy Bishop lay on his bed, naked, covers thrown back, resting. Not sleeping, for he rarely felt the need to sleep. Indeed, it was only habit and boredom that drove him to inertness on this night; the day had been so filled with life-regenerating sunlight that he felt bursting with energy, like a fully charged battery. He experienced the same problem each summer and had learned that he shouldn't expend that energy merely for the sake of it. He sometimes became reckless with the joy of renewal and allowed that joy to overcome the restraint that usually kept him from indulging in his greatest and darkest pleasure. Also his most dangerous pleasure.

So he lay still, listening to the sounds of the city through the open window and idly watching the curtain sway in the warm breeze. When his phone pinged and the screen lit up to announce a message received, he didn't turn to it immediately. He had been waiting so many years, so many hopes had been dashed, that he had stopped anticipating the only message that he yearned to receive.

By the time he languidly turned onto his side and stretched out one hand to retrieve the phone from the bedside cabinet, its screen had darkened. He turned onto his back and held the phone above him while he pressed a button to relight the screen. When he saw who the message was from, he sat bolt upright and a low whistle escaped his lips.

"Milandra," he breathed. "At last."

He quickly opened and read the message. His tanned features twisted into a grin that contained no humour. The grin of a wolf.

"Mercy is not an option?" Bishop snorted. "As if *I* need to be told that…"

In downtown Los Angeles, the background hum of traffic increased as the rush hour began in earnest. Diane Heidler had only recently moved from Beverly Hills and had not yet grown accustomed to the noisier environment. Traffic was much heavier here, even outside the rush hours, the strident klaxons and wails of emergency vehicles more prevalent. She had even heard the occasional sounds of gunfire while she lay awake in the small hours.

Diane had chosen to move after growing bored with the opulence of the Hills and what she considered the plasticity of its people. She was becoming increasingly fed up with L.A. in general and was considering moving further south, maybe to San Diego. She had already tried the north; had lived for many years in San Francisco, watching it grow and burn and grow again.

But she couldn't leave California; it was her area, her responsibility when the time came, though another shared the responsibility. He lived in Sacramento and would take care of the northern part of the state before pushing into Oregon. Sometimes she could sense him.

Diane would look after the southern half of the state and would then head east towards Las Vegas, taking a winding, circuitous route to take in as many townships and smaller settlements along the way as she was equipped to handle.

It wasn't only boredom that had driven Diane to move

downtown. Restlessness had grown in her of late. A restlessness that had to do with more than the tedium of her friendless, joyless existence. A sense of urgency was growing inside her; a sensation she had felt before, but not for many, many years. Something momentous was about to happen, she knew, without knowing how she knew.

It therefore did not come as a huge surprise when her laptop made a sound like a light hammer blow on a tin bathtub that signalled the receipt of a message.

Diane rose from the settee where she was sipping a morning coffee and strode across the small living area of her apartment to where her laptop sat on a leather-topped desk. She opened and read the message.

Expressionless, she stared at the screen for a few moments. She didn't know how to feel so she felt nothing. She sent a response to the message; one word.

She finished her coffee before starting to pack.

All around the globe, in most major cities, in many major towns and in various places in between, in almost five thousand locations all told, home computers and laptops and smart phones and pagers bleeped, pinged, flashed, vibrated or buzzed to signify that a message had been received.

Not every recipient was within earshot of the receiving medium; not every medium was turned on; not every message was received instantly it was sent: some had to be routed through a network of servers before reaching their destinations. But they all would arrive and be read within seven hours of Milandra pressing the send button.

Almost without exception, every recipient responded to the message within minutes of receiving it. Almost.

Chapter Two

The large woman whose apartment overlooked Central Park in midtown Manhattan had only a first name. She had never needed a surname and so had never taken one. Though wealthy beyond measure, she held no bank accounts. Though she owned this swish apartment and another, equally salubrious, in Palm Beach, Florida, she was not named in any deeds or land transactions. She had no social security number or driving licence. Though widely travelled, she held no passport. National authorities were not aware that she existed.

She spent most of the winters in Florida, only returning to New York for the two weeks or so leading up to Christmas. There was something about Christmas that fascinated her. Not the religious significance or mythological aspect, but the spirituality that she sensed at this time of year; the general feeling of being part of something bigger, something more significant, more *cosmic*, that was shared by people of all races, religions and creeds. This sensation was stronger in the massed humanity of New York City than in Florida and attracted her back to the city at Christmas year after year. It reminded her of home. Of course, she also sensed the underlying cynicism, the desire to make a fast buck, the despair and loneliness that came to the fore during this season. Strangely, this too attracted her, making her marvel at the contradictions in mankind. She also wondered at herself; whether she was growing soft and sentimental. She could not afford to indulge such weaknesses.

Within seconds of sending the e-mail around the world, she started to receive replies. They were terse and along similar lines: *Acknowledged and complying* or *Message received and understood* or *Will action immediately*.

For thirty minutes, she sat in front of the computer and read each response, her face set grim. Only a couple of the replies gave her any pause. One was from California; only a one-word reply:

Obeisance. Her eyes narrowed slightly while she stared at that word; for some reason that she could not put her finger on, it caused her a little disquiet.

Then she read the response from Sydney in Australia and her frown deepened. The message was from Troy Bishop: *Yes! At long last! It will be my great and undiluted pleasure to begin at once. Whoo-hoo!!!* The last thing that Milandra expected or wanted was for anyone to derive pleasure from what they were about to do. She made a mental note to keep an eye on Bishop.

The replies came thick and fast. The computer had been programmed to check each response against the addresses to which the original message had been sent and display at the side of the screen a list of recipients who had not yet responded. While her inbox rapidly filled, that list grew shorter.

Milandra eased her bulk from the computer chair and moved back to her favourite armchair, again causing it to creak ominously when she settled into it. She pulled her cell phone from the pocket of her housecoat and speed-dialled a number. It rang once before being answered.

"Milandra?" The voice was deep and resonant, the accent cultured.

"Jason, listen. I've been contacted. They are coming. It is in motion."

She heard a deep intake of breath and waited. He did not disappoint her.

"Okay," said Jason. "I'll contact the others. We'll stock up on perishables. We'll be with you by lunchtime."

"Yes," she said and broke the connection.

She smiled, gratified by his reaction. No questioning whether she was sure; no panicking; no superfluous words. When she had chosen Jason Grant to be her immediate right-hand man, she had chosen well.

Grant was one of four of what she liked to refer to as her 'Deputies'. He would now be contacting the other three and they would go shopping for fruit, vegetables, dairy products and other short-to-mid-term perishable items. In addition to the refrigerator she had for everyday use, the kitchen in her apartment contained two industrial-sized refrigerators and freezers for the very purpose of storing all this produce that the Deputies would shortly be bringing. Her villa in Florida had a custom-built walk-in refrigerator for the same reason, though it would never now be employed for this purpose.

Milandra remained in the armchair, listening to the pinging of the computer as more responses arrived. Even through the triple-glazing she could hear the faint sounds of New York on a December morning: the dull thrum of traffic; the honk of horns and squeal of brakes; a distant siren; a muffled shout. The rumble and grumble of a city alive and seething.

Another look of deep sorrow creased her face.

Tom and his teaching assistants bustled about the classroom straightening furniture, washing paint pots and brushes, feeding and watering guinea pigs, all the while chatting about the Nativity and which child should play which part.

By four o'clock, they were almost finished.

"Any plans for the weekend, you two?" Tom asked.

"I'm meeting up with some old school friends tonight," said Mark Davies. "Not seen them in a while so it'll be good to catch up."

"And a couple of pints while you're at it?"

"Oh, one or two." Mark returned Tom's grin.

"What about you, Lisa?"

"Um, nothing much tonight," said Lisa Jones. "A spot of Christmas shopping in Cardiff tomorrow and…" She paused, cheeks dimpling as she smiled, green eyes twinkling mischievously. "Tomorrow night I have a tryst planned with my secret lover."

Tom felt colour flare in his cheeks and hoped that Mark hadn't noticed.

"Oh," he said. "Well, good. Good for you. Anyway…" He

made a show of consulting his watch, momentarily forgetting about the wall clock. "Anyway, Mark, why don't you get off? There's nothing much left to do and Lisa and I can finish up. Since you're the only one going anywhere tonight…"

"Okay," said Mark. "Cool. Have a great weekend, folks. Don't do anything I wouldn't."

Mark grabbed his coat from the row of pegs near the door and shrugged it on as he left. Lisa went to the door and glanced out into the corridor. She walked back to Tom and wrapped her arms around his neck.

"Mmm," she murmured. "Can't wait for tomorrow night, Mr Evans."

"Me, neither," said Tom. He placed a kiss on her nose, but as she tilted her head to bring her lips towards his, he pulled back, unwrapping her arms. "Wait until tomorrow, Miss Jones."

Lisa folded her arms and pretended to pout. "I wish we could go out," she said, "instead of having to skulk away as if we're doing something wrong."

Tom sighed. "We've been through this. We can't risk being seen. Not until we've told Ross the Boss. It has to come from us, or from me anyway. If he were to hear about us from someone else…" Tom shuddered.

Mr Ross was the headmaster of Penmawr Primary School. Sometimes jovial but more often crusty, he was a stickler for doing things the right way and it didn't pay to get onto his wrong side. Having a relationship with one of his teaching assistants would, Tom reckoned, very much get him onto the wrong side of Ross.

"Then let's tell him," insisted Lisa. "Before the staff party. Then we can go to the party, and leave it, together."

Tom grimaced. "The party's only two weeks away." He breathed out heavily. "Oh, cripes! Yeah, I'll tell him next week."

"Why not now?"

Tom didn't have a good answer. Lisa was right: they weren't doing anything wrong. They were both single, both adults in their twenties, Tom at twenty-seven Lisa's senior by three years. They weren't breaking any hard-and-fast rules, but he knew that Ross would frown upon a classroom relationship. He had seen Ross beetle his bushy brows and didn't relish being on the receiving end.

He shrugged. "Next week? Please? I need to psych myself up."

Lisa laughed. "Okay. I don't think he's all that bad, you know. Bark worse than his bite, I reckon."

"He'll still insist that you change classes."

It was Lisa's turn to shrug. "I know." She glanced around the classroom. "I'll miss the reception kids…" She smiled. "Though not their little accidents. Still, most of them are toilet-trained now." Her expression grew serious. "I'll miss being with you throughout the day. But if it means we can be seen together the rest of the time, it'll be worth it."

Tom nodded. "Yes. It will."

Troy Bishop dressed simply: canvas cargo shorts with deep pockets, tee-shirt and rubber deck shoes.

He stepped to the wall in his lounge, the exterior wall, made of solid brick and breeze block. He swung aside the print of Munch's *The Scream* to reveal the sturdy-looking safe built into the wall. His hands shook a little when he spun the safe's dial, and he had to reset it and start again, forcing his breathing to slow down and his hands to steady.

This time he spun truly and the safe clicked open.

Bishop reached in and withdrew a silvery-metal canister that glinted in the moonlight entering his apartment through the uncurtained windows. In that pale, milky light, he imagined the canister to be a futuristic artillery shell for some sci-fi heavy-duty plasma weapon. In less fanciful moments, he thought it resembled a sleek vacuum flask.

He carried it to his desk, holding it carefully like an overfilled glass that might spill. He set the canister down and sat before it, his bearing as tense as taut wire.

Quickly at first, then forcing his hands to slow, he reached for the top of the canister and unscrewed the lid. As it came loose, internal pressure released with a low hiss and Bishop smelt an aroma, dark and sweet like scalding caramel.

He pulled the lid aside—it remained attached to the body of the canister by a length of black polymer plastic. They had not been permitted to open the canister before now to avoid the risk of contaminating and harming the efficacy of the contents; this was the first glimpse he'd had of the interior of the canister.

There wasn't a great deal to see. Just below the lip of the canister's exposed neck lay a silvery disc that filled the gap. Set into the disc were two shallow grooves, forming a raised portion between them which could be gripped by thumb and forefinger. On the smooth metallic surface on either side of the grooves was engraved in small but clear block capitals: CAUTION: KEEP UPRIGHT AND OPEN ONLY IN CALM, DRY CONDITIONS.

Bishop did not feel calm—excitement bubbled below the surface like a geyser readying to spout—but he guessed the engraved admonishment referred to the environment in which the canister was being opened, not to the condition of the person opening it.

He reached forward, grasping the raised portion of the disc with his right thumb and forefinger. With his left hand he tightly gripped the canister, the surface cold and smooth against his palm. He twisted the disc.

It turned with surprising ease, like a freshly-oiled wing-nut. Three complete turns and another hiss of releasing pressure. Another waft of sweet darkness. Half a turn more and he was able to lift the disc away. He placed it carefully to one side and pulled the canister closer until, by craning forward, he could peer inside.

Bishop's apartment was equipped with all modern conveniences including, of course, electric lighting, but he rarely turned the lights on at night. He was therefore accustomed to darkness and had developed a highly-tuned night vision. The ambient moonlight amply illuminated the interior of the canister for him to clearly see what it contained.

Earlier versions of the canister had been replaced every few years as their contents were upgraded. This canister had been in his possession, locked away in the safe, for around eighteen months. During that time, the contents had settled and their surface now lay about an inch below where the disc had been.

That surface resembled a smooth, circular expanse of creamy-white chalk. If the person gazing in didn't know better, he would think that the contents were solid and could be coaxed out of the canister, by turning it upside down and tapping its base, in a cylindrical rod. But Bishop knew better.

He slowly lowered his right index finger into the canister until it met the creamy surface… and continued through it. He pressed his finger down for maybe an inch, then withdrew it. The top of his finger down to the second knuckle was coated in a creamy powder, so fine it was almost translucent, each grain too minuscule to be identified individually.

Bishop turned his finger, admiring the silkiness of the powdery coating, able to make out the cuticle of his nail through it.

He grinned once more, his tongue lolling out to wet his lips, almost slavering. That and the moonlight combined to make him appear more lupine than ever.

Bishop moved his hand over the canister and used his thumb to flake away the powder on his finger. It came away easily, like chalk dust, and fell back into the canister in a fine drizzle.

Abruptly he stood. He strode into the kitchen and extracted a large sandwich bag from a drawer: a polythene bag, the type that self-seals. He unsealed the bag and shook it, making it billow as it filled with air, before moving back to the desk. Forcing himself to move deliberately, he turned the bag and placed its open end over the top of the flask. Carefully—he didn't want to waste any—he slowly upended the canister, keeping the bag in close contact with the canister's smooth sides. Gently, oh so gently, he shook the canister to discharge the creamy powder into the bag. When he judged that the bag was three-quarters full, he righted the canister, making sure that the bag also remained upright while it slid off.

He placed the canister carefully to one side, expelled the remaining air from the bag and sealed the opening. Next came the most risky part of the process; the part where, if he acted hastily or impatiently, the bag might tear.

Slowly, slowly, slowly, he eased the bag into the front left-hand pocket of his cargo shorts. Tapping gently at the sides of the bag with his left hand, while maintaining a sure grip on it with his right, he was able to ease the bag in without mishap. He heaved a long sigh. Since he had been careful about not overfilling it, the bag fitted inside the pocket comfortably, not making any strange bulges that might attract unwanted attention.

Around half of the canister's contents had been transferred to the bag. Bishop replaced the disc into the neck of the canister and fastened it tightly. Then he added the lid and screwed that on firmly, too.

Grabbing his keys, he almost bolted from the apartment, only pausing to lock the door securely behind him. In the lift on the way down to the lobby, he reached into his pocket and undid the seal on the sandwich bag sufficiently so that he could dip his fingers in.

By the time the lift stopped, the wolfish grin had returned.

The morning rush hour was in full swing in downtown Los Angeles when Diane Heidler shrugged the knapsack onto her back. It didn't contain much: a change of clothes, a bottle of water and a few toiletries. She could buy whatever else she needed on her travels. Money wouldn't be a problem.

She paused at the doorway and glanced back at the apartment. The laptop stood, screen open, on the desk. Diane had no further use for it. She had deleted the message from Milandra and her response, and disabled the internet connection. If a neighbour wandered in and wanted to take it, they were welcome to it and anything else she was leaving behind. She turned her back on the apartment and walked out, leaving the door wide open behind her.

Diane caught a bus uptown to her bank. She grabbed a coffee from a nearby Starbucks while she waited for the branch to open. If there was one vice Diane possessed, it was an over-fondness for coffee. Caffeine did not stimulate her. On the contrary, it had a soporific effect, calming her thoughts, dampening her emotions, making existence more bearable.

She was the first customer through the doors of the bank when it opened.

Firstly, she approached the cashing desk where she arranged to transfer all funds from her savings account to her checking account.

"Expecting some major expenditure, Miss Heidler?" the cashier enquired.

"Mmm, something like that," she replied in what she hoped was a non-committal tone that would discourage further chat.

Secondly, Diane cashed a cheque for twenty-thousand dollars. The cashier raised one eyebrow but made no comment. Diane stuffed the bills into her knapsack.

Thirdly, she arranged to close her safety deposit box. She was shown into the room off the rear of the banking hall that contained small curtained cubicles where deposit boxes could be opened in privacy. Her box was brought to her by a smiling clerk, who placed it on the table in a cubicle and drew the curtain closed as he left her alone.

Diane withdrew a small brass key from a pocket of her jeans and inserted it into the lock on the front of the box. She turned it and lifted the lid.

There was only one item inside: a silvery, metallic canister, a little like a vacuum flask.

Diane hefted the canister in one hand, considering its weight. About the same as a bag of sugar, she guessed. Then she placed it in her knapsack on top of the money, turned and walked out.

There seemed little point in closing the lid of the safety deposit box or removing the key, so she didn't bother.

~ ~ ~

Similar scenarios played themselves out in almost five thousand towns and cities throughout the world. From Reykjavik to Wellington, Beijing to Cape Town, St Petersburg to Mumbai, an e-mail was received and replied to. The recipients recovered from their places of safe-keeping silvery metallic canisters resembling vacuum flasks. Then, canisters or only their creamy, powdery contents in their possession, the recipients left their places of abode and went to work.

All except one.

Chapter Three

In a village west of Cardiff, at the edge of the South Wales coal field, less than five miles from the village where Tom Evans was tidying his classroom ready for the weekend, a mobile phone played a jingle that signified the receipt of an e-mail.

The phone sat on top of an old oak dresser in the main living area of the tiny miner's cottage. Two doorways led off the living area: the peeling front door that opened directly onto the street; a curtained doorway at the rear that led into a small kitchenette. A ramshackle staircase led from the living area to the basic bathroom, and bedroom large enough for a single bed and slim wardrobe.

Aside from the dresser, the only other furniture in the downstairs living area was a threadbare two-seater settee, a basic television stand and, upon it, an incongruous, state-of-the-art 36-inch plasma television.

Peter Ronstadt, who occupied the sagging settee, could afford something—almost anything—much grander, but the cottage suited him. He had rented it three months previously, complete with furniture. The only change he had made was to add the television and satellite box which sat on the lower shelf of the TV stand.

He picked up the remote lying on the settee next to him and switched off the television. He had been enjoying an afternoon quiz show, but forgot about it the moment the phone sounded.

For a few moments he sat where he was. In the silence created by switching off the television, other noises started to intrude: chattering children walking past the window on their way home from school; car engines straining while they climbed the steep hill; the drip drip drip of the kitchen tap; the sizzle and crack of the log fire in the grate opposite the settee.

Peter didn't leap to his feet to read the e-mail. He knew who it was from—only one person knew his telephone number—and he had a fair idea what it would say. His gaze flickered involuntarily to the ceiling. Above, crammed under his bed, was a battered suitcase. Inside the case, wrapped in an old flannelette shirt, was a silvery canister.

It was already growing dark. The neighbouring houses in the street were larger and more modern than the cottage Peter occupied. The other cottages that had once also lined the road were long-gone, along with the mining industry they had serviced. Peter had no idea why his cottage had been allowed to remain, set slightly away from the bigger houses like a disgraced child. He had meant to discover the cottage's history, to give himself something to do as much as anything, but hadn't yet got around to it. He didn't suppose it mattered now.

Soon the other houses would light up when their owners switched on the fairy lights that adorned the Christmas trees standing proudly in front windows and porches, when candle arches were illuminated, when blue and white plastic icicles dangling from eaves and window sills were turned on.

Peter sighed heavily and rose slowly to his feet. He took two or three steps to the dresser, reached for the phone and read the message. A little unsteady on his feet, he stepped back to the settee and sank into it.

He had known this moment would come. He had known, when it came, that he would have to decide. Rather, he had already made the decision, deep inside where his true convictions nestled, but had put off admitting it to himself. He could delay no longer.

"No," he murmured. Then, a little louder: "No. I won't do it. I *can't* do it."

He looked down at the phone in his hand and frowned. He deleted Milandra's message, then turned the phone over. Grunting a little with concentration, he fiddled at the plastic cover with his fingernails until he managed to remove it. Again with a little effort—his fingernails weren't long enough to easily fit into tight spaces—he prised up the battery and placed it on the settee. Clutching the phone, he rose once more to his feet. This time there was no trace of unsteadiness.

He crossed quickly to the hearth and flung the phone into the flames.

Troy Bishop had entered the lift and descended to the lobby of the apartment block, powder in pocket, within thirty minutes of receiving Milandra's message. When he stepped out of the lift, he almost collided with the man waiting to get in. It was someone he vaguely recognised: another tenant who lived in one of the cheaper apartments on a floor below Bishop's.

Ordinarily, Bishop would not have favoured him with a second glance. But tonight was different. Bishop stopped outside the lift entrance, blocking the man's path, and regarded him. The man was in his early thirties. His lower eyelids looked heavy and dark, his expression a little vague. He returned Bishop's gaze with no sign of interest.

"All right, mate?" Bishop said.

"Hmm? Um, yes, suppose so." The man tried a smile, but it seemed half-hearted and quickly faded.

Bishop thrust his left hand into his pocket and poked his middle finger into the powder.

"Hey, mate," he said, withdrawing his hand and holding it, middle finger extended, to the man's face. "Take a whiff of that. It's a new talc I just had from my girlfriend. It's kind of different, you know?" Bishop moved his finger until it was under the man's nose. He nodded his head and smiled encouragingly.

If the man felt any alarm or unease, nothing showed in his expression. If he wondered why Bishop should be walking around with talc in his pocket, he didn't express it. If anything, his eyes had grown more hooded and he looked ready to fall asleep where he stood. As though barely aware of his actions, the man inhaled quickly through his nose in a somnambulistic snort.

"Ngh," he muttered. "Toffee."

Bishop nodded and grinned. "That's right, mate. Toffee!" He

stepped aside to allow the man to enter the lift and clapped him on the shoulder while he shuffled past. Bishop watched the lift door close, the grin never leaving his face or reaching his eyes.

Then he turned and walked jauntily across the lobby to the exit. He let himself out of the building, rubbing the powdered finger onto the door handle, and headed into the city.

A few blocks away from the bank, Diane Heidler came across a small park with one corner devoted to a children's play area. She entered and sat on a bench inside the entrance. The park was edged with trees that would in summer provide leafy shade from the dry heat of the day. Now the trees stood forlorn and skeletal beneath a gloomy December sky. It hadn't rained for a few days. That might soon change, Diane thought. It probably explained why nobody else was in the park.

She knew what the canister contained and didn't want to be opening it in rain. She pulled the knapsack onto her lap and opened the zip. The canister lay within, nestling on crisp dollar bills. She stood it upright, keeping it within the knapsack to shield it from the light breeze, and held it tight with her left hand while she unscrewed the lid with her right.

With a slight hiss, the lid came away and she allowed it to drop to one side, though it remained attached by a black plastic strip. She quickly unscrewed the disc that covered the neck of the canister. With another small exhalation of air, the disc came free. Tapping it on the rim to shake off any clinging dust, she removed it and placed it on the bench by her side. As Bishop had done a couple of hours earlier on the opposite side of the globe, she dipped a finger into the canister, then withdrew it and held it up for inspection.

The powder covered the top half of her finger like cement, except that this powder wasn't grey. In the daylight it seemed almost colourless, translucent as water. In strong sunlight it would be all but invisible. She turned her finger this way and that, seeing the occasional flake lift away to be immediately lost on the breeze. Most of the powder, however, remained on her finger, clinging to it like pollen to a bee's leg. It had been designed this way.

Diane moved her hand back to the top of the canister and rubbed at her index finger with her thumb. Although the powder could not be easily dislodged by moving air, it readily dropped away under the friction of her thumb. She nodded, satisfied.

She changed grips, using her right hand to hold the canister, and lowered her left hand towards the opening.

Anyone describing Diane's physical appearance would use words like 'dainty' and 'petite'. Her hands were no exception. Fine-boned and narrow, they, like the rest of her, showed no signs of her age.

By pulling her left thumb in towards her little finger, bringing all five digits together in a tight cluster, she was able to comfortably lower her entire hand into the body of the canister. She thrust it down, deep into the powder, wiggling her fingers a little, covering her hand to the wrist. While she withdrew it, she continued to wiggle her fingers to dislodge any excess.

Avoiding touching anything with her left hand, she placed the canister between her left arm and chest. Clutching it tightly under her arm, she used her right hand to replace the disc and lid. Happy that the canister's contents were secure, she dropped the silvery flask back into the knapsack and rezipped it. Still only using her right hand, she shrugged the knapsack over her shoulder.

One corner of the park was taken up with the children's play area. A slide, two sets of swings, a merry-go-round made of wood with a running board and steel arms for clinging onto while it whirled around.

Diane walked over to the play area, stopping first by the merry-go-round. She stretched out her left hand and touched one of the cold steel arms. The mechanism was well-maintained and the merry-go-round began to turn easily. She moved her hand to the next steel arm and touched that, too, making the ride turn a little faster. She repeated the process, touching each arm with her left hand, before allowing the ride to ease gently to a standstill.

First glancing around to make sure she was still alone, she peered closely at one of the steel arms. She could see smears of the powder where her fingers had brushed the metal, but only because she knew they were there. Each smear was faint and almost transparent, even in this gloomy light. She doubted that anybody else would even notice them; even if they did, she doubted whether they would cause any concern. Not yet, anyway.

Next she walked to the slide and ran the back of her left hand over the metal handrails that children used to help them climb the steps. Again, the powdery residue that she smeared on the metal was barely discernible to a casual glance.

Finally she moved to the swings and ran her fingers along the guard rails that younger children would cling to while they swung, allowing the chains of the swings for older children to slide between her fingers, removing the powder that lay in the gaps. She stopped at the last swing and sat, setting it in motion with graceful movements of her slim legs, before allowing the swing to slow of its own accord. She stared out at the city, barely aware of the noise of traffic and distant cries of children in some school yard.

The breeze freshened and she clutched her jacket more tightly to her. A light shower should have little effect on her handiwork. More persistent rain or a heavy downpour may undo it, but it rarely rained heavily in L.A., even in December.

A young woman entered the park, clutching the hand of a child of about three or four. The child was clad in a padded green anorak and matching woolly hat with ear flaps secured by a ribbon tied beneath his chin. He tugged at his mother's hand, eager to reach the slide.

Diane watched the child ascend the steps to the top of the slide under the alert eye of the woman, tightly gripping the handrail as he climbed. He reached the top and clambered awkwardly—as though he wasn't accustomed to being hampered by an anorak—onto his bottom. Before he pushed off, the boy wiped the palm of his hand across his nose.

"Jarod!" the woman called sharply. "How many times do I have to tell you? Don't use your hands to wipe your nose."

Jarod pushed himself off and swooped down the slide, almost shooting off the end but managing to arrest his forward motion in time by planting his legs either side of the chute. He staggered to a halt in a series of short, stuttering steps. He turned a flushed, happy face towards his mother, who was by his side in an instant, wiping at his nose with a handkerchief. Then she wiped his hands before allowing him to toddle back to the steps for another go. Before replacing the handkerchief in the pocket of her coat, the woman wiped her own nose briefly.

Diane stood and left the park without a backward glance at the mother and child. She turned to the north, towards Hollywood.

She kept as far as possible to the more populated areas: pedestrian thoroughfares, shopping malls, parks. While she walked, she'd stretch out a hand from time to time and let it trail along handrails or across handles to doorways. She entered shops selling trinkets and browsed for a few minutes, picking items up and replacing them. She made purchases, extracting notes from her knapsack, fingering them as though deliberating whether or not to proceed, before handing them over. Her purchases she deposited into the next litter bin she passed.

Occasionally she'd stop and rummage in her knapsack, thrusting her hands deep inside, fiddling with something before continuing on her way. She passed a homeless beggar and paused to deposit some coins into his outstretched fingers.

It took her a couple of hours to reach Hollywood. After visiting the Chinese Theatre and placing her powdered hands into the prints of the stars, she stopped in a bistro to eat, borrowing the salt cellar from an adjoining table and returning it to be used by the family of diners seated there. She made sure she used the pepper pot that was on her table, though she disliked the flavour of pepper. Again she paid with well-handled cash.

A light shower started when she left the bistro. It didn't daunt her. She turned west, towards Beverly Hills. She looked forward to leaving her mark there.

The air in Central Park was cold and crisp, making Milandra's breath billow while she walked. She breathed easily, in spite of her bulk and the frosty weather. She didn't intend going far, but she felt the need to take in the winter air and feel the sun, however weak, on her head before the Deputies arrived. She didn't think they would allow her to leave the apartment for the next few weeks.

She strolled south in that peculiar rolling gait, like a ship in a heavy swell, past Strawberry Fields, and chose a bench within sight of the park entrance where the horse and carts were plying their trade to the never-ending streams of tourists. Tourists that would likely be leaving within a day or two or three, returning to their homes all over the world.

It was mid-morning and the park was, as always, busy. Only heavy, drenching rain or extreme sub-zero temperatures seemed to discourage visitors to the park, and even then the occasional hardy soul could be seen braving the conditions. Central Park had that magnetic effect, drawing visitors and natives alike.

A group of Japanese tourists walked past her bench, cameras at the ready. Milandra looked away, not wanting to catch anyone's eye and be asked to take a group photograph. Ordinarily she would have been happy to oblige, but not today, despite it being the last chance she would have to interact with ordinary people. Or perhaps because of it.

She could not shake the vague feeling of disquiet that had settled into her ancient bones since she had pressed the send button on her computer. It was not a feeling to which she was accustomed nor that she could afford. She bore a great responsibility on her shoulders and needed to remain steadfast for the sake of her remaining people. That responsibility would be relieved, perhaps even removed—she could only hope—when the others arrived, but that would not be for another five or six months. Until then, it was hers, and hers alone, to bear.

So she cast her gaze upwards at the pale, almost colourless, sky, or at the bare trees, or towards the Plaza Hotel and Fifth Avenue. Anywhere other than at the passing people.

The man approached from the north, from the direction of her apartment. She sensed him coming long before she could see him. She looked in that direction, waiting for him to come into sight. He could, she knew, sense her presence, too. When he appeared, walking briskly, arms swinging by his sides, he was scanning the path ahead, looking for her. He found her and their gazes locked. Neither made any sign of acknowledgement.

Milandra watched him approach, wondering whether he would walk on by. When he drew nearer, she could see that he carried a small knapsack on his back.

The man slowed, as though debating whether to halt. Then he walked up to her and stopped before her. He did not sit.

"Milandra?"

"Yes."

She did not require his permission, not in her position, but she sought it anyway. She probed gently, merely nudging the surface.

The man nodded and she probed a little deeper, just far enough to see it. There! A small worm of doubt, mirroring her own that she was trying so hard to quell.

Milandra withdrew and smiled up at him, a smile that hinted at shared grief.

"Be strong," she said. "We have to be strong."

"I've come from Harlem," the man said. His tone was expressionless. "Going to work my way down through Midtown, then West Village and Greenwich. Battery Park by evening and on to Staten Island."

Milandra didn't need to hear this—she knew without being told—but she let him continue.

"Tomorrow Brooklyn and Queens," he said. "Then a Greyhound to Albany."

She glanced down at his ungloved hands. His right hand

glistened faintly in the weak sunlight, the only hint of its powdery coating.

The man followed her gaze and held up his hand self-consciously. His smile was almost embarrassed, sheepish.

"The hand of God?" he muttered. He dropped his arm back to his side and stood silently for a moment.

"Well," he said. "I guess I'd best be on my way."

"Me, too," said Milandra. "I've dallied here long enough. Good luck. We'll meet again soon. At the airport."

"Yes," said the man. "Till then."

He turned away and began to stride purposefully toward the park exit. Milandra watched him until he crossed the road and was lost to sight down Seventh Avenue, heading for Times Square.

She turned her face up to the sun and closed her eyes for a few moments. Then she stood and walked back to her apartment.

Chapter Four

It had passed four o'clock by the time Troy Bishop returned to his apartment, foot-sore but exultant. The first hint of dawn was streaking the sky when he let himself in, locking the door behind him.

He extracted the polythene bag from the pocket of his shorts. Almost a third of the powder remained, which pleased him. The way it gleamed faintly in the moonlight when he rubbed it onto things had caused him to christen the powder 'Moondust'. He had already covered a large part of the city, jogging and pausing to touch things and jogging again, and would probably only use half of what remained in the bag in finishing Sydney off. That would leave him with a plentiful supply for the airport and the capital, Canberra, then every coastal settlement between Sydney and Melbourne.

By the time he reached Melbourne, half the population of Sydney would likely already be dead and the other half dying.

Bishop threw back his head and laughed long and hard. Tears of mirth squeezed helplessly from his eyes and rolled down his chiselled cheekbones. The fit of laughter became so prolonged that he had to sit on the bed until at last it passed, leaving him with an aching stomach and a general feeling of weakness that he didn't like one bit and that drove away the last vestiges of humour.

He needed to be in the sun.

He began casting around the apartment, deciding what he would need on his journey, though he preferred to think of it more as a crusade. A giggle rose unbidden in his throat and he quickly banished it.

A few changes of clothes went into a suitcase—he may have limited opportunity to buy more as he travelled. He paused at his dressing table, eyeing his collection of gold jewellery. Monetary value would soon become meaningless, but he liked the weight of the bracelet on his wrist and the pendant around his neck.

Shrugging, he put them on. Gathering the rings and watches (by Cartier, Rolex and Hublot) and chains, all gold, all satisfyingly heavy, he chucked them into the case on top of the clothes.

Into another case he packed bottles of water and foodstuff, mainly tinned and dried. The suitcases were small—his car was built for speed, not storage—but they held sufficient for his needs.

Finally, he retrieved a small holdall from the top shelf of his walk-in wardrobe. Into this went a couple more bottles of water, a few thousand dollars in cash and the silvery canister. From the drawer of his bedside table he removed a black semi-automatic pistol, a box of cartridges and a couple of spare magazines. The handle of the pistol was smooth and gleamed as though well-handled. The pistol, magazines and box of cartridges went into the bag, too, alongside the canister. The polythene bag went back into the pocket of his shorts.

He attached the shoulder strap to the holdall and hoisted it over his right shoulder. At the door, he looked back at his apartment. He liked this apartment; loved this city, despite its people. He had every intention of one day returning. Even if he couldn't, he did not want anybody else intruding on his space.

He unlocked the door, thrust it wide and moved the suitcases into the corridor. He locked the door, listening to the satisfying clunk of the deadlocks engaging.

Hefting a suitcase in each hand, he headed for the basement car park.

The telephone began to ring as Tom let himself into his house. He knew who it was; she was the only person who ever rang on the landline and the only reason he bothered to keep a handset plugged into it. He dropped his bag in the hallway and hurried through to the living room to answer it.

"Hi, Mam," he said.

"Tom? Tom? Is that you?"

"Who else calls you 'Mam'?"

"Well, no one. You're an only child."

Tom tried manfully to keep the impatience out of his voice. "Exactly."

"I'm ringing to see if you're still coming to tea."

"Yes, Mam. I told you last night I'm coming."

"Oh, good. I'm making your favourite. Sausages and mash with baked beans."

"Mmm," said Tom. He felt it impolitic to mention that this had been his favourite meal twenty years ago and his tastes had grown a little more sophisticated. "Look, I've just got in from work. I'll have a quick change and then I'll be on my way. Be with you within the hour, all right? By six at the latest."

"All right, love. Drive carefully."

"Yes, Mam."

Tom replaced the handset and sighed. He felt like collapsing in front of the television with a takeaway and bottle of wine, and that in turn made him feel guilty. Guilt: an all too frequent emotion of late when it came to dealings with his mother.

Years of working underground in the coal mines had eventually caught up with his father six months ago. His mother had still not grown used to not having her husband around—she had relied on him for virtually everything from taking care of their finances to gardening and jobs around the house. Tom helped her as much as he could: showing her how to reconcile her monthly bank statements, mowing her lawns, arranging to pay her bills by direct debits so she wouldn't have to remember to pay them. It never seemed to be enough and he sometimes resented the unspoken demands she made of him. And he then hated himself for feeling that resentment.

Tom removed his coat and went upstairs to change. Ten minutes later, he was back in his car heading towards Swansea.

His mother lived in a terraced property on the outskirts of the city. Tom had to hunt for a parking space and ended up leaving his car almost half a mile away. It was turning six when he reached his mother's front door. He had a key and could have let himself in, but part of him refused to acknowledge that he and his mother were that trusting of each other. He knocked.

She answered the door in her apron, wiping her hands in a tea towel.

"Tom! There you are," she said. "I didn't think you were coming."

Tom stepped forward and kissed her cheek, bending a little. Every time he saw her, she seemed to have shrunk a bit more, somehow diminishing before his eyes. But some things never changed: she still smelled of apples and lavender and wintergreen, though overlaid by the aroma of fried food.

"I *told* you I was coming," he said. "Traffic was heavy and I had trouble parking as usual."

He followed her through to the kitchen, leaving his coat on the end of the banister. She wouldn't let him help prepare the meal—there were some things she would never accept help with—and so he sat and watched her, drinking a cup of tea, only half-listening to her chatter about the neighbours.

After they had eaten, Tom insisted on doing the dishes while his mother wiped and put them away. Then they retired to her living room, fresh cups of tea in hand. The tang of pine resin—his mother always insisted on a real Christmas tree—brought to mind childhood Christmases.

"Mam," Tom started after they had settled in. "Have you thought any more about what we discussed?"

"What's that, love?"

"You know. Selling this place and either moving closer to me or—"

"Oh, Tom, you're not going to go on about putting me in a home again, are you?"

Tom started, almost spilling his tea. "Mam, I wasn't talking about a home!" He took a deep breath. "You don't need to go into a nursing home. You're not ill. I was talking about sheltered accommodation. You'll be sixty in February. That's old enough to go into sheltered. I've looked into it. You'll have company. Other people to talk to. And there's a warden in case you need help with anything."

"But you help me, Tom." Her voice had grown smaller and Tom had to fight to keep his tone level.

"I know, but I live twenty miles away and I work. If you fell or something… Oh, Mam, don't get upset."

She took a handkerchief from the sleeve of her jumper and dabbed at her eyes with it. Tom placed his cup and saucer on the occasional table next to his armchair and sat forward, clasping his hands between his knees.

"Look, Mam, why don't you at least arrange to see the council? Find out a bit more about it before making up your mind. I'll come with you, if you like. It'll have to be in the Christmas holidays, though."

Without lifting her head to look at him, she nodded. "Whatever you say."

"Right. Okay. That's what we'll do then. I'll ring the council on Monday during my lunch break and arrange an appointment."

When Tom drove home later, it was with a heavy heart.

Across the world, almost five thousand people with silvery canisters left faint, barely-visible, powdery hand-prints and finger-prints on handrails, door handles, pedestrian crossing buttons, hand-dryer switches in restaurant and bar restrooms, sugar cubes in bowls, cruet sets on tables, napkins in holders, park benches, telephone handsets, books in libraries, knick-knacks in shops, taxi and train and tram seats and hand straps, cans and packets on supermarket shelves, trolley handles, electronic key pads, parking meter dials… Any object that was likely to be touched by someone else.

In churches in Italy and Spain and Greece, and in countries across Latin America, powdery residue appeared on the feet of statues of saints and Madonnas and Christ on the Cross, feet that would be kissed by the faithful.

Hand-prints of the famous in Hollywood (courtesy of one Diane Heidler) and Leicester Square in London bore faint dusty traces.

In Ireland, a woman braved the stomach-churning drop of Blarney Castle, thickly coating her lips with powder while the guide's attention was elsewhere, before being helped upside down through the gap where she planted a full kiss on the Stone.

Across the world, unsuspecting people collected unnoticed particles of powder—Moondust, as Troy Bishop now called it—on fingers, palms, wrists, clothes, hair. In most cases, sooner or later, those particles would find their way into the person through their mouth or nose. There, in the moist warmth of throats and nasal passages, the particles activated.

And so it began.

On Saturday morning in Sydney, in the same apartment block from which Troy Bishop had departed almost six hours earlier, Nicky Moran awoke with a muzzy head and sore throat. He had slept solidly for nine hours, but didn't feel any the better for it.

The previous day he had worked a fourteen-hour shift as a sous chef in the upmarket, waterfront restaurant, a stone's throw from the opera house, where he had been employed for the past two years. Fourteen hours on his feet. It would be worth it if he was promoted to Head Chef when that lazy, grumpy bastard Maitland decided to retire. Or was given the push. If Nicky owned the restaurant, Maitland would have received his marching orders months ago.

Nicky wasn't working the lunchtime shift today so, after a visit to the bathroom to empty his bladder and slurp some water to ease his raspy throat, he went back to bed. Before drifting off to sleep, he replayed the incident that had occurred when he'd returned to the apartment building last night. He had only the fuzziest recollection of standing in front of the lift, wanting only to get to his apartment and fall into bed, but having his way barred by that cobber from upstairs. The one who occupied the penthouse and dripped gold whenever Nicky saw him, yet never seemed to go out to work. The one who usually didn't so much as glance at Nicky if they encountered each other in the lobby.

Oddly, Nicky seemed to recall that the man had greeted him like an old friend and asked him to smell something. Something sweet. Something that was on his finger. Very strange…

When Nicky awoke again, it was late afternoon and he had developed a tickling cough.

By the time he finished his shift in the restaurant that night, the cough had become a nagging, rasping bark and Nicky had unwittingly infected four waiters, two diners and three fellow chefs, including Head Chef Maitland. Nicky's wish for Maitland to cease to be Head Chef would come true much quicker than he had thought. Sadly, Nicky would not himself be around long enough to derive any satisfaction from the grumpy bastard's demise.

Nicky Moran was the first person in the world to become infected by what would soon become known as the Millennium Bug, so christened by some wag on a current affairs programme during the first days before the scale of the problem had begun to be truly appreciated.

If it ever was.

Peter Ronstadt watched the phone sizzle, crackle and pop, melting and blackening into running blobs of molten plastic and misshapen metal. Destroying the phone had cut off one possible method of them tracing him. If they attempted the other method, he would know about it.

Now that his decision was affirmed and accepted, he felt lighter, at ease with himself. He would play no part in what was to come. At the same time, a dark contradiction twisted inside him like a barbed hook. Although he would play no part, it would nevertheless happen; was probably already happening.

That knowledge sickened him.

He should not harbour such human feelings, but the ability to control his emotions had left him many years ago. And as that control had at first loosened and then let go, empathy and compassion had taken its place.

Peter sat back in the settee and reached inside his shirt. He drew out a heart-shaped locket attached to a fine silver chain. An onlooker might have considered the locket to belong to a woman, not a man of such muscular stature, and that onlooker would be correct to an extent: the locket had once belonged to a woman. Peter had removed it from her neck while placing a tender kiss to her cooling lips.

He flicked open the locket with practised ease. Each interior half of the locket contained a protective cover of thin glass, held in place by two tiny metal clips on each side that could be swung aside to remove the glass.

Beneath the glass on the left was a photo: a sepia-tinged image of a middle-aged woman with greying hair pulled back into a tight bun; she wore a high-necked blouse with a frilly collar like a choir boy's ruff. The photograph was necessarily small and cropped to fit into the locket, and thus details of the woman's features and expression were only suggestions. Peter only needed suggestions. One glance at her face conjured up the complete woman in his mind, from the fresh-rosehip scent of her hair to the mountain-spring tinkle of her laughter. Another glance recalled the forest-pool depths of her green eyes and the ember-warmth of her embrace.

The other half of the locket contained a curled lock of fair hair. It was her hair, snipped when she was a teenager, held safely beneath the glass ever since. Peter had often felt the urge to remove the glass and stroke the lock of hair, but resisted, afraid that it might disintegrate to dust under his caress.

"Sleep well, Megan," Peter whispered, then clicked the locket shut. He concealed it once more beneath his shirt in the thick mat of curly hair that lay within.

He turned his thoughts back to the present, to what he should do next. They would know that he had not fulfilled his part in the operation. At some point, he would have to face consequences. He did not think those consequences would be severe; at least, not fatal. All he was guilty of so far was a failure to act as he should. An omission. He doubted they would even bother coming after him. Not yet, anyway. They would be far too busy over the coming weeks and months to worry about one rotten apple. Maybe he could use that to his advantage…

Looking deeper within himself, he began to wonder: how far was he prepared to go? He recognised that he was completely powerless to affect what was going on. The non-use of that one shiny canister nestling in the suitcase under his bed would make not a scrap of difference in the overall scheme. But later, when it was over, there might be things he could do that would influence the eventual outcome. Yes, certainly things he could do. The question was, what did he want the final outcome to be?

Despite being possessed of those alien emotions of empathy, of compassion, this was a question that Peter was not yet capable of answering.

The buzzer next to the front door sounded, announcing visitors. Milandra, already aware of the approach of the Deputies, stood ready by the door. She pressed the button that would release the magnetic catch on the main entrance to the brownstone apartment building.

She waited for them to cross the lobby, call the elevator and ride up to the sixth floor. When she sensed their approach, she unlocked the door and threw it wide.

Jason Grant strode in, grinned briefly in greeting and made for the kitchen. In his brawny arms he clutched four brown, bulging bags, bearing them effortlessly as though they contained popcorn.

Close behind Grant came the other Deputies: George Wallace, slighter than Grant, carrying a grocery bag under each arm and a flight bag over his shoulder; Lavinia Cram, the beauty of the group with her olive complexion, raven hair and smouldering eyes, also carrying a grocery bag and flight bag; Simone Furlong—the Chosen—burdened with two brown bags.

All three nodded at Milandra and headed wordlessly for the kitchen. Milandra closed and locked the door, and followed them.

Nobody spoke while they unpacked the brown bags and loaded the refrigerators with fresh produce: vegetables, fruit, dairy.

Grant broke the silence. "Wallace and I will head down to the markets at dawn and load up with meat and fish."

Milandra nodded. "Get what you can carry, but don't sweat it. We've plenty of canned stuff. Enough to last us months. We should only need it for weeks."

Simone uttered a short, high-pitched titter. "Then there'll be plenty of stuff just… lying about the place."

Milandra glanced at the Chosen. "Indeed." She pushed aside the slight unease that Simone's brief hilarity had stirred within her. "Anyway, to business. We must Commune. Then we'll eat."

"One moment," said Wallace.

He reached for the flight bag he'd brought, hefted it onto a granite work surface and unzipped it. Lavinia did the same with the one she had carried in. An acrid smell of oil filled the air.

Wallace reached into the bag and withdrew an object, wrapped in a greasy cloth. He unwrapped the cloth to reveal a black, stubby submachine gun. He reached back into the bag and withdrew a magazine that he slid smoothly into the pistol grip of the weapon.

"Uzi," he said. "There's one each. Er, except for you, Milandra."

Milandra grimaced and held her hands up to her chest, palms outward. "I don't even want to touch one. They make me nervous as hell."

Lavinia reached into her bag and withdrew a pistol. "One of these each, too," she said. "Semi-automatic. Walther PPK. Like that James Bond guy."

This drew another titter from Simone. Milandra glanced

sharply at Grant, who raised his eyebrows as if to say, 'Search me'.

"Good," said Milandra, addressing Wallace and Lavinia. "But let us hope that we never need to use them. Now, please, put them away."

"But," added Grant, "keep them close to hand."

Wallace did not remove the magazine from the submachine gun, but checked that the safety was on, before stashing it back in the flight bag. Lavinia did the same with the pistol. They hefted the bags once more and carried them to the front door, leaving them on the long, narrow table that stood next to it. They left the bags unzipped.

Milandra's apartment was much larger than her needs. She tended to occupy only a small part of the living space. She had her armchair and television and computer desk all in one corner where the best of the afternoon and evening sunlight could be enjoyed through the picture window that overlooked the Park.

The larger, seldom-used portion of the living space was taken up by a six-seater oak dining table and chairs; nearby, two low-slung, Oxford-green leather sofas faced each other over a smoked-glass coffee table. An armchair in the same leather was placed at the head of the table, between the two sofas.

Milandra sat in the armchair, making the leather creak under her weight. On the sofa to her right sat Grant and Lavinia; to her left, Wallace and Simone.

Lavinia glanced to the furthest side of the room where Milandra's laptop still emitted the occasional ping.

"Replies still coming?" she asked.

"Yep," said Milandra. "They've slowed somewhat, but are still pretty steady as you can hear."

"So," said Wallace. "It's really happening."

"Yes," said Milandra. "But we still have to reach the others. The ones without internet access."

"How many?" asked Grant.

"Two hundred and forty-three," Milandra replied, without having to think about it.

Simone sighed. "Who doesn't have access to the internet these days?"

Milandra looked at her closely. Simone wasn't looking back at her; she didn't appear to be looking anywhere in particular, but gazed vacantly at a point somewhere above Grant's head, chewing on a strand of her shoulder-length, not-quite-ginger hair. To Milandra, she resembled a slightly bored, slightly ditzy teenager. Again that sense of unease that this time she found harder to ignore. She resisted the impulse to probe: she needed all her mental energy for the task they were about to perform.

Grant took it on himself to answer the Chosen's question. "Well, Simone, as I thought you knew, we have people in countries whose governments block, or make difficult, access to the outside world. Television, radio, the internet are all state-controlled or disabled or made inaccessible. Countries like North Korea and Venezuela to name but two. And many areas of the world are too remote. We have people in the frozen wastes of Alaska, Canada, Siberia, both Poles. In deserts in Africa, Asia, Australia. In the Himalayas, the Urals, the Amazonian rainforest—"

"Why, Jason?" Simone interrupted.

"Huh?"

"Why do we have people in these far-out places?" Simone's gaze turned towards Grant, and Milandra, despite the unnerving naivety of Simone's question, was relieved to see that the Chosen's expression had lost some of its vacuity, had regained some vitality.

"Well…" Grant kept his tone level, but Milandra sensed that he was struggling to keep his patience. "It's obvious why we need insiders in places like North Korea. It's so isolationist that there would be no guarantee that our, um, little surprise would ever reach it. And as for the remote regions, well, again, they are too out of the way for us to reach them indirectly—the winds may not be strong enough or blowing in the right direction; the *surprise* may prove too effective so that no carriers ever make it to those regions. And many humans populate them, albeit sparsely. In aggregate, there may be too many to risk them coming together and forming some sort of rebellion. So, our people will make sure that can't happen."

"Provided they are told to act," Milandra said. She leaned forward, making the leather creak again, and rubbed her hands briskly together. "Enough talk. It is time to Commune." She glanced at each of them in turn. "Ready?"

They all nodded and closed their eyes. Milandra closed hers… and probed.

Immediately she felt the power of the other four intellects and absorbed them into her own, melding them, forming one whole more potent than the sum of its parts.

It was not necessary that she and the Deputies join hands or form a circle or recite incantations. All that was required was the joining and the reaching out to two hundred and forty-three receptive minds dotted about the world.

Milandra *reached*… then sagged back into the armchair, her ample bosom heaving beneath the housecoat while she sucked in air.

The four Deputies leaned back in the sofas, also breathing hard. They remained that way for a few minutes, considerably longer than the thirty seconds or so that the Commune had lasted.

"Okay," said Milandra, when her breathing had grown more regular. "It is done. Now…" She smiled at her Deputies. "I'm ravenous. Let's eat."

Chapter Five

Two hundred and forty-three people, in some of the most isolated and inhospitable regions of the world, abruptly stopped whatever it was they happened to be doing. Their faces became blank as if their minds had, without warning, deserted them. Within seconds, though, awareness reappeared and they shook themselves like men and women awaking from a peculiar dream. Those who happened to be in company met the concerned looks of their companions with disarming smiles, and comments such as, "Sorry, must have drifted off there for a moment."

Two hundred and forty-three silvery metallic canisters were retrieved, either immediately or at the first opportunity to do so unobserved, and opened.

The creamy powder, which had already been distributed through much of the densely-populated areas of the planet, now began to be smeared on banisters, door knobs and so on and so forth in cities like Pyongyang and Caracas, and in scientific and military outposts in far-flung regions. The powder appeared, though barely discernibly, in the thin air of mountainside villages and on oil rigs and in military island bases and other remote communities.

Many of the two hundred and forty-three people in possession of the canisters also held positions as research and field scientists, or high-ranking military advisors and personnel—army, air and navy—or elevated civil servants and personal assistants to such. Background positions that kept them out of the limelight, but that allowed them relative freedom to move about in areas where such movements are closely monitored or restricted.

Some had become traders between or, if possessed of the necessary racial characteristics, members of remote rainforest tribes or nomadic desert dwellers or the Inuit. Others had infiltrated cults or religious communities that preferred to live in out-of-the-way places with no modern conveniences.

No sizeable human settlements escaped the contents of the canisters. No humans that came into contact with the powder, or with someone already infected, were unaffected by it.

The gun-metal grey Mazda MX-5 Roadster eased in and out of the Saturday morning traffic around the suburbs of Sydney, describing an ever-widening series of arcs centred on the harbour. Bishop had the soft top down, enjoying the sun on his face and the breeze in his hair.

He stopped frequently, dipping his hand into the bag within the holdall on the passenger seat next to him, getting out and wandering around as though to stretch his legs, touching things.

Occasionally, when he drove through built-up areas, he'd dip his hand into the bag and then raise his hand above the level of the windscreen, rubbing his fingers to dislodge the Moondust and allow the wind to whip it away to settle he knew not where, but settle it would. He laughed while he did this.

If he noticed pedestrians looking at his car, and it drew many admiring or envious glances, he waved and grinned at them. One youth, slouching along in vest and cut-off jeans, gave Bishop the finger. Bishop waved to him and laughed harder. On another day, Bishop would have been tempted to screech to a halt and have a little 'chat' with the youth, but not today. Today nothing could shake his agreeable mood.

As the morning stretched on, he made for Palm Beach and stopped for lunch at the golf club for what would probably be his last visit—he doubted he would receive an invitation to renew his membership in January. He ate heartily of freshly-caught red snapper and left an extremely generous tip, the dollar bills glistening lightly under their thin coating of Moondust.

This was the furthest point north of his crusade and now he headed south, driving past the harbour and opera house for one last time, sprinkling a little more Moondust as he went for luck. He took a quick detour to Bondi Beach where he smeared powder to be collected by the fingers of the bodies-beautiful.

By late afternoon, he was satisfied that he had deposited sufficient Moondust to ensure that nobody in the metropolitan area was likely to avoid encountering it, either directly or indirectly, unless they happened to be a reclusive health freak inhabiting a sterile environment. He had stopped at half a dozen golf clubs—he was a member of many golf and sailing clubs—for a coffee or fruit juice, tipping well and leaving near-invisible, powdery calling cards.

He left Sydney by the coastal road, driving south to Wollongong. There he took dinner and a late evening stroll. A stroll that took in some of the town's residential areas and was accompanied by much touching of handrails and pedestrian buttons and benches in parks and bus stops.

On his way back to the car, he approached three youths who were standing together beneath a street lamp, smoking cigarettes. As he drew nearer, he noticed one of them glance at him and nudge his companions. All three of them turned to face him, spread across the pavement, blocking his way.

Bishop had changed from shorts to chinos to have dinner and wore a short-sleeved shirt that he hadn't tucked into the trousers. Thrust into the waistband of the chinos, in the small of his back and hidden by the shirt tails, was the smooth-handled pistol.

His hand moved towards the pistol, then back to his side when he changed his mind. He was walking through a residential area—he could hear people talking and laughing in their gardens, enjoying the balmy night air—and the sound of gunfire would bring people running, he had no doubt. He did not want to risk being delayed.

He reached the youths and stopped a few yards away from them. The one standing in the centre was shorter than his companions, less gangly, and sneered at Bishop, who sensed immediately that this was the leader. Cow this one and the others would give no trouble.

"Good evening, fellas," said Bishop.

The leader took a step closer. "Got any spare cash, mate?" His tone was confident, cocky. Bishop almost laughed.

"Yeah, plenty," he said.

The leader's eyes widened and he glanced at his companions, who seemed a little nonplussed. He looked back at Bishop, narrowing his eyes like a gunfighter in a western film trying to face down the sheriff.

Now Bishop did laugh. He doubted that this would improve the situation, but he couldn't help himself.

The youth took another step closer. Bishop knew that he was backing the boy into a corner, forcing him to act to save face in front of his friends.

He looked at the youth and probed. He sensed the barrier: an angry, scared barrier. The boy was about to do something rash; his hands had curled into tight fists.

Bishop's left hand had been in his pocket, fingers dipped in Moondust. Now he withdrew it. He raised his hand to his mouth and blew. A puff of Moondust flew into the boy's face.

"What the— Oh man, what is that?" The youth flapped one hand in front of his face. His other hand was no longer balled into a fist.

Bishop pushed with his mind, pressing against the barrier. The boy blinked. Bishop pushed again, harder. The boy took half a step back, his gunfighter expression dissolving in confusion.

It was Bishop's turn to take a step forward. The leader stepped back again, rejoining his friends who shared his look of bewilderment. Wordlessly, they retreated to the hedge that bordered the pavement, leaving room for Bishop to continue on his way.

As he walked past them, Bishop grinned at the youths; the leader cringed.

"Evening, fellas."

Bishop grinned all the way back to the Mazda. He gunned the engine, enjoying the feeling of power.

He glanced down at the smooth-handled pistol, now settled

once more within the open holdall on the passenger seat. He was glad he had brought it with him—it was a comfort to have by his side—even though he felt it unlikely he would need again to put it to its former use. For many years, Bishop had been responsible for a trail of unexplained killings throughout New South Wales and southern Queensland. The pistol had been the tool he employed to carry out the killings—he considered them to be executions—in the majority of cases. Now and again, for variety or if he needed to be quiet, he used his bare hands. He knew how to break a man's neck from behind, but preferred to strangle his victims. That way, he could watch their expressions while they struggled vainly for breath.

The police must have connected the murders—the simplest of ballistic tests would confirm that each shooting was carried out with the same weapon—but had never launched a public man-hunt. The papers weren't full of articles damning the police for failing to catch a serial killer or lurid headlines making the killer out to be some sort of celebrity with a suitably macabre nick-name. Maybe a team of detectives *was* working on the case, but Bishop doubted they were working too hard. Apart from the ballistics, they would have very little else to go on. Bishop made sure he left no DNA calling cards. If he employed strangulation as his extermination method, he would first disable the victim's hands so no fingernails could gouge his skin. Besides, no DNA test on his tissue would give results that any human scientists would find reliable.

And he was careful in his choice of victims: usually lone vagrants, druggies or alcoholics, inhabiting the underbelly of Australia that the more affluent pretended didn't exist. If nobody cared about the victims, they wouldn't try too hard to catch the perpetrator. Or so Bishop hoped and, so far, it had proved.

Now Bishop had discovered a new method of execution, one that wasn't messy, posed no risk to him and which the victims weren't aware was happening, even as they breathed in the deadly powder. Maybe not quite the thrill of watching the victims' faces turning blue or their brains spraying from their heads, but a different sort of satisfaction. Yes, Bishop was satisfied. For now.

He grinned and gunned the engine again. He would now continue south along the coast before heading inland for the capital. He meant to reach Canberra by the morning.

In Los Angeles, a young boy by the name of Jarod, who had spent a happy morning playing with his mother in a local park, had developed a hacking cough and complained of a sore throat. Mom, while sympathetic, was herself feeling a little under the weather. Her throat felt as though it had been rubbed with powdered glass and her nose had begun to drip. She was forced to constantly wipe it, and it had become red and swollen like the nose of an alcoholic.

That afternoon, she and Jarod had infected the waitress in the coffee shop where they'd had lunch (who in turn infected the short-order cook, seven customers and her boyfriend), nineteen mothers and children in the Mothers and Toddlers Club, Jarod's grandparents who they called in to see on their way home, and three fellow bus passengers.

Meanwhile, Diane Heidler had left Beverly Hills and made her way through Century City to Santa Monica. She was footsore and heartily fed up of walking. While she sat in a beachfront coffee house, gratefully sipping a large latte with an extra shot of espresso, she decided that it was time to mobilise.

Diane did not enjoy driving. It scared her. Particularly in the traffic-choked roads of the city. But she still had a lot of ground to cover before she could leave L.A. and driving herself would be quicker than using public transport. Besides, she would need a car to reach Las Vegas. Although it would be many days before the contents of the canister lost their potency, she had the feeling that staying in L.A. for longer than necessary might turn out to be a bad move.

While she worked her way through Hollywood and Beverly

Hills, Diane had been aware of the multitude of CCTV cameras mounted on nearly every street corner and civic building; on many privately-owned properties, too. Although she imagined it would take the authorities days to suspect that the disease had been spread deliberately, if they suspected at all, it was inconceivable that nobody would think to check CCTV footage, or that she had not been captured on at least one camera reaching into her bag then trailing her fingers along things, leaving powdery smears. Even though her actions would not look suspicious to anybody watching her now, they would tell a very different story if viewed in the wake of a purposely-started plague. All the more reason not to use public transport to travel to Vegas.

Diane finished her coffee. She touched the sugar bowl and ran her fingers along the edge of the table before leaving.

The Pacific Ocean twinkled and sparkled in the late afternoon sunlight. Soon the sun would dip into the ocean and Diane doubted that she'd easily find a vehicle rental store that would still be open. But find one she would, even if it meant having to travel out to the airport. Car hire was available there almost twenty-four hours a day.

Her mind made up, she walked off in search of a cab.

Tom slept badly Friday night. He dreamed of his mother. She was walking away from him, towards a dark tunnel. No matter how his dream-self tried to catch up with her, to pull her back from the darkness, he could not gain on her. At the last, before she disappeared into blackness, before he awoke panting and perspiring, she looked back at him. Tears rolled down her face and her eyes filled with reproach.

He lay in bed, feeling his skin prickle as the sweat dried. His duvet had been kicked to the floor. He reached down to grab it and glanced at his bedside clock: 7:42.

Pulling the duvet over his cooling body, he turned to his side and closed his eyes, but it was no good. He could not shake the image of his mother stepping into that dark tunnel, and he knew that he and sleep were done with each other for the night.

With a grumbling sigh, he got up.

Downstairs, cup of tea and slice of toast in hand, he sat in front of the television and watched the news on BBC 24. It contained the usual doom and gloom about wars and murders and famines and recessions and job losses. Even the supposedly more light-hearted items didn't particularly lighten Tom's heart: the odds on a white Christmas were shortening; the race for the Christmas Number One was hotting-up with the winner of some reality show the favourite, despite the winner not even having been yet decided; medical experts were confidently predicting a flu-free winter after an extensive programme of inoculation against the most recent virulent strain.

That last item got him thinking about his mother again. He'd had a battle to persuade her to get her flu jab; a battle that he'd won, eventually, but at some cost in irritation and exasperation. He checked the time: it was after nine and he knew she would be up.

Tom picked up his mobile and called her land line. She owned a mobile—he had bought it for her two birthdays ago—but was obdurate in her refusal to learn how to use it.

The line rang and rang. Frowning, he disconnected the call.

He tried every half an hour or so throughout the morning, but did not get an answer until early afternoon.

"Yes. Hello?"

"Mam! Where've you been? I was worried."

"Who is this?"

"It's me—Tom."

"Oh, yes."

"Have you been out?"

"I've been to the shops with Betty. We had lunch at Marks'. I'm tired now."

"Look, Mam. About last night, what we talked about, you know, sheltered accommodation."

"Oh, yes?"

"Well, I've been thinking some more and maybe we should leave it for now. Get Christmas out of the way. Talk about it again next year. See how you feel then."

"Whatever you say, Tom."

Tom sighed. "Mam, I only want what's best for you. You know that, don't you?"

"Yes, love. If you say so. I'm going to have a lie down now."

"Okay. I'll ring you in the week."

"Bye."

"Bye, Mam. Oh, and…" But she had already gone.

He'd had a sudden impulse to tell her that he loved her, something that he probably hadn't said to her in more than fifteen years. He stared at his phone for a moment, before shrugging. Perhaps it was better that he hadn't; maybe she'd have felt embarrassed, or was he projecting his own discomfort onto her? Later, he would wish that he'd rung her back and spoken the words, no matter how it made either of them squirm.

Nobody spoke much during the meal, each too intent on replenishing strength. The Commune had been fleeting, but had consumed a vast amount of mental energy due to the distances it had covered.

Everyone ate heartily, except for Simone Furlong. The Chosen picked at her food, staring into space for long moments at a time.

Away with the fairies again Milandra thought, watching the girl. *She'll never gain the necessary girth with the amount she eats.* Milandra mentally shrugged. Simone had plenty of time to fill out; Milandra had no intention of relinquishing her position just yet.

Something else nagged at Milandra. While she and Grant filled the dishwasher, she mentioned it to him.

"We've lost one."

Grant blinked. "Dead?"

Milandra shook her head. "Closed his mind. Or her mind. I don't know who it is yet."

"Will we need to Commune again?"

"No, that won't be necessary." She nodded towards the desk where her computer stood. The pings as messages were received had all but ceased. "That should tell us who it is."

"I was afraid we'd lose more than one."

"So was I. Still, I'd rather have not lost any."

Grant's brow furrowed in thought. "Will we need to do something about him, or her?"

"That depends. On what they do. If they don't try to interfere…" Milandra shrugged. "If they do, well, that's an entirely different matter."

On Saturday morning, Peter caught the train into Cardiff. The steady drizzle had not deterred the Christmas shoppers. Throngs of people crowded St David's Centre and it was impossible to walk in a straight line down Queen Street due to the sheer volume of bag-laden pedestrians.

Peter visited his bank and transferred all the money in his savings account to his current account. Unlike most of his kind, he had never been interested in the acquisition of riches. Nevertheless, by most standards he was an extremely wealthy man.

He responded to the bank clerk's enquiry with a shrug and a smile.

"May as well spend it. Can't take it with you." He refrained from adding that money would soon be worthless. "Now, I need some cash and a banker's draft…"

He left the bank with a thousand pounds in twenty-pound notes in his pocket and a banker's draft for one hundred thousand pounds in favour of a car dealer on the outskirts of the city.

Peter did not often go shopping, but knew the layout of Cardiff well. He had lived in the city for many years. It would have been partly his responsibility to deposit the contents of the canister that lay under his bed around the capital's streets, concentrating on the north of the city, before heading up to

Caerphilly and Pontypridd and Merthyr Tydfil, then up through Mid Wales. Another person would deal with the city centre before heading east towards Newport and on to Chepstow.

He wondered whether the towns north of Cardiff would escape the worst of what was to come because of his lack of participation, but doubted it. Many of the people shopping and working here today would be returning to the northern valley towns, some of them carrying the infection with them. The evening would bring another contingent of folk from those towns, coming into the city by bus and train for a night out. They would awake the following morning with more than hangovers.

In fact, it was likely that many people in those towns were already infected. If the other person had acted immediately on receiving Milandra's message, the city centre would have been contaminated by the previous evening and the Friday night revellers would have taken home more than they'd bargained for.

Peter also wondered about that other person, probably now on his or her way east, perhaps even now wandering around Newport city centre. Touching things.

He felt a crazy urge to run through the streets, shouting at people not to touch anything, to get out, grab their loved ones and disappear into the remotest parts of the planet they could find. But he didn't. Even if the most likely outcome wasn't that he would be locked up as a madman, it was already too late.

Instead he made for a camping and outdoor equipment shop. His purchases included waterproof clothing, a rucksack, a pair of sturdy hiking boots and a camping stove. He stood for some minutes staring at an olive-green dome tent, debating whether to buy it. He decided not to on the basis that he should never be short of places in which to shelter and rest, and if he ever needed to disappear into some wilderness, acquiring a tent at that point should not be too difficult.

When he left the shop, he was too heavily laden to buy anything else in the city centre, though he had many more purchases in mind. They would have to wait until next week, by which time he would have a vehicle.

That couldn't wait. He found a taxi and ordered the driver to take him to the Land Rover dealer on Penarth Road. He asked the driver to wait with the meter running and left his camping purchases on the back seat of the taxi.

He entered the showroom and scanned the gleaming new vehicles. One caught his attention immediately, bronzed and glinting under the showroom lights. He walked over to it and around it, examining and admiring the sleek yet functional bodywork, waiting for the inevitable approach from a salesman. That was heralded by a polite clearing of a throat.

Peter turned and faced the young man. The salesman glanced down at Peter's shabby jeans and scuffed shoes, then back up, no doubt mentally noting the worn overcoat and generally unkempt appearance. Peter had never taken much notice of what he looked like. He wore clothes which felt comfortable and tended to wear the same things until they fell apart.

The young man cleared his throat again. "Can I help you, sir?"

"Yes," said Peter. "I'd like to buy one of these." He inclined his head towards the vehicle.

"But, sir," spluttered the young man. "It's the latest Range Rover. These *start* at seventy-one thousand pounds."

"That's for the three-litre version, I believe," said Peter. "I want a four-point-four-litre, please. Eight-gear. Four-wheel drive, naturally. V8, yes?"

"Yes, but… Sir, may I ask how you intend financing the purchase?"

"You may," said Peter. He didn't normally take pleasure in other people's discomfort, but found he was enjoying watching the young man squirm inside his Italian suit.

"Um, so how…?"

"Banker's draft," said Peter and turned back to the vehicle. "This is a four-point-four-litre, yes? Is it sold?"

"No, but—"

"I would like it fully road-tested, please," said Peter. "If they're not already, I want all-terrain tyres fitted. If it doesn't come equipped with a spare tyre—not those nonsense temporary things—then I want one fitted. I want it delivered to my home address—I'll write it down for you—on Tuesday. Full tank of fuel, please."

The salesman blinked. "Sir, I'll have to check with my manager. Um, he's in the office. I'll go and get him… um."

Peter nodded and flapped his hand as though shooing a bothersome fly. The young man scooted away.

Peter tried the door handle of the vehicle and was pleased to find it unlocked. He got into the passenger seat, hearing the unworn leather crackle satisfyingly beneath his weight, and breathed in the heady aroma of luxurious newness. He was still sitting there when the young salesman returned with an older version of himself. The older man cleared his throat.

"Good morning, sir. I understand that you are interested in purchasing this vehicle?"

Peter got out of the car. "That's right," he said.

"My assistant Justin here mentioned that you intend to pay by banker's draft?"

"Correct." Peter reached beneath his overcoat and dug his wallet from his jeans pocket. He flipped it open and extracted the draft. He unfolded it. "This should be more than adequate to cover the price and my few additional requirements. You may keep any change." He held the draft out to the man.

The manager took it and read it. His eyes widened. "Indeed, sir, this will be more than adequate. Would you like to follow me to my office? Justin, two coffees, please."

Peter smiled and followed.

Chapter Six

It starts with a tickle at the back of the throat. The tickle becomes an irritation and the throat grows sore, like a scraped knee. It becomes painful to swallow; most sufferers can only manage thin foods like soup and porridge.

The cough begins: a dry, rasping bark that irritates the throat further. The cough becomes more phlegmy, more moist, as fluids start to build in the lungs.

Eyes stream and vision grows a little blurred. The nose begins to run, freely at first but then slowing down like a brook in summer as the fluids thicken.

A slow, dull ache begins behind the eyes. Gradually, as insistent as spilled molasses, it spreads through the skull until the whole head aches and takes an effort to hold upright. Light is too bright. Crusty eyes want to close and remain closed.

Joints and muscles grow heavy. Leaden. Listlessness and lethargy steal in like squatters. When it feels as though arms and legs have become too heavy to lift, most retire to bed where they will, in the main, remain.

The cough grows more severe, more compelling, expelling thick gobbets of mucus during violent bouts. The head aches so poundingly that it feels it must burst if only to release the incessantly-building pressure. Curtains and blinds are drawn tightly shut; gaps are filled with dark tape or bin bags or towels—anything that will block the last of the light, that piercing, blinding, hating light.

Sleep is the only refuge, but not even that comes easily. Burning, icy, sweating, shivering fevers take hold, causing delirium and fitful wakefulness. Stomachs cramp while bodies muster their last defences and desperately try to eject invading organisms through whatever channels seem expedient. By now, the hosts are too weak to get out of bed for the toilet, and many slip into the last stages lying in their own shit and piss and vomit.

When the wracking, hacking cough at last breaks, it is too little too late for any relief to be enjoyed. For around now the brain barricades itself for a last stand and the host withdraws quietly into a coma.

The last few hours are calm, peaceful, almost serene. The only sound made by the body is shallow, irregular breathing; the only movements are the soft rise and fall of the chest, the occasional flutter of crusted eyelids and the odd involuntary spasm caused perhaps by a deep dream of happier times.

Breathing becomes more ragged, wetter, as though air is being forced through a throatful of water. When the water becomes too much, too dense, the breathing ceases.

An averagely fit, middle-aged person takes around six days from the first tickle to be felt at the back of the throat to expel that last breath. The very young, elderly and infirm may succumb within three days; the very fit within eight. But succumb nearly everyone will, drowned in their own bodily fluids.

Milandra sat at her computer, reading the last of the responses received to the e-mail she had sent over twenty-four hours ago. It had taken her most of the night to plough through them all.

The Deputies had amused themselves by watching DVDs or playing video games or monitoring the internet on tablets and smart phones. Although sorely depleted, their psychic energy could easily cope without further depletion with mentally undemanding pastimes like watching films or playing games.

They interrupted their activities frequently to snack. This was particularly true for Milandra. Her psychic power had been boosted by the Deputies', but she had nevertheless taken the biggest hit. While she sat and read the last of the e-mails, she munched absentmindedly from a jumbo bag of salted peanuts. She could feel, though barely, her levels of mental energy replenishing; it was a little like filling a swimming pool with a garden hose. Sunlight would be the better cure, but she was confined to quarters until this was over. It would take probably another twenty-four hours and a lot more food before she would feel mentally strong enough to attempt another Commune; not that she foresaw any reason to have to.

Occasionally, Milandra glanced out of her window at Central Park. Another cold but dry morning had brought out the usual crowds of tourists and locals, taking in the wintry air, scarves and gloves and thick overcoats the order of the day. For now, it looked like any other Saturday morning in Central Park. Give it a few days and she doubted very much that the scene from her window would present any appearances of normality.

She looked back at the computer. The list of e-mail addresses to the left of the screen, which had been shrinking as replies were received, had now been reduced to one.

A voice spoke from behind her.

"Is that the one we've lost?" It was Grant.

Milandra sighed. "That's the one."

Grant bent forward to peer over her shoulder. "prond12@hotmail.co.uk," he read. "Who is it?"

"Peter Ronstadt. He's in Wales in the U.K. I last saw him, oh… eighty, ninety years ago? It was some time before World War II anyhow. He came to see me in Florida when his ship was in port. He was in the merchant navy."

"And did he show any signs…?"

Milandra thought hard. The current dilapidated state of her mental powers did not adversely affect her memories; it was simply that she had so many of the darned things. Had he given any clues, any insight that he would one day break away?

"I don't think so. Though… hmm…"

Her brow furrowed as a memory tried to break through. She could see Ronstadt sitting in front of her on the veranda of the villa, iced drink in hand, and something had bothered her. Something about him that seemed obtuse, clouded, as though he was concealing something. Yes, she had…

"I probed," she said. "Just a little. But I met resistance. Peter looked flustered, but the resistance receded and there was nothing there of concern. Nothing at all. Except…"

She thought harder, trying to snag that wisp of memory. Grant knew better than to interrupt.

"That's it," she said. "There *was* something there, something that he whisked away as soon as he felt me probe. But not before I'd caught a glimmer. It was something to do with a woman."

"A *human* woman?" asked Grant.

"Yes. I am very much afraid that it was."

"What shall we do?"

Milandra shook her head. "This changes nothing. If he was involved with a human, she'll be long dead. No. We'll leave Peter alone. So long as he doesn't try to interfere."

"So how was your day?" Tom asked after he had taken Lisa's coat and thrust a glass of wine into her hand. She sipped it gratefully.

"Oh, that's good," she said. "Well, the world and his wife were in Cardiff today. You'd swear shopping is about to be banned or something. And it rained the whole time I was there. Think I've caught a chill. My throat's really sore."

"Oh, dear," said Tom. "Come on through to the living room and relax. There's chicken and jacket potatoes in the oven. They'll be ready in about an hour."

"Mmm. Smells good."

Lisa went first, Tom following close behind. He watched her backside move beneath the tight skirt and couldn't help wondering whether the sheer, dark nylon covering her calves belonged to tights or stockings. He swallowed hard.

They sat together on the settee and chatted about work and Christmas and family. Lisa also lived in the village, with her parents and younger sister, about five minutes' walk from Tom's house.

Over dinner they opened another bottle of wine. Tom noticed that Lisa occasionally grimaced as she swallowed a mouthful of food.

"Is your throat getting worse?" he asked. "Or is my cooking that bad?"

Lisa sighed. "Is it that noticeable?" She put down her knife and fork, and raised a hand to her neck, rubbing it. "Feels like it's been scrubbed with sandpaper and then had acid poured down it." She glanced down at her half-empty plate. "Tom, this is really delicious, but… I feel awful. Do you mind?"

"No, Lisa, that's fine. I'll warm it up tomorrow for my lunch."

"Oh, you're a gent." She reached across and grasped his hand. "You'd best keep your distance this evening. Don't want you coming down with it, too, do we?"

Tom pretended to consider for a moment before shrugging. "Think I'll take my chances," he said.

Lisa smiled and gave a low chuckle.

It turned out that she was wearing stockings.

Later, as she was leaving, Lisa reached up and clenched her hands behind Tom's neck. She kissed him.

"Thank you for a lovely evening," she murmured.

"Are you sure you won't stay?"

She nodded. "You know what it's like when you're feeling under the weather. You only want to sleep in your own bed. Although my throat feels a little less sore now. Probably all the wine." She giggled, but pulled away from Tom when the laughter broke into a brief coughing fit.

"At least let me walk you home," said Tom.

"Don't be daft. It's only around the corner. Besides, I've lived in Penmawr all my life. I know everyone. If someone tries to attack me, I'll scream and people will come running. Anyway, who's going to attack me in this village? It's too dull."

Tom placed a kiss on the mole on her cheek; her Monroe mole he called it. "Okay, Miss Stubborn. But text me when you're home."

"Yes, Dad."

"Hey, less of that! I'm nowhere near old enough to be your father."

"True. Three years older is about perfect. When we're old and doddery, you'll be the first to go and I can live like a queen off your pension."

"Killing me off already? And who said we're going to be together when we're old and doddery?"

Lisa raised her eyebrows and smiled. She leaned forward and kissed him again.

Tom watched her walk away, her breath pluming in the cold night air. Before she was out of sight, she turned and waved. Then she was gone.

Canberra is relatively small by the capital city standards of London, Paris or Mexico City and Bishop had it covered without incident by Sunday lunchtime. Civil servants and politicians arriving for work on Monday, only days before the Christmas recess, would be spreading more than seasonal joy when they returned home to their families for the holidays.

On his way out of the city, he called at the airport for good measure and transferred Moondust to handles of trolleys and keypads of ticket machines.

He drove in a gentle south-easterly direction back to the coast. Allowing for stops to distribute Moondust at settlements along the way and to refuel both himself and the Mazda, Bishop reckoned to be in Melbourne by Tuesday.

As he headed towards the ocean, the afternoon sun on his face, the wind whipping his hair, Bishop whooped. He turned the radio up and bellowed along to some rock tunes, keeping time with his hand on the steering wheel, occasionally sprinkling specks of Moondust from his fingers while he drove through some one-horse burg not worthy of a stop. A little more than one-third of the contents of the canister remained. Plenty to finish off Melbourne. Bishop suspected that by the time he arrived at the city, the disease would have beaten him there.

He lifted his chin to the sky and let out another long *Whooop!*

After decades of inaction, of boredom, of being burdened by a pressing sense of impotence, Bishop was once more a man driven by purpose. Life was once again good.

If asked, Diane Heidler wouldn't be able to say with any confidence what type of car she rented in L.A. International Airport. She'd wave a hand vaguely and reply, "Oh, it's a Mercedes or a BMW, or something like that…"

In truth, she had chosen it for its colour: a rich, metallic red like deep-vein blood. And it looked comfortable. She told the clerk she needed it for a week or two and paid two weeks' rental in cash. She said she'd drop it back to the airport and didn't blush in the slightest at the lie.

Diane left the airport, knuckles white on the steering wheel while she negotiated the evening traffic. She drove in a wide loop back to Downtown and, by the time she was close to her former apartment, she had relaxed somewhat as she grew accustomed to the car. Nevertheless, she drove hesitantly, like a lost tourist, and was honked at more than once by impatient drivers.

She circled until she found a parking space at the side of the road large enough that she didn't have to reverse into it, got out with her knapsack, and spent a little time walking and touching things. She passed her apartment building and considered going in, but almost immediately dismissed the notion, instead settling for grabbing the worn chrome door handle with powder-dusted fingers.

The sky was beginning to darken when she returned to the car, the other people on the sidewalks were becoming more sinister-looking, at least to her eyes, and she was glad to regain the plush interior and lock the doors. She was aware of one or two young men eyeing her car and could feel their calculating regard as she drove thankfully away.

Diane turned south and made for Long Beach, stopping once or twice along the way, not venturing more than ten yards from the car, but far enough to run her fingers along a bench or wall or railing.

At Long Beach she repeated the process, not straying out of easy reach of the car. In the halogen wash of the streetlights, it looked the colour of ripe cherries; in unlit areas, like the stain of dried blood.

She followed the coast for miles, stopping at the various beaches that she passed—Huntingdon, Newport, Laguna—and marinas and viewing points, never staying long enough to draw attention to herself, unlikely as that was: most places were virtually deserted on this December night grown chilly with the promise of another shower.

By the time she picked up the San Diego Freeway west of Dana Point, Saturday morning had dawned.

Although they were not yet aware of their peril, almost one twentieth of the residents of Greater Los Angeles had already caught the Millennium Bug; some from direct contact with the powdery smears Diane had left in her wake; many, many more from contact with those already affected. Within another twenty-four hours, that figure would increase tenfold so that every other resident was infected.

By Monday, as Diane left San Diego on Highway 15 to travel back towards Los Angeles, the incidence of infection was fast approaching ninety per cent and the first deaths had already occurred.

Lisa Jones did not attend work on Monday. The school secretary popped her head around the classroom door while Tom was taking the morning register to let him know that Lisa had rung in sick. Three pupils were also absent, including Janie Rees, who Tom had earmarked to play the part of Mary in the Nativity.

"So much for my speech on Friday about staying well," Tom muttered to Mark Davies, his teaching assistant.

"Can't be helped, I guess," said Mark. "There's always

something going around this time of year, no matter what they say on the telly."

"You sound a little croaky yourself. Are you feeling all right?"

"Oh, probably overdid it at the weekend." Mark grinned, but it lacked his usual sparkle.

While Mark organised the children into groups, Tom noticed that he coughed once or twice and winced as though his throat hurt to swallow. Throughout the morning, Tom also noticed that a few of the children were developing coughs. One or two seemed listless; not even the prospect of taking a part in the Nativity could raise their spirits.

At lunchtime, Tom was on playground duty, but managed to grab a word with the other teachers. Each class had at least two pupils missing. One teacher and three classroom assistants were away. The headmaster, Ross the Boss, was thick-throated and teary-eyed, but it would take more than a touch of flu to make that old goat go on the sick.

As home time approached, Tom called it a day for rehearsals and allowed the children to sit quietly and colour. More of them had fallen into lethargy and most coughed while they crayoned.

Mark's eyes looked as though he had lined them liberally with a reddish-purple eyeliner. Tom sent him home at the same time as the children.

He cleared up, alone with his dark thoughts.

A three-year-old boy named Jarod Oakley was the first citizen of the United States to perish of the Millennium Bug. He was admitted to L.A. County Hospital as Sunday was slipping into Monday, accompanied by his frantic mother. Her eyes were red-rimmed and bloodshot, not solely through anxiety.

By the time Jarod was seen in E.R. by a young intern, who took one look at the child struggling wetly for breath and ordered immediate isolation protocol, the paramedic crew and three members of the nursing staff had been infected. The young intern himself, who enjoyed taking in the winter air on a nearby park bench and smoking cigarettes during his breaks, was already experiencing a tickling cough and sore throat. When he reported to his senior resident, he unwittingly infected his colleague by letting out a huge and unexpected sneeze while he explained why he had ordered the toddler to be isolated.

The senior resident looked in at the boy, now encased in an oxygen-rich and germ-containing polythene tent, and concurred with the intern. He didn't think to check on the couple of elderly patients admitted that same night with flu-like symptoms until they had infected a doctor, five nurses, the admissions clerk and four other patients.

At 3:54am, Pacific time, Jarod Oakley let out a weak, wet breath, little more than a sigh, and didn't draw another. The crash team, gowned and masked, worked on him inside the tent for forty-seven minutes, while his mother infected the nurse who tried to keep her calm.

Jarod's mother returned home in daylight, dazed and coughing. She would die there alone four days later. By then, hospitals had ceased functioning. Bursting at the seams with dying patients, trying to operate on a skeleton staff with running eyes and hacking coughs, they had become little more than repositories of the dead and soon-to-be dead. Mortuaries were full. Bodies draped in green or white sheets occupied gurneys in corridors. There was nowhere and nobody to take them.

Soldiers in full-body environment suits and gas masks stood guard at entrances, allowing nobody to enter—or leave. Their weapons contained live ammunition and they were under orders to employ them in lethal force if necessary. In what circumstances such action would be necessary was not so clear. 'Containment' seemed to be the keyword from on high, but it was patently obvious to soldier and civilian alike that this horse had long bolted.

Many of the soldiers surreptitiously rubbed at their throats when they thought nobody was looking, or tried to muffle tickling coughs. Eyes behind gas masks were red, running and scared.

Chapter Seven

Unlike most of his kind, Peter Ronstadt had acquired the habit of sleeping. He could manage perfectly well without it, but had grown to enjoy the sensations of drifting into slumber and the slow wakefulness of morning. It had taken him many years to master. He had first to overcome the irrational feeling that he was somehow surrendering his sovereignty by allowing himself to slip into unconsciousness, placing himself at a disadvantage that could easily be exploited.

Although he had eventually mastered the art of falling into slumber, he was never able to stay under for longer than two or three hours. He had also, during a fifty-year period, become accomplished at faking sleep, but had not needed to employ that skill for the past seventeen years. Neither did he *need* to continue retiring to bed and willing himself to sleep each night, but he continued nevertheless. He enjoyed it and derived some measure of comfort from it: the process reminded him of her.

This December morning, as was his practice during winter months, Peter waited until four o'clock to sleep so that he would awake around first daylight. He liked to stay in bed awhile, yawning and stretching, allowing his senses to return gradually to full alertness, enjoying the cosiness of his bed. Unless a full bladder drove him out sooner—rare, due to the efficiency with which his body extracted every last microgram of nutrition from what he consumed—he'd lie there until he could hear the chattering of children passing on their way to school.

Those sounds appeared later than usual this morning and were quieter than normal—muted, subdued.

Peter got up, dressed and descended the creaking staircase. He had laid the fire before retiring to bed and he lit it before making breakfast. The day was chilly.

He switched on the television and flicked between news channels while he ate his breakfast. It didn't take long to find what he was looking for; only a brief report, a snippet, but it had begun.

To stock footage of ambulances, doctors wearing face masks and patients attached to drips lying in hospital beds, the newscaster said, "Reports are coming in from Los Angeles of an outbreak of an as-yet unnamed flu-like illness that seems to be striking down the very young and the very elderly. Seven people are said to have died of the illness in Los Angeles County Hospital, while other unexplained deaths are being investigated to establish whether they, too, can be attributed to the mysterious disease. A spokesman for the hospital said, 'This could be merely a minor outbreak of influenza that is quite usual for this time of year. It is possible that the victims had not been immunised. There is no cause for concern.' In the meantime, four people are reported as having died in Sydney, Australia from a similar, flu-like illness. This report has not yet been confirmed."

The programme moved on to other items. Although the living room had warmed up somewhat as the fire did its job, Peter shivered. He turned the television off and finished his breakfast to the sound of logs spitting in the hearth.

He had just finished washing the few breakfast dishes when there came a knock on the front door. Peter opened it to find the manager of the Land Rover garage in Cardiff on his doorstep. Behind him at the side of the kerb stood Peter's Range Rover.

"Mr Ronstadt, sir!" The manager brought his heels smartly together. "Your chariot awaits." He brandished a set of keys and stood aside.

Peter smiled and took the keys. He stepped outside and gave the vehicle a cursory examination. He opened the large boot and checked on the presence of the spare tyre. He nodded, satisfied.

When he turned back, the manager was gazing at Peter's cottage, a thoughtful expression on his face. As Peter watched him, trying not to smile, the man sneezed. He took a handkerchief from his pocket and wiped his nose. Then he coughed. Peter's urge to smile faded.

"Everything to your satisfaction, sir?" the manager enquired.

"Perfectly," said Peter.

"Splendid. Er, Mr Ronstadt, if you don't mind my asking, are you some sort of eccentric millionaire? Um, if that's not too presumptuous a question…"

Now Peter did smile. "Something like that," he said.

A Rover saloon drew up behind the Range Rover. It was driven by a young man in a suit, though not the young salesman who had first approached Peter in the showroom on Saturday.

"Ah," said the manager, wiping his nose again. "My lift back to Cardiff. Not young Justin, though, I'm afraid. He rang in sick this morning."

"You don't look so good yourself," said Peter.

"Yes. Seem to be coming down with something. And only last week on the news they were saying they weren't expecting a flu outbreak this year." He rolled his bloodshot eyes. "Bloody experts, eh?"

"Listen, um… I don't even know your name."

"Musgrove, sir. Adrian Musgrove."

"Listen, Adrian. Do you have a wife? Children?"

"Why, yes. The wife's off work today. A bit poorly. And both children are home from school. Running high temps."

"Go home. Shut up the showroom or leave someone else in charge. Whatever. But go home. Be with them."

"What? I can't do that. Impossible."

Peter stepped forward and laid his hand on the man's forearm. The manager's eyes widened under the intensity of Peter's gaze.

"You need to be with your family, Adrian," Peter said quietly. He *pushed*, a little, not so much that the man would be aware of the intrusion, but enough that he might be influenced. "Go home."

A look of confusion passed across the man's face. Then his eyes cleared. "Go home? Hmm… yes, maybe I should do that."

"Yes, you most certainly should." Peter released his forearm and shifted his grip to shake him firmly by the hand.

He stood and watched Adrian climb into the passenger seat of the saloon. While the car pulled from the kerb, Adrian sneezed, startling the driver and making the car jerk slightly before it moved smoothly away.

The reception class of Penmawr Primary School was down eight pupils and one teaching assistant on Tuesday. Mark came in, but his voice was husky and he frequently had to blow his nose.

Tom abandoned the idea of a Nativity concert. Not one of the remaining ten children even mentioned it.

The classes of older children fared slightly better, but each class had on average five pupils missing. Two teachers and three classroom assistants had rung in sick.

Tom popped into the school office during morning break to ask if Lisa had called in. The school secretary shook her head.

"No, Tom, she hasn't. But I spoke to her yesterday and she sounded terrible. There's some bug doing the rounds and no mistake." She coughed. "I think I've got a touch of it myself."

Before returning to the classroom, Tom sent Lisa a text: *How r u feeling?*

She hadn't responded by lunchtime and he felt a small worm of anxiety stir in his stomach.

That afternoon, Tom arranged for three pupils to be collected by their parents. They had gone downhill drastically, eyes and noses running freely, weeping for their mums and shielding their eyes as though bathed in bright summer sunshine, not grey December gloom. The remaining seven children in the class had become withdrawn and listless. Tom and Mark had never had it so easy, but Tom would have swapped it at the drop of a hat for a class full of unruly, healthy five-year-olds.

Mark, too, was deteriorating: his cheeks had become sunken and sallow, dark shadows had appeared beneath his eyes and a persistent cough had acquired the rough edges of a bark.

Tom sent him home again at the children's home time.

"Mark," he said, as his assistant shuffled to the door. "Unless you're feeling much better in the morning, don't come in."

Mark attempted to smile, but it seemed too much effort and it became a grimace. He passed through the doorway and was gone.

Tom never saw him again.

On Tuesday morning, the local cable news channels in the Los Angeles area showed a fuzzy still of a woman. She had been photographed from above, her right arm outstretched to a door as though about to enter the building. She was glancing up towards the camera, which had captured her image face-on.

It was difficult to determine the woman's age, though some estimates gave it at somewhere in her mid- to late-thirties. She was dressed in faded jeans and a thick, dark coat. A scarf covered her neck. Her hair appeared in the still to be mousey-brown or dusky blonde, reaching an inch or two below her shoulders. Over her left shoulder she clutched a small backpack.

Why the police wanted to talk to the woman was never quite made explicit. It was hinted that it had something to do with the recent outbreak of the mystery virus affecting some local inhabitants, but without linking her directly.

Even if the photograph had been clearer and closer, the woman it showed had neutral, nondescript features and would never stand out in a crowd, though quite how it was possible to stand out in a crowd in Los Angeles was in any event a moot point. Needless to say, the news stations received hundreds of calls naming possible candidates as the mystery woman, but not one of them by the name of Diane Heidler.

The woman who bore that name was motoring along Highway 15 in a blood-red car, heading north away from Los Angeles towards the Mojave Desert.

The Range Rover handled like a dream. Peter drove into the countryside, choosing twisty, winding B roads and hilly areas, growing accustomed to the gearbox. The steering was light and responsive for such a heavy vehicle, the brakes sharp and effective. Coming across a rutted farm track with the gate thrown wide and nobody in sight, Peter flicked the four-wheel drive switch and set off across the field, testing the vehicle's suspension and ability to handle rough terrain. Both proved extremely satisfactory.

He visited a supermarket and stocked up with enough bottled water and canned goods to last a month's siege. Although late morning on a weekday and he hadn't expected the shop to be packed, the aisles were unusually quiet. The shoppers were mainly middle-aged to elderly, quietly going about their business, exhibiting no obvious signs of illness. Yet, there seemed to Peter—and he was looking out for it—a certain antipathy, a listlessness, about the shoppers, as though they were merely going through the motions of normality.

The shelves holding fresh bread were nearly empty. They looked like they do when snow is forecast and there is a rush of panic-buying, though there was no sign of feverish shopping activity. Peter asked a passing employee about it.

"Short-staffed in the bakery, love," the woman replied. "In fact, we're short-staffed everywhere today. Lucky it's not very busy."

"Some sort of virus doing the rounds, I expect," said Peter, regretting that he had engaged the woman in conversation. He had to fight the urge to reach out and hug her.

"Aye, I expect so," said the woman. "Are you all right, love? You're looking a bit peaky."

"I'm fine, fine," said Peter, turning away. "Thanks for your help."

"Righto, love. Well, take it easy." She went about her business, leaving Peter to brush angrily at the corners of his eyes. If holding a brief, banal conversation with a supermarket employee was going to affect him like this, how the heck was he going to get through the next few weeks?

He added a loaf of fresh bread to his trolley. He didn't have a freezer—his kitchenette was too small to hold one—and a loaf usually lasted him a few days, so it was pointless buying more. He purchased as much meat—steaks, sausages, pork chops, a chicken—that he could fit into his tiny fridge and cook when required so he wouldn't have to live off canned food alone for the next week. Finally, he added as much fresh fruit and vegetables as he calculated he would be able to eat before they started to rot.

On his way to the checkout tills, he passed a display of batteries. He paused for a moment considering, then with a shrug added most of them to his trolley.

He deliberately avoided engaging the checkout boy in conversation. This seemed to suit the boy, who did his job disinterestedly and made no comment on the number of batteries, tins or bottles of water that he passed over the barcode reader. The boy sniffed frequently and coughed occasionally. He didn't cover his mouth with his hand, not even when he sneezed, although he at least had the courtesy of turning away from Peter, instead spraying the back of the girl operating the till behind him.

Having placed his purchases on the back seat of the car, an idea occurred to Peter. He went back to the supermarket and made for the electrical goods section. When he returned to the Range Rover, he was carrying a boxed DVD player and sixty-three DVDs—every title that had caught his eye.

Next, he visited an out-of-town shopping outlet that sold five-gallon plastic fuel containers. He was fortunate that the man who served him was red-eyed and coughing since otherwise Peter would have been unable to persuade him to sell more than four of the containers; something to do with Health and Safety, according to the man. As it was, the salesman's defences were severely depleted and Peter, with the aid of a mental shove, talked the man into selling him ten.

"It's okay," Peter assured him. "I'm not a terrorist."

He paid cash.

It took him five trips between the shop and the Range Rover, but he was soon on his way home, the containers booming and echoing in the vehicle's substantial boot. He stopped at the garage nearest home and filled each container with petrol. At the same time, he topped up the Range Rover's tank. He was pleased to note that the engine coped with the additional weight without complaint.

The cottage had no garage, but a rough hardstanding to the side was large enough for Peter to pull the vehicle off the road. He reversed it in and carried the supermarket purchases into the cottage. The fresh food went into the kitchenette; the water and cans he trudged upstairs with and stored them in the corner of his bedroom; the DVD player and films he placed on the floor next to the television stand.

In the pocket handkerchief back garden of the cottage stood a sturdy, brick-built outhouse. It contained a stack of rough-sawn logs, a full sack of coal that Peter had been saving for when he needed it most, like now, a large sheet of tarpaulin and years of accumulated dirt.

With a grunt, he hefted the sack and staggered into the cottage. He dumped the sack in a corner of the kitchenette, leaving just enough room to open the door to the fridge. Then he made several journeys, bringing the logs inside and stacking them on the hearth.

He lifted the tarpaulin, raising a cloud of dust and spider skeletons. Outside, he shook the worst of the dust out of it, stepping smartly back to avoid being enveloped. He threw it to one side—the breeze was strong enough to make the edges flap, but there was no danger of it being blown away—while he emptied the car's boot. Now that they were full of petrol, Peter could only manage one sloshing container at a time. He placed them in two rows on the dirt-covered concrete floor of the outhouse. It was dry and free of vermin, its door old and solid, despite the contrary appearance of its coating of flaking green paint. Peter secured the door with a sturdy padlock that he had purchased on Saturday during his shopping expedition to the city. He attached the padlock key to the keyring holding the car keys.

Finally, with the last of the day's grey light leaking from the sky, he spread the tarpaulin over the Range Rover. It didn't cover it entirely, but would serve to keep out the worst of the elements and might act as a deterrent for any would-be looters. He secured the corners of the tarpaulin around the tyres using lengths of coarse string cut from a ball he kept in a drawer in the kitchenette.

Satisfied that the vehicle and supply of petrol were as secure as he could make them, Peter went indoors. It was only when he was inside that he realised that he hadn't heard the usual excited sounds of children returning from school.

He made sure that the front and back doors to the cottage were securely locked and all windows tightly fastened. He drew closed the curtains over the windows in the living room and kitchenette, and banked the fire.

He switched on the television in time for the main evening news on the BBC. There had been another terrorist outrage somewhere in the Middle East; it was reported almost perfunctorily, with a certain degree of detachment, as though such events were now *de rigueur* in the run-up to Christmas. Or maybe the news team was keen to get to the second story in that evening's schedule.

They were already calling it the Millennium Bug. Deaths had been reported in London and Birmingham, though the British medical authorities were remaining tight-lipped about the cause. The death toll in Los Angeles had jumped to sixty-five; that they were all the result of the same illness had now been confirmed. Reports of similar deaths in American cities such as New York, San Francisco and Dallas were trickling in. The earlier reports from Sydney had now been confirmed and more deaths had since been recorded. Rumours of a fatal disease spreading like wildfire throughout Asia and Africa were being received from foreign news agencies…

Peter changed channels, deciding that from here on in he would avoid the news. He would watch sport and comedies and films and documentaries until broadcasts ceased. Then, for so long as the electricity supply lasted, he would watch DVDs.

He was as prepared as he could be to ride out the storm.

~ ~ ~

Lisa had not replied to Tom's text message by the evening. He rang her, but the call went immediately to voicemail.

"Hi. You've reached Lisa's phone. Leave a message and… oh, you know how it works."

"Lisa, it's Tom. I hope you're okay. Call me, please."

Tom disconnected the call. After a moment's thought, he called his mother. He didn't expect her to answer. Tuesday night was bingo night. She and Betty would be sipping port and lemon, gossiping like two old fishwives while they marked their bingo cards.

The call wasn't answered and Tom disconnected.

Since watching the evening news, he had been feeling increasingly uneasy. Some sort of superflu was sweeping the country. Hell, it seemed to be sweeping the world. The Millennium Bug. People were dying in the hundreds.

He wondered if this same bug was responsible for the absences in school. He had put it down to another winter virus—how could the same virus affect the whole world at the same time?—but now wasn't so sure. Lisa might have it.

He hadn't spoken to his mother since Saturday. She might…

Tom shook himself, trying to get rid of the sense of foreboding. He wondered briefly if he ought to jump into his car and take a drive to Swansea; make sure she was okay. On the other hand, he was tired and she would not thank him if she arrived home from bingo to find him sitting yawning in her living room. She would be suspicious and he would get cranky and they would end up arguing. He'd drive home in a mood and have trouble sleeping. They had played out that scene too many times.

No. He would ring her tomorrow.

Tom would regret that decision for the remainder of his days.

The roads into Melbourne were quieter than normal. The same

could not be said for the roads out. Bishop passed cars and trailers and vans, piled high with people and possessions, fleeing the city.

He laughed at them and sprinkled Moondust into his slipstream. Some of it may find its way in through open windows and air ducts, he reasoned, although he suspected it was a futile gesture on his part. It was evident that the Millennium Bug had beaten him to the city by a couple of days, perhaps transported there by air from New Zealand or Fiji or further afield. It was all they were talking about on the radio; they were already hesitantly calling it a pandemic. People were dying throughout the world.

Bishop listened and laughed until he grew bored and found a station that was still playing rock music.

"Fools!" he yelled at the streams of vehicles heading in the opposite direction. "Where are you going? Nowhere is safe." He whooped joyously and sprinkled a little more Moondust above his head for good measure.

He pondered his assertion. Maybe those not yet infected might find safe areas, but they would have to seek out the uninhabited regions. *They* tended to be the most inhospitable areas, places like the deep Outback. He guessed that groups of people who headed into the wilderness might survive if they had plenty of provisions and means to provide shelter from the desert heat and hostile environment. But if only one of their number—only one-—was unwittingly carrying the Millennium Bug with them, then their goose was cooked.

"Hell, yes!" he shouted, banging the steering wheel with the palm of his hand. "Not just cooked. Burnt to a crisp. Incinerated! Whoo-hoo!"

If any of the passing motorists or passengers noticed him, they glanced quickly away, a shadow passing over their hearts.

The gun-metal grey Mazda drove through the suburbs of Melbourne in early evening sunshine. Bishop slowed occasionally and sprinkled more Moondust into his slipstream. He didn't have much left; maybe around half an inch had remained in the canister when he'd last stopped and he hadn't been able to reach it with his fingers. He had transferred the remaining powder to the plastic bag and it was into this that he now dipped his fingers to spread his version of seasonal greetings to the world.

Four or five times on his drive into the city, at children's playgrounds and public parks, he stopped the car to perform the routine of pretending to stretch his legs, while smearing Moondust on benches and swings and picnic tables. In truth, he no longer believed it necessary to spread any more Moondust, but he was nothing if not a thorough man and would rather spread it unnecessarily than allow some to survive through lack of diligence on his part.

The steady stream of traffic heading away from the city slowed as Bishop neared the centre. He had started to fear that the city would be snarled with people fleeing, but it seemed that those who had decided to get out had left in an orderly, civilised fashion. Visions of thoroughfares choked with cars full of dying people, the stench of corruption on the evening breeze, did not materialise. If he had been forced to abandon the Mazda and walk into the city centre, the exertion wouldn't have bothered Bishop. But he would have been vulnerable, even with the pistol.

Another concern proved to be unfounded. He had wondered whether the city would be rife with civil unrest: rioters and looters roaming the streets, random acts of violence born of fear and frustration. Although he enjoyed watching mindless violence—had himself indulged in it frequently—he would make a prime target for the crazies in the open-top Mazda. As a precaution, the gun lay within easy reach in the open holdall on the seat next to him, safety catch off.

Bishop never paused to consider that violence had once played no part in his make-up and was abhorred in his culture. That the worst excesses of humanity had rubbed off on him did not occur to him, except perhaps in some remote part of his sub-consciousness that he kept firmly subdued. He was not a man readily given to introspection.

If there was any unrest in the city, he managed to avoid it, by luck if not judgment. Once or twice he heard sirens, but far away and he never encountered their source.

He suspected that these things may still occur; that trying to leave Melbourne by road over the coming days would grow increasingly difficult and that venturing into the streets would become unwise. Once he reached his destination, he had no intention of doing either.

As it was, the city seemed calm. In fewer numbers, maybe, but people were still going about their business; the al fresco restaurants that he passed were open, though there were many empty tables in evidence.

Bishop was close now to his favourite haunt. He had spent a lot of time in Melbourne over the years, had seen it expand and thrive, and even kept a small apartment here. But he wanted to spend the last days of humanity in luxury; watch mankind's death throes from the comfort of a five-star hotel.

As he neared the business district, he reached to the holdall with his left hand and withdrew the bag containing the last of the Moondust. Putting pedal to metal down a straight stretch of road, he lifted the bag above the windscreen and let the slipstream whip the remaining powder away. Giving the bag a last shake, he released it and saw it sail to the street in the rear-view mirror.

He turned into the Park Plaza Hotel and pulled up in front of the entrance. He switched off the engine and closed the zip on the holdall, hiding the handgun from view. A concierge appeared.

"May I help you, sir?"

Bishop held out the car keys. "Two cases in the trunk." He motioned to the holdall. "I'll take that. Park it up for me and close the hood."

Bishop stepped out of the car, holdall in hand.

"Oh," he said. "Fill up the tank and *then* park her up. This should more than cover it."

He held out two hundred-dollar bills.

The concierge took them and made them disappear into his grey suit.

"Certainly, sir," he said. "And which grade of parking would you prefer? Standard or executive? Executive is in a more secure area and includes a complete valeting service. It, ahem, costs a little more, of course…"

"Executive, naturally."

"I shall see to it, sir. Enjoy your stay at the Park Plaza."

"Oh, I will," said Bishop. "Arrange for the keys to be delivered to my room."

He stepped into the air-conditioned, marbled opulence of the hotel lobby and approached the desk. The clerk, a pretty woman of Asian origin, looked up and smiled.

"I'd like to check in," said Bishop. "I'll be paying cash up front."

"Certainly, sir," said the woman. "How long will you be staying with us?"

"Oh, a week initially. With perhaps an option to extend." He didn't add, *if there's anyone left alive to take more money from me.*

"And what grade of room would you be interested in? I can offer a special rate on our standard twin?"

"I want your most expensive available room."

The woman didn't miss a beat. "Ah, then you'll want our Ambassador Suite. Fortunately, sir, we have such a room available due to a late cancellation. Illness." She coughed and, for a fleeting moment, her mask of professional efficiency slipped. Bishop caught a glimpse of haunted eyes and sensed the fear coming from her like a rotten smell.

"Yes," he said. "I hear there's a lot of it about."

He handed over a small fortune in cash and refused the woman's offer to summon a concierge to show him to his room.

The Ambassador Suite was larger than Bishop's Melbourne flat. It offered stunning views of the city skyline, now lit up as night-time took hold. He dropped his holdall onto a thickly padded armchair and hunted for the room service menu. He rang down and ordered a lavish meal.

He then placed a call to the airport. It took a while to be put through to the person he wanted to speak to—apparently there were a lot of staff off on the sick—but he was connected eventually.

"Hello," he said. "This is Troy Bishop. Reference ACJ319/4708… Yes, I'd like the aircraft safety-checked, fuelled and ready to go… Yes, fully fuelled, including the extra tanks… Europe… Stocked for forty passengers… No… Not sure precisely when. But within the next few days… Yes... Usual account. Be sure to do a thorough job."

He replaced the handset, a satisfied grin on his face. Then he kicked back and settled down to wait.

Chapter Eight

Out of almost two hundred pupils, only eight turned up for school in Penmawr on Wednesday morning. Out of more than twenty members of staff, only four showed up: Tom, one other teacher, a teaching assistant and the headmaster.

Tom trod the echoing corridor towards his classroom, feeling a sense of disassociation. The building was normally bustling at this hour with running feet and laughter, chit-chat and the bellows of teachers ordering pupils to walk, not run, but this morning he walked it alone.

He turned into his classroom, expecting to find it empty. Sitting at one of the tables, head cast down, fingers fidgeting on the table, was a boy.

Tom dumped his briefcase and crossed to the boy in three long strides. He crouched at his side.

"James?"

The boy turned his head to look at him. His eyes were red-rimmed and weepy; a thin line of snot ran from his nose and collected in a puddle on his top lip. Judging from the damp stain on the boy's sleeve, his jumper made a useful handkerchief.

"James, how did you get to school? Did your mum bring you?"

The boy shook his head. He coughed and winced as though it hurt.

"Did you walk? On your own?"

The boy nodded. The action made the snot run over his lip and into his mouth. He swiped at it with his sleeve, smearing it across his cheek.

Tom frowned. This lad had no brothers and sisters, and no father; at least, not one that the boy knew.

"Where's your mum, James? Has she gone to work?"

"No, sir." It was barely audible, not even a whisper. "She's… not very well."

A sob hitched in the boy's thin chest and his eyes filled up.

Tom reached out and gathered the boy to him, hugging him close. This was against all protocol that forbade teachers from having any physical contact with their pupils, but at that moment Tom couldn't give a stuff for protocol.

He waited until the boy's shaking had subsided somewhat, then stood and took him by the hand.

"Come on, James. We need to get you home. I don't think there's going to be any school today. Where's your coat—in the cloakroom?"

The boy nodded. He coughed again and wiped his nose in his jumper.

Tom walked with him back down the corridor, retrieving the boy's coat on the way. They stopped at the headmaster's office.

The door was open and a deep, bellowing coughing came from within. There was not much point in knocking. Tom entered, still clutching the boy's hand.

Mr Ross sat behind his desk, almost doubled over with the coughing fit. He half-straightened and Tom gasped. The man's face, usually quite florid, was now the colour of a ripe plum. Tears streamed from puffy eyes and the cheeks had sunk in on themselves like subsiding ground.

The headmaster coughed again into a handkerchief that looked damp and sticky. He took short, sharp breaths, struggling to get the coughing under control.

"Mr Ross? Is there anything I can get you?" asked Tom, more to say something than from any expectation that he could actually help the man.

Mr Ross shook his head. "No," he managed. "When it catches me, I have to go with it. Ride it out. It's easing now." He sat up straighter and looked at Tom's charge.

"Hello, young James," he said. "We'll soon sort you out. Be a good lad and wait for me in the corridor while I talk to Mr Evans."

James nodded and let go of Tom's hand. He turned and trudged out of the office.

"I know that one's mother," said Mr Ross. "She went to school with my eldest granddaughter. I'll take him home. Maybe sit with them for a while."

"You're closing the school?"

"No bloody point staying open. You're the only person who's turned up today fit and healthy." Despite his swimming eyes, Mr Ross was still capable of fixing Tom with a piercing glare. "Haven't been able to get hold of anyone, mind." He motioned to the phone on his desk. "Education department, governors, even tried the Welsh Government Education department in Cardiff. No bugger's answering."

"This thing seems to be widespread. Worldwide. Everyone's coming down with it."

"Except you, eh?"

"Apparently so… I feel fine at the moment."

"Well, I hope it remains that way, Tom. Trust me, you don't want to feel like this. Tell me, are you a religious man?"

"Um, not really."

"No? Me neither. I was brought up with the chapel, but stopped going twenty years ago when my Elsie died of cancer. I could no longer believe in a god that would allow such a terrible thing to happen."

Tom didn't know what to say so said nothing.

"I wonder," continued the headmaster, "whether it's too late to find that path again."

"I don't think it's ever too late, is it, sir? Forgiveness and all that."

"Hmm. I suspect I shall find out sooner rather than later. Do me a favour, will you, Tom? Help an old man to his feet."

Tom stepped around the desk and gripped Mr Ross under his arm. The man felt hot. Feverish. With a grunt, he stood. Tom helped him around the desk where the headmaster shrugged into a heavy overcoat.

"Right, where's that young James? Let's get you home, young man." Before stepping out of the office, he stopped and looked back at Tom. "You and Lisa would have made a lovely couple.

Pity."

"You knew?"

Mr Ross smiled. "Good luck, Tom. Whatever fate has in store for you, meet it head on."

"Er, okay. Good luck to you, too, sir."

"Oh, I think luck will play no part in my future."

Tom followed him and James out of the building, and watched them get into the headmaster's car. He waved as they disappeared down the school drive. Neither Mr Ross nor the boy waved back.

The desert at night in December is a cold place, but the vehicle's air conditioning was efficient and kept the interior temperature to a comfortable sixty-eight degrees Fahrenheit. Diane drove through the night, enjoying the emptiness of the highway, barely going above fifty miles per hour.

She pulled in at every rest stop. If fuel was available, she'd fill up, smearing the pump handle with dust from her canister. If not, she'd pretend to use the WC, leaving smears on door handles and faucets. If, as was more often the case, the joint was locked up in darkness, she'd stride over to the doorway and grip it briefly as though to confirm the place was closed, before walking smartly back to the car and driving away.

At one point, her headlights picked out a rough dirt track leading away across the desert towards some low hills. Had she chosen to turn off the highway and follow the track, it would have eventually led her to a low building enclosed behind a well-maintained chain-link fence topped with barbed wire. A camera mounted above the locked gate would have swivelled towards her and a disembodied voice would have enquired about the nature of her business. If she had no business there, the voice would have politely suggested that she turn around and return to the highway.

The building and the land upon which it stood were in private ownership. The government was aware that it existed and every five years or so carried out an inspection, but had never turned up anything that gave cause for concern. The locked cabinet inside the main door contained a small selection of firearms that were all licensed and properly stored. The variety of chemicals used for research and to maintain the sterile environment were, too, fully logged and stored according to regulation.

The land was registered to a corporation that gave its address as a swanky building in Manhattan which housed a firm of attorneys that prided itself on acting for the extremely rich and famous, and providing extreme discretion if so required. Such was required, very much so, in this case.

As far as the government was aware—and it had tried to dig further without success—the corporation was the public face of a group of reclusive millionaires who wished to remain anonymous, but who desired to use some of their wealth for altruistic purposes. One such purpose was to conduct research into the gene which caused cancer and that is what the building in the Mojave Desert was used for.

Every five years, the government inspectors were treated to a guided tour of one of the most advanced laboratories in the world, staffed by a team of half a dozen research scientists. The gleaming laboratory equipment was state of the art, so the inspectors thought. In fact, a few items of equipment, disguised as a spectrometer or hidden within a centrifuge or masquerading as an electro-magnetic microscope, went way beyond state of the art, employing technology unknown to man.

It was from this building that, eighteen months or so ago, a shipment of silvery metallic containers, somewhat resembling vacuum flasks, had departed, bound for destinations throughout the world.

Now the scientists within continued to work, ostensibly trying to isolate and manipulate that elusive gene. An unannounced inspection would not uncover anything suspicious. Yet the work was a sham. The scientists in that laboratory knew exactly how to isolate and manipulate the gene. They could have eradicated cancer in a heartbeat.

What they were actually doing was awaiting the call that would see them drop everything and head east, following the same route as Diane Heidler. Two SUVs stood ready in the dusty yard, fuelled and packed with food and water for the trip east.

As the virus spread and the worldwide death toll rose into thousands, political tensions increased.

For a twelve-hour period on the Wednesday two weeks before Christmas, mankind teetered on the edge of adding nuclear war to its list of woes.

North Korea postured and threatened a full-scale nuclear attack on the United States, claiming that the West had waged biological warfare upon it. The West responded cautiously, pointing out that it had in fact been the first to suffer casualties and the virus appeared to be a world problem, divorced from political ideology, killing democrat, republican, communist, anarchist and liberal indiscriminately.

China entered the fray, followed by Russia and Iran. Soon every major world power had something to say about the Millennium Bug, fingers were pointed, fists shaken and warheads armed.

The world held its breath.

Then, while the virus raged unabated, the absurdity of the claims and counterclaims seemed to strike home. Either that or the upper echelons of state themselves were feeling too ill to be bothered getting into a fight. Warheads were disarmed. Troops stood down. Besides, they were needed to deal with the increasing domestic unrest to which not even North Korea was immune.

Floods of panic-buying had cleared most shops of fresh produce; tinned goods were next to fly from the shelves. Restocking ground to a halt as shop workers, warehousemen and delivery drivers fell victim to the Millennium Bug.

The usual militant factions saw their opportunity and stirred up unrest, leading to protests and rioting and looting. Many governments reacted strongly, imposing martial law, but the riots were short-lived in any event. It is difficult to muster enthusiasm for rioting when the light is too bright, limbs feel like they've been scooped out and filled with concrete, and bed seems a much more attractive proposition than lobbing a brick through a shop window.

Martial law was nevertheless retained and extended by most administrations in a vain attempt to curb the further spread of the virus. Quarantine areas were set up, buffer zones established, firebreaks attempted. People attempting to flee quarantined areas were peremptorily executed.

International flights were cancelled by one country after another until the skies had fallen silent. All except for the occasional drone of military aircraft.

Most experts agreed that these attempts were futile, that the damage had already been done. One prominent medical expert, speaking on BBC's *Panorama*, described the measures as, "not so much slamming the stable door after the horse has bolted, but more like after the horse has been captured, shot and turned into glue."

In the New York apartment overlooking Central Park, Milandra let out a deep sigh and pressed the off switch on the TV remote.

"Well, that was a close call. A lot closer than I'd have liked."

She and her Deputies had spent all day in front of the television, watching the world draw close to nuclear annihilation and then pull back from the brink.

Wallace grunted. "Our people wouldn't have let it happen."

"It is as well we took the precaution. It was nevertheless a close-run thing." Milandra shuddered.

Simone spoke in a voice of one just waking up. "Um, what precaution did we take?"

Milandra exchanged a glance with Grant and allowed him to explain.

"Simone, don't you recall? We have people in top advisory positions in most volatile governments throughout the world.

Their job wasn't to disseminate the virus, but to exert influence at the very top to try to prevent any overreactions. It seems that they were successful. Barely."

The girl tittered. "Oh, yeah. They were to stop everything going *Boom*!"

Grant raised his eyebrows. "That's about the size of it. They had by far the most dangerous jobs to do. And the most crucial… We could only hope that in the extremity of facing the decision of whether or not to press the button, the minds of world leaders would be open to influence and would fail to detect their wills being manipulated. It appears that—"

A loud, insistent banging came from the front door.

Wallace and Lavinia were at the door in moments, standing to either side, guns at the ready. Milandra and Simone remained seated, but turned to watch. Grant rose and strode to the door. He glanced at Wallace and Lavinia, who both nodded and released the guns' safety switches.

Grant called out, "Hello? What is it you want?"

The banging stopped. A woman's voice, thin and quavering, muffled through the heavy door, came back. "Please? Help me."

"I'm sorry. There is no help for you here. Go home."

"*Please*! My daughter…" The voice broke into a fit of coughing.

Grant glanced again at Wallace and Lavinia. They nodded once more, tensed like cats about to pounce.

Slowly, deliberately, Grant reached out and started to turn the locks on the door. Milandra arose from her chair and moved to stand behind him.

Grant lowered his hand to the door handle and pressed it down. While he swung the door open, he stepped forward to prevent the person on the other side from entering the apartment. Wallace also moved forward when the door swung towards him so that he stood near its edge, ready to spring around it if needed. Lavinia adopted a marksman's crouch against the wall, handgun held forward in both hands, poised to emerge and fire in an instant.

A pale, dishevelled woman in her mid-twenties stood in the corridor, face damp with snot and tears. In her arms she held a child, wearing a disposable diaper and nothing else. The child appeared to be asleep, its breathing shallow and laboured.

The woman held the child out towards Grant in supplication. "*Please…*"

She coughed again, spittle flying from her mouth and dangling from her chin. Her gaze moved from Grant to Milandra, who was peering into the gap between her Deputy and the door jamb, and then back to Grant.

Milandra looked beyond the woman, but the corridor was otherwise empty.

"Where have you come from?" Grant asked the woman.

"Number seven. It's three floors down. You're the only one who's answered..."

"Do you have a husband?"

She nodded and spittle dropped from her chin onto the front of her already-stained blouse. "He's…" A sob hitched in her chest. "I think he's dying." She took a deep breath and it all came out in a rush. "I've called our doctor but he won't answer and the hospitals are full, the paramedics won't come and my daughter is only eleven months old, it's her birthday next week, her name's Holly, she was nearly a Christmas baby and *I don't know what to do…*"

The woman still held the child out towards Grant, as if she hoped he would take her and heal her. He pressed his hands to hers, gently but insistently pushing the child back to the woman's midriff. Her face crumpled and a thin wail came from her mouth.

Grant silently posed a question to Milandra who immediately answered it in the affirmative. Together they probed…

The wail tailed off and the woman's eyes widened. She drew her daughter close to her chest.

"Go home," Grant said gently. "Be with your husband. Be with Holly. Be together."

The terror and helplessness faded from the woman's face. She nodded, now calm, almost serene.

"Yes," she murmured. Then she turned and walked away.

Grant and Milandra watched her go along the corridor until she disappeared down the stairwell.

Tom walked home from school Wednesday morning through a village that seemed to be asleep. Barely a vehicle moved on the roads. He encountered only one other pedestrian, a man walking his dog, someone he vaguely recognised as one of his neighbours. The man was middle-aged and walked with a slight limp. Tom recalled another neighbour telling him that the man had been injured in an accident at work and now lived off the compensation he had received.

The dog wagged its tail as Tom approached them. Tom was no expert on dogs, but thought that the mutt was probably some sort of mongrel, like a cross between a border collie and a Labrador.

He nodded at its owner. The man barely glanced at Tom. Beads of sweat stood out on his forehead and cheeks, despite the near-freezing temperature. His limp seemed more pronounced than normal and his breathing was laboured, but he walked with chin thrust forward as though determined to keep up appearances of normality.

Before Tom could enquire whether he was okay or needed any help, man and dog were past him. Tom turned and stared after them for a moment, troubled, before continuing on his way.

As soon as he was in the house and had removed his coat, he took out his mobile and called his mother. It rang and rang. No sooner had Tom disconnected than his house phone rang, making him jump.

He snatched up the handset.

"Mam?"

Silence. Then, "Tom? Is that you?" The voice was faint, as if the caller held the phone too far away.

"Yes?"

"Oh, Tom. It's Lisa."

"Lisa! I've been trying to get hold of you."

"I got your message. I've been sleeping a lot. The signal's not very good here."

"*Here*? Aren't you at home?"

"No, I…" There came a sound that it took him a moment to realise was the sound of sobbing.

"Lisa! What's the matter?"

She took a deep breath as though trying to compose herself. When she spoke again, her voice was stronger. "Tom, listen! I probably won't be able to speak for long. They… Look, I'm at the sport centre in town."

"The sport centre? What—"

"Shush, Tom, and listen! My parents and sister aren't well. I'm not well. I think… I think my mother's dying. And my dad. And, oh God, my sister, too. Tom, I think *I'm* dying…" Her voice broke and she took another deep breath. "We rang for an ambulance but they said the hospital was full and to come here. I drove us down. They've got us all in the sports hall, the big one. It's full of camp beds. Tom, there are soldiers here. They're wearing masks and weird suits… it's like something from a horror film. And they're carrying guns."

"Huh! Guns?"

"I think they're stopping anyone else coming in. Or leaving. I heard gunshots from outside. And people are dying. The corridor is piled with bodies under blankets. I peeped around the corner. A soldier saw me and made me come back inside. He… he pointed his gun at me."

"That's outrageous! I'm coming to get you. I'll—"

"No! They won't let you in. Stay away." There was a pause and Tom heard a sharp intake of breath. "One of them has noticed me on my phone. He's coming over. Tom, say a prayer for me. I—" Tom heard a voice in the background; a harsh, muffled voice.

"Lisa! Put him on. Let me speak to him."

There was a shriek and the line went silent.

"Lisa! Are you okay? Lisa!"

But the line was dead.

Tom replaced the handset and dialled Lisa's number on his mobile. It was answered after the first ring.

"Lisa! Is that you…?"

A robotic voice intoned: "This number is currently unavailable. Please try again later."

Tom lowered the phone and stared it for a long moment, his mind awhirl, trying to take in everything Lisa had said.

Then, grabbing his coat and car keys, he ran from the house.

Chapter Nine

The desert sun rose higher and Diane was able to turn down the car's air conditioning. She became aware of a steady increase in traffic in both directions. A continuous line of traffic headed away from Las Vegas; another stream of cars and vans passed her, coming from Los Angeles. The vehicles all had one thing in common: they were packed with possessions and people.

She wondered idly where everyone was going. If those coming from Vegas thought they might find safety on the west coast, they couldn't be more mistaken. And those overtaking her might as well have stayed put as make for Vegas. If the virus hadn't yet reached Vegas, it soon would, coincidentally at about the same time as she arrived. Diane snorted; it was the closest she had come to laughing in months.

The rest stops were busy with people wanting fuel, food and toilet facilities. Diane continued to stop at each one and stretch her legs. She kept the fuel tank topped up and paid each time with well-fingered cash.

As she continued eastwards, Diane considered, merely to pass the time, where she would go if she was in their shoes. North, she decided. Deep into Nevada, then on to Idaho, sticking as far as possible to back roads, ignoring rest-stops unless she needed to stop for gas, then remaining in the car, tipping the pump boy handsomely, but feeding cash though a slightest crack in the window and turning her head away when he reached for it in case he coughed or sneezed.

Then she would continue north to Canada, drive through British Columbia and not stop until she reached the permafrost of Yukon. Maybe that's where she would make base. Or head into Alaska. Either way, she would construct a cosy little log cabin for herself, and hunt moose and bears.

She did not allow the fact that she had not the slightest notion how to build a log cabin, and had never so much as hunted rabbits, let alone creatures with long teeth and sharp claws, to spoil her fantasy. She expanded it, inventing ingenious ways to melt ice and snow to provide a permanent supply of running water, then imagining methods of cultivating the frozen ground and building a loom so she could spin her own clothes from bear fur…

It kept her amused all the way to Vegas.

Like their political counterparts, religious leaders weren't averse to a spot of finger-pointing and chest-thumping. Islam blamed Christianity for the Millennium Bug. Catholics blamed Protestants. Sikhs blamed Hindus. Everyone blamed the Jews.

But the Millennium Bug did not favour one religion over another, one denomination above others. It killed almost everyone, ruthlessly and efficiently, whatever deity they chose, or chose not, to worship.

Unsurprisingly, most religions were in accord that the virus represented humanity's Final Judgment: man has been measured and been found wanting, was the common theme.

Religion, both mainstream and at the margins, organised and off-the-cuff, gained a massive, though all too brief, swell of popularity. Atheists became agnostics; agnostics became believers; believers became zealots.

In Britain, New-Ageism enjoyed a revival. A mass celebration of the Winter Solstice was planned to take place at Stonehenge. A tentative suggestion that, perhaps, it might be wise to go ahead and hold the celebration immediately, rather than wait for the actual Solstice in case, you know, there's no one left to celebrate it was, unwisely, ignored.

Churches and chapels, mosques and temples throughout the world had never been so full, the congregations so fervent, except those that had been hastily converted to makeshift hospitals or mortuaries, though they, too, did not lack for attendees.

Throughout those first few days of realisation that a deadly pandemic was sweeping the planet, huge religious rallies took place at which bold, and ultimately inaccurate, pronouncements were made that only the true followers of that particular doctrine would survive.

These meetings and marches and gatherings faded as quickly as they had sprung up as followers took to bed and had to settle for making peace with their maker alone.

While spiritualism provided solace for many hundreds of thousands, possibly millions, of people as they lived out their final hours, the more sinister aspects of cultism and extremism made a blessedly short-lived appearance.

Bombs were set off in Cairo, Mexico City and Rome, killing hundreds; the tolls would have been far greater had not the streets been so deserted.

The Middle East erupted in violence when Arabs and Jews took their last chance to air ancient grievances and hatreds, but this soon died down like a guttering flare since there was nobody left fit enough from either side to continue. So ended one of the world's most bitter religious conflicts.

In Utah, Zimbabwe and Brazil, hundreds of people encouraged or forced their children to gulp down orange juice laced with strychnine or cyanide, à la Jonestown, before swigging it themselves.

In Brighton on the south coast of England, a hundred people of both sexes and most ages crowded the Royal Pavilion where, under the startled gazes of those well and brave enough to venture outside into the winter weather, they proceeded to dance and chant and remove their clothes, before strolling calmly down onto the beach and into the sea. They kept walking until they disappeared beneath the waves.

In New York City, thirty-seven members of an extreme Christian cult stormed the Empire State Building, overpowering the security guards, who were short-staffed due to sickness absences, and ascended to the observation platform armed with powerful bolt cutters. There they jammed the elevators and doorways to the stairwells, before cutting through the curved safety railing that extended around the perimeter of the deck, removing it on two sides of the square, shrugging off the few half-hearted attempts to interfere by watching tourists. Those tourists clasped their hands over their mouths, some looking away, as the cult members climbed unsteadily onto the waist-high wall to which the railing had been affixed. They formed a chain with their hands and stood gazing out over Manhattan, the wind ruffling their hair and clothes. On a count of three, they stepped off the wall together. Two passers-by were killed on Fifth Avenue.

There were many other random and isolated acts of madness, but in the main people preferred to slip away amidst their loved ones or alone and did not attempt a last grand statement of whatever.

Tom drove the three miles to town in a daze. He passed only one other vehicle on the way, a khaki jeep being driven rapidly in the opposite direction. The armed soldier sitting in the back stared at Tom while the jeep went by.

As he turned down the road leading to the sport centre, Tom slowed down. He resisted the urge to rub his eyes in disbelief. A hundred yards ahead, completely blocking the road, was an army truck, parked sideways across both carriageways.

He drove on, slowing to a crawl as he approached the truck. A man stepped from behind it and motioned to Tom to stop. The man—at least, the figure had the build of a man—wore a protective suit of some shimmery material that extended over the head. His face was covered by a gas mask. Across his chest he held a short-barrelled rifle.

Tom brought the car to a halt and stepped out. Immediately, the soldier raised the weapon and pointed it at Tom.

"Whoa!" said Tom, automatically raising his hands in a placatory gesture. "What are you doing? I just want to get to the sport centre."

"Negative. Turn around and leave." The soldier's voice

sounded metallic and inhuman from behind the mask.

"What is this?" Tom pointed behind the soldier. He could make out the flat roof of the centre. "My girlfriend's in there."

"This area is under martial law," said the soldier. "Turn around and leave. Now."

"Hold on a minute," said Tom, taking half a pace forward. "This is Britain, not some tinpot—" He froze when the soldier cocked the rifle and raised it, sighting down it at Tom's chest.

"Leave. Now. This is your last warning."

Tom felt afraid to move. He gazed at the soldier's face, trying to make out the man's eyes behind the Perspex of the mask. All he could see was a grey reflection of the sky.

"Okay," Tom said, though it came out as more of a croak. The bore of the gun barrel looked deep and dark, like infinity. A word crept unbidden from the depths of Tom's mind: carbine. That's what the weapon was called. A carbine. As if it mattered.

He took a tentative step backwards. The soldier didn't move. He took another and another until he could see his car door from the corner of his eye.

The soldier didn't relax his stance until Tom had performed a three-point turn, hands clammy on the steering wheel, and driven back the way he had come. He could see the soldier in the rear-view mirror slowly lower the weapon as Tom moved further away, but he was still staring after him through the faceless mask when Tom pulled out of sight.

He slammed on the brakes and slumped over the steering wheel. His hands and shoulders shook like leaves in a summer squall. He sat like that for minutes, waiting for the shock to pass, before he felt capable of driving again.

The sun moved behind her as Diane neared Las Vegas. The stream of traffic leaving the city had dried to a trickle by the time she passed through. She arrived on the Strip in the early evening.

She had filled up with gasoline, bottles of water and snacks in the city. At the same time, she left smears of powder from her fast-diminishing supply, despite it being clear that her task had already been accomplished. If the number of vehicles fleeing into the desert hadn't fully convinced her that the Millennium Bug had arrived days ahead of her, the scarcity of people and symptoms of illness amongst those who remained completed the job. There was little reason for her to tarry. She had visited Vegas once as a tourist and had hated every inch of its glitz and glamour.

Last time she was here, the Strip had been a parade of stretch limos and Continentals and fin-tailed Buicks, dropping off the rich and the beautiful and the brash to whichever casino they preferred to give their money to. Flat-bed trucks carrying billboards advertising topless bars and high-class call girls had driven slowly up the Strip, turned around and driven slowly back down again, pretty much all day.

Now, apart from the occasional straggler leaving town, the Strip was empty. Diane was able to pull over to the side without any difficulty. She turned off the engine and got out.

Although the sun was dipping towards the horizon, the evening was still bright and none of the neon lights had yet come on. It was warm, too, for December and she didn't need her coat. She stood for a moment, the wind rustling her hair, marvelling at how quiet it was. The clanging chimes of slot machines and fanfares and announcements designed to lure the undecided inside had not yet begun their nightly clarion calls, and the only sound she could hear was the wind. She walked towards the centre of the road and stood looking first one way, then the other. Not a vehicle moved. If a bolt of tumbleweed had come rolling down the Strip, it would have been fitting. It seemed she had the place to herself. Then a truck turned out of a side street and the illusion was broken.

Diane stepped back to the sidewalk. She could not see any people, apart from what looked like a hobo shuffling down the sidewalk away from her on the other side.

More out of curiosity than anything else, Diane walked to the nearest hotel and entered the lobby. The casino was beyond. She pushed against the door and peered around it.

The rows of slot machines flashed and bleeped and pinged, but nobody paid them any attention. Looking beyond them, Diane could see a roulette table with a croupier and three customers. The table was in operation, but none of the players seemed particularly animated. She suspected that if she moved closer, she would be able to hear them coughing and see them wincing as they swallowed their drinks. None of the other tables—blackjack, crap, poker—was occupied. Out of habit, she moved inside to the nearest machine and ran her fingers over the flashing buttons, smearing them with the last of the powder on her fingers.

She left and walked back to her car. Leaning over the driver's seat, she removed the canister from the knapsack on the passenger seat.

The Strip was quiet again. She walked to the outside of the three-lane stretch of road and took one last glance around to make sure nobody was watching her. Then she unscrewed the top of the canister, removed the inner disc and held the canister horizontally in her right hand. Tipping it forward, Diane spun on the balls of her feet. The remaining creamy-white powder poured out to be immediately caught by the wind and dispersed behind her, settling on the verges of the Strip and beyond.

Diane stopped spinning, feeling a little dizzy. She looked into the canister.

"All gone," she remarked to no one in particular.

She replaced the disc and top, returned to her car and threw the empty canister into the back.

Setting the car to the east, Diane drove away from the setting sun.

Tom turned on the radio and made for the motorway. The radio was full of the news that Parliament had sat in emergency session and declared the United Kingdom of Great Britain and Northern

Ireland an area of martial law, effective from nine o'clock that morning. Never before had martial law been declared on mainland Britain.

All routes into and out of the U.K. had been suspended. Civilians were being advised to remain in their homes.

The M4 was all-but deserted. He saw maybe ten civilian vehicles during the twenty-minute drive to Swansea, but twice as many military vehicles. He received stares but no interference.

Tom pulled up outside his mother's house when it was approaching noon. There were no free parking spaces so he left the car blocking the road. It didn't matter; he hadn't seen a moving vehicle since leaving the motorway. He strode up the path and rapped on the front door. Nothing. The house was as silent as the street.

Fumbling his keys from his pocket, he found his mother's and inserted it into the lock.

The stench hit him immediately. He stumbled and almost gagged. The acrid smell of urine mixed with the cloying stink of vomit. Smells he associated with hospitals. Death smells.

Holding a hand over his nose, he glanced quickly into the kitchen and living room, neither expecting nor finding them to be occupied.

He took the stairs two at a time, almost slipping onto his face, and gained the landing. The stench here was stronger, so thick he could almost see it.

Swallowing hard, he faced his mother's bedroom. The door was closed.

"Mam?" he called, softly. Then louder, "Mam?"

He strained to hear if there was any response, then placed his fingers to the door, unable to put off the moment any longer. He pushed and the door swung open.

The air that met him was humid and foetid in equal measure. He swallowed hard again, but did not gag. His nose was growing accustomed to the assault.

Stepping into the room was like entering a greenhouse whose

contents had spoiled. And it was dark. He could barely make out the vague shape of the bed in the pale light spilling through the open doorway.

He moved to the curtains and tugged them open. It took him a moment to realise why the room was still in darkness. Black polythene bin bags had been taped to the window frames. He tore them away and at last grey, wintry light could enter the room. He turned to the bed.

Tom's mother lay on her side in the foetal position, facing away from the window. A duvet covered her to the waist and a stained nightdress clung damply to her back. He stepped around the bed so he could see her face.

Her chest rose and fell in time with her short, shallow breaths. Tom let out a heavy sigh, hardly realising that his own breathing had been shallow from fear that she was already gone.

Her eyelids quivered—her lashes were encrusted in thick, orange muck—and she moaned. Sallow, sunken cheekbones; dark hollows beneath each eye.

Tom placed a hand on her shoulder, almost recoiling from the heat. He shook it gently.

"Mam? Mam? It's me. Tom."

Her eyelids flickered again but did not open.

Tom reached for his phone and punched in 999. He couldn't remember ever dialling that number before, but he was pretty sure he wasn't supposed to get a recorded message. The voice was tinny, reminding him of the soldier with the rifle:

You have called the emergency services. All lines are currently busy due to unprecedented demand. Please consider whether the reason for your call is, in fact, an emergency. If so, please state clearly after the tone which service you require, the brief reason why and the address, including postcode, at which you require the service.

As Tom waited for the *Beep*, he rummaged on his mother's dressing table for an item of mail or anything containing her postcode.

"Er, yes, I require an ambulance for my mother. Urgently. It's definitely an emergency. I think she might be in a coma. The address is…"

He grabbed at the bank statement hiding beneath a pile of old letters and read out the address and postcode. The line beeped again and he pressed the disconnect button.

A thought struck him and he started pulling open the dressing table drawers, looking for clean night clothes and underwear so that he could make up an overnight bag for her. A slight noise behind him made him whirl around. His mother had turned onto her back and was trying to open her eyes. Tom reached the bed in two strides and sat next to her, clutching her frail right hand in both of his.

"Mam? It's okay. I'm here. There's an ambulance on its way."

Her eyelids flickered again, more urgently, and Tom realised that she was struggling to part them because of the orange gunk. He ran to the bathroom, grabbed a flannel and soaked it under the tap. He hurried back to her side and wiped gently at her eyes, softening and removing the crusted matter.

Her eyes fluttered open and closed again immediately. Then, scrunched up against the light, they parted a fraction and she peered at him.

"Mam. It's me. I'm here."

A ghost of a smile formed on her cracked lips. They moved. It was barely a whisper and Tom had to strain to hear what she said. Only two words.

"My boy."

Her eyes closed as the effort of holding them open even a crack grew too much. They didn't open again.

Tom stayed at her side, holding her hand, until the end. It didn't take long.

The President of the most powerful nation on earth made a live televised address that was beamed around the globe at 9:00am Pacific Time.

Viewers gasped at how haggard he looked; he seemed to have aged thirty years in less than a week. The make-up that he wore for the TV cameras couldn't completely mask the dark shadows, the red bruising around the eyes, the hollow cheeks.

The President fixed the camera with his famous glare, which did a better job of hiding his illness than the make-up girl had done, and addressed the world.

"My fellow Americans… No, strike that. This is going out live to every free nation on this planet and it is my fervent hope that it will be seen in many of the less free nations. We're all in this together. So let me start again…

"My fellow *humans*. It is my grave duty to address you on the eve of mankind's swansong. A virus that some have dubbed the Millennium Bug has caused worldwide sickness and death. Every one of you has lost someone precious. I have lost someone precious. The First Lady slipped away six hours ago. I was at her bedside."

The President paused, blinked, coughed and took a sip of water before continuing.

"Every one of you is likely to have someone precious suffering from this virus as I speak. So have I. Both my children are currently in bed, too sick to have even gotten up to be with their mother at the end…"

His voice broke. He took a moment and another sip of water to compose himself.

"I have not long come from a meeting with my Joint Chiefs of Staff—at least, those who were well enough to be conscious—and the top medical advisors this great country has to offer. We made the decision for me to address you now, while I still can. They wanted me to treat this like any other speech, but I refused to have it scripted." He made a noise in the back of his throat; a snort.

"Votes, popularity, opinion polls…" He held up his hands, palms upwards, and shrugged. "What does any of that matter now? The only thing that matters is that I share the truth with you. Everyone deserves that much.

"So. The truth. This administration has been in constant consultation since the start of the crisis with leaders of every other major nation on this planet. Even when nuclear war was a very real threat, we continued to converse—behind the scenes, as it were, in some cases—with each and every one of those nations. All the top scientific minds in the world have been working on the problem constantly. Even when they have fallen ill, these wonderful men and women have worked from their sick beds. We have pooled our resources. Every country has shared everything they can about this threat. Nothing has been held back.

"Every effort has been made to find a cure for this disease.

"Nevertheless..." The President paused and his expression became, if that was possible, even graver.

"Nevertheless, it falls on me to inform you that we have failed. I am told—I am no scientist—that this virus is like nothing we have encountered before. It is wholly resistant to every treatment known to man. If a drug shows any signs of being effective, the virus mutates into something else, constantly shifting the parameters within which it attacks the human body, making sustained treatment impossible. It is as though the virus has been created specifically for killing humans—it appears to have no adverse effect on other creatures, not even members of the ape family.

"We do not possess the technology to artificially create such an organism. No country on earth has such technology. That being the case, there is no need for mistrust of our neighbours. We can say with absolute certainty that the Millennium Bug is not man-made. From where, then, did it come? From outer space? There are theories, but they amount to little more than idle speculation." He grunted. "No one can say for sure and I see little point in speculating further."

Pause; cough; sip of water.

"I am told that if we could slow down the effects, then a cure might be possible in three, four, maybe six months. But even then, a cure is not guaranteed. Our knowledge of the structure of DNA and its manipulation would have to increase tenfold… maybe a hundredfold, before we could even begin to experiment with possible cures. The harsh reality is that we may never find a cure if we had another hundred years to spend searching. And many of us may not have a hundred hours remaining…"

The President removed his spectacles and rubbed tiredly at his eyes, before sliding them back on.

"I appear before you as a sixty-three-year-old. Heck, I feel ninety-three! I will stop speaking shortly, but first I want to address a special group of people.

"It is possible—maybe even likely—that a small percentage of humans will survive the Millennium Bug. Please don't let this raise false hopes. I am advised that even if such a miracle comes to pass, that we are talking about a fraction of a fraction of one percent of the entire pre-virus world population. That equates to roughly one and a half million people. Sounds a lot—it isn't. They will be spread thinly across the planet. It is likely to include a proportion of the elderly and infirm, who may struggle to survive the deprivation that will inevitably follow.

"In other words, the human species, even if that infinitesimal survival rate actually materialises—and I pray to God that it does—will become what the scientists refer to as 'functionally extinct'."

The President took a deep breath, went very still and gazed intently into the lens of the camera before continuing.

"I speak now to the people who are going to live through this. You won't know you're one of them—I'm told that even that tiny percentage who will survive will probably fall sick—but please hear my words and, if you should pull through, please try to remember them.

"I urge you to forget about race and nationality, creed and colour. Forget politics. Forget religion. Forget property and ownership. Such concepts held sway in a planet teeming with seven billion people; they will become meaningless in a world whose population numbers less than two million. The only meaningful ideology, the only ideal worthy of pursuit, will be simple survival of the species."

His gaze intensified further; the millions of viewers worldwide watched in tense silence.

"If you turn out to be one of those people, the future of humanity is in your hands. I beg of you, do not hide away in fear of other survivors. Seek them out and extend the hand of friendship. If you don't speak the same tongue, invent a common one. Heck, draw pictures in the dirt if you have to. But find one another and then find more. Protect and nurture each other. Rebuild communities."

The President paused for the last time. His hands were clasped firmly together on the desk in front of him, but some sharp-eyed viewers noticed that they were shaking.

"Hundreds of thousands of people have already died. Millions more… billions, are dying. To those lucky few who survive: I am issuing instructions that all power plant facilities and food production sites and medical supplies, and whatever else occurs to us, be left running and unlocked. Use them for good.

"Please… take this opportunity to build a better world.

"I beseech you."

His shoulders sagged. "I am out of strength. I am out of words. All that is left to say is goodbye and good luck."

The picture faded, but not before the same sharp-eyed viewers noticed the single tear run down the President's cheek.

In New York, Milandra switched off the television.

"That was really quite moving," she said. "Could almost feel sorry for them."

"*Almost*," said Grant.

"Yes," said Milandra. "Like I said."

In the Ambassador Suite of the Park Plaza in Melbourne, Bishop laughed and flicked a peanut at the television as the President's face faded.

"Wanker," he said.

Tom Evans did not watch the President's address. He was too busy digging a hole in the wet, heavy soil of his mother's back garden.

The ambulance had never turned up. Tom had tried again to ring the emergency services, but once more reached a recorded message. He disconnected before the voice could finish speaking.

He rooted around until he found the telephone number of his mother's GP. No reply; no recorded message.

Next he tried the local hospital. Same result.

Finally, in desperation, he tried the number of a Swansea funeral director. After about ten rings, he was about to hang up when it was answered.

"Yeah, hello?"

"Er, is that the funeral director?"

"Yeah, but we're closed."

"Closed? But, it's my mother. She's… dead."

"Sorry, mate. I can't help you."

Tom did not know what else to say.

"Look," the voice continued, "we're backed up. Same with the morgues. You'll have to make your own arrangements, or…"

"Or what?"

"Leave her where she is. Sorry, don't want to sound harsh—"

Tom hung up.

For a moment, a fleeting moment, he considered walking away and leaving her in bed. He immediately felt guilty and started to hunt for a shovel.

Drawing a blank, he went outside and knocked on neighbours' doors. When nobody answered, he hammered on the doors, making them rattle in their frames. Not so much as a curtain twitched in response. The streets remained deserted, the city silent.

He returned to his mother's terraced house and went out of

the back door. He climbed the fence into the neighbour's garden and approached the shed. The door was secured with a sturdy padlock, but the wood from which the shed had been constructed was of poor quality, flimsy and partially rotted by frequent Welsh rain. When Tom took a firm grasp of the padlock and pulled, the clasp tore away from the wood with a screech. It was still daylight, but nobody challenged him. If anybody saw or heard what he was doing and called the police, they'd be lucky if the police came. *Besides,* he thought, *let them come. They can help me dig the hole.* His mind baulked at calling it a grave.

Inside the shed he found a garden spade. After a moment's hesitation, he grabbed a pickaxe, too.

By the time he had finished digging a pit that he hoped was deep enough, Tom's arms and back felt as though someone was whipping them with red hot wires. Night had fallen: the pitch darkness of deep winter, only marginally relieved by distant street lamps.

He trudged into the house and upstairs to his mother's bedroom. Even with the window thrown wide open, the room still smelled of defecation and death.

Tom bent, the muscles in his back screaming in protest, and gently turned back the duvet, revealing his mother's face. She looked as peaceful as he had ever seen her. He placed a light kiss on her cool brow, stopping himself from instinctively bringing his sleeve up to wipe his lips as he drew back.

He wrapped her in the duvet and lifted her. He expected his back to scream some more, but it had settled into a dull ache that the slight weight of his mother's frail frame did not inflame.

He made his way slowly downstairs, being especially careful of his footing on the stair carpet, and through the kitchen, trying with only partial success not to bump his mother's flopping head on the work surface while he passed.

His grief had been subsumed in the anguish of trying to find someone to help dispose of her body and the exertion of digging the hole. It would no doubt bubble to the surface at some point, but for now he moved purposefully, methodically, as though burying a friend's dog, not his mother.

Tom stood over the hole and knelt at its edge. Back and arms complaining anew, he lowered the wrapped form. The opening was not quite long enough, but by manoeuvring his mother in such a way that her knees bent, she slipped in and landed at the bottom with a small splash where ground water was seeping in.

The horror of what he was doing threatened to overwhelm him. Tom scrabbled on his knees away from the hole and vomited a thin, acidic stream into the grass. Knowing that he needed to act quickly before his mind shut down, he stumbled back and began to shove the pile of extracted earth, clay and stones into the hole with his bare hands. He didn't feel his grasp on reality begin to return until the last of the duvet was covered.

An hour later, muddy and sobbing, he patted down the mound with the back of the spade and threw it aside.

He didn't have energy remaining with which to go hunting for materials to fashion into a cross. He bowed his head for a moment.

"Goodbye, Mam," he whispered. "Although I can't remember the last time I told you, I did love you."

Tears coursing flesh-coloured tracks down his filthy cheeks, Tom returned to the house. His mother had a spare bedroom upstairs, but he made straight for the living room settee and collapsed into it without pausing to remove his mud-caked shoes.

He awoke nine hours later to thin daylight and a cold breeze coming through the open back door. He stumbled to his feet, stiff and aching, shut and locked it.

It was only while splashing water onto his face and into his dry mouth that he realised it was not only his back and arms that were sore: so was his throat.

He decided to drive straight home. This time the only vehicles he saw were military, but only one or two and only in the distance. He had the M4 to himself.

As he neared the exit road that meant he was merely a few

miles from home, the tickling cough began.

Part 2: In the Bleak Midwinter

Chapter Ten

Silence.

Silence of a world gone to hell.

Awareness seeped in, but he did not attempt to open his eyes. He wasn't yet certain where he was. He wasn't yet certain *who* he was.

He started by listening to himself. A faint, regular sigh of exhalation. At least he was breathing. He extended his aural senses.

A *tip*, a *tap*… a brief cacophony of *tips* and *taps*… drops of water. Rain. Rain spattering against a window pane.

Further away, fainter, a *whooshing* sound, building swiftly, fading instantly to nothing, the crescendo coinciding with the spattering rain.

Wind. Gusting wind.

No other sounds. Only his breathing, rain and wind.

Other senses, then.

Smell. He closed his mouth and breathed in. Nothing… no, something. An odour: sour, unpleasant, familiar…

He rolled his tongue around his mouth, trying to taste. The mouth was dry, the teeth coated and furry. He tried to swallow, but there was nothing to go down. Water; he needed water.

For the first time since awaking, he moved. First, his fingers. He spread them flat and moved his hands from side to side. A material of some sort. Cotton? Warm. Damp. Next, his feet. He wriggled his toes against more material, thicker, also warm and damp. A duvet? Finally, his eyes.

They wouldn't open.

He brought up a hand—it felt heavy to lift—and touched his face. Bristly hair rasped faintly when his fingers stroked it. Beneath the bristles, the skin felt tightly stretched, like an over-taut drum. Cheekbones jutted, so prominent they felt likely to break through if he pressed too hard against the skin.

His fingers brushed the eyes, against crustiness resembling the surface of a cooled crème brûlée. Tentatively, the fingers explored the crust. With a fingernail, he scratched at it; gently at first, then more vigorously, feeling the material begin to crumble away. He gasped when a larger chunk broke off, searing the eyelid, probably taking eyelashes with it.

His other hand came up to work on the other eye. More pain. With it came a memory: a beach; a young boy running along the sand; a man watching, coughing thickly into a handkerchief.

The pain in his eyelids—and the memory—stimulated his tear ducts and what remained of the crust softened, coming away more easily, like fresh putty.

The first memory had been the first drip from a breached dam. The last of the crust came free and other memories returned: a trickle, a stream, then a raging torrent as the dam burst.

He gasped again and dropped his hands to his sides.

Now he knew where he was; he knew who he was.

Tom Evans opened his eyes.

Inaction did not suit Troy Bishop. He preferred to be on the go, a man of purpose and intent, a man who made things happen.

Being cooped up in the hotel for almost a week was driving him a little stir crazy. The television channels had stopped broadcasting old shows and movies a couple of days ago. The last local news broadcast had gone out that morning. A teary, coughing technician—all the usual presenters were dead or comatose—had mumbled incoherently for twenty minutes, expounding his theories on why the plague had come, as if there was anyone left who gave a shit. Bishop lobbed wads of moist tissue at the screen, roaring with laughter when he scored a direct hit on the man's face.

Now there were emergency messages on two channels, playing on a loop, exhorting any survivors to collect as much water and tinned food as they could carry and flee the cities, where pestilence from decomposing flesh was otherwise likely to finish what the

Millennium Bug had started. On the other channels, blizzards played to the sound of a clearing throat.

While there had still been a skeleton staff manning the hotel, Bishop had made full use of the room service facility. He gathered that he was the only fit guest. When the last remaining member of staff solemnly informed him that she was leaving her post to go home and to bed, she handed to Bishop her master key that would allow him access to any part of the hotel.

"Thanks," Bishop said. "I hope the fridges are well stocked."

The girl looked at him wonderingly from streaming eyes. Bishop sensed the puzzlement in that look and also something more. Resentment? No, strangely no resentment. What, then? Pity? Yes, that was it… pity.

A cold fury ignited in Bishop. How dare she feel pity for him! His hands clenched into fists and he took a step forward, but the girl had already turned and was trudging down the corridor. For a moment, Bishop considered going after her and showing her who should pity whom. But he stayed still and allowed the fury to seep away. Now was not the time to allow the primal instincts of another species to dominate him. He needed to keep a cool, calm head. There was still much to be done. Soon, he would be able to get on with doing it.

In the meantime, he roamed the hotel, finding his way to the kitchens. They were indeed well stocked and he would eat like a king for his short remaining stay. He did not need to break into any of the provisions he had brought with him.

He made his way to the roof and sat in the sun in the small terraced garden that he found there. This became his favourite place to while away the hours, looking out over the glittering city, soaking up the bright sunlight, feeling his cells react to the energy, absorbing, strengthening. Bishop had lived all over the world, but had settled for the last seventy years in Australia, attracted by the climate and the outgoing nature of the populace. Well, the second factor would no longer be relevant, but he still wanted to return here after the Great Coming. He now considered it to be home, a concept that Bishop still struggled to fully embrace.

The noise of the city diminished with each hour that he spent on the roof terrace. At first, he could still hear the hum of traffic while stragglers fled the city, but soon all sound of road traffic ceased. It was replaced by the distant wails of alarms that he could only hear if he turned his head in certain directions. Whether vehicle or building alarms, he couldn't tell and didn't care. Within a couple of days they, too, had ceased.

He heard the rattle and pop of gunfire one afternoon. It had died away by the evening.

The wide blue emptiness of the skies was only punctuated by the occasional drone of a police or military helicopter. They swept the city and hovered over the streets. Sometimes the faint echo of a metallic human voice reached Bishop's ears when the aircraft addressed the city over their PA systems. A military chopper passed low over the roof of the hotel, close enough for the occupants to be able to see Bishop sitting in the sun, and he waved a hand lazily in its direction. It did not deviate or respond in any way. Bishop laughed and gave it the finger.

After a few days, he stopped seeing or hearing any aircraft and the sky became the sole preserve of birds and insects.

The city became calm and peaceful. A state of serenity settled over it like a balm, a state that had not existed here since before the first European settlers had started to encroach on the region. Bishop found it a little tedious.

He spent the last couple of days of confinement amusing himself in other ways. He outfitted himself in designer clothes from the hotel's boutiques. He visited each of the hotel's three-hundred and forty rooms. Around three-quarters of them had been occupied during the outbreak. Of those, perhaps a hundred rooms had emptied, presumably when the occupants decided to leave the city in a vain attempt at avoiding contamination. Thirty or so rooms had been occupied by people with the presence of mind to lock them securely from the inside before retiring to what they must have thought were merely their sick-beds, not their death-beds. Bishop pressed his ear to these doors but could hear nothing from within any of them. He moved on. There were plenty of rooms to which he could gain access.

The occupied rooms announced their status as soon as Bishop opened the doors. The stench made him grimace at first, but he quickly became accustomed to it. Without exception, these rooms had their blinds and curtains tightly closed. Some had blankets thrown over the windows, too, secured by packing tape. Most occupants lay putrefying in bed, a process hampered by the hotel air conditioning that continued, for now, to pump out cool air. Bishop was therefore able to remove gold watches from wrists that had swollen and blackened, but had not yet begun to grow furry and weep and slough away.

Rings on fingers he ignored—the only way to remove them was by also removing the swollen fingers that the bands had sunk into. It wasn't that Bishop didn't possess the stomach for such a procedure; he merely didn't feel that his need was that great to go to the trouble. In truth, he had no need for any of the items he took back to his room and placed in one of the suitcases. For years he had been accumulating a cache of gold against the day when paper currency became worthless. When gold and silver and precious stones became the new world currency, Bishop would still be extremely wealthy.

Besides, there were plenty of such items lying on bedside cabinets or stuffed into underwear drawers. Also, the hotel safe, once he had found the combination on a sticky note on the back of a cupboard below the reception desk, had provided a treasure trove of diamonds, rubies and precious metals. He left the passports and cash there.

Not all occupants had died in their beds. Some lay blackening on bedroom floors, maybe having fallen out of bed in a death throe or having got out to go to the bathroom before discovering that they no longer possessed sufficient strength to make that journey or to get back into bed. One man he found sitting naked on the toilet, hunched forward with forearms resting on knees.

Bishop prodded him curiously on one cold shoulder. The man toppled sideways and into the open shower, rigor mortis ensuring that the corpse retained its hunched posture.

In the unoccupied rooms, Bishop amused himself by eating peanuts and chocolate from the mini-bars, or taking a shower and using the free range of toiletries, or jumping up and down on the beds as though they were trampolines, or smashing mini bottles of wine and spirits against the walls or against television screens. He had no other use for the alcoholic beverages—the only alcoholic drink he could tolerate was beer and he preferred the taste of lemonade. If there was one thing, apart from the sexual act, for which he slightly envied the human species, it was for their obvious enjoyment of alcohol. It merely made him piss more while his body ejected the poison.

It was in almost the last room that he entered, the room closest to his own, that he found the woman. His senses were assailed by the usual sour stink when he opened the door, but with a small difference. The stench in this room was warmer, moister, fresher, as though the air conditioning had more than a rotting corpse to contend with.

"Interesting," Bishop murmured.

As usual, the occupied room was tightly shuttered against daylight. Bishop flicked the light switch, casting away the gloom. From the doorway, he could see that the bed was empty, the bedclothes thrown back. He strode into the room and glanced at the floor either side of the bed. Empty, too. The bathroom door was closed. He approached it and turned the knob. Locked.

To enable parents to extract children who had managed to lock the bathrooms but could not then unlock them, the locks were designed with a groove into which the edge of a coin or butter knife could be inserted and twisted to disengage the lock. Bishop scanned the room and located a woman's purse. He opened it and glanced at the credit card: Miss A. Anderson. He grabbed a coin and threw the purse onto the bed. In a few seconds, the bathroom door swung open, then stopped when it hit an obstruction. The gap was wide enough for Bishop to squeeze around and, with a grunt, he was in the bathroom.

A young woman lay on the bathroom floor. She wore a dirty white nightdress that had pulled up, exposing lithe, creamy thighs. Her chest rose and fell in short, shallow gasps. Her eyes were closed and a dribble of spittle ran from her open mouth to pool on the tiled floor.

Bishop knelt at the woman's side. She was of slight build and Bishop barely grunted as he got one arm under her knees, the other under her shoulders, and lifted her. Nevertheless, she was starting to feel heavy by the time he climbed the last few stairs and emerged onto the roof terrace.

As soon as the bright sunlight hit her face, the woman moaned and turned into the crook of his arm, trying to escape the glare.

Bishop carried her to the wall that ran around the terrace. It came just past his midriff and formed a wide ledge that he had to bend as far forward as he could manage in order to see over. The hotel was seven storeys high and if Bishop had been one to suffer from vertigo, he would not have been happy to gaze over the ledge; the pavement below looked a long way down.

He placed the woman on her back on the ledge, his arms burning a little, glad to be free of her weight.

She immediately turned her head towards him, away from the sun. Her eyes flickered, struggling to open due to the orange gunk that had formed a crust where the lids met.

"Help me…"

It was little more than a croak. Her lips were caked in dried phlegm.

"What's your name, Miss Anderson?" Bishop said. "Anne? Amy? Amelia?" He laughed. "Let's be honest, is there anyone left who cares?"

"Please…" Her eyes at last opened and Bishop was struck at their greenness; cat's eyes. She must have been quite a stunner before she fell ill. "Help me…"

"Course I'll help you," said Bishop in what he imagined was

the tone employed by a friendly uncle.

The faintest hint of a smile touched her lips and her eyes fluttered closed.

Bishop shoved her off the ledge and craned forward to watch her descent.

Her nightdress flapped out like a failed parachute.

She didn't scream.

Milandra gazed out of the picture window at Central Park. Nothing much moved out there except litter, blown about by strengthening winter winds, and squirrels, who seemed to be enjoying having the park to themselves. She watched them scurry here and there, leaping onto benches and off, emboldened by the absence of people. She yearned to be out there with them.

Jason Grant and Lavinia Cram *were* out there. They had left almost two hours ago on a scouting mission. Milandra had tried to persuade all four Deputies to go, but Grant had insisted that George Wallace and Simone Furlong remain with her.

"In case unwelcome visitors come calling," Grant had cautioned. "Me and Lavinia will be quite safe." He patted the Uzi that hung against his side from a shoulder strap.

Milandra did not argue. She knew that he was right: he and Lavinia were more than capable of taking care of themselves, with or without guns. On the other hand, so was she, and the main reason for her suggesting that the other two Deputies go with them was that she would welcome a little time on her own. Although Milandra had never truly been alone—as the Keeper, she was in constant connection with the rest of her people here on Earth—she enjoyed being physically alone. In this open plan apartment, solitude was almost impossible to find except in the bathroom or one of the bedrooms, and Milandra did not want to disappear into her bedroom too often. Once or twice, when the girl wasn't away with the fairies, she had caught Simone regarding her in a cold, calculating manner, as though measuring her, and she did not wish to give the Chosen any excuse to find weakness. Now was not the time for challenges. Besides, the girl had a lot—an infinity—to learn before she would be ready.

The return of Grant and Lavinia brought her out of her reverie. Wallace let them in and Milandra moved to the armchair at the head of the couches around the coffee table to hear their report. The Deputies took their places around her.

Not one for preliminaries, Grant launched straight into his report.

"There are no indications that there is anyone alive in this building. Most apartments are locked and silent. We could sense no signs of life from within."

He glanced across at Lavinia, who nodded. Milandra thought briefly about the woman who had knocked on the door of her apartment. Holly, that had been her daughter's name. She pushed the image away.

"Three apartments," Grant continued, "had been left unlocked but are deserted. The concierge desk is unoccupied. The main entrance to the building is still secure. When the power fails, that will no longer be the case, but it won't much matter. So far as we could see and sense, there's no one out there alive to cause problems."

"In any case, we'll be gone soon, right?" said Wallace.

"Right," said Grant. "Though *how* we're going to leave is something we need to decide. Let me continue.

"We scouted round some of the other apartment buildings. No signs of life. Most windows we could see from outside have been blocked against the light."

"We heard a dog barking," said Lavinia. She folded her arms across her chest. "Grant wouldn't let me find it."

Grant nodded. "It sounded far away and towards the Hudson. Not the direction we need to take. We went across the Park. There's only squirrels moving about in there now."

"And penguins," added Lavinia. She grinned.

Grant grinned back. "Yep, we took a detour and, ah, liberated the animals from the zoo." His smile faded. "Those that were still alive."

"That was an unnecessary risk," said Milandra. "I've seen those polar bears. Captivity has driven them crazy."

"Yes," said Grant. "Though crazed may be a better description. There was no risk. I could have handled them both on my own. With two of us, no problem."

"I told them to go north," said Lavinia. "We caught them some squirrels. Man, they was *starving*."

Grant chuckled. "They sure were. Never seen a bear chew on a squirrel before with such relish. Anyways, the bears have gone. Headed for Canada last we saw them.

"After the zoo, we went along East 65th to 1st. From there, we went down to the 59th Street Bridge. Everywhere we've been, the roads are empty. It worried me a little. Where had all those vehicles gone? The answer, or part of it, we found at the bridge. It's completely blocked. Both directions. Something must have happened on the Queens side. An accident maybe? Shit, even a truck breaking down and blocking one lane might have caused it, the number of cars trying to get off this island. There are a lot of people still in them cars. Rotting people." He shrugged. "Whatever, we ain't getting out that way."

"What about the Midtown Tunnel?" asked Wallace.

Grant shook his head. "There was a lot of smoke coming from that direction. Difficult to tell with the wind, but it might have been coming from the U.N. building. I think we should avoid it. And tunnels in general. If we are going to encounter anything that might cause us problems, I'd rather do it in the open air. Not trapped like rats underground."

There was a general murmur of agreement.

"North, then?" said Milandra. "The RFK Bridge?"

"I think so," said Grant. He sighed. "It's a pity we weren't in Florida when the message came. We'd have had much further to travel, but it would have been a hell of a lot easier."

There was no hint of it in his tone, but Milandra sensed the mild rebuke nevertheless. She *could* have waited for them to pack and return to Florida before sending the e-mail; a day or two's delay would not have made any difference. She couldn't tell him the real reason why she had sent the e-mail immediately: every minute that she delayed meant another minute during which she could invent excuses to delay further, which meant more minutes to come up with reasons not to send the message at all.

"Yes, well…" She sighed. "We had no control over when the message would arrive. So. North?"

"I think so. We'll have no problems reaching FDR Drive. If there are blockages, that's where we'll encounter them. I think we should take the flatbed, with the bikes on the back. If the bridge is blocked, we may be able to get through on those."

"Why not start on the bikes?" said Simone. Milandra had almost forgotten she was there.

"Well," said Grant, speaking slowly as though addressing a child. "We can travel together on the truck and carry more equipment. If we're lucky, we can take the truck all the way to JFK and not have to dump anything along the way. If we need to switch to bikes, some of our stuff is going to get left behind." He shrugged again. "Nothing we can't cope without, but still…"

Simone tittered. "Cool. Okay."

Milandra sat forward. "Is that decided then? The flatbed. As far as we can take it?"

Everyone nodded.

"Good," she said. "The only thing left to decide is when to set out. There's no hurry. Others are coming in from all over the country and Canada. We'll have to wait in JFK for them to arrive. Nevertheless, I for one would like to get going as soon as possible. I think we're all going a little nuts cooped up in here."

"As far as I can see, there would no advantage to be gained by delaying," said Grant. "If there's anyone still alive out there, they'll be in no condition to cause us any problems."

"Okay," said Milandra. "Unless there are any objections, I suggest we head out tomorrow. At first light."

Nobody objected.

With each passing day, Diane Heidler encountered more and more obstacles during her cross-country trip. The route she had chosen was intended to make maximum use of interstate freeways, but she frequently had to retrace her steps when she found the way blocked by a tangled wreckage of vehicles. This was especially true near larger settlements and she could always tell when she was approaching a city by the number of abandoned or crashed vehicles she encountered.

It seemed that many people had decided to flee the cities in a last desperate attempt at survival, even though they were already ill. Quite possibly, many of the pile-ups she saw had been caused by drivers passing out at the steering wheel and careering across lanes, causing mayhem.

Whenever she left the main highway, she'd find an alternative route to bypass the obstacle and rejoin the main road as soon as she could.

On more than one occasion, she had been forced onto the hard pan to the side of minor roads to skirt an accident scene. During one of these detours, for a few heart-stopping moments the car's wheels had spun in loose sand and the engine's pitch rose alarmingly, before the tyres had found traction in some harder material beneath the surface and the car shot forward. As Diane thankfully rejoined the paved road, her hands had been shaking. It would have been no joke having to abandon the car in the desert midst or plains of Utah or Colorado or Kansas. She would no longer be able to call a recovery firm. It was evident from the bodies strewn around crash sites or still sitting inside cars that emergency services had ceased operating days past.

She guessed that it might have been possible to take one of the cars that had been pulled to the side of the road when, presumably, the occupants became too ill to go any further, but the thought of having to drag putrefying bodies from them first made her shudder. Hand on heart, she didn't know if she would have been able to do it.

Fortunately for her, she never had to. She always managed to find an alternative route, a way of skirting around the major obstructions. She became adept at judging the optimum moment to leave the main highway and find circuitous roads, sometimes meandering back roads, that avoided the approaches to the main cities like Denver, Kansas City and St. Louis where the congestion was worse.

Sometimes, she saw thick, bellowing smoke in the distance that usually marked a town or city and that served as her signal to exit at the next ramp and head south or north until the smoke was behind her and she could make for the main highway again.

In this manner, driving day and night, Diane passed through seven states in four days.

That is when she began to notice the next, and more serious, problem. More and more of the rest stops and filling stations were closed. Some had hand-scrawled signs saying things like, 'Closed until further notice' or, more starkly, 'Shut—Plague!' Many more had simply been abandoned. She had been lucky to come across an abandoned filling station off Route 64 in Illinois whose former owner had not bothered shutting off the power to the pumps. She was able to fill the car's tank, but all the stations she found from then on—and she stopped at them all, in case—either had their power turned off or it was already down.

Outside of an operating theatre, where she had extensive experience as a nurse, Diane was not a practical woman. Even had she heard that there was a way of manually pumping gas from the tanks beneath the forecourts, she would not have known where to start.

By the time she entered West Virginia, her gas tank was almost empty once more. She pulled off at the next filling station and switched off the engine. More in hope than expectation, she pulled a gas gun from its holder, but no pump clicked into whirring motion. She depressed the trigger a few times experimentally, but not so much as a drop trickled out.

A battered grey estate wagon stood at another pump. Diane walked over to it and peered in. A family had owned the car: they were still inside it. The father sat slumped forward against the steering wheel. A woman—his wife?—occupied the passenger seat, head hanging forward onto her chest, still strapped in by the seat belt. A teenage girl lay on her back across the rear seat, staring sightlessly at the car ceiling. The trunk was jam-packed with belongings, on top of which lay a basket containing a cat. It was still alive. It noticed Diane peering in and began to mewl and scrabble at the wire caging of the door. The creature was probably starving, Diane thought.

Something else caught her eye. A coiled length of clear plastic tubing lay next to the cat's cage—like a garden hose for a model village. What Diane didn't know, and wouldn't have cared even if she'd been told, was that the father had recently undergone a colostomy. When the family had been frantically packing the car to flee their home in the suburbs of Columbus, Ohio, the father had picked up the spare surgical tubing that he had for carrying out emergency repairs to his colostomy bag and that, thankfully, he hadn't yet needed to use. He had paused for a moment, fighting back the tickling cough that made his head ache, considering whether to take it. He already knew that repairing his colostomy bag was likely to be the least of his problems. With a shrug, he had chucked it into the back, next to Candy's basket.

Diane tried the handle of the back door. With a creak it came open, letting out a gust of foetid air. She stepped smartly back, coughing and clutching her nose.

Taking a deep breath, she held it and ducked through the doorway, placing her knee carefully on a space on the rear seat not occupied by the girl's corpse, and reached for the tubing.

The cat spat and tried to claw at her.

Diane grabbed the tubing and backed out of the car. She thought for a moment, then repeated the process, this time grabbing the cat's cage. The creature yowled and threw itself at the wire. Diane laid the basket on the ground and knelt on the tarmac to peer in. The cat was scrawny and bare patches of pink skin showed through its tawny fur. The floor of the cage was thick with the cat's waste; its paws were stained and soaking. At least one of its claws had come off when it had attacked the caged door. One of its ears was tattered and bleeding where it must have snagged on a protruding wire in its frantic efforts to escape.

"Shhhh," murmured Diane and probed. She could sense a swirling, livid vortex of feral need to feed, underlain by sheer terror. The cat's mind had come unhinged during its confinement in the trunk of the car.

"Hmm, you're one hungry, angry kitty, ain't you?" she said.

The cat continued to hiss and swipe at the wires, trying to reach her.

"Will you survive, I wonder, if I let you go…" She glanced past the shuttered service station, to the fields that stretched away beyond. "There'll probably be mice and rats out there. Snakes, too. Maybe *they* will get *you*." She shrugged. "*Que sera sera.*"

Diane reached for the door catch, but drew her hand back in a hurry when the cat yowled and made a leap at her, thudding into the wire mesh.

"Oh, my. You're gonna come for me, ain't you, kitty? It won't matter that I'm more than twenty times bigger than you. Let's put you straight on that score, shall we?"

She stared intently at the cat. It laid its ears flat against its skull, but stopped hissing and mewling. It stared back at Diane, its eyes large and black. She implanted the image of her bashing the cat's head into a bloody pulp with a rock. The creature backed into the furthest corner of the basket, lowering its body so that it cowered in its own filth.

"There," said Diane. "That should discourage you." She reached out again and unfastened the clasp. She pulled the door open. The cat did not move.

"Off you go then, kitty." Diane shuffled back a couple of paces on her knees.

The cat looked at her. It took one tentative step towards the door. When Diane made no movement, it slunk forward, belly fur brushing through excrement and urine. With one last terrified glance at Diane, the cat gained the forecourt and looked desperately around, not knowing where to run.

"Over there's your best bet, kitty," said Diane, pointing towards the fields and starting to rise to her feet.

The cat took off, streaking across the forecourt. It skidded to an ungainly halt at the edge of the brush that marked the start of the field and looked back, its tail whipping back and forth like a live cable.

Diane took one step in the cat's direction. It turned tail and fled into the fields.

She smiled, but it quickly faded when she remembered that she was almost out of gas. She glanced at the roll of tubing in her hand.

Of course, Diane had heard of syphoning and had seen it done in the movies. She needed to poke one end of the tube into gasoline and suck hard to start a flow of liquid. So long as the open end of the tube was below the level of the covered end, the flow would continue.

Diane stepped back to the station wagon and opened the driver's door. The key was still in the ignition and she turned it to accessories. Trying to ignore the stench that came off the driver in thick waves, and supporting her weight by grabbing the central pillar to avoid touching him, she leaned across him until she could see the fuel gauge. Almost half a tank. It clearly wasn't the need for gasoline that had caused the father to park up on this forecourt.

Judging from the intensity of the reek rising from the bodies, the car had been parked here like this for days. Assuming that there had still been other people around a few days ago, strange that no one had tried to help the family. Diane did not waste time pondering the question—she had witnessed so many instances of man's brutality to man that apparent indifference towards a dying family did not completely surprise her.

She walked around the station wagon, trying to find the gas tank cover, before thinking to open the trunk. There it was, tucked into the sill that ran around the trunk.

Diane went back to her car, started it and drove it to the back of the station wagon, lining up her gas tank cover near the station wagon's. She parked and turned off her engine.

She uncoiled the tubing and fed one end into the wagon's gas tank. She had no idea how far down it went so gave an experimental suck on the end still in her hand. She gasped as the fumes burned her throat, and took deep breaths before she fed the tube in further and tried again. This time, she could not suck. She let out a deep breath and sucked again, harder. Nothing except more stinging fumes. Another deep exhalation and another huge suck… and she was gagging on the most disgusting liquid she had ever tasted.

Coughing and spluttering, she whipped the tube from her mouth and clamped her thumb over the end. She doubled over, spitting and retching, desperate to expel the burning, foul taste.

When at last she could straighten, she used her free hand to unscrew the cap to her gas tank and then held the tube over the opening. She could see the liquid inside the tube; it looked like pale urine. Moving her thumb away from the end of the tube, she quickly fed the tube into her tank. Now she could feel the liquid flowing down the tube.

She held it in place until the flow stopped. Only then did she grab a bottle of water and rinse her mouth.

Once back behind the wheel, the tube stashed safely in her trunk where she would not notice the fumes it gave off, she started the engine. The needle on the fuel gauge crept up to a quarter and continued, hovering just below half. The station wagon probably had a larger tank, but she had succeeded in syphoning most of its contents into her own car.

Diane did something very much out of character: she threw back her head and uttered an almighty *WHOOP*!

Chapter Eleven

It had been a few days since Peter had heard any sign of life outside; two days since the man appeared.

Electricity still coursed through the cables, water still ran clear from the taps, but he didn't think either would for much longer. He had watched all the DVDs with varying degrees of interest and enjoyment. His supplies of fresh food were exhausted. The weather had taken a turn for the worse and wind-driven rain spattered the cottage windows. A few degrees' drop in temperature and that rain would turn to snow. He still had enough logs and coal to keep the cottage warm, but that was insufficient reason to stay. In truth, he was bored.

There were also, of course, other considerations. Soon the others would be on the move, heading this way. He didn't think they would set out just yet. They would need to make sure that the virus had finished its work. But neither would they want to delay for too long.

Some would be coming by air and the longer they waited, the more chance of something going wrong with the ground and satellite guidance and communications systems upon which modern aircraft so heavily relied. Like the electricity and water supplies, these systems would continue to operate for a period without being maintained, but not indefinitely. Indeed, some would fail when the electricity failed and he was already anticipating that occurring.

Nevertheless, it would be a few weeks yet until they began to arrive in any numbers. They were coming from all around the world and it might take up to a month for everyone to get here. Peter intended to be far away by then.

For now, he felt it was time to be out and about. See if there were any survivors in the vicinity. It was a risk, but one that he wanted to take. Falling in love with Megan had taught him the pleasure—and pain—of loving another. Living with her for sixty years had taught him to care for others; more specifically, for humans. If he could find some survivors, there was a chance that he could save them.

Provided he could convince them of the truth. That was a problem he would have to try to overcome as and when it arose. It wasn't something that he could plan for so it was pointless trying to.

Peter went into the kitchenette to make a cup of tea. Might as well, he thought, while he still could. Tea would be one thing he would miss when the electricity failed.

While he waited for the kettle to boil, he looked out of the window. The rain had stopped, for now. *He* was still there.

The man hadn't been the first to try opening Peter's front door, but the first to bang upon it when finding it securely locked. Peter had ignored the rattling of the door knob, but paused the DVD he had been watching when the banging started. He sat there quietly, waiting for it to stop. When it had, Peter stood and crept upstairs to the tiny window in the bathroom at the front of the cottage. He peered through, but the street seemed to be deserted. He moved to the window in his bedroom, at the back of the cottage.

He could see from this vantage point the back end of the Range Rover. A man came into view, moving around the vehicle, pulling at the tarpaulin. Peter stepped back a little into shadow so he would be hidden if the man happened to glance up.

The man was in his forties; tall, balding, rough-shaven. He paused now and again to lean forward and cough, resting his hands on his knees and expelling large wads of phlegm when each fit of coughing tailed off. The man straightened and began tugging at the tarpaulin again, but it didn't move. Peter knew that the man would have even less success in untying the knots in the string which he had used to secure the tarp—he had learned many things in his years in the merchant navy; tying knots that could not easily be undone was one of them. Of course, not even his knots would defeat a keen blade, but the man did not seem to possess a knife for he gave up tugging at the tarpaulin and walked unsteadily to the outhouse.

He grasped the padlock and yanked on it. Peter stayed still, watching from the shadows, not in the least concerned that the man would be able to break the padlock open with his hands alone—he had bought a sturdy one with this sort of scenario in mind.

The man let go of the lock, turned to one side and vomited. He looked down at the small puddle for a few moments as if fascinated by what he saw there.

Then he stepped to the side, like a drunk trying to walk a straight line. For a few paces, he stumbled sideways onto the small lawned area, until his legs became entangled with each other and he fell. The man stayed where he was, flat on his back, arms spread wide in the shape of a crucifix.

That had been two days ago and the man still lay there, face turned skywards. Although he didn't look as though he'd moved since he'd fallen, there had been some small changes: his left hand was now missing three fingers; one of his cheeks had been torn away, leaving a flap of skin that fluttered in gusts of wind. Foxes, probably. Maybe dogs or cats, already going feral.

The kettle boiled and Peter made a mug of tea. While he sipped it, he came to a decision. Tomorrow, he would venture out. He wouldn't go far, only a two- or three-mile radius for now, taking in the neighbouring villages. Depending on what he found there, he could increase the range, but he would only explore the surrounding areas for the next two weeks.

Then, he was leaving.

After the girl in the nightdress, Bishop did not find any more survivors in the hotel. He had explored every inch of the Park Plaza and spent his last night there sitting on the roof terrace, enjoying the balmy summer air.

With nightfall, many areas of the city remained in darkness as the Grid started to fail. Within a night or two, the only lights would come from places, like hospitals, that had their own emergency generators. They, too, would fail soon enough with no one to refuel them.

Even while Bishop watched, lights in parts of the city winked out. He knew it was coming; sure enough, the floor-level subdued floodlights that gently lit the terrace flickered and faded.

Bishop went inside and made his way down the staircase to the Ambassador Suite, the darkness relieved only by the soft glow of the hotel's battery-powered emergency lighting. The key-card no longer worked, but that was all right since the room doors defaulted to unlocked in the event of total power failure.

His suitcases remained packed. New clothes, food, drinks—he had been well provided for by the hotel and hadn't needed to open the cases except to add jewellery and other precious items he had scavenged, though he preferred to think of it as salvaging. He had taken the pistol from the holdall and spent a morning thoroughly cleaning and oiling it using the small kit he kept in a side pocket of the holdall.

After a moment's consideration, he clicked off the pistol's safety and placed it back inside the holdall, on the top. He would once more keep the holdall unzipped and within easy reach on the passenger seat next to him.

Hoisting the holdall over his shoulder by its strap, a suitcase in each hand, Bishop made his way to the basement car park, stepping carefully in the dim light. His footsteps echoed in the cave-like space.

The Mazda had not been tampered with. It was parked alongside some other expensive vehicles in a caged area of the car park. The electro-magnetic lock that secured the steel-mesh gate to the small compound had unlocked in the power failure. Bishop swung it open with a gentle kick.

He unlocked the car and squeezed the cases into the boot space. The concierge had been true to his word and had raised the polyvinyl hood. Bishop decided to leave it in place. His only real concern about driving to the airport was encountering some crazy survivor who had managed to arm himself with a firearm. Leaving the hood up would make him a more difficult target.

As he settled behind the wheel and gunned the accelerator, nodding to himself that the period of inaction did not sound as though it had done the engine any harm, he glanced at the holdall on the seat beside him and had second thoughts. He reached in and extracted the pistol. He placed it in the door well next to his right thigh. From there, he would be able to draw and level the weapon with his right hand quickly and, if needs be, unobtrusively.

Bishop set off for Melbourne Airport.

He was familiar with the layout of the city and found alternative back-street routes with ease in the few places where abandoned vehicles blocked his path.

During one of his detours, not far from the banks of the Yarra River, he approached a snarl of cars and vans that were blackened as though they had been torched. The wreckage partially blocked the road ahead, but the Mazda was small enough to squeeze past. He slowed down to ease the car past the last of the burnt-out vehicles and noticed a pile of bodies lying in the road beyond the wreckage. There must have been twenty or thirty men and maybe half as many women thrown higgledy-piggledy on top of each other. At the same time that he noticed the bodies, the stench of putrefaction swept through the open window and he hurriedly closed it.

When the passage of the car disturbed the multitudes of flies that had settled on the piled corpses, they rose buzzing into the air like a plague of locusts. Bishop gave a wry smile, relieved that he had closed the window and kept the hood on the Mazda raised.

He waited until he was well clear before winding down the window again.

Not long after that he encountered a living person. The man emerged on the run from a side street and stopped in the road ahead of him. Bishop considered for a moment simply mowing him down, but curiosity got the better of him and he slowed down.

The man looked to be in his late thirties, unshaven and straggle-haired. He watched Bishop approach, unmoving but poised to spring away like an alert hare.

Bishop brought the Mazda to a halt alongside him, a few feet away. He dropped his right hand from the steering wheel and allowed it to rest on the grip of the pistol. He probed, too briefly and gently to be noticed, but sensed no danger, only bewilderment and fear.

"G'day," Bishop said.

The man's face immediately broke into an expression of relief and he almost bounded to the car. He bent forward, hands on thighs, to look in at Bishop.

"Man, oh, man, oh man, am I glad to see you!" he said.

Bishop regarded the man curiously. His skin was sallow, dark troughs below the eyes, but the eyes themselves, though a little wide and staring, were clear and dry. He did not cough or sniff.

"You survived, then," Bishop murmured.

"Yeah, man. I fell ill but…" He shrugged as though he hadn't considered this until now. "I got better."

"It appears so," said Bishop.

The man's face creased and it took Bishop a moment to realise that he was fighting back tears. "Everyone I know is dead, man. Can I… can I come with you?"

Bishop's fingers tightened around the butt of the pistol, then relaxed when he had an idea. Maybe this man, fatigued as he was and close to tears, would be more open to suggestion. Maybe Bishop could persuade him to jump into the Yarra or step off a rooftop.

He looked intently at the man and… *pushed.*

The man's eyes opened wider. "What the fuck…?" He took a step back, then another. "What are you doing?" The man's eyes narrowed. "What are you?"

Bishop frowned. He had hoped that the man's mental resistance would be so eroded as to be easily overcome, but it seemed they could still keep him out, at least one-on-one. No matter; they would not be able to resist the combined force of his people. And after the Great Coming…

"What am I?" said Bishop. He laughed. "I am the thing under your bed. The monster in your closet. The bogeyman…" He raised both hands, fingers waggling, and made a *whooo* sound. "I am your creator and your doom."

The man stumbled back another couple of paces. Bishop grinned at him. With a cry of fear, the man turned and disappeared down the alleyway from which he'd emerged.

Bishop was still chuckling to himself when he arrived at the airport twenty minutes later.

Tom stared at his reflection in the bathroom mirror. He appeared wan, washed-out, and could do with a shave. The skin covering his cheeks and brow looked as thin as tracing paper.

His stomach rumbled. He made his way downstairs slowly, legs shaky and unsteady, one hand clutching the banister, the other holding his duvet around his shoulders like a king's robe. At the bottom, he sat back on the second stair to catch his breath.

Only vague recollections of the last few days remained in his mind. Shadowy images of sweats and shivers, tottering expeditions to the bathroom to relieve himself and splash water on his fevered brow, nightmarish encounters with Dracula and Freddy Krueger and Lisa… He tried to imagine that burying his mother wrapped in a duvet in her garden was also the product of delirium, but he knew better. The callus on the palm of his right hand attested to the blister the handle of the borrowed shovel had made while he dug deep into the heavy soil.

Tom blinked and swallowed quickly when the water he'd greedily drunk threatened to come back up. He swayed a little, thankful that he was sitting down.

He glanced at his front door; at the mat below it. He had no idea what day it was or for how long he had been ill, but the mat should be covered in mail, even if most of it was junk. But there was nothing there, not even a circular.

The feeling of nausea passed and he rose unsteadily. Hand leaning against the wall for support, he stagger-walked to the kitchen. The digital clock on the cooker showed the time as 14:51, but the room was cast in gloom. Rain fell heavily from rolling, black clouds and dashed against the windows like gravel. Although the blinds were open, it was more like evening than early afternoon and he flicked the overhead light switch. It was only when the room was bathed in the warm glow of the ceiling spotlights that he realised the full import of the clock and overhead lights working: the electricity was still on.

Tom breathed out heavily. He had imagined during his delirium that Armageddon had come and he was the last man to be left alive. One obvious consequence of such an occurrence would be power outages. Permanent ones if he was truly the last man standing. Tom possessed only the most hazy notion of how services like gas and electricity arrived in people's homes and would not have the first idea where to even begin to reconnect the power if it went out.

His stomach rumbled again. He moved to the fridge and opened the door, wrinkling his nose in anticipation. The smell of sour milk was bad, but not unbearable. He took the carton out of the door and shook it. By the thick sludgy sound, he guessed that the milk had coagulated. He didn't intend to open the carton to find out. Placing it to one side, he took a quick inventory: three cartons of yoghurt days past their use-by date; an opened tin of baked beans covered in clingfilm; a plastic container of tomatoes that had begun to dimple and shrivel; a chunk of cheddar cheese that had started to grow a skin of blue mould that could easily be cut away; a couple of onions that felt firm enough; a three-quarter full bottle of cola; an unopened bottle of lemonade; three cans of beer; a half-drunk bottle of white wine; assorted tins of meats and fish; jars of pickles and chutneys.

Could be worse. The yoghurt, beans and tomatoes would have to go, but he could make some sort of meal from the rest. The small freezer section of the fridge contained a box of fish fingers and a loaf of sliced bread. A cupboard next to the sink contained a few cans of soup, a tin of chopped tomatoes, a bag of dried pasta and a box of rice.

Letting the duvet fall to the floor, Tom opened a can of corned beef, his fingers struggling with the key, but hunger lending them strength. He turned the block of meat out onto a plate and sliced it. Almost dribbling with desire, he brought a slice up to his lips. He bit off a chunk and chewed, eyes closed, savouring the fatty flavour.

He made himself pause after finishing the slice before taking the next one; although his instinct was to wolf down the meat, he didn't want to make himself sick.

While he chewed and swallowed the last morsel of that first divine slice, and in order to divert his attention from the rest of the corned beef, he took stock.

Clearly he had fallen ill with some sort of flu-like disease. He could only assume it was the same one that had killed his mother—he hurried his thoughts along at this point—and had led to martial law being introduced to the U.K. He had survived. Here he was, weak as a new-born foal, but free of sniffles and coughs and fever. And if he had survived, then maybe it wasn't as bad as he had imagined…

He shivered, but that was because the house was cold. He picked up the duvet and threw it around his shoulders. Feeling a little stronger already after only one slice of tinned meat, he walked over to the boiler and flicked the central heating switch on. A pause, a loud click and the heating whirred into motion. He smiled.

Pausing to collect the plate of corned beef, Tom walked through to the living room and turned on the television and a couple of lamps. He crammed a whole slice of meat into his mouth and settled back on the settee with the remote control.

The TV was tuned to the sports channels, as usual, but only flickering, snowy static showed on the screen. That didn't surprise him too much—the sports channels would, he supposed, be the last things to be reinstated after a world crisis. The BBC, that's what he needed to watch. If anyone could tell him how far the recovery was underway, he could rely on the good old Beeb.

The channel changed to BBC1 and Tom stopped chewing while his lower jaw dropped. The screen showed a dark red background over which was printed a few sentences; an expressionless voice spoke the same sentences over and over in an unending loop:

This is an emergency announcement. The Acting Prime Minister, General David Banning, has issued a nationwide order that any infected person found in a public place be shot on sight. He urges anybody currently unaffected by the Millennium Bug to remain where they are and not to attempt to have contact of any sort with any other person. May God be with you…

This is an emergency announcement. The Acting Prime Min—

The television screen and the lamps went off simultaneously. The whirring and clicking of the boiler that Tom could usually hear in the lounge when the TV was off also stopped.

Tom sat in the gloom, listening to the rain lash against the windows, and forced himself to finish the corned beef, though his appetite seemed to have disappeared with the electricity.

By the time she reached the outskirts of New York City, Diane Heidler had become an old hand at syphoning gasoline from abandoned vehicles. She could start the flow with one suck, and knew exactly when to whip the tube out of her mouth and clamp the ball of her thumb over the end to minimise loss through spitting or spilling. She had even grown accustomed to the foul, fiery taste. In fact, she sometimes welcomed it for it banished the stench of the putrefying occupants of the vehicles. She had quickly learned that syphoning only seemed to work on older-model vehicles. It wasn't a problem—she was spoilt for choice.

She approached the city via New Jersey. She had not seen a living person for three days and he had been almost dead, slumping towards her when she opened the car door and half-falling to the road with a weak groan. She'd had to step over him to check his gas gauge and release his fuel cap. When she had finished syphoning his fuel, she poked him with the toe of her right foot. He groaned again, but did not open his eyes. The other occupant of the car—an old woman; his mother?—had been dead for a day or so judging from the smell and the way her body was swelling.

The number of stalled vehicles began to rise when she drew nearer to the city and the fear of finding her way blocked began to grow. If she came across an obstacle that she could not find a way past, she would have to walk, a prospect that held no attraction. Diane had a slight frame that would cope with a long hike, but she would much prefer to avoid it. Physical exercise was not an endeavour that she particularly liked to pursue. Added to which, it had been raining steadily for most of the morning.

Her luck held at first. The toll road and bridge to Staten Island, though blocked in the other direction, was clear heading onto the island. She had to slalom around a couple of cars, but made it to the island without mishap. Her luck ran out trying to leave Staten.

She had almost made it to Brooklyn, when she found the road blocked by a snarl of silent vehicles. She stopped the car and thumped the steering wheel in frustration.

"Damn! Damn! Damn!" she muttered. "Oh, well. Only one thing for it…"

Diane got out of the car and leaned back inside to retrieve her knapsack from the passenger seat. Buttoning her jacket tightly and muffling her neck with a scarf, she opened the rear door and grabbed a couple of bottles of water and a few snacks that she thrust into the knapsack. She considered the length of plastic tubing for only a moment, before closing the door on it. She didn't even notice the empty silvery canister on the floor. With a glance of regret at the car—she would have to get one in precisely that colour when all this was over—she turned her face to the drizzle and began to walk.

The stalled traffic formed two solid lines, but there was ample space for a lone pedestrian. Once or twice, Diane had to pick her way around or over rotting bodies. If she had given it any thought, she might have guessed that these people, too, had decided to walk, but had died where they fell when illness overcame them. But she didn't speculate; the bodies were simply more obstacles, smelly, oozing obstacles, in her way.

She passed a motorcycle, its former rider gone, keys still in the ignition. She stopped and considered for a moment, but only for a moment since she had absolutely no idea how to ride one—and now, with no one around to pick her up when she fell, probably wasn't the best time to try to learn. She shrugged, making water drip down her neck, and continued on.

Her jacket, designed more to keep out cold than rain, had become heavy and the clothes beneath damp as she stepped onto Brooklyn. The cause of the traffic jam became evident a mile or so on when she came to the exit ramp. A container truck had jack-knifed, blocking the highway in both directions as effectively as a cork in a bottle. Boxes of whatever the truck had contained had spilled out, and lay sagging and bloated in the rain. She gave them no more than a cursory glance. Whatever was in the boxes held no interest for her.

Having left the expressway, Diane did not have to walk much further. She came across a yellow taxi standing at an angle with its front tyres against the kerb as though it had trundled to a halt. A man's body lay face down on the grass verge a few yards away. She glanced inside the cab. No corpses. No keys.

She tried the driver's door and it swung open. The interior light came on, looking strong, indicating the car's battery was still good.

Diane walked over to the prone man. Breathing through her mouth, she grasped the body by the shoulders and half-turned it so she could reach into the pockets of the bomber jacket that he wore. Although the jacket was thick, Diane fancied that the shoulders beneath felt a little squelchy and she grimaced.

The first pocket was empty. Turning the body the opposite

way, she reached into the other pocket of the jacket. Her hand encountered something sticky and she withdrew it sharply. A quick glance and sniff at her fingers revealed that the sticky thing must be a roll of sweets. Nearly ready to give up and resume trudging, she thrust her hand inside the pocket again, deeper, past the sweets, and came out holding a bunch of keys.

She stood, ran back to the taxi and lowered herself into the driver's seat. She inserted the key into the ignition—it went in smoothly—and turned it. The engine coughed, spluttered, then roared into life.

Diane shrugged out of her wet jacket and flung it in the back. She drove the rest of the way to JFK without incident.

Chapter Twelve

The flatbed truck moved northwards past Central Park, then turned east through Harlem, without difficulty. The roads remained virtually deserted until they reached FDR Drive, but even here they encountered stalled vehicles only in patches and were easily able to manoeuvre around them.

Milandra entrusted the driving to Grant's calm assurance. She sat on the bench seat in the cabin next to him, with Simone on her right next to the passenger door. In the back, wearing waterproof jackets beneath which they kept the readied Uzis out of the rain, rode Wallace and Lavinia. They shared the flatbed with five motorcycles, a tarpaulin secured to protect them from the worst of the elements.

There came a moment, while they searched for a way past knots of entangled vehicles onto the Robert F. Kennedy Bridge, when Milandra thought they would have to abandon the truck and take to the motorbikes. It wasn't a thought that filled her with delight. Although her Harley had been custom-made to comfortably support her bulk and she could ride like a veteran Hell's Angel, she didn't derive the thrill from riding a motorcycle that the others, particularly Wallace and Simone, seemed to. It made her feel vulnerable. Mortal. Not something she liked to be reminded of.

"It's okay," Grant said. "I think I can see a way past."

Inching forward and using the front end of the truck as a sedentary bulldozer, Grant nudged the obstructing vehicle out of the way and their route onto the bridge was clear.

They crossed the East River onto Randalls Island and turned south, joining the road from the Bronx. The route remained clear, the occasional stalled car failing to hamper their progress.

It was only when they approached the East River again, to cross into Queens, that they began to encounter more and more abandoned vehicles, forcing Grant to slow down and weave a path through them like negotiating an obstacle course.

Slower and slower he drove, not much more than walking pace, but still he was able to find a way through.

"I don't like this," Grant muttered. "It's almost as though these cars have been set out like this deliberately... *arranged*, to slow down any approaching vehicles."

There's something not right here he sent. *Be alert!*

Grant lifted his right hand from the steering wheel and banged once on the roof of the cabin. Immediately, an answering thud sounded from above.

Milandra added a note of caution. *Only use the weapons as a last resort* she sent. *We don't want to draw attention to ourselves.*

Another thud sounded on the roof and Milandra smiled.

"Why?" said Simone.

"Huh?" said Milandra.

"Why not draw attention to ourselves? I thought most everyone else was dead."

"Yes, Simone, most are. But there *will* be survivors. Some of them may have already found each other. Started banding into groups. They'll be scared and angry. The last thing we need is to draw survivors to us at this juncture."

Grant grunted in agreement, not taking his eyes from the road. He looked tense and Milandra realised that she felt the same. She glanced at Simone. By contrast, the girl seemed relaxed, one jeans-clad knee drawn up in front of her, foot resting on the benchseat, hands clasped around her knee. She looked out of the windshield, then out of the side window, as though close to boredom.

Milandra sensed Grant stiffen. "Here we go," he muttered.

Ahead through the drizzle, Milandra could see the outside lane blocked by a car that had stopped, or been moved, so that it was tight to the concrete central barrier. A maintenance truck with cones and warning signs in the back was pulled alongside the car, blocking the next lane. They were passing beneath one of the grey suspension girders and the highway was four lanes wide. An RV, a white one that looked shiny and new, had been parked sideways across the remaining two lanes, providing a complete barrier.

Grant pulled the flatbed to a halt five yards from the RV and engaged the parking brake. He left the engine running and the windshield wipers on.

"What now?" said Simone. She lowered both feet to the floor and sat forward, peering through the drizzle. Milandra sensed excitement flowing off her.

"Now we wait," Milandra answered. "Let them see that we're not aggressive."

They didn't have to wait long. A man appeared from behind the RV, squeezing through the gap between it and the maintenance truck. He wore a dark green military cape and looked to be in his late fifties. Drops of water clung to the faint wisps of grey hair that criss-crossed his head like a spider's web. In the crook of one arm, the butt and workings wrapped in clear plastic, only the black muzzle open to the elements, the man held a sawn-off shotgun.

He stopped in front of the RV and regarded them.

Milandra was about to probe the man, surreptitiously, to see if she could ascertain his intentions without alarming him, but Simone beat her to it. The Chosen had sat so far forward, her butt was at the edge of the benchseat and her nose almost touched the windshield.

The man frowned and his posture stiffened. He raised the shotgun to chest height, aiming at the cabin of the flatbed.

Help me sent Simone. *He's too strong. Can't do it on my own.*

She flung open the passenger door and stepped out into the rain.

Reacting instinctively, Milandra lent her intellect to Simone, and felt Grant, Wallace and Lavinia follow suit.

Simone approached the man. His features contorted into a grimace of surprise and fear. He still held the shotgun pointed at the truck, but it looked as though he was trying to bring it to bear on Simone. His mouth twisted with effort while he willed his arms to obey his instructions. The shotgun didn't move.

Milandra made as though to follow Simone, but Grant laid his arm on hers.

"Let her handle it," he muttered. "Not much you can do with her taking the lead..."

Milandra sagged back into the seat, knowing he was right. With Simone controlling their combined intellects, there was only a limited amount any of them could do until she released them.

Simone reached the man and walked slowly around him, inspecting him with a look of frank curiosity. The drizzle started to flatten her hair and she brushed it away from her eyes absentmindedly. Having completed the circle, she stopped in front of the man.

Even with the combined force of five psyches, it didn't appear as though Simone's control was complete. The man's body and limbs had frozen, but his face still worked, expressing at turns fear and loathing and anger and bewilderment.

With the part of her mind that remained her own, Milandra sensed what Simone intended to do. She wanted to stop her, to persuade her down another path, but would need the others to all be in accord to override Simone's wishes. That clearly wasn't the case. All she could sense from Grant was indifference; Wallace and Lavinia were in agreement with Simone and were performing the mental equivalent of a cheer lead.

Milandra was powerless to do anything except sit and watch.

Summoning the power of all five intellects, Simone *pushed...*

The man's eyes blazed with hatred and he tried to spit at Simone. The spittle barely left his mouth. He lowered his arms and turned the shotgun around and upwards, placing the muzzle under his chin. His movements were jittery as though he resisted with every last ounce of strength he possessed.

Simone took a step backwards. The man pulled both triggers and the reports reverberated around the confined space created by the vehicles.

The white side of the RV was sprayed with blood and thick globules of skull and brain matter that slid down its rain-slickened surface.

Simone watched the man's body fold up and crumple to the road. She turned and smiled. Only then did she release them.

Milandra breathed out deeply, feeling a little sick. She clambered out of the truck. Grant followed her. Wallace and Lavinia jumped down from the back and they all approached the RV.

"How cool was that?" said Simone.

"Yeah, baby," said Lavinia.

Wallace nodded and grinned.

Milandra said nothing. Her reaction to what had happened disturbed her. She must quell these emotions of compassion and mercy. With what lay ahead, she could not afford to give them any room. She had grown weak and she needed to be strong.

She glanced sideways at Grant. He was considering her with a thoughtful expression that she didn't much like, but she resisted the urge to probe him.

Grant looked away and walked to the other side of the RV.

"All clear," he called. "The keys are in the ignition. I'll move it out of the way."

Milandra's nausea had passed, washed away by the rain like the man's blood.

"Come on," she said to Simone, "let's get out of this drizzle."

She and Simone resumed their seats in the cabin of the truck. Wallace and Lavinia waited while Grant reversed the RV towards the central barrier, leaving it parked in front of the car and maintenance truck, clearing the inside lane for them to pass.

They resumed their places on the bed of the truck and Grant sat back in the driver's seat, wiping water from his face.

"Right," he said. "Hopefully, next stop JFK."

It took Tom the best part of forty-eight hours to feel he had built up his strength sufficiently to consider venturing outside.

He slept and ate and tried to keep despair at bay.

The terrors that came while he slept were born not of

delirium, but of the hazy memory of burying his mother and the fear that he was the only person alive. In his dreams, he feverishly dug holes and ran from a faceless stalker, and tried over and over to breathe life into his dead mother, but her face crumbled under his touch.

When the electricity failed, he filled saucepans from the cold tap, then went upstairs and ran the cold tap into the plugged bath until, with a clanking of pipes, the flow spluttered to nothing. The bath was nearly half-full. He reckoned he also had a hot-water tank full of water if he needed it.

He would not die of thirst, but his food was already running low—he had been eating as though food was going out of fashion, which he supposed in a manner of speaking it was.

The phone lines were dead. Without electricity, his desktop computer was useless and he had left his laptop in school. His mobile phone, though the battery held some charge, had no signal. The internet connection didn't work. His sense of isolation was complete.

Tom wasn't usually one for reading fiction, though the previous year had worked his way through a novel Mark had lent him. It was by a German author, about a man who wakes up to discover he is the only person left alive on the planet. Tom enjoyed the book, but scoffed at the notion. Now he felt as though he was that man. The story had not ended well—the man stepped off a very tall building.

The idea of ending his life had occurred to Tom, especially in the black hours when he awoke thrashing and shouting, cold sweat covering his body. Lying in the silent, frozen darkness, clutching his duvet tighter while his breath condensed around his head, he considered methods.

Plunging from a great height like the man in the novel was impracticable: there were no buildings within a ten-mile radius tall enough to ensure that he wouldn't end up dying in immobilised agony of starvation or exposure with broken legs or back. And he was terrified of heights; he couldn't climb a ladder past his own height without his knees locking and refusing to go any higher. Even if he were to find a building tall enough, his body would betray him, refusing to let him approach the edge, let alone cast himself over.

Overdosing on sleeping tablets seemed a painless way to go, though he didn't have any and would have to root around in neighbours' medicine cabinets. A possibility.

He already had the means to slit his wrists or hang himself, but neither option appealed much: he seriously doubted he possessed the courage to go through with either.

No, sleeping tablets it would have to be if he reached that level of despair. Maybe he ought to secure a good supply. Just in case.

With that purpose at the back of his mind, Tom wrapped up in thick clothes and unlocked his front door. He stepped outside into a biting winter wind that took his breath away; he was immediately glad of his thermal beanie that he pulled lower to protect his ears.

He locked the door behind him from habit, without wondering whether he needed to, then stood for a moment, listening. Nothing, except the occasional rattle of a street lamp casing when the wind shook it, and the howl of the wind itself.

Tom's house stood in a small development of identical box-like structures that opened onto a shared path. Wooden side gates led to tiny back gardens, surrounded by high wooden fences that discouraged neighbourly interaction. Tom, therefore, barely knew his neighbours. An elderly couple lived next door, but he wasn't even sure of their names.

He walked to their property and rang the doorbell. No chimes sounded. Not surprising, given that the door bells ran off mains electricity. He knocked, the sound dull and muffled beneath his gloves. He knocked harder, making the door rattle in its frame. The Christmas wreath that had been tied to the door knocker jumped a little. Tom lifted it and let it drop, the door knocker making a noise like a pistol shot. Finally, he stooped and pushed open the letter box.

"Hello?" he called through the gap, feeling a little foolish. "Is anyone home?"

He pressed his ear to the opening. Nothing. He put his nose there and sniffed. The smell was faint, but unmistakable. The same sweet, cloying odour that had filled his mother's house.

He stood and tried the door handle. Locked.

It was the same at the next three houses: a young couple expecting their first child; a single mother with two young children, the younger of which had been in Tom's class two years previously; a middle-aged bachelor with a fondness for brewing his own beer. No sight or sound of life from any of them, only the faint odour of decay.

At the fourth house, the front door swung open at his touch. Tom hesitated, glancing around, afraid of being observed, but there was nobody to observe him. He stepped inside.

"Hello?" he called. "The door was open…"

He tailed off as the now-familiar waft of death assailed his nostrils. It was much fainter here and Tom thought he could detect the reason why: a constant draught blew through the house as though every window had been left wide open. The odour that he could smell was coming from upstairs. He went up and glanced into the main bedroom. The curtains were closed—taped closed judging by the almost total darkness in the room—and the stench was much stronger. He closed the bedroom door without going in.

Before going back downstairs, he looked in the bathroom cabinet. Painkillers, anti-inflammatories, indigestion tablets, anti-histamines and cream for piles. He pocketed the painkillers.

He went downstairs to the rear of the house. The back door that led from the kitchen had been wedged wide, allowing the wintry wind open access. A large part of the garden was taken up by a wooden shed, the door to which was also open, held in position by a rusting iron hook. Tom walked over, avoiding the piles of excrement that dotted the lawn, guessing what he would find inside.

Sure enough, lying on its side in a basket in a corner of the shed, was a dog. It looked up at Tom and tried to wag its tail, but it seemed too much effort. It uttered a faint whine. Tom recognised the animal: the border collie-Labrador cross he had passed when walking home from school what seemed a lifetime ago. He guessed that the body of the person lying in the bed upstairs belonged to a middle-aged man who walked with a limp.

Tom stepped over to the dog and bent down. He removed a glove and placed a hand on the animal's side. The dog lifted its head and tried to lick Tom's hand, but again gave up as if it was too much effort. Tom stroked the animal's side and could feel every rib. The dog was starving.

He glanced around the shed. Two food bowls and a water bowl stood on an old newspaper against the shed wall. All three were empty; licked clean by the looks of them. On a shelf he found half a dozen tins of dog food and a tin opener, alongside four empty tins. He quickly opened one and emptied its contents into one of the food bowls. Using the sharp edge of the top of the tin like a knife, he chopped the food into a gelatinous mess.

Tom lowered the bowl.

"Here, boy," he murmured. "Get on the outside of this."

The dog's nostrils flared, but it lacked the energy to stand to eat. Tom dug his fingers into the meaty mess and smeared a little on the dog's lip. Its tongue came out and licked at Tom's fingers until they were clean. He repeated the process and again the dog licked his fingers clean. He kept doing this until the bowl was nearly empty.

"Good boy," Tom said and this time the dog made a more concerted effort to wag its tail.

When Tom stood up, the dog whined.

"Won't be a minute, boy. Gonna find you something to drink."

Tom picked up the bowl marked 'Water' and went back into the house. He turned on the cold water tap in the kitchen. The thin stream that issued was brown and quickly petered out. He tried the hot water tap, but nothing came out.

He opened the fridge and recoiled a little at the smell, but he was growing accustomed to foul odours. He was in luck. An unopened litre bottle of spring water stood in the door, alongside a carton of milk congealed to cottage cheese.

He returned to the shed and sloshed water into the bowl. The dog sniffed at it and lurched unsteadily to its feet. While it lapped at the water, Tom stroked its fur, sleek in spite of its owner's deprivations.

"A coat as black as coal dust, eh, boy? Hmm… coal dust. How about Dusty for a name?"

The dog lifted its head from the bowl and gave Tom's cheek a cold, wet lick.

"That's settled then. Dusty it is."

Tom returned once more to the kitchen and rummaged around until he found some carrier bags. Into them he placed cans of food that he found in a cupboard, a packet of chocolate digestives, three more litre-bottles of spring water, a dozen more cans of dog food to go with the five remaining in the shed, and a box of dog biscuits. He also found the dog's collar and lead. Turning over the collar, he found an inscription: 'Chester'.

"Chester?" Tom shrugged. "Oh well, you're Dusty now." He left the lead and collar where he'd found them.

Back into the shed and Dusty had drained the bowl. He looked up at Tom, one ear cocked expectantly.

"Still hungry, eh?" Tom bent and ruffled the dog's head. "Well, I'll sort you out with some more food in a moment or two. First, we need to get you to your new home. From now on, that's going to be wherever I am. Okay?"

Dusty wagged his tail and Tom took that as agreement.

The private Airbus jet was owned by a corporation of which Troy Bishop was the Managing Director. The corporation chartered the plane to oil and gemstone companies, or to whoever else could afford it, on a frequent basis so that the craft was regularly used and maintained. On occasion, Bishop himself took the controls to keep himself familiar with the way she handled.

The Melbourne Airport staff had followed his instructions to the letter—they were well paid to—and the plane was good to go. With the extra fuel tanks fitted and filled, it had a range of 12,000 kilometres and would reach London with one stop for refuelling in Hong Kong. A groundcrew of five would be awaiting them there—until recently, they had been spreading Moondust throughout eastern China—and would come aboard for the second stage after refuelling the craft.

Of the thirty-five people catching the flight from Melbourne, ten had flown in from New Zealand in a sleek Lear jet that Bishop eyed a little enviously. *I'm gonna get me one of those* he thought. The Lear pilot, a sandy-haired woman by the name of Tess Granville, would serve as co-pilot of the Airbus. Eighteen more, including Bishop, had arrived by road from various places in Australia. The final seven were en route, having the most arduous journeys across the vast desert interior.

Bishop only half-listened to the chit-chat about the operation to spread the Millennium Bug. He paced the corridors of the airport or the baking tarmac of the runways, anxious to be away. The transformers that still provided power to the airport wouldn't do so indefinitely and he wanted to leave while he could take advantage of the airport's navigation systems. Not that it would be a disaster if the power went before they left; they wouldn't have to worry about missing a flight slot.

The stragglers at last started to arrive, pulling into the airport in dusty four-by-fours and camper vans.

"It's gone well," said a voice behind Bishop. "Don't you think?"

He turned to the smiling face of Tess Granville.

Bishop shrugged. "Long way to go yet."

"Ye-es," agreed Tess. "But it's gone well so far."

"Won't mean jack-shit if something goes wrong during the flight, or if any of the others should have a mishap."

Tess frowned. "Yes, it will. We'll have still done our bit. The whole is greater—"

"—than the sum of the parts," finished Bishop. "Yes, I know how it goes."

"Hmm… maybe it wouldn't hurt to keep reminding yourself now and again. You know, for the greater good." She raised her eyebrows.

Bishop didn't respond. He looked away to where a dust-streaked jeep was pulling in.

"There's the last one," he said. "The weather's perfect. Light tailwind. Let's go."

Without waiting to see if she'd follow, he started to stride towards the Airbus, barking orders at people to embark.

A similar scene was taking place thousands of miles away in JFK Airport, only on a larger scale and without the dazzling sunlight.

Diane sat in a corner of a concourse in the terminal designated as the gathering point, and watched people arriving in dribs and drabs. Most were bedraggled from the rain that swept down from grey skies. A few were joyful, jubilant, greeting people with hugs. Many more seemed a little tired and listless, like Diane.

She sat straighter, though did not rush forward like the others, when Milandra and the Deputies arrived. She didn't join in the clapping and cheering and back-slapping that accompanied their entrance into the concourse. She didn't stand with a rapt expression on her face while Milandra spoke a few congratulatory words. She didn't add to the triumphal pandemonium that greeted her words.

Later, when Milandra and the Deputies strolled about the concourse, chatting and smiling and holding the occasional serious-faced discussion with some or others of their fellow arrivees, Milandra passed nearby and glanced at Diane, holding her gaze for a moment. Milandra stopped and motioned for her companions to continue without her. She came closer.

"It's Diane Heidler, isn't it?" she said. "You were in Los Angeles."

Diane nodded.

"Yes. You sent a one-word response to my e-mail. Um, let me see…"

"Obeisance," said Diane.

"Yes, obeisance. Curious choice of word. Different shades of meaning."

Diane shrugged. "It simply means 'I'll do what you ask' as far as I'm concerned."

"I wonder…" Milandra stared at her intently.

Diane felt the briefest flutter and slammed the door shut. Milandra blinked.

"I'm tired," said Diane, standing. She stood a good three inches above Milandra. "Not seen the sun for a few days. Think I might need a nap to recharge. I'm going to find somewhere quiet to get my head down."

"Sleep well," said Milandra.

Diane could feel her regard on her back while she walked quickly away.

Chapter Thirteen

The car didn't like to start in cold weather at the best of times. When it hadn't been used in almost two weeks, Tom had no chance of coaxing it to life.

It didn't much matter. He had the run of the neighbourhood and there was a street nearby of older, larger houses with walls and gates and drives and huge, mature gardens that Tom could not imagine having to tend. Most of these houses had double garages containing at least one car, often two, shut away from the elements.

He gained entry to each of his immediate neighbours' properties by smashing the glass panes in the back doors with a lump hammer. The first one had been the hardest. Tom gasped at how loud the breaking glass sounded and looked around guiltily, though he knew he was alone. He removed from the houses all usable food and drinks. Some of the neighbours had kept pets—dogs, cats, guinea pigs, hamsters—but none had had the foresight of Dusty's former master, who had at least given the dog a chance by opening four tins of food and leaving the doors unlocked.

He roamed further afield, to the larger houses, only stopping when he had collected sufficient food and drink to withstand a siege.

Tom did not enter the darkened bedrooms of the houses, from where the smells emanated. He only went upstairs to empty bathroom cabinets of sleeping pills and painkillers; soon, he had accumulated quite a collection. Enough to do the job, he hoped.

In each house he paused for a moment before each Christmas tree. Many had presents beneath them. One such present, a chocolate orange by the size and feel of it, had the name 'Mr Evans' printed on the tag in a childish scrawl. Tom thought he knew which child this house belonged to and could not bring himself to go upstairs, not even to inspect the bathroom cabinet, for fear of seeing the tiny, rotting body. He replaced the present under the tree; it somehow seemed wrong to take it.

Tom and Dusty ate and drank their way back to strength, the dog's presence helping to keep the black pit at bay, though not banish it completely. As their weakness receded, they took to going for longer and longer walks in the empty countryside, though Dusty seemed to enjoy them more than Tom. A sense of solitude pressed down on him, making him feel insubstantial, a ghost. This sensation came to a head one late evening when the air was unseasonably mild and the moon hung full and low in a clear sky.

As he strolled through parkland at the furthest reaches of town, Tom came to a suspended wooden footbridge spanning a lazy stretch of river that was brown in daylight, black at this hour, leading to more parkland beyond. Dusty had gone ahead, snuffling through the sparse undergrowth at the river's edge.

Tom stepped onto the bridge and walked down the centre strip, the boards faintly echoing beneath his boots. The raised sides of the bridge were formed of thick wooden beams, like railway sleepers, and steel girders with cross struts, giving the structure a feeling of solidity that overcame the contrary sensation caused by the slight give in the boards.

He had crossed the bridge before, had sometimes brought his class to this park on summer outings. But it no longer seemed familiar. He felt like an intruder.

He paused before he reached the end of the bridge. The rectangular arch that supported the cables formed a perfect frame for the moon. Its light spilled over him and he glanced behind at his shadow that stretched back down the bridge like an elastic man. Or an alien.

An abrupt feeling of utter desolation threatened to overwhelm him. He glanced at the girdered sides, estimating the ease with which he could scale them. From the top, he could topple to the blackness below, probably knocking himself unconscious in the impact with the surface or the river bed. The water would finish the job.

Tom looked ahead, knowing that he lacked the courage to throw himself over, despising himself a little for recognising that fact. He shivered, regretting his decision to come out without a jacket. Calling to Dusty, he turned and walked away from the moon. He did not venture far on foot again.

On the day that Tom awoke and felt as healthy as he ever had, he nudged Dusty, who slept on the top of the duvet next to him, and said, "Hey, boy. How do you fancy a ride in a Jag today?"

The dog wagged its tail and yawned.

When they stepped outside, it was onto a thin covering of snow. It wasn't deep enough to leave a track, crumbling and melting away under the pressure of a boot or paw, but it was snow nevertheless. Dusty lowered his head and sniffed hard, causing a sharp, snotty sneeze.

"Well, Dusty, my old boy," said Tom, placing a gloved hand on the dog's head, ruffling his ears. "Did you know that according to the calendar on my watch it's Christmas Day today? Merry Christmas."

Tom gazed at the smattering of snow.

"At least the bookies got something right," he muttered. "I'm dreaming of a white Christmas… I guess nobody will be taking their decorations down this year so it'll be Christmas every day. Ha! Roy Wood got his wish."

Dusty sneezed again in reply and Tom glanced down, suddenly concerned.

"Hey! Don't you dare come down with something. Let's get you into the car. Correction. The *Jag*."

Parked at the pavement where Tom had left it the previous night sat a pale blue Jaguar XJ6. Tom didn't care much for the colour, but cared very much for the smooth purr of the engine, the worn leather upholstery and the walnut dashboard. The engine had roared into life with the first turn of the key. Tom drove it out of the garage and the few streets to his house, feeling like royalty.

Now he was itching to sit behind the wheel again, even if he dreaded going where he intended to go. The car had over half a tank of petrol: plenty to take a drive for pleasure afterwards.

He opened the driver's door and held it wide. Dusty glanced up at him.

"Come on, then," said Tom. "In you get."

With an effortless bound, the dog leapt into the car and stepped over to the passenger seat as though he knew the driver's seat was for Tom.

Tom got in and closed the door. It made a satisfying, silky clunk.

The thin coating of snow on the road crunched lightly under the Jag's wheels, but was too shallow to affect the tyres' grip on the surface.

Tom saw many vehicles on the drive to town, but all were parked outside houses or on driveways. He saw no evidence of mass panic. Apart from the fact that everywhere was deserted, all seemed orderly. The only incongruous sights he noticed were the rear end of a camper van sticking out of a deep ditch and a small pack of dogs, maybe half a dozen of mixed sizes and breeds, some wearing collars, that stopped to watch the Jaguar go past. Tom looked in his rear-view mirror while he pulled away: the dogs watched the car for a few seconds and then, as one, they set off again, running in the opposite direction.

Dusty pricked up his ears when they passed the dogs and uttered a small whine, but otherwise was still. He seemed to be accustomed to riding in cars, though not perhaps one as posh as the Jag, and took it in his easy canine stride.

The traffic lights in town had stopped working and Tom felt that strange sense of disassociation once more. Quite why the non-working traffic lights should have that effect Tom had no idea, but the haunting feeling that he was the only person alive returned.

He turned into the road that led to the sport centre and slowed the Jag's speed, remembering the last time he had driven here. The road block was still there and more military vehicles were parked behind the truck that blocked the road. A soldier in uniform and gas mask sat on the road in front of the truck, rifle laid across knees.

Tom's stomach began to churn, but he drove slowly forwards, dropping his speed to crawling pace, staring intently at the soldier. He stopped about ten yards away from the truck and cut the engine.

The soldier hadn't moved. Tom glanced at Dusty and rubbed his head.

"Stay here, boy," he said.

He opened the door and stepped out. He closed the door softly. This time the clunk did not seem so silky; instead, it seemed incredibly loud to Tom's heightened senses and he glanced anxiously at the soldier. He—or she; it could be a she under that mask and uniform for all Tom knew—didn't so much as twitch.

Tom did not expect the rifle to be raised and to stare down the infinite blackness of the barrel again, but he feared it, too. He stepped forward, one deliberate pace at a time, pausing between each as though taking part in a bridal march. Or funeral.

When he was only a few paces from the soldier he realised that his fears were unfounded. The shoulders of the soldier's tunic, the top of the full-head mask and its snout-like nose piece, the rifle, the legs and toes of the black boots, all were sprinkled in a light dusting of snow.

Not aware that he had been holding it, Tom let out his breath in a deep sigh and felt his shoulders sag like a marionette whose strings have been cut. He stepped around the soldier and the back of the truck.

The car park in front of the sport centre wasn't littered with parked cars or rubbish or military equipment, but with bodies. Soldiers and civilians—men, women, a few children. Despite the cold, they had bloated and discoloured, and gave off the sweet stench, though it was less noticeable here outside.

As Tom picked his way between the corpses, a movement caught his eye. Big black birds, crows or some such, feasted on the bodies. With a cry of disgust, Tom ran at them, making them take to the air with startled caws.

He was gaining a fair idea of what he would find inside the building, but he made for the entrance anyway. Not all of the bodies scattered about the car park had died of the Millennium Bug; at least, not the civilians. Most of them were surrounded by pools of blood; some had severe injuries that not even the savage beak of a crow could inflict. Scattered on the ground around many of the soldiers were spent brass cartridges.

Tom reached the side entrance to the main sports hall. The emergency doors were propped open by a tangle of blood-soaked bodies; people had been shot when they tried to leave.

The stench here was much stronger and Tom held his hand to his nose while he stepped over corpses, trying to avoid treading in congealed blood, finding it impossible not to. The thin winter daylight only penetrated a few yards into the hall. The rest stretched away, hidden in darkness like the inside of a cave.

The sounds of scrabbling and squeaking came to his ears. He yelled. The shout died almost as soon as it left his lips, swallowed by the stinking blackness. The scrabbling and squeaking, if anything, increased. He didn't yell again.

When he took a few more paces in, flies buzzed up at his face. Maybe they could feast and lay eggs here where it was a little warmer, shielded from the wind and snow.

At the furthest edge of illumination, before the darkness proper began and Tom's courage ended, he found what he was looking for. She lay face up, almost unrecognisable if it wasn't for the mole on the cheek, the Monroe mole, the one he had kissed the last time they had been together.

Tom looked down at her for a long moment.

The scrabbling in the darkness came closer, or Tom's imagination made it sound that way, making his skin crawl with revulsion. He knew that he ought to drag her out of there. Afford her a decent burial if he could manage to dig a grave in the frozen earth.

His physical strength had returned, but he required a different sort of toughness to bury another person dear to him. A toughness that he had surprised himself once by demonstrating, but that he doubted he would ever possess again.

"Goodbye, Lisa," he whispered. Then he turned and ran from the sports hall.

Gaining the fresh air, he stopped and doubled over, gulping in cold air. When he thought he must lose his breakfast, the wave of sickness passed.

"Got to get away from here," he muttered and made his way at a trot-march back to the Jaguar.

He opened the driver's door and looked in.

Dusty gazed back at him, tail thumping against the leather upholstery.

"Let's go for a drive, shall we?" said Tom. "See what this baby can do."

For a moment, Tom thought that Dusty's ears pricked up and his head cocked at the sound of his voice, but then he heard it, too.

The sound of an engine, heading their way.

Five hundred people descended upon JFK Airport, coming from all points of the United States and some from further afield in Canada and Central America.

A fully fuelled and safety-checked Jumbo stood ready on the wind- and rain-swept runway. The flight crew preferred to wait for an area of low pressure in mid-Atlantic to move away before departing.

The weather forecast systems were still operational. The main meteorological centres in the U.S.A., South America, Canada and the U.K. were manned by skeleton staffs. The American staffs would keep the centres operational until the last flight had departed continental America and would then follow in readied private jets that stood waiting on local airstrips.

The airways were clear and the only risk would be encountering another of their flights on its way to Heathrow. Geostationary satellite systems for navigation and communication continued, for now, to be fully functional. The aircrafts' onboard radar systems would remain effective and there was no reason to suppose that a mid-air collision was a realistic worry; less so than before the Millennium Bug.

The flight crew's main concern was the weather. Although the Boeing was capable of flying through an electrical storm, the crew would much prefer avoiding any sort of weather systems that might knock out an engine or any of the onboard safety systems. It wasn't so much the remainder of the flight that would be risky, but the landing in London without a full fire and safety groundcrew on standby. Milandra assured the Captain that they would not depart until he was satisfied that the way was safe.

"There's no desperate hurry," she said, "although we can't delay here too long. We need to hold the Commune before the survivors get their act together. Once they start grouping, controlling them will become problematic."

The Captain, a veteran of over seven hundred international flights on 747s and many more on their predecessors, nodded. "Understood. A window is likely to open within the next few hours. Folk need to be ready to board at a moment's notice. Has everybody arrived?"

"Only a few more to come. The ones who've had the furthest to travel. But they aren't far away."

"Okay. Let me know when they're here. I'll be in the control tower. And Milandra..." He paused as if choosing his words carefully. "What we've had to do, it *was* essential, wasn't it? It's, well, I kind of grew fond of some of them..." He tailed off, looking at her anxiously. She didn't need to probe to sense his need for reassurance.

She placed a hand on his forearm and squeezed. "You weren't the only one," she said. "But, yes, it was essential. If there'd been some other way..." She shook her head. "There wasn't."

"I know. Guess I needed to hear you say it. Okay..." He was

brisk and business-like again. "Call me in the CT when they get here."

Milandra removed her hand from his arm. "Will do."

She was turning away when she received from Grant: *Main entrance. I think you should see this.*

As Milandra neared the entrance, she heard a commotion. Raised voices and laughter. A small crowd had gathered in front of the doors. Milandra saw Grant standing to one side, watching her approach.

Simone Furlong stood at the front of the knot of people, clapping her hands with glee, her gaze fixed on a young woman. The woman—more a girl, probably still in her teens—crawled on the dirty tiled floor on her hands and knees. Now and again, she lifted her head and howled like a wolf. Tears streamed down her cheeks.

Milandra probed. The girl was under the power of Simone and half a dozen or so others in the crowd behind her. With the girl's mind wide open, it took Milandra only a moment to see the girl's anguish at watching her family die; her own descent into blackness and emergence again into the light; her spotting one of Milandra's people and following them to the airport; her dashed hopes of finding comfort and companionship and safety…

The girl stopped crawling and knelt. Mouth twisting in a grimace of humiliation, she pulled her sweatshirt over her head. She was braless and her small breasts glinted in the fluorescent lighting, tears spilling down them.

"Is this what we've come to?" said Milandra in a loud voice. "Are we now animals?"

Without releasing the girl, Simone glanced at Milandra. "No," she said, nodding towards the girl. "*They* are the animals and we once more have dominion over them."

A murmur of assent rose from the people in the small crowd behind the Chosen. Milandra gazed at each of them in turn. One or two cast their eyes down and withdrew their minds from Simone's, but most glared defiantly back. Simone retained sufficient psychic support to make the girl do whatever she wanted.

Simone's attention returned to the girl, making her tweak her nipples until they started to bleed.

"You don't need to do this, Simone," Milandra said quietly.

The Chosen shrugged. "Now. Later. Makes no difference."

Milandra glanced at Grant. He was still watching her, his expression grim but calculating. He hadn't needed to call her over.

He's trying to teach me a lesson she thought. *Maybe he's right…*

She walked over to him and stood by his side. They didn't speak. Milandra watched as Simone made the girl strip naked. She watched as she made the girl climb onto a check-in counter and balance there, tying one arm of her sweatshirt securely around an overhead stanchion. She watched as Simone made the girl tie the other arm of the sweatshirt around her neck.

When the girl took a step backwards off the counter, Milandra looked away.

Peter's circle of exploration of the area surrounding his cottage grew wider and wider when he found no sight or sound of any living person. He stopped at each small settlement and sounded his horn in the main street. The only reactions to the sound were raucous cries of crows and seagulls, complaining loudly at being disturbed in their carrion-feasting, and the distant barking of dogs, though Peter only saw one: a mangy, half-starved creature that slunk away at the sight of the Range Rover.

He stepped out in larger villages and explored a little on foot. The only living things he encountered were scavenging birds and rats and, more rarely, unseasonal flies. In one house he peeked into, seven or eight cats peered balefully back at him before resuming their gnawing on the body of a man. Peter left them to it.

He quickly grew accustomed to the smell of putrescence; it wasn't as though he had never encountered such odours before.

For weeks in the trenches of Belgium, he had lived amidst mud and ordure and decomposing flesh. These smells took him back to that time as if it had happened only last year; in a way, to Peter's sense of time, it had.

As the days wore on and he failed to glimpse another living person, Peter began to share Tom Evans's feeling that he was the only person alive. Unlike Tom Evans, Peter knew this not to be the case, but he still found it difficult to shake the sensation.

His journeying brought him to a town. It had snowed a little overnight, but it would have to come down considerably heavier for it to affect the handling of the Range Rover, and then he had the four-wheel-drive to utilise if necessary. He drove slowly around the snow-sprinkled streets, the driver's window wound down, listening for sounds of life.

Silence.

He headed out of town on the opposite side to which he'd entered and almost missed them. The snow itself was so faint on the road that tracks made by another vehicle were almost invisible, but his eyes must have taken in the double parallel strips of black tarmac showing through the light dusting for, twenty or so yards further on, it registered in his mind.

Peter pressed hard on the brakes, bringing the vehicle to a smooth halt. Not certain if he had imagined it, he reversed until, sure enough, he could make out tracks on the road. Assuming the vehicle that had made the tracks had been travelling in the direction that traffic would normally have been heading on this side of the road—not a failsafe assumption, he knew—he turned the Range Rover and followed the tracks.

They weren't easy to see, even now he knew they were there, and he was forced to go slowly not to lose sight of them. So intent was he on keeping his gaze fixed on the dark twin strips that he didn't notice the vehicles blocking the road until he was almost on them. Once more, he brought the Range Rover to an abrupt halt.

An army truck was parked side on, blocking the road in both directions. A long, light-blue car was parked near it. Something moved in the passenger window—a dog? Peter had no time to consider this any further. All of his attention was suddenly fixed on the muzzle of the gun pointing at his face.

The driver's window was still wound down, giving Peter an uninterrupted view of the weapon and the man who wielded it. A young man, tall, with sandy, curly hair starting to recede at the temples. He was dressed against the cold in a thick ski jacket. If he had been wearing gloves, they had been removed the better to handle the weapon. The index finger of the man's right hand was curled around the trigger.

"Switch off the engine," said the young man.

Peter did as he was told. In the silence, he could hear the man's heavy breathing.

"I mean you no harm," said Peter. "You're the first person I've seen in days. Weeks."

The man watched him closely. Peter considered probing to ascertain the man's intentions, but thought better of it. Not while a gun was being held in his face. He waited.

"Who are you?" said the man.

"My name's Peter. Peter Ronstadt."

"Okay," said the man. "Where've you come from?"

"Not far. A small village a few miles north of Cardiff. I've been looking for survivors. You're the first—"

"Survivors? You mean, there are survivors?"

"Well, like I said, you're the first I've found, but there will be others."

"How do you know? How do you know that we're not the only ones left?" The words came out in a mingled rush of hope and fear, as though the man wanted to hear affirmation, but wouldn't believe it.

"It stands to reason," said Peter. "If *we* are still alive, there are bound to be others."

"Others…" It came out in almost a whisper. The gun wavered from side to side as though the man had forgotten about it.

Peter hadn't. "Look, I meant what I said about not meaning

you any harm. Why would I want to hurt you? I'm really pleased to see you. What's your name?"

"My name? Uh, Tom."

"Well, Tom, I'm very happy to meet you. I'd be even happier if you'd lower your weapon."

Tom blinked and looked down at the gun. He grunted. "I grabbed this from a dead soldier when I heard you coming." For the first time, he smiled. It was a wan smile, little more than a grimace, but it made his face light up like a child's. "I'm not sure how to use this. Don't even know if it's loaded." He lowered the muzzle until it pointed at the ground.

Peter opened the car door and got out, moving slowly and deliberately. Tom watched him and took half a pace back, but he didn't raise the gun. Peter stood and held out his right hand. After a moment's hesitation, Tom stepped forward and gripped it. They shook.

As they released hands, Peter grinned. Tom returned it and a tear slid down his cheek. He swiped it away.

"Look at me," he said. "Blubbing like a baby. I thought I was the only one left…" He shook himself. "Let me get rid of this—" he motioned at the gun "—before I shoot myself in the foot. Then you must come and meet Dusty."

"Your dog?"

Tom nodded. He stepped to the side of the road and lowered the gun carefully to the ground, leaving it propped against the kerb. Side by side, the two men walked to the blue car.

Chapter Fourteen

The man sitting next to Diane during the flight tried to engage her in conversation, until he took the hint from her monosyllabic replies and left her to her thoughts.

Those thoughts were a jumbled morass that Diane tried to pick her way through while the 747 headed across the Atlantic Ocean. Though Diane had never felt any great love towards the human race, she had never felt any particular animosity either and her indifference to what she had done to spread the virus puzzled her. In the years leading up to the moment that she had opened the canister and infected the child in the park, she had often dreaded what she would have to do, anticipating that it would sicken her. She had sometimes worried that she may not be able to go through with it.

In the event, it came as easily as applying lipstick. While wandering the streets of L.A., smearing powder as she went, she had even started to enjoy herself, especially when she worked her way through Beverly Hills. The idea of infecting what she thought of as The Plastic People gave her the kind of excited jolt that she rarely experienced.

The excitement had not lasted long. It had soon been replaced by the familiar emptiness that she had come to accept as her normal state of being.

Diane had long lived a solitary existence, preferring her own company. She had wondered what it would be like to be once more amongst her own kind; whether that would stir up more sociable longings within her. The answer turned out to be negative. Here she was, surrounded by five hundred of her people, and still she yearned for solitude. Not even the promise of being part of a much greater whole if the Great Coming was successful filled her with particular anticipation.

She knew that she would have to play her part, the dutiful servant as she thought of it, though no doubt Milandra would never agree with that assessment. Yes, she would play her part and after the Great Coming she would be free to go wherever she wanted and be alone. And there would be a world of choice. Unlike before, she wouldn't be forced to inhabit a certain, limited area. She could find somewhere warm, a tropical island, somewhere with coconuts; she would live off them and fish.

Her happier contemplation was interrupted by the sound of Milandra's voice coming over the aircraft intercom.

"Ladies and gentlemen," said Milandra, sounding tinny. "Your Captain informs me that we are almost midway across the Atlantic. Radio communications are still operational and Heathrow is ready for our arrival. Some snow has fallen on the U.K. in the last few days, but the runways are clear and the conditions are perfect for a safe landing. So if any you are not too keen on flying—and I sense that to be the case—then have no fears. We are in good hands.

"Now, as you all know our operation to, er, cleanse Earth Haven has gone well. The virus developed in Nevada by our small team has proved to be as effective as we could have hoped. Dr Samuels, take a bow."

A few rows in front of Diane, a small man stood and gave a short bow. A round of spontaneous applause broke out. Diane did not join in, drawing a glower from the man in the seat next to her. She ignored him.

Milandra's voice came again over the intercom. "Some of you may have found what we did distasteful. Some of you may have grown fond of humans. I confess that I held a certain fondness for them myself. But we cannot afford to feel sympathy for them. We were ruthless in carrying out the cleansing. We must maintain that ruthlessness in our coming dealings with the survivors.

"Greater London had a population of a little over eight million people. The estimated survival rate is 0.02 per cent. Assuming an even spread, around one thousand, six hundred people will have survived in the greater metropolis of London. Many of those may have already left the city, but there will undoubtedly still be survivors there. Our presence may flush them out. If you encounter any survivors in London, *do not* eliminate them. There is a great deal to be done and we need to put them to work.

"As I speak, almost five thousand of our people are making for the U.K. When all are assembled, we shall hold a Commune. We will call out to all surviving humans in Britain and draw them to us. While they are splintered and afraid, they will be unable to resist.

"However, as they answer the summons and begin to group together, we must exercise extreme caution. Until the Great Coming, our numbers are insufficient to control groups for any length of time. Humans in combined strength are too powerful still for us to bend completely to our will. Yet there is a way of weakening their intellects, of overcoming their resistance so that they will be powerless to resist our command. A medical unit will be established near the airport. A temporary unit to deal with the first survivors we find. As more come in, a more permanent unit will be established, probably in a local hospital."

In front of Diane, a man stood up and began to mime the actions of a shambling zombie from some cheap-rate horror flick, to much amusement. Diane did not so much as smile, drawing another glower from the man next to her.

"To be clear," continued Milandra, "do not harm any survivors you encounter once we're on the ground. You don't need to try to control them; if you're alone, you'll probably find that you won't be able to. If any survivors *are* controlled, they are to be sent to the medical unit. From there, they will be set to work. We will need places to stay. The hotels near Heathrow will do for now. Bodies will need to be cleared and burned; food and water will have to be collected. These are the first tasks we shall set the survivors to do.

"We can all remember when we held complete dominion over humanity. We considered them to be no more than drones, created to do our bidding. We now once more hold sway over them. We must now, like we once did, treat them as drones. We are to show them no mercy. Is that understood? No mercy."

~ ~ ~

Milandra's estimate of the numbers of inhabitants of Greater London who had survived the Millennium Bug wasn't too far off the mark. In fact, one thousand, four hundred and seventy-three people fell ill, but pulled out of the fever, feeling weak and hungry but very much alive. Of those, over three hundred had already fled the city in a doomed effort at outrunning the virus. Another four hundred had since left, fleeing the stench of decomposing flesh. Twenty-seven people had given in to black despair or guilt and taken their own lives.

That left around seven hundred survivors in the city, most of them struggling to come to terms with the fact of having survived and living a hand-to-mouth, dazed sort of existence. Most still had not ventured far from their homes and remained unaware that they were not the sole survivors. If they had known that there were others, that they would soon be faced with another threat and that banding together may increase their chances of surviving again, maybe they would have made more effort at seeking each other out.

Or maybe not. A torpor had descended over the survivors like a shroud, making them unable to contemplate life beyond today, hoarding any food they came across automatically, not with any thought of long-term survival in mind. This was true of most of those who had survived across the world, not only in London.

The same could not now be said of Tom Evans. For the first time since the death of his mother, he allowed a faint bloom of hope to settle in his breast. Faint, yes, but hope nonetheless.

He was back behind the wheel of the Jaguar, driving towards his house. In the rear-view mirror, he could see the Range Rover following.

"Well, Dusty," he said, stretching out his left hand to ruffle the dog's ears, "I'm not the only survivor, after all. There's a turn-up for the books. Not sure that you're very impressed by our new friend, mind."

The dog's reaction to Peter puzzled Tom. Dusty hadn't wagged his tail, hadn't barked a greeting or exhibited the slightest excitement at seeing another person. In fact, other than flattening his ears, Dusty hadn't reacted at all, merely sat very still while Peter patted his head. Tom put it down to the animal still being traumatised by his ordeal, though he had not displayed any other ill-effects of nearly starving to death.

Tom parked the Jaguar in front of his house. The Range Rover pulled in behind and Tom showed Peter into his home. Dusty ran in ahead of the men, making for his food bowl. When he found it empty, he gave a small enquiring bark and Tom emptied a can of food into the bowl. He topped up the water bowl from a saucepan. He was running short of water that he'd collected from the cold tap, though still had almost half a bathtub-full upstairs and hadn't touched the water in the hot tank. There was no cause for concern since he had accumulated plenty of bottles of spring water on his explorations of neighbours' houses that he was saving for when the tap water was all gone.

He opened a tin of beans and a can of luncheon meat.

"We'll have to have them cold, I'm afraid," he told Peter. "I haven't yet come across a camping stove on my travels. That's something I could have got today in town, but meeting you drove it clean from my mind."

"No worries," said Peter. Tom could detect no obvious accent in the man's voice. "I have a camping stove and plenty of fuel for it, but I left it in my cottage. I'll be going back there to collect my stuff before…"

"Before?"

"Well, I'm thinking of heading north. To look for other survivors."

"North? Why north? It's cold enough here."

"Yes, I've noticed it's cold in here," said Peter. "Don't you have any means of generating heat?"

Tom shook his head. He noticed that Peter had side-stepped his question, but decided not to pursue it for now. "Modern house. Gas central heating. No fire place. I keep my coat on to stay warm and Dusty sleeps on my bed. We help keep each other warm in the nights."

"You'll be using a lot of energy to stay warm like that. You'll go through your food a lot quicker."

"Hmm… hadn't thought of that. Haven't thought of many things, to be honest. Here you are." He handed Peter a plate of beans and meat. "Let's go eat in comfort."

They carried the food through to the living room and spent the next few minutes in silence. Tom surreptitiously studied Peter while they ate.

Medium height, muscular frame. The skin of his face was lined and tanned, as though he had spent many years in much warmer climes than those of South Wales; the face itself had an open aspect, suggesting that its owner would struggle to conceal deception. Dark brown hair, thinning on top; pale blue eyes, like washed-out denim; indeterminate age, though Tom would guess, if pressed, at early fifties.

Tom carried their empty plates to the kitchen. Dusty had cleared both his bowls and lay in his basket, showing no interest in joining the men. Tom returned to the living room, carrying two bottles of lager he'd purloined from a neighbour who no longer had any use for them.

"Fridge doesn't work, but they're still nice and cold," he remarked, handing Peter a bottle.

"Thanks." Peter tipped his bottle towards Tom's. "Cheers!"

They clinked bottles and both took a sip.

"Ah," murmured Tom. "That hits the spot. I haven't felt like one of these until now. So, Peter, tell me a little of yourself. If you don't mind, that is."

"Not at all, though there's not much to tell. I used to be in the merchant navy. Fell in love with a Welsh girl and settled in Cardiff. Left the city when she died. I moved about for a while, but now live alone in a cottage in a small village. What about you, Tom?"

"Even less to tell. I teach… I *used* to teach, in the primary school here in the village. Single. There was a girl, but…" He shrugged.

"Virus?"

"Yep. Is that how your wife died?"

"No. Megan went seventeen years ago." Peter hesitated, as though choosing his next words carefully. "Natural causes."

"She must have been very young."

"No. Not really." Peter shifted a little in the armchair.

Tom said nothing, though it was clear that Peter was holding something back.

"Do you have any plans, Tom? Any ideas about what to do now?"

"Like I said, I haven't given much thought to anything. Making plans beyond surviving each day seems a little pointless."

"What about planning *not* to survive?" Peter shot a pointed glance at the boxes and bottles of pills piled on the telephone table next to the settee.

Tom felt himself colour, but didn't drop his gaze from Peter's. "Yes, I've certainly thought about that. Less so since finding Dusty. Perhaps less so again since meeting you. But, it's still an option."

"That's your prerogative. However, I'd like you to give some thought to coming with me. Help me find more survivors."

"What then? Supposing we do find more. What then?"

"One step at a time. They are out there, Tom. The trick will be finding them."

"But you said you were going to head north. Why north? Why not go south where it's warmer?"

"Well, the largest part of this island lies to the north and that's where I intend looking first. Maybe later, when we've found everyone who wants to be found, we can head for warmer climes."

Tom thought for a moment. Peter's explanation seemed to make sense, yet…

"There's something you're not telling me," he said. It was a statement, not an accusation.

It was Peter's turn to look thoughtful. He tipped back the bottle of beer, drained it, and let out a belch.

"Oops. Beg your pardon." He grinned, but it quickly faded. "Tom, the truth is that there's a great deal I'm not telling you. I will, but you'll have to be patient. I'm not even sure where to start." He let out his breath slowly. "I guess I could show you something. Fetch Dusty and I will."

Tom frowned, but stood and walked to the kitchen. The dog was still in his basket, lying still with head on paws. His dark eyes watched Tom, but he didn't wag his tail. Tom lowered himself onto his heels and scratched the dog behind his ears.

"Dusty, come with me, boy." He stood and tapped his thigh.

Dusty looked at him and, for a moment, Tom thought that he'd have to pick him up and carry him into the living room. Then the dog stood, shook himself and trotted to Tom's side.

"Good boy."

Tom walked back into the living room, Dusty following, and stopped in front of Peter. Dusty sat and regarded Peter quietly.

"Tom, if you could sit down. And, please, there's no need to look so worried. Dusty will come to no harm."

Tom sat on the edge of the seat of an armchair and watched.

Peter looked intently at Dusty for a moment. He held his right hand out in front of him, index finger extended. The finger made a quick downward movement and Dusty lay down. The finger made a circular motion and Dusty flipped onto his back. Then Peter moved his hand, his finger making a larger circle in the air. Tom gasped when Dusty mimicked the movement, describing his own circle, scrabbling with his paws at the carpet while he pulled himself around, his nose almost touching his tail.

Peter stopped and so did Dusty. The finger flicked upwards and Dusty rose to his haunches. It flicked upwards again and Dusty stood. It beckoned him forward and Peter patted him on the head.

"Good dog. That's enough."

Dusty turned and trotted over to Tom. He nuzzled at Tom's hands before lying down at his feet.

Tom looked at Peter.

"What just happened?" he said.

"Well, the finger was for your benefit. It would have worked without it."

"You were controlling him? Are you a dog trainer or something?"

Peter smiled, but it seemed to Tom a sad smile. "No. I've never even owned a dog. Megan was more of a cat person."

"Then how…?"

Peter tapped the side of his forehead. "Power of the mind, Tom. I can control most animals."

"Could you hurt Dusty if you wanted to?"

"Yes. I could make him run into a wall. Or step into fire. And he knows it, which is why he's wary of me. Yet he can also sense that I mean him, and you, no harm."

"Huh! If I hadn't seen it with my own eyes…"

"Quite. If I had told you rather than shown you, you wouldn't believe me. There are other things I will need to show you. Some you will need to take on trust. But not now."

"When?"

"One step at a time, Tom. One step at a time."

From all over the world they came. Almost five thousand people converged on London by plane and boat and car.

Ferries set sail from Le Havre and Calais in France, Ostend in Belgium, Esbjerg in Denmark and Dublin in Ireland. Coach- and carloads headed for west London by road from ferry ports in the north and south of England, in Scotland, and in the north and west of Wales.

Planes landed from all points of the compass. Planes of all shapes and sizes, though none so large as the 747 that flew in from

New York.

The last aircraft to touch down was an Airbus that had flown in from Australia, via Hong Kong.

Bishop was glad to arrive, not because he was tired from piloting the plane all those thousands of kilometres, but because he would at last be able to escape his co-pilot's inane and constant cheeriness.

Tess Granville had wittered away for the entire journey, or so it felt to Bishop. And he was a captive audience. On more than one occasion, he'd handed over the controls to escape to the bathroom, even if he didn't need to go, just so he could have a break from the incessant chatter. It was either that or throttle the woman, but he was very careful to conceal his feelings. He didn't think that she would try to probe him without his consent. Unless you were Milandra, to do so was considered extremely bad form and this woman appeared far too conformist to commit such a faux pas, but it wouldn't hurt to be guarded from here on in.

Tess was a sociable person, she told Bishop about fifty times, and missed living amongst her own kind.

"Oh, you know, humans are all well and good—better than being completely alone—but they are so individualistic, don't you think?"

Bishop grunted non-committally, which Tess seemed to take as a sign to continue.

"Despite all their talk of community spirit and altruism, and their crowding together in cities, they're really a bunch of individuals only interested in bettering their own situations. Yeah, okay, sometimes the greater good is improved at the same time, but the bottom line is that they are totally self-serving. Don't you agree?"

Bishop grunted again. He had quickly learned that this was all he needed to do. Thank heavens for small mercies.

"And what is it with humans and religion…"

Bishop tuned out. So long as he remained alert to when he should insert a grunt, he could stop listening to what she was actually saying. Besides, she would be surprised, nay shocked, if he revealed his true feelings to her.

Many, many years of living in their midst, away from his own kind, had changed Bishop. He had come around to thinking that humans had got it right; that it was all about striving to improve your own lot in life and bollocks to the rest. So returning to become part of the whole once more did not fill Bishop with the same delight that infused his co-pilot.

Still, he needed to play the game, show willing and all that. Then, first chance he got, when the Great Coming had succeeded—or failed; Bishop found that he didn't much care either way—he would leave. Return to Oz and pick up the reins of his old life. Live in isolated splendour until the country became populated once more. Then live like a king on the pickings he would garner from an abandoned continent.

Bishop taxied the Airbus to the main terminal building where a groundcrew with steps awaited. He grabbed his two suitcases—one had grown much heavier with the weight of gold and other items he had collected in Melbourne—and was forced to put one down again when Tess held out her hand to shake his.

"Thank you, Troy," she said, "for a safe journey and for being a good listener."

"No worries," he replied, and shook her hand, resisting the temptation to squeeze until she squealed.

"For the good of the whole," said Tess, releasing his hand and raising her own, fist clenched.

"Yeah, sure." He picked up the suitcase again.

"London awaits. Our family awaits. Can you feel the excitement, Troy?"

"Er, yeah."

"We should join them. No doubt I'll see you around."

"Yeah." *Not if I see you first* he thought.

Chapter Fifteen

Armed with a sharp carving knife from Tom's kitchen, Peter left the house and visited the gardens of the neighbouring properties. It didn't take him long to find what he was looking for. Rooting around in a small shed, he uncovered a coiled garden hosepipe. He cut two lengths each of around five-feet from the pipe. He also picked up a couple of sturdy screwdrivers before returning.

Tom raised his eyebrows in enquiry when he saw what Peter was carrying.

"Refuelling kits," said Peter. He held up the screwdrivers. "For prising open the covers over the fuel caps. It'll be much quicker than hunting around for keys." He held up the lengths of coiled green tubing. "For syphoning petrol. I already have a supply back at the cottage, but it won't hurt to top up the tank as we go along." He noticed the other man's doubtful expression. "Have you never syphoned petrol before?"

Tom shook his head. "Though I understand the principle. I've only ever done it with water. I show— used to show, my kids how to do it in school."

"There you are. It'll be exactly the same, except you'll want to spit out whatever gets into your mouth straight away. You might throw up the first time, but you'll soon get used to it. There are plenty of cars around here. Only go for the older models, mind. Most modern cars are fitted with anti-syphoning valves."

"You're very organised, Peter. It's almost as if…"

"As if I knew this was going to happen?"

"Yes." Tom had grown very still.

Peter sighed. "I knew. But I didn't take any part in it."

"Take any part… What are you talking about?"

Peter looked at him. Tom's mouth had formed a ring of surprise. He seemed to realise that his mouth was agape and closed it with an almost audible snap.

"Tom, there's something I can show you when we reach my

cottage. I'll tell you everything, but you need to hear little bits at a time. You're going to find it very hard to believe."

"Wait a minute, wait a minute. Are you saying that this virus, this plague, was *deliberate*?"

Peter nodded.

Tom sagged back against the kitchen counter as though he'd been punched in the stomach. Colour drained from his face.

"Tom, I won't say any more now. Wait until tomorrow."

Tom nodded, but didn't look up.

"Okay," said Peter. "I'm going to bed. Shall we set out at first light?"

Tom nodded again. Still he didn't look up.

Peter climbed the stairs to the spare bedroom with a heavy heart.

The people who had been based in the U.K. had been busy. Those already in London had begun the preparations. When others from around the country started arriving, they pitched in.

Two hotels to the north of the airport had been cleared of bodies; soiled linen and mattresses replaced. Clearance had begun on the residential properties in the area. On nearby playing fields, pyres had been lit and rotting bodies cremated. The fields were far enough away that the pungent smell did not reach the cleared areas.

It was slow, dirty work and those doing it longed for the Commune so that the drones could take it over. Four surviving humans had already been found and put to work. After they had visited the medical station. A temporary station had been set up in one of the hotel lobbies. It wasn't much: a couple of hospital gurneys with leather straps and an electro-therapy machine that had been hooked up to a series of car batteries. Not much, but enough.

The four drones went about their work with slack-jawed efficiency, never questioning or complaining. If they needed to use the toilet or eat, they did so, quietly and quickly, before returning to the task in hand. They didn't care what they ate, though seemed to be able to distinguish between what was and wasn't edible. Someone had tried feeding one of them grass. The young woman had put a handful into her mouth and chewed briefly, before opening her mouth and allowing the congealed mass to fall out, staining her already filthy blouse with a green blotch.

A fleet of vehicles had been obtained and fuelled and made available at the airport concourse for ferrying people from the airport.

As more people arrived and more houses were cleared, more survivors were found, and soon the number of working drones had increased to sixteen. A dozen were given the task of picking up decomposing corpses, wrapping them in sheets to contain the ooze and placing them in the back of transit vans or ambulances. Sopping, stinking mattresses and bedding, and the occasional ruined armchair or settee or carpet were also loaded into vans for burning. The vehicles were driven to the playing fields where the remaining four drones unloaded them and built pyres. Depots and warehouses had been raided for supplies of lighter fluid that the drones used to douse the corpses before setting them alight. It rained frequently, interspersed with the occasional flurry of snow or hail, and the bodies burned much easier with the lighter fluid.

Thick black smoke billowed above the playing fields before being dispersed in the fresh winter winds. Those driving the vans and ambulances wore damp cloths over their noses and mouths to lessen the stench of the insides of the vehicles and the air at the playing fields. But still it was a job that nobody wanted to do for long and the drivers were rotated frequently.

Diane Heidler found a small flat free of corpses and installed herself there. She returned to it each evening, weary and filthy, pausing at the entrance to strip off her clothes and deposit them for collection and burning, then sluicing her body from head to toe with a bucket filled from a barrel of rainwater. Teeth chattering, she would wrap herself in a towel and climb the stairs to the flat where she would outfit herself in a brand-new set of clothes taken from a nearby shop.

Once or twice, she had been lucky to avoid driving duty and had instead joined others in collecting tinned food and bottled water from supermarkets and warehouses, stockpiling it in the hotel kitchens where anyone could go and take what they needed. On those days, she had been able to avoid the shivering sluicing down and had worn the same set of clothes the next day.

She was always glad to shut and lock the door to the flat behind her.

Troy Bishop had been annoyed to find that the best suites in the hotels had already been taken. He was reduced to scouring the area until he found a deserted apartment that wasn't quite in keeping with the standards he was used to enjoying, but would do for now. He, too, was forced to take part in the clean-up operation, as to refuse would have betrayed his true feelings. He was, however, more fortunate than Diane in being among the last to arrive so he only had to endure a couple of days of getting his hands dirty.

With everyone now in London, the Commune could take place.

Unlike Dusty, who showed no ill-effects of the tricks he had performed at Peter's bidding, Tom did not sleep well. He wondered how Peter had made Dusty behave as he had. Tom had no idea whether the animal had ever been formally trained, but even if he had, Peter had no way of knowing. Then the answer occurred to him: hypnotism. Peter had stared intently at Dusty while he controlled him, and he'd made some remark about the power of the mind. Yep, that must be it—hypnotism.

What disturbed Tom's sleep more was the man's assertion that the Millennium Bug had been caused deliberately. Tom did not, *could* not, believe that, in which case the man must be lying. Yet, Tom didn't gain the impression that he was; Peter's countenance was too open—a lie would be too easily read. Insanity, then. The man must be deluded, believing that virtually the entire world's population had been wiped out in little more than a week by an illness that had been spread on purpose. Yet, again, he did not appear to be crazy. If anything in the short space of time that Tom had known him, Peter presented as one of the most calm, rational men Tom had ever met.

Dark thoughts resurfaced in the predawn hours; the cold, dark hours. Tom almost welcomed them like old friends.

He had reached no firm conclusions by the time they sat and ate tinned rice pudding for breakfast. In winter dawn's pale half-light, Tom watched the other man eat. Peter glanced up, but Tom did not look away.

"Wondering whether I'm nuts?" said Peter, with a tight smile.

Still Tom did not look away. "Frankly, yes," he said. "It's the only sensible explanation for what you claimed last night."

Peter shrugged. "I'll show you. At the cottage. You're still coming with me?"

"I'll come as far as your cottage. After that…"

"That's entirely up to you. I would like you to come north with me. It will be to your advantage to do so, but I won't try to coerce you. But know this: I intend heading north this afternoon. I would have gone yesterday, but I bumped into you. I have already tarried a day or two longer than I'd intended."

"What's the rush? If there are other survivors out there, it's not as if they're going anywhere."

"Oh, but they will be. And very soon, I fear. They will be called." Peter held up his hand to forestall Tom's question. "Soon. I promise."

Hand-printed notices went up around the cleared areas informing people that the Commune would take place the following afternoon at an area of parkland to the east known as Cranford Park. Clearance and salvage work were to be suspended for the morning and people were urged to use the time to rest and eat to build up their strength.

Milandra could, with the help of her Deputies, have simply *sent* the message—it would be a lot easier now that everyone was closely confined—but she and they needed to conserve every ounce of mental energy for the Commune.

"Everything has gone like clockwork," she remarked to Grant in the hotel suite.

"That's what worries me."

"It worries me a little, too. I still can't quite believe that here we all are in London, everyone's gotten here so quickly and we haven't lost a single person in the operation."

"Not in the operation, no. But we have lost one, don't forget. That worries me, too."

"Hmm… yes, Ronstadt," said Milandra. "I had almost forgotten about him."

"We need to decide what to do about him."

"If anything."

"Yes. If anything. But we need to decide."

"Okay. So let's decide."

"Not you and me. The other Deputies, too."

"But..." Milandra broke off under the intensity of Grant's regard. She sighed. "No, you're right. As usual. Fetch them."

Grant rose and strode to the door. He opened it and called into the adjoining room. "Please would you all come in for a moment."

Simone, Lavinia and Wallace walked in and Grant closed the door behind them. Milandra motioned to the armchairs that were arranged in the same formation as in the New York apartment: a horseshoe shape with her at the apex.

When they were all seated, she cleared her throat.

"As you all know, we're holding the Commune tomorrow. We'll be reaching out to the surviving humans. First those in the U.K., that we estimate to be over ten thousand strong, though I hope they'll be anything but 'strong' since they outnumber us two-to-one."

"It's the main reason we've had to move so quickly," said Grant. "We need to get to them while they're still spread out, still weak and bewildered. Once they start to regroup, we may lose them again."

Milandra nodded. "We'll be persuading the U.K. survivors to make their way here immediately. A couple of miles north of here is Hillingdon Hospital. We'll establish a much larger treatment centre there, one that can cope with a large influx of drones."

"And zap 'em!" said Simone with one of her flighty giggles.

"Quite," said Milandra. "Once we've contacted all the U.K. survivors, we'll cast the net wider to the whole world. With them, we can only suggest they begin clearing up their local areas. As we've previously discussed, it would be far too risky at present to get them to travel here. Too many of them are liable to group together and start resisting. By persuading them to remain where they are, the chances of them grouping are slim. Besides, once the Great Coming has taken place, it won't matter."

"We already know all this," said Wallace. "Why have you called us in here?"

"Straight to the point as usual, George," said Milandra. "Okay. What you don't know is that we've lost someone. Not dead. Closed his mind off."

"Who?" asked Lavinia.

"A man by the name of Peter Ronstadt."

"Did he take part in the operation?" asked Wallace.

Milandra shook her head.

"Fucking traitor!" Wallace almost spat the words. Lavinia uttered a low sound in the back of her throat, like a growl. Simone nodded in agreement with Wallace.

"I have no reason to believe he has done anything to hamper the operation," said Milandra. "Or that he will."

"But we can't be certain," interjected Grant.

"No," said Milandra. "We can't be certain."

"Do we know where he is?" asked Lavinia.

Milandra nodded. "He's here in the U.K. In South Wales, last I knew. He was due to infect Cardiff. During the Commune, I should be able to pinpoint precisely where he is now. And who he's with. What we have to decide is what we do about him, if anything."

Wallace's response was immediate. "Hunt him down. Kill him."

Milandra frowned. "To what end? We are not violent people. He has done nothing to hurt us."

"But he could do many things to hurt us," said Grant. "He could shield any survivors with him from the effects of the Commune."

"True," agreed Milandra. "But not many. Three, four, maybe five at most. More than that would be very difficult. He is but one against almost five thousand."

"He could intercept others while they make their way to London," said Lavinia.

Milandra nodded. "Again, true, but they will be flocking here from all over the mainland. He cannot possibly hope to intercept more than twenty or so. Even that will take a great deal of luck. And he may find that there is little he can do to undo the effects of the Commune. If we get it right."

"He could head to the continent," said Grant. "Find survivors there. Band them together. Try to interfere with the Great Coming. He'll have time to try something."

"Pah!" said Milandra. "What can he possibly do to interfere with that?"

"Nevertheless," said Grant, "is that a risk we're willing to take?"

Milandra was about to argue, but closed her mouth. She could see from the expressions on her Deputies' faces that further debate was futile.

"Okay, then," she said. "Let's vote. All those in favour of doing nothing about this Ronstadt?"

Her hand was the only one to rise.

"All those in favour of hunting him down and killing him?"

Four hands rose.

Milandra sat back with a sigh. "So be it," she said.

Peter was right about Tom's first effort at syphoning petrol: he threw up. Despite this, he succeeded in almost filling the Jag's tank.

As they prepared to leave, Peter said, "There are a number of small towns and villages north of here. I want to drive back to my cottage that way and approach my home village from the west. Keep your eyes peeled for signs of human life."

Tom nodded and got behind the wheel of the car. He glanced into the back. Dusty lay in his basket on the broad rear seat. Tom had agreed to pack as if he wasn't returning. All the food and drink, including dog food, that he'd accumulated were boxed away in the boot, together with a small suitcase that contained his hiking boots, a pair of trainers and some spare clothes. He had accepted Peter's assertion that getting kitted out in new outfits wouldn't present a problem so he had left most of his clothes behind. Also in the case were his collection of sleeping pills and painkillers, and the first-aid box from his bathroom cabinet. If Peter noticed that the pills had disappeared from the telephone table, he didn't mention it.

The Range Rover pulled past him and Tom started the engine of the Jaguar, delighting again in the silky purr. It had rained a little overnight and the last of the dusting of snow had disappeared. The sky glowered grey and low, acting like a blanket that would keep the temperature high enough that ice shouldn't be a problem during their journey.

The light-blue Jaguar pulled off behind the bronze Range Rover and they left the village of Penmawr in convoy. Although he had packed as though he was never returning, Tom had every intention of coming back. Maybe not today—on that much he was still undecided—but one day, and he had locked his house securely. He guessed he owned it outright now. There was unlikely to be anybody left in the bank to enforce the mortgage; no judge to make a possession order; no bailiffs to change the locks. On the other hand, this wasn't such a big deal bearing in mind that he could pretty much take his pick of any house he fancied: cottage by the sea; country mansion; swanky townhouse. Heck, he could probably move in to the Hilton in Cardiff if he wanted. Live out his days in five-star surroundings, even if the five-star service wasn't available.

The two vehicles made their way up the valley to the north of Penmawr, passing through villages that clung ribbon-like to the mountain sides.

Reaching the head of the valley, Tom followed the Range Rover through winding mountain roads, the Jaguar handling the bends effortlessly. They passed through thick forests and across wild moors, chunks of granite poking through the bracken like broken dentures.

The only times they had to slow were to avoid sheep, grown brazen by the lack of traffic, and to curve around the occasional abandoned vehicle. One car still had the driver inside, grinning and clutching the steering wheel in a death grip with fingers through which yellowing-white bone showed. Tom swallowed, but it seemed tame compared to what he had seen at the sport centre. Once they had to drive close to the edge of a precipitous drop to avoid a burned-out police car, but there was enough room for them to squeeze between the blackened wreck and the crash barrier without scratching the paintwork on either vehicle.

As they dropped into the next valley, they passed the still-bleeding, mangled corpse of a sheep. Tom glanced in his rear-view mirror, craning his neck to see Dusty, fast asleep in his basket. Mild-mannered and friendly as the dog was, Tom couldn't help but wonder if Dusty would by now have resorted to savaging sheep if he had been freed to roam by his former owner. Probably, he concluded. Without man's interference, the brave new world would see a shuffling in the previous order of things when the fittest overcame the weakest. Claw and fang would become king now.

Mid-morning and they drove on through more winding settlements and more twisting mountain roads. They dropped down into the Rhondda valleys, famous for exploitation of coal and men alike.

Peter chose a circuitous route, driving through hamlets, villages and small towns that covered the valleys like a rash. It was while they were leaving one such village, had almost passed the last of the grey-stone terraced houses lining the road, that the Range Rover's brake lights lit up for no apparent reason and the vehicle came to an abrupt halt. The former owner of the Jaguar had kept the car well-maintained and the brakes were sharp; Tom was able to comfortably stop without danger of ramming the Range Rover, though Dusty's basket thudded against the back of the passenger seat and the dog uttered a small whine.

"Sorry, boy," said Tom. "I have no idea why we've stopped here."

Tom wound down his window and poked his head out, looking enquiringly towards the Range Rover. Peter was craning back, pointing excitedly to something to Tom's left. Tom pulled his head back inside the car and leaned over to peer through the passenger window. With a gasp, he saw what Peter had noticed.

The terraced houses were set back from the road behind stone walls and peeling iron gates. The front gardens sloped upwards so that the ground floors of the houses were raised above the level of the road. Tom had to dip his back and crane his neck to see it, but the last-but-one house had smoke pouring from its chimney.

Tom felt his stomach give an excited flip. "Oh, shit," he said.

He switched off the Jaguar's engine and got out. He closed the door, leaving Dusty sitting in the back. Standing in the open air, freed from the noise of engines, it suddenly seemed too quiet to Tom. Although the sky had lightened, it remained steadily overcast and the day had not grown appreciably colder. Nevertheless, Tom shivered. Peter stepped out of the Range Rover and stood by the bonnet, gazing up at the house. Tom joined him.

Sometimes when Tom felt nervous or unsure, he resorted to stating the obvious.

"There must be someone in there," he said.

"Come on," said Peter, and started walking towards the house.

Tom followed. The creak when Peter opened the gate sounded like a sound effect in an early Hammer horror film and Tom found himself glancing wildly around, certain that someone—or something—would come lumbering down the street, attracted by the noise. He forced himself to look ahead, to breathe slowly, to stop reacting like a ten-year-old.

The house was narrow. A navy-blue painted door faced them at the top of the path. To the right of the door was a window.

Peter walked to the front door and knocked upon it. Three sharp raps. Tom stood at the gate and held his breath.

No answer. Peter looked back at Tom and motioned to the window.

Reluctantly, Tom walked up the path, trying not to creep, and turned behind Peter where the path continued past the window to the stone wall separating the house from the end house. He stopped in front of the window and peered in.

Curtains were drawn tightly across, leaving no gap in the centre or on either side through which Tom could see anything of the interior. A plant in a china pot sat on the inside windowsill. Judging from the blackness of the soil, it had recently been watered.

Tom glanced across at Peter and shook his head.

Peter stooped and poked his fingers through the letter box, opening it, and placed his mouth to the gap, much like Tom had done days ago at his elderly neighbours' house.

"Hello!" Peter called. "Hello? My name is Peter. My companion's name is Tom. We're looking for survivors. We've only found each other so far. And you. Tom has a dog; his name is Dusty. Hello?"

Tom stared at the white lining of the curtains, expecting them to twitch apart, wanting them to yet dreading it. They didn't move.

Peter tried once more. "*Please.* Won't you at least speak to us? Tell us your name? We mean you no harm."

He turned so that his ear was pressed to the opening. After a few moments, he released the letter box and straightened. He looked at Tom and shook his head slowly.

"Doesn't look like they want to be friendly," Peter said. "Don't suppose we can blame them." He beckoned Tom. "Come on. We need to get going. The day is wearing on."

Tom left the window and followed Peter to the gate. He shut it behind him, the creak not sounding so ominous now. As he turned towards the car, he heard a voice.

"Wait."

He turned back to the house. The blue front door had half-opened. Peering around it was a woman.

The park was wide, wet and windy. Many had brought rugs or plastic sheets that they spread on the grass and sat on. Most who hadn't, stood; some sat anyway.

They formed a rough circle around a space occupied by Milandra and the Deputies, who sat on five plastic chairs. The Deputies formed a square in the middle of which sat Milandra. The chair creaked when she settled her bulk onto it and she felt the legs sink into the sodden soil, but she put it from her mind. It had far more momentous matters to occupy it.

There was little preamble. The Deputies rose to their feet and faced the crowd, holding their arms out straight in front of them. The babble of whispered conversation died immediately. The Deputies sat back down. The damp air almost crackled with anticipation.

Milandra spoke briefly, her voice resonant in the silence.

"You all know why we are gathered here. We must Commune. This may be the last time we need to do this before the Great Coming, so give me your all."

Almost five thousand pairs of eyes watched her intently. Nothing moved except the breeze and the drizzle. She drew a deep breath and closed her eyes.

"Now."

Milandra cast her mind free. Instantly it was joined by almost five thousand other minds. Like a feather caught in an updraught of warm air, her psyche spiralled upwards and outwards. Buoyed and strengthened many multiples more than five thousand, it spread like a vast blanket or a stormfront, moving faster than the strongest hurricane, covering the British Isles in a heartbeat, catching everyone in its path.

A moment later, almost five thousand intellects melded into one—squeezing, grasping intellects—Milandra *pushed*...

The woman's name was Ceri; Ceri Lewis. She, too, had fallen ill, but not before watching her husband and ten-year-old son die in the hospital. This was in the first days of the pandemic, when hospitals still took in patients, though the corridors were rapidly filling with sufferers. When Ceri walked, red-eyed and dazed, through the hospital doors, soldiers were already patrolling the grounds, turning the dying away at the main gates.

"If it had been a day or two later, they probably wouldn't have let me leave," she told them in her gentle, lilting voice.

She was thirty-five, a dinner lady at the local comprehensive school. Tears brimmed in her brown eyes while she told them her son had been due to start at the school in September.

"I wasn't even able to give them a burial," she said, her voice breaking.

Peter and Tom sat in the darkness of her living room, the only light coming in from the open front door and the flames from the log fire in the hearth. The afternoon was stretching towards evening; it would soon be dark outside. Peter had glanced at Tom once or twice while the woman's head was bowed, and motioned at his wrist, but Tom shook his head angrily. It was clear that the woman needed to get a few things off her chest before she would even begin to think straight.

Tom stiffened as a high-pitched howl reached his ears. Both Peter and Ceri turned towards the front door while Tom ran to it.

He had left the driver's window of the Jaguar open when he had come to investigate the house and it was due to this that the dog's howl reached the house as loudly and clearly as though Dusty was standing on the path outside the front door. Tom glanced wildly around but could see nothing out of place. No one and no thing had approached the car. So why—?

A rough hand grabbed Tom by the arm and yanked him back into the house.

"Quick!" hissed Peter's voice in his ear. "Grab my hand! No time to explain!"

"But—"

"GRAB MY HAND!"

The force of Peter's yell shocked Tom into obeying and his right hand was engulfed by Peter's. In the gloom, he could just make out that Ceri grasped Peter's other hand, her face twisted into a grimace of terror.

"HOLD HANDS! FORM A CIRCLE! DO IT!" While he shouted, Peter yanked them towards each other.

Tom reached out his left hand and grabbed hold of Ceri's free hand.

"What—" he began, but wasn't silenced this time by Peter. Something slammed into his mind with the force of a runaway truck. He gasped. Vaguely, he was aware that Ceri was making a high-pitched keening sound. From somewhere further away, he could still hear Dusty howling. Next moment, such considerations became irrelevant.

His mind was being examined. An intelligence, far superior to his own, *infinitely* superior, was probing, deeper, deeper…

The gloom deepened to blackness and he felt his knees begin to buckle. He was going to slide senseless to the floor and was powerless to prevent it.

Then, as abruptly as it had come, the pressure lessened, lifted like removing the lid of a pressure cooker, and was gone.

Tom sank to his knees, still clutching the others' hands. He looked to his left. Ceri had also fallen to the floor; her head hung down to her chest and she gulped deep convulsive sobs.

Dusty had stopped howling. Other than the sound of Ceri's sobbing and his own ragged breaths, silence returned.

Tom looked up at Peter. Peter's eyes glittered darkly in the firelight while he returned Tom's gaze with a grimness Tom hadn't seen before.

"I have delayed too long." Peter's voice was as toneless as a broken whistle. "They are coming."

Part 3: Auld Lang Syne

Chapter Sixteen

The nation that had stood almost alone against the might of the Third Reich and had refused to bow even when defeat to the mighty Nazi war machine had seemed inevitable, was brought to its knees—rather, flat on its dying face—by an organism invisible to the naked eye.

In England, Scotland and Wales, the Millennium Bug had left alive a little under eleven thousand people out of a combined population of fifty-nine million. Around three thousand of those had since perished by suicide or starvation or accident. Nearly all of the remaining eight thousand now headed for London.

Not many had tried to resist the calling. Minds still numbed by shock and loss had proved an easy target, wide open to intrusion. Those who did resist performed a brief exercise in futility: the sheer mass of intellect brought to bear against their comparatively puny minds made it a one-sided contest.

Cars, vans, motorbikes, bicycles… whatever was at hand was utilised in obeying the compulsion to head to England's capital. One middle-aged man, paralysed from the waist down in a skiing accident, travelled the sixty miles from his home in Northampton in his wheelchair, forcing himself up steep inclines until his hands were raw and bleeding. An elderly woman, who could not drive, set off from Portsmouth on foot, a trek of around one hundred miles; she almost made it as far as the M25, the motorway that rings Greater London, when her heart gave out near Guildford.

Despite a few incidental deaths like that of the elderly lady, the vast majority reached London alive. The calling of the Commune had not been sufficient to override the survivors' basic instinct to keep on surviving. Minds that might have been open to suggestions to walk off a cliff or slit wrists had already taken those and similar options.

No, the Commune did not possess the strength to achieve mass suicide. Not yet.

~ ~ ~

She stared out of the car window while they passed through villages and skirted around towns. The car juddered over potholes that had appeared during the cold snap in November and would never now be repaired. The wind had strengthened, whipping up old newspaper and crisp packets that had come free from bin bags deposited at the roadside and never collected, torn open by cats and birds.

Scrawny dogs and stringy cats darted away at their approach. Cows and horses watched them from fields, surviving on grass and rainwater. Sheep blundered across roads in search of richer pastures. Birds rose at the sound of the vehicles and circled until they had passed. But she saw no people.

"A land of song that's lost its voice," she murmured, too quietly for her companion to hear.

Strings of forlorn fairy lights swung in the wind; plastic Santas and snowmen leaned crookedly in gardens; they had to slow down to steer around an almost life-sized plastic sleigh and reindeer that had been blown into the roadway.

"My dad was in a choir," she said, a tear trickling down her cheek.

"Sorry?" said Tom.

"My dad. He was in a male voice choir," said Ceri. "He and Mum went almost immediately. Neither of them had been well for a while so the virus got them within hours. I think..." She paused to swipe angrily at the tears. "I think they must have infected Paul. He came with me to the hospital. And Paul infected Rhys."

"Paul's your husband?"

"And Rhys was my son."

Tom said nothing more and they lapsed into silence for a few miles. They were heading north, through the middle of Wales. They had started off following the A470 towards the Brecon Beacons, but had found it blocked near Merthyr by a multi-vehicle pile-up that they could not find a way around. They had been forced to backtrack, the further delay making Peter jittery judging by the anguished look he'd shot them when he'd turned the Range Rover around, and had since been following winding B roads and lanes.

"Peter knows about the virus," said Tom, breaking the silence.

"What do you mean?" She half-twisted in her seat to face him.

"He knows how it started."

"How?"

"I don't know. But he said it was started deliberately. I'm not sure whether to believe him." Tom continued to look straight ahead, following Peter's Range Rover closely. "He said he has something to show me. When we stop I'll make him show me. Show us."

When they had arrived at Peter's cottage the previous evening, Peter had refused point-blank to discuss anything. He had looked drawn and haggard so Tom hadn't pressed it. As soon as they had loaded the Range Rover with the containers of petrol, food and water, and camping equipment, Peter had wanted to leave, but it was Tom's turn to be obstinate.

"Absolutely not," he said. "I'm shattered. That thing that happened in Ceri's, it's left me feeling exhausted. It was as much as I could do to drive here. I can't drive any more tonight, especially through the dark. And look at Ceri. She's drained. Truth be told, you look like shit, too. We all need to rest."

Peter opened his mouth to argue, then closed it again and his shoulders slumped. "You're right. But we have to leave at first light. Put some distance between us and here. *Then* we'll talk."

They had spent a fitful night, Ceri in Peter's bed, the men on the settee and armchair, but all looked slightly improved in morning's light. They left Peter's village a little after eight o'clock and had been driving constantly since.

Ceri craned her neck to look into the back of the Jaguar. "Dusty's still fast asleep," she said.

"Good," said Tom. "I was worried that he'd be affected by all that howling, but he seems fine. Just tired, like all of us."

Ceri drew in a deep breath. "That—whatever it was yesterday in my house—I think Peter stopped it doing something to us."

"I think so, too. But I want some answers. Are you hungry?"

"A little."

Tom pressed the heel of his hand into the centre of the steering wheel, sounding the horn. When Peter slowed down to glance back at them, Ceri mimed forking food into her mouth and Peter stopped in the middle of the road. Tom did likewise and killed the engine. He glanced around. Dark spindly fir trees grew to the edge of the road on one side; on the other was a drystone wall with empty shrubland beyond.

"Hmm…" said Tom. "The middle of nowhere."

Ceri smiled. He wasn't much for small talk, but she was starting to like Tom. She had been very unsure at first, had very nearly allowed them to drive away. It maybe had been the shock of discovering that she wasn't the last person left alive, but she felt glad that she had come out of it in time to call them back. She hadn't done so with any intention of going with them; she merely craved human company after almost two weeks of grief and solitude. Until that invasion of her head, if that's what it had been. If the other man hadn't been there to do whatever it was he'd done, she dreaded to think what would have become of her. She had felt her sanity beginning to slip away like sand through fingers…

After that, going with them had seemed the obvious thing to do. She barely gave a glance at her house after she closed the door behind them. It had stopped feeling like home when she had returned from the hospital a widow and mother without a child.

Ceri opened the car door and got out, glad to be able to stretch her legs. Peter had spread a tarpaulin in the middle of the road and was setting out tins, bottles of water and plastic plates.

"A proper little picnic," she said. "*Da iawn*."

"I know that one," said Peter with a smile. "'Very good'. I married a Welsh girl."

Tom also got out and opened the rear door. Dusty bounded

out, seeming to grin, and almost knocked her over in his delight at seeing her. She noticed that he didn't run over to Peter. Instead, the dog ran to the treeline and squatted.

"Erm," said Tom, looking from Dusty to her. "I'm going to nip into the trees for the same thing. Ah, not *precisely* the same thing, you understand. What I need can be accomplished standing up…"

"Well, I'm going behind that wall," she replied. "Either way, I'll be *twttying* down."

"*Twttying* down?" said Peter, eyebrows raised. "Don't recall that one."

"Squatting," she said and almost uttered a giggle.

While she protected her modesty with the stone wall and conducted her business, Ceri wondered at how good it felt to smile and joke, no matter how feebly. It didn't make the grief and pain disappear, but pushed them away a little. For a few moments, she felt human again.

Joe Lowden was a northern boy through and through. Born and raised in the fishing town of Grimsby, he had never been further south than Nottingham. That had been on a school trip to Sherwood Forest when his class had been studying the legend of Robin Hood. Joe hadn't been particularly impressed; perhaps unsurprisingly, the forest had amounted to little more than a bunch of trees. The ancient oak in which Robin was reputed to have hidden from the dastardly Sheriff of Nottingham was fenced off so that Joe couldn't do the one thing he had been looking forward to: climbing inside. The best part of the trip had been the journey home when he and his classmates shot at each other with the plastic bows and arrows they'd bought at the gift shop, until the spoilsport teachers confiscated them. It hadn't been Joe's fault that one of his arrows had ended up stuck to the driver's bald head—the boy he'd been aiming at had ducked.

Academia had never been Joe's strong point. He left school the first chance he had when he reached sixteen. He told the careers officer that he intended going to work on his father's trawler, but that was a lie. His father had once or twice suggested that as a possible career path for Joe, but without conviction. He knew that the sea didn't run in Joe's blood like it did in his own. If that made him wonder about the source of Joe's blood, he never mentioned it to Joe. In truth, he never mentioned much of anything to Joe, which suited Joe just fine. The less interest his father took in him, the more he could pursue his own ambitions.

His mother, even when sober, paid little attention to her only child. Occasionally, she'd thrust a tenner into his hand for him to run down the offie for a packet of fags or a bottle of cheap wine, telling him he could keep the change. Most of the time, she sat drinking in front of the TV or had her awful friends round and they'd all get drunk together.

When his father came home, filthy and stinking of fish, they would row, he would start drinking and occasionally slap her, then they'd storm off to separate bedrooms.

Joe tended to stay out until late into the night, creeping back to his tiny bedroom long after they had passed out, her from wine and vodka, him from whiskey and exhaustion.

Unlike many boys his age, Joe had no love for football or sport in general. He didn't read, though he could so long as the author hadn't used too many big words; he simply couldn't see the point. He didn't have a computer or games console. He occasionally went to the cinema to see an action film or anything with zombies; they could keep the arty-farty stuff, though.

Nevertheless, Joe had developed an interest; one he had discovered when barely into his teens and one that, now he was approaching eighteen, had become an all-consuming passion. Not one that he could share with his parents, though they unwittingly funded it in part by helpfully leaving purses and wallets lying around the place, and by not being careful enough with their valuable items of jewellery. Petty theft and the occasional burglary provided much of the remaining necessary cash. Any shortfall he made up with his fortnightly benefits—as if they seriously expected him to use it to try to find a job.

The onset of the Millennium Bug and the swift demise of his parents and everyone else he knew had given him a new freedom to indulge his passion. He fell sick himself, but barely noticed. He spent most of his days in a fug of delirium anyway; a touch of flu made little difference.

He wondered briefly if his parents had found release from the pain of their existence, then found that he didn't much care. Quite why his maker had deemed it fit to spare him, he spent not a moment pondering. He had no time for traditional gods. He worshipped the gods of cannabis, ecstasy and mephedrone. Soon, he would graduate to the higher deities: the gods of cocaine and heroin.

Joe knew where most of the dealers in Grimsby and surrounding areas lived. He had never passed a driving test, but that needn't stop him now. The Filth had gone the way of everyone else and he could drive where and how he pleased. And if he banged up a few cars along the way, who was there to give a monkey's?

Within days of the streets falling quiet and deserted, Joe had accumulated a suitcase-full of every leisure drug that had been doing the rounds in the North-east when the virus hit. He took the case to the poshest hotel in Grimsby, to the poshest room that didn't smell like an abattoir, and indulged. Boy, did he indulge!

When the wave of mental energy hit him like a brick one afternoon, Joe was lying on a king-sized bed, eyes open but glazed, dreaming of rainbow bridges and flying serpents and subterranean lakes of molten white gold. As he slowly came out of the fugue, he felt a longing to go to London.

He didn't pause to wonder why he suddenly had this urge, but it seemed as good a place as any to find more drugs. *No* he chided himself *Better. The best. London—where the streets are paved with marijuana.*

An image, as clear as a multi-pixel photo, shone bright and

clear in his mind. Plastic bags of weed and amphs and angel dust and blues and… everywhere his mind's eye looked, the bags waited, on pavements, on walls, in bus stops, to a backdrop of St Paul's dome and Big Ben and a red double-decker bus, for him to pick up.

Clutching his suitcase of somewhat depleted goodies, he headed out of the hotel, found a car containing petrol and set off for the Big Smoke.

Lunch consisted of cold beans and meat, followed by tinned pineapples. Tom suggested heating the beans with Peter's camping stove, but Peter insisted they didn't have time.

Ceri passed on the pineapples. Instead, she took a battered packet of cigarettes from her pocket. She offered it to her companions who both shook their heads.

"Yeah, it's a bad habit," she said, "though don't suppose it much matters now." She lit the cigarette and gave a satisfied sigh. "I can stop feeling guilty about fags now."

Tom smiled at her, then turned to Peter. "So where exactly are we headed?" he asked.

"North," said Peter. He avoided Tom's gaze. Tom suspected he knew why.

"I'm not going any further, you know," he said quietly. "Not without some answers."

Tom was aware from the corner of his eye of Ceri pausing in mid-drag to watch the two men closely.

"I meant to talk to you about that," said Peter. Now he did look at Tom. "They're coming after me. You and Ceri may not be safe. Perhaps it would be better if we separated."

"*Who* are coming after you, Peter?" Tom still spoke quietly and deliberately. Otherwise, he felt, he would explode with his need to know.

Peter sighed. "Okay. I suppose it's time to tell you a little more." He glanced from Tom to Ceri, then back to Tom.

"Showing you would be better. And quicker."

Tom nodded. He glanced enquiringly at Ceri who also nodded. "Show us."

"Come closer," said Peter.

Tom scooted across the tarpaulin to where Peter sat cross-legged and took a similar pose facing him, a little to his left. Ceri took a last drag on her cigarette and flicked it to the side of the road. After a slight hesitation, she followed suit, sitting a little to Peter's right.

"It makes it easier if we hold hands," said Peter, holding his out. Tom and Ceri each grasped one. "And you two." Tom took hold of Ceri's hand, completing the triangle.

"Right," said Peter. "You need to relax your minds. And when you feel me trying to get in, don't resist."

"Hold on one second," said Ceri. She released her grips on their hands and hugged herself as though cold. "I really don't like the sound of this."

"You'll come to no harm," said Peter. "But it's entirely up to you, Ceri. If you're not comfortable with this, I can show Tom on his own."

Tom grabbed Peter's free hand. "I'm fine with that," he said.

"No, wait!" said Ceri. She peered closely at Tom. "Do you trust him?"

Tom regarded Peter for a moment. He gazed calmly back. Tom looked at Ceri. "Yes, I do. I have nothing to base that on except gut instinct. But I believe that he means us no harm. Remember what happened in your house."

"Yes," said Ceri. "Forgive me, Peter. It's just that I barely know you."

Peter shrugged. "It is okay to be cautious. There will come a time when caution will have to be cast to the wind, though it is not upon us yet. But we need to get moving…"

"Okay." Ceri took hold of their hands again. "Let's do it."

Peter looked down. Immediately Tom felt it and heard Ceri utter a small gasp. Then all his concentration focused inwards.

A fluttering sensation inside his head, as though a butterfly was flapping its wings in there. Tom could have stopped it going any further, thrown up shutters that would have made the fluttering cease, but he didn't. Images appeared, flickering like a badly tuned TV, then growing stronger. So strong they were like a high-definition movie and his face was pressed to the screen. Then he passed through the screen and became immersed in the images. Experiencing them.

A vast black ship rising from black sand, glinting redly in the light of a baleful sun. He was inside the ship, moving away from the dying star, speeding up as it passed beyond the gravitational field. An idea glinted at the edge of his consciousness. He grasped at it, snagged it fleetingly. The craft was riding a current that pulled it like a leaf in a storm-swollen stream. He felt entire solar systems pass in the blink of an eye. He sensed that time as he knew it had no meaning here. The ship crossed great gulfs of the universe in heartbeats.

He moved deeper inside the ship. He stood on a balcony looking down onto row upon row of glass coffins that stretched away into the impossible horizons of this cavernous interior. Each coffin contained a figure submersed in fluid, pulsing to the rhythm of unseen pumps. Each figure had a sloping brow, a pronounced jaw and a coarse pelt that rippled like the fronds of sea anemones.

The craft slowed, became almost pedestrian. He looked out once more and saw another star, a white flaming ball of hydrogen that flared fiercely, making the first star appear old and tame in comparison. A planet filled his vision, swirling blue and green and grey as the ship headed towards it. Into it. Too quickly.

Tom's perspective shifted. He was on land of sorts, amongst the creatures. They sensed the coming like an approaching storm. Some fell with dread and sank to the floor of the swamp. Others fled, instinctively heading for high ground.

Clouds covered the skies in a seething orange mass. The wind rose, became a hurricane, a hundred hurricanes, tearing up forests, gouging canyons, raising gigantic waves.

The clouds broke apart when the craft descended. As large as a continent, it landed on the ocean, *in* the ocean, creating a tidal wave that swept the circumference of the planet and opened fissures in the earth's crust with the might of its passing.

He was back inside the calm of the ship, looking out at the devastation; then his vision moved inwards and he saw a man smiling serenely at him. It was Peter…

Tom gasped as the vision winked out. He looked at Peter, who was regarding him calmly. He glanced at Ceri. Her mouth hung open and her eyes were wide. He could feel her shaking.

"What was that?" he managed. His throat felt dry; he let go of their hands so he could reach for a bottle of water.

"Are you all right?" Peter asked. "Are you okay to drive?"

Tom swallowed half a bottle of water in four large gulps. "I'm fine," he said.

Peter turned to Ceri, who was wiping weakly at her mouth as though she had dribbled. "Ceri? You okay?"

She nodded and took the bottle of water from Tom.

"You didn't answer my question," said Tom.

"We have to get moving," said Peter, rising to his feet.

Tom didn't move. "What was that?" he repeated deliberately.

"Absorb what I showed you. We'll discuss it later."

"But—"

"Later, Tom. One step at a time." Peter began to collect together their things and pack them into the Range Rover.

Tom watched him for a moment. Then, with a sigh, he rose to his feet and helped. Ceri stood shakily and walked to the Jaguar.

When they had packed everything away, Tom called to Dusty. He appeared panting from the trees, pine needles sticking to his black coat. He shook himself to dislodge them.

"Good boy," said Tom, bending to pick out a few needles that had refused to budge. "Into the car with you then."

The dog bounded to the Jaguar and Tom let him into the back seat, where he settled down in his basket. Ceri was already installed in the passenger seat, seat belt on, gazing out of the window over the scrubland.

Peter called over. "We'll stop to refuel at the next bunch of cars we pass. You and Ceri discuss what I said. About whether you really want to be accompanying me. You may be placing yourselves in danger."

Before Tom could say anything, he turned and climbed into the Range Rover. Tom got back behind the wheel of the Jag and they set off once more.

It took Milandra a full day to recover sufficiently from the rigours of the Commune to take an interest in her surroundings. The calling of the inhabitants of Great Britain hadn't been too difficult; they were, after all, within very close reach. It was the remainder of the Commune that had completely drained her.

Satisfied that she had called every British survivor—apart from two—she had spread in every direction simultaneously, crossing oceans and continents until the combined psyche of almost five thousand people covered the world like an invisible mist. It homed in upon the survivors, probing, smashing down feebly-erected barriers, installing a subliminal message that the recipients would be virtually powerless to ignore. The message was simple:

Do not seek out others. Remain where you are. Burn bodies. Do not seek out others.

Simple it may have been, but delivering the message worldwide exhausted her to such an extent that anything more complex or requiring greater persuasive effects would have been beyond her ability without larger numbers to boost the combined psyche.

With the last of her mental strength, Milandra reined it back in and released the other psyches. She slumped down in the plastic chair, making it lurch to one side. She might have fallen if Grant, Lavinia and Wallace hadn't rushed to her side and supported her. She retained sufficient cognisance to note that the Chosen remained seated.

It was left to Grant to thank everyone for their efforts and to bring the assembly to a close. He invited everybody to attend a great feast in the main concourse of the airport.

He helped Milandra back to their vehicle and drove her back to the hotel. When she was settled into an armchair, he placed a platter of food on her lap.

"Eat," he said.

Milandra needed no second invitation. She filled her mouth with food and laid her head back against the chair, closing her eyes while she chewed.

When she opened them, Grant was watching her intently. She could sense concern flowing off him. Weakly, she flapped a hand at him.

"I'm okay," she said. "Go join the feast."

"It went well."

"Yes," she said. "Now go."

"If you're sure. But first…"

He walked out and returned carrying another platter piled high with food that he placed on a table by her side. He went out again and returned with two large bottles of cola. These, too, he deposited on the table. Finally, he placed a candle on a saucer and a box of matches on the remaining space on the table top. It would soon be dark.

"Thank you," she managed around the fresh mouthful she had just crammed in.

Grant left and did not return with the other Deputies until some hours later. By then, Milandra had eaten her way through both platters and drunk most of the cola.

"How are you feeling?" Grant asked.

"A little stronger. What I could really do with is sunlight, but more food will have to do."

Grant turned to Lavinia and Simone. "Fetch more food, will you? I'm going back out. I have an idea. Wallace, come with me."

They were gone for a couple of hours. When they returned, they struggled in carrying a large box and six car batteries. Grant opened the box and extracted a full body solar lamp, while Wallace fiddled with the batteries.

After a couple of false starts, the room was bathed in a blue-tinged light. Grant stood the lamp next to the armchair, directing the light onto Milandra. He blew out the candle.

"The batteries will only last a couple of hours," he said. "And obviously it's not as good as the real thing. But it should give you a boost."

Milandra lay back and allowed the warmth from the light to wash over her, feeling her cells soaking it up.

"Mmm," she murmured. "It's wonderful."

By the time the batteries gave out, it was almost dawn and Milandra felt a lot stronger. By morning and after munching her way through yet more food, she was beginning to feel like her old self. She struggled up out of the armchair for the first time since settling into it and used the bathroom. The bodies of Milandra and her kind were far more efficient than the human body, extracting every speck of nutrient from food, able to utilise many more minerals than humans can, so producing very little waste. Nevertheless, the sheer volume of food that Milandra had consumed over the last eighteen hours meant a large volume of waste products by her standards and it had become a case of make room or burst.

Grant was waiting for her when she returned to her chair.

"Visitor asking for you," he said. "You up to it?"

"A visitor?"

"Troy Bishop."

"I had a hunch he'd turn up here sooner or later. Show him in. Oh, and better get the Deputies in here, too. This is about Ronstadt."

Wallace and Lavinia came in and drew up chairs. Simone soon followed, looking bored. Grant came close behind, accompanied by a man. He was tanned and slim and muscular, but the overall effect was spoiled by an expression that suggested it was permanently sardonic.

He strode into the room and stopped in front of Milandra.

"Good to see you again, Milandra. It's been a long time."

"Millennia," said Milandra. "Please. Sit down."

Grant had pulled up three more chairs. He and Simone took two of them. Bishop took the last one so that they formed a rough circle.

"What's this about?" said Milandra, though she knew full well why Bishop had come.

"The Commune," said Bishop. "We have a rogue. I saw him. He protected two drones."

"Yes," said Milandra. "I expect everyone saw him. And your point?"

Bishop grinned. "You already knew about him, didn't you? And you've already decided he has to go. What's his name?"

"Peter Ronstadt," said Grant. "Yes, we've already discussed him. And you're right, we've decided it's too risky to allow him to live. But how does this concern you?"

I want to do it Bishop sent.

"No!" said Milandra. "Speak, please. I'm still too weak from the Commune."

Bishop's grin grew wider—it gave him a predatory look. "It really takes it out of you, does it? My, the burden of leadership."

"Why do you want to do it?" asked Grant.

"Well, let me first commend you on making that decision, though it was a non-brainer if you ask me. He's a traitor."

A growl of assent came from Wallace.

"So why you?" insisted Grant.

"For a start, I didn't see a queue forming of people offering their services. Second, I've served in the military—"

"As have many of our number," interjected Milandra. She could barely remember Bishop, had not known him well before and had not seen him for many long years, years that had wrought changes in them all, but felt a strong dislike for the man seated before her.

"Very true," said Bishop. "But I have special forces training. I've been involved in many 'In, kill and out' missions, acting solo and as part of small hit squads. I can fly—planes and choppers—and I can handle modern firearms." He shrugged. "Also, I'd enjoy taking down a traitor."

"And that," said Milandra, "is precisely what makes you unsuited for this task. The reason there's no queue outside that door is that most decent people would find no pleasure in killing one of our own. A necessary evil, at best. You enjoyed watching humans die, didn't you?"

"Absolutely. And I make no apology either. They're drones, don't forget." His eyes and smile narrowed. "Do I sense an unhealthy degree of sympathy towards our fellow planet-dwellers?"

"There's no sympathy here," said Grant. "Though you won't find much gloating either."

"I think he's perfect for the job." This came from Simone, and Bishop beamed at her.

"Why, thank you, Chosen," he said. "You're spot on. I am perfect."

"I agree," said Wallace.

"Me, too," said Lavinia. She turned towards Milandra. "You can find others to do it. You only need ask and most wouldn't refuse. But why send someone whose heart isn't in it when we have a willing volunteer sitting right here?"

That was quite a speech for Lavinia and it took Milandra a moment to gather her thoughts. She glanced at Grant who merely shrugged.

"It seems you have the backing of my Deputies," she said. "I disagree with them, but I won't try to overturn the majority." She sat forward so she could fix Bishop with her most piercing glare. "But hear me, Troy. Don't take too much pleasure from this. If you find him, make it quick. Make it painless. We are not savages."

Bishop raised one eyebrow, making his expression even more sardonic. "*If* I find him? Were you not able to pinpoint his position during the Commune, Milandra?"

"Of course. He was in Cardiff in South Wales, but had already reached Bristol when we found him. From there, he intends heading south, to Plymouth. He's going to commandeer a boat and sail to France."

From the corner of her eye, Milandra was aware that Grant was watching her and wondered if he knew she was lying. But she quickly dismissed the thought. Even in her weakened state, no one could probe her without her knowledge. And there was only one who might have witnessed, without her knowing, what had passed between her and Ronstadt during the Commune—she glanced quickly at Simone, but the Chosen was staring off into space, having apparently made her only contribution to the discussion and lost interest.

Bishop nodded. "Okay. I'll need someone to direct me to the nearest RAF base. And can I take someone with me on the mission?"

"Yes," said Milandra. "No more than one. Do you have someone in mind?"

"Not yet."

Wallace stood. "I'll go with him."

"Absolutely not," said Milandra. "This is one task for which the Deputies are not eligible."

"Agreed," said Grant and she shot him a glance of gratitude.

Wallace's shoulders slumped in dejection.

"Though any of you may assist him in finding the airbase," she added.

Bishop stood and gave a mock bow. "Thank you, Milandra. I'm going to hunt me some traitor!"

She couldn't help it. She felt her face crinkle as though she had bitten into a lemon.

Bishop only grinned all the more.

Chapter Seventeen

They picked up a main road and headed east along it before turning north once more. They travelled through rolling countryside—farming country—making for the English border.

They didn't speak for the first few miles. Ceri sat staring out of the passenger window as though lost in her own thoughts. Tom did not like to interrupt; he had enough thoughts of his own to keep him occupied: dark, swirling thoughts.

They passed a large signpost and it was Ceri who broke the silence.

"We're heading towards Hay-on-Wye," she said. "They hold a big literary festival there. Always wanted to go."

"I've been," said Tom. "To the town, not the festival. Never seen so many second-hand book shops." He shrugged. "I do occasionally, but I'm not really one for reading books."

He sensed Ceri consider him for a moment. "A teacher who doesn't read books?"

Tom felt his colour rise. "I teach four- and five-year-olds. Don't need to read books to do that." He heard the defensive tone in his voice and felt his colour deepen. "But never mind books. We need to talk about what happened back there."

"I guess we do." She gave a deep sigh. "Did you see a big black spaceship?"

"Yep."

"A huge sun. Red and, er…"

"Dying?"

"Yes. Dying."

"I was on the ship," said Tom. "Looking out. It was travelling fast. Impossibly fast."

"Did you see the people? Hairy people in glass caskets?"

Tom nodded. "They looked Neanderthal."

"Then the planet. The creatures—did you see the creatures?"

"Yes. And the tsunami. I think it wiped them out."

"But did you *see* the creatures? What they were?"

Tom glanced across at her. She was staring at him as though her sanity depended on his answer. "Dinosaurs," he said.

She expelled her breath in another deep sigh. "Thank God. I thought I must be going crazy."

"The last thing I saw…"

"Peter."

"Yes."

"So what does it mean?"

Tom uttered a short humourless laugh. "I guess he was trying to tell us something. But it's utter nonsense. Dinosaurs were wiped out millions of years ago by an asteroid that struck somewhere near Mexico."

"Millions of years ago? Or thousands?"

"Millions. A lot of millions. Every year my class did a project on dinosaurs. But thousands, millions, what's the difference? Even if he was trying to tell us that the extinction was caused through a spaceship crash landing, he couldn't have been there." He laughed again. "It really is complete bullshit. He must be off his rocker."

"But the image, vision, whatever it was—it was so real. I was there, seeing it happen before my eyes."

"Yes. It's a neat trick, I'll give him that. But that's all it is. Some sort of mental conjuring trick."

"Well, it's a very realistic one." She didn't sound convinced.

"Look, we'll tackle him about it when we stop for the night, okay?"

"Okay. After all that's happened, I don't think anything would surprise me any more…" She tailed off and Tom realised that she was close to tears.

Ceri resumed staring out of the window. Tom didn't disturb her. He had no idea what to say.

A black Audi wound its way south down the M1, weaving from side to side. A dent in the front wing attested to a close encounter with the crash barrier. Behind the wheel sat Joe Lowden, grinning while he peered blearily through the windscreen.

A stalled car loomed large in his vision and he twisted the steering wheel, scraping the car with the Audi's bumper as he went past.

"Oops," he said, chuckling.

Sitting in the front seat of the car he'd scraped was a rotting corpse that seemed to grin at him. Joe waved and beeped the horn.

He slowed the car to a crawl and reached into the open polythene bag on the passenger seat. Using his knees to keep the vehicle's course in more or less a straight line, he rolled himself another joint.

When he reached the M25, he turned onto the anti-clockwise lanes and headed south-west. He had never been to this neck of the woods before and wasn't sure why he had turned off the M1, but he knew it was the right thing to do.

"Hinningdon Hospital," he muttered. "No, that's not right. Hillingdon Hospital. Yeah…" He chuckled again.

Quite why he was making for a hospital he had no idea, but it seemed as good a place as any to start. Hospitals had drugs by the bucketful, sitting there, waiting for someone to come along and pick them up. Well, that someone would be one Joe Lowden, a northern lad. He would collect everything he could find, even if he never had any use for it himself. If there were other survivors, he may be able to trade what he didn't want. Start an empire. He'd soon become more important than either of his parents had ever dreamed of being. Ha! He'd show them.

Visions of the new order with Joe Lowden as the Godfather-type head of the organisation playing happily in his mind, Joe eventually eased the Audi through the congested roads of Hillingdon. There was always a gap he could squeeze through—almost as if abandoned vehicles had been moved out of the way—and he was able to drive into the hospital's car park.

He brought the car to a halt. Walking towards him was the first living person he had encountered in, well, he didn't know how long, but it must be a week at least.

Joe opened the car door and stumbled out into the fresh air. It made him cough. A woman had nearly reached him. She was slim and tanned. Jean-clad, firm-looking thighs; perky breasts straining against the material of her jumper. Hanging by a shoulder strap, a machine gun bumped against her hip. When she spoke, it was in a strange accent: Australian, maybe.

"Welcome. I'm Tess Granville. Hope you had a good journey." Although her face wore a friendly expression, her tone suggested that she didn't really care whether he'd had a good journey or not. "If you could make your way to the Accident and Emergency Department." She motioned with one hand towards the hospital building. "It's signposted."

Joe eyed the gun, then moved his gaze up to her chest.

"Nice gun, nice tits. Hey, baby, do you want to join my gang?"

"Mate, if you could make your way to—"

Joe lurched towards her, holding out both hands to that luscious chest. The indulgence of the past few days had made him incredibly horny.

The woman took a smart step back and raised the gun, pointing it in Joe's face. He juddered to a halt.

"Hey! Hey! No need for that, baby. I'm just being friendly, you know."

The affable expression left the woman's face. Her eyes narrowed and her mouth set in a firm line.

"Then take this as a friendly warning," she said. "Don't make any attempt to touch me again. Make your way inside the hospital. Go to the Accident and Emergency Department. Do it now."

"Okay, okay. Hey, baby, fancy a smoke?"

The gun didn't waver. "Go. Now."

The first alarm bells were managing to pierce the fog that shrouded Joe's mind, but he was barely aware of them yet. He stumbled past the woman—she took a couple more paces backwards to remain out of his reach—and made for the hospital entrance. A man stood by the door, also holding a gun.

"Hey, brother!" said Joe. "How you doing?"

The man didn't smile. "Inside please, sir," he said in an American accent. "Follow the corridor to the E.R."

"Huh?" said Joe. "That's a TV programme, isn't it?"

"Yeah, right," said the man, his face expressionless. "Accident and Emergency Department. That's where you need to go."

"I don't need to go there, brother. I'm not injured."

The man's voice grew lower, almost a whisper. "Call me brother again and you will be." The knuckles on the hand gripping the butt of the gun whitened.

Joe edged past him. "What is it with people round here?" he said. "Where's all the love?"

The alarm bells in Joe's mind had set up a clanging, jangling racket and at last he began to pay attention. Uneasiness helped clear away more of the befuddlement and Joe became almost clear-headed for the first time in many months. He stopped in the corridor. A sharp smell of antiseptic and something else filled the air, clearing his mind further. That something else was familiar: an acrid smell that he could almost taste, metallic against the back of his throat, like an electrical discharge.

"Keep moving, please," said a voice. Another gun-toting man stood against the corridor wall. Further down, Joe could see another. "Down the corridor to your right, please."

Joe stumbled on, passing two more men and a woman holding guns, motioning him onwards.

He turned into a wide room, laid out with cubicles formed by drawn blue-patterned, plastic curtains. A line of bedraggled people, maybe twenty long, men and women, stretched from the doorway to a wooden desk on wheels—more like a lectern—behind which stood a stern-faced woman. Two or three people with guns wandered up and down the line. A group of unarmed people, four or five strong, watched the line intently. The sharp smell of ozone grew stronger.

An armed woman stood inside the doorway. "Join the queue, please," she told Joe. Her voice contained no hint of emotion.

Robotic, almost.

Joe hesitated. "Um, I'd like to talk to someone about this."

The woman flicked the gun, a submachine gun, towards him.

"Join the queue," she repeated. Joe noticed that she had dropped the 'please'.

Joe opened his face into what he hoped was his warmest smile and took half a step towards the woman.

"Hey, is that a Thompson?" he said in a buddy-buddy voice, pointing to the gun.

The woman's finger moved to the trigger.

"Last chance," she said. "Join the queue."

"Jeez, okay, okay." Joe backed away. He turned to the queue and shuffled to the end.

He nudged the man in front of him. "Hey, man, what's going on here?"

A drawn, pale face turned to him. The man's breath was sour, like spoiled milk, and Joe felt his stomach lurch.

"Everyone has to go behind one of those curtains and—"

He broke off and turned away when a shrill scream rent the air. It cut off almost immediately. Joe watched the curtains. One of them quivered and a woman shuffled out. The hair at her temples had been gelled down and her jaw hung slackly. A line of spittle dangled from her lower lip. She looked neither right nor left, but half-walked, half-stumbled to the other end of the room and disappeared through an open doorway.

Another waft of sour milk hit Joe as the man in front turned back to him.

"That's how everyone leaves," he said. "Go behind the curtain normal. Come out like that."

The line shuffled forwards while the woman in the front of the queue walked slowly towards the cubicle vacated by the slack-jawed woman. From her bearing, she appeared to be terrified, an impression confirmed when she cast a wide-eyed glance behind her at the people standing in line. She reached the curtain and paused. Although she was many yards away, Joe clearly heard her gasp and saw her clutch at her head. She stepped forward and the curtain twitched closed behind her.

Joe nudged the man in front.

"Hey, man, why don't we make a break for it?"

The man's haunted eyes turned his way again.

"They've got guns," he said. "Anyway, someone tried that before you got here. See them?" He nodded towards the unarmed group that continued to scrutinise the queue like customs men looking for drug-smugglers. Joe had an idea that they had started to focus on him. "A woman made a break for that back door. All they did was stare at her and she stopped in her tracks like she'd run into an invisible wall. They carried on staring at her and she turned around and walked into the cubicle. But she didn't walk normally. She jerked about like a puppet."

"But that was only one woman, right? If we all make a run for it at the same time…"

The man shook his head. "Then they'd use the guns. Besides, you're assuming that we don't all want whatever lies behind those curtains. I for one welcome it."

Joe stared at him. "It could be oblivion, man."

"I sincerely hope so," said the man and turned away.

Joe glanced at the unarmed group again. They had definitely turned their attention to him.

"Fuck this for a game of soldiers," he muttered.

He stepped to one side, trying to look casual, and took off towards the nearest armed person. If he could grab the gun, he might stand a chance.

He had only taken two paces when something slammed into his mind and he skidded to a halt three yards from his intended target. The armed man in question glanced in his direction, his mouth turning up in a sneer, before resuming his pacing.

Joe tried to get his legs moving again, but they refused to obey. Then they did start to move, but towards the curtains. Struggle as he might, he had no control over them. He tried to move his arms, but they swung uselessly at his sides. He tried to cry out, but his mouth and throat had stopped working, too. The only things he could move of his own volition were his eyes. They swivelled towards the unarmed group of people. Each member of the group was staring at him intently.

The man he had been talking to glanced at him while he passed. A told-you-so grimace was his only reaction.

Joe walked, or was walked, to the curtains. The man's description had been accurate. Joe's legs moved in quick jerks; he must resemble a puppet in the hands of an inexperienced puppeteer.

He came to a halt in front of a curtain. A slack-jawed man appeared and shuffled away. Joe was marched inside and onto the plastic-covered bed that dominated the cubicle. His nose must still have been his own since it filled with the ammonic smell of urine. A yellow puddle had formed on the plastic sheet. Joe lay down on it.

A machine stood next to the bed, equipped with a small array of dials. Wires ran from the machine to two metal-tipped electrodes held in the grip of a man.

A woman stood the other side of the bed. When Joe lay back, she bent over him and smeared some sort of gel onto his temples. The man brought the electrodes forward.

Joe's limbs remained out of his control, but his vocal cords were suddenly released from whatever had held them. He used them to scream as loudly as he could.

Bishop was sitting in his apartment cleaning his pistol when the knock came on the door. He opened it to find Simone Furlong standing there.

"Chosen," he said. "I thought Wallace was going with me to the airbase. We're not leaving till the morning."

She stepped forward, forcing Bishop to move back, making a gap for her to squeeze past him. She skipped into the living area, looking around like a child in a toy shop.

"Cool apartment," she said.

Bishop closed the front door and returned to his seat, walking through the waft of expensive perfume that she trailed behind her.

"What is it you want?" he asked.

"A direct man. I like that." She whirled around to face him. "Milandra lied to you."

"Ah. Are you sure?"

"Oh, yes." Her voice had a faraway, dreamlike quality that Bishop was beginning to suspect masked a sharp intellect. "I don't yet possess the talents that she has, but I can do things most people can't."

"Go on."

"Milandra sympathises with the drones."

"I could sense that much. So?"

Simone smiled. Bishop noticed that she had green eyes, flecked with gold. Cat's eyes. "So I watched closely during the Commune when she made contact with the traitor."

"So did I," said Bishop. "All I saw was him close his mind and protect the two drones that were with him."

"That's all she wanted anyone to see. However, being the Chosen has certain advantages. I could see what really happened. And the best part is that she had no clue I was watching." She tittered.

"Okay. Why are you telling me?" Bishop had sidestepped the real question of what she had witnessed deliberately. He wasn't the sort of man who liked to ask for what he wanted. He preferred to take it.

Simone shrugged her slight shoulders. "I want you to catch them."

"Them? There's only one traitor."

"The drones that are with him. Kill them, too."

"You hate them that much?"

Her eyes blazed and she almost spat the words. "Yes, I fucking hate them!" She breathed deeply for a few moments. "This is our world and they've taken over."

"Not for much longer. If the Great Coming succeeds…"

"And if it doesn't? It'll be two less to hunt down and kill later."

Bishop considered for a moment. "Okay. The traitor is my number one priority…"

"Of course."

"… but if the drones are still with him, they're as good as dead."

Simone smiled. "I had a feeling we'd see eye to eye. Now for what I saw…" *I can show you* she sent.

Bishop shook his head. "Uh-huh."

Simone took a step closer and placed a finger to his temple. He didn't flinch. "Hmm… what secrets do you want to keep hidden, I wonder?"

Bishop raised his hand and caught her arm by the wrist. Her eyes opened a little wider. He brought his head forward until it was an inch or two from her face. "No secrets," he said. "But I ain't letting you in."

He released her arm and she stepped back, bringing her other hand across to rub her wrist where he'd gripped it. Bishop half-turned away and picked up the pistol and cleaning brush. He started to clean the barrel.

"You're a bit of a bastard, aren't you?" said Simone.

"Better remember it," Bishop said, concentrating on the weapon.

There was a long pause and Bishop knew that she would now say what she had come to say. "They're not going south to Plymouth. During the Commune, they were still in Wales, around ten miles north-west of Cardiff. They're heading north. She warned Ronstadt. Told him that someone would be coming after him."

"If he has half a brain, he already knew," said Bishop. "North. Okay."

"Make sure you get them."

"Close the door after you."

He didn't look up until the door had slammed behind her.

Then he grinned and bent back to his task.

A few minutes later, another knock came on the door.

Bishop's eyes narrowed. He placed the gun on the table and strode to the door. He yanked it open.

"What—"

But it wasn't the Chosen come back to salvage some injured pride.

"May I come in?" asked Diane Heidler.

Chapter Eighteen

The temperature dropped to freezing and the sky lowered while the afternoon wore on.

"Think we might be in for more snow," Tom remarked.

Ceri merely grunted.

They drove on, making better time, only needing to slow down occasionally to steer a cautious path around knots of vehicles. Tom had stopped noticing the rotting corpses that still occupied some of the cars.

Now and then, Peter would stop at these vehicles and insist that he and Tom top-up their fuel tanks. Each time, Peter would refuse to engage in any conversation other than to plan the immediate journey.

Late afternoon, they crossed the border into England. Tom commented on this to Ceri, but again only received a grunt in response. The woman had withdrawn into herself and Tom didn't know what to do to bring her back to the surface. Not that he spent much time worrying about it. His own thoughts had turned dark once more while he pondered how best to force Peter to tell them what he knew. On more than one occasion, Tom's thoughts strayed to the boxes and bottles of pills in the suitcase in the boot.

As night fell, they left the main road and drove down a lane to a quaint village. Peter pulled up in front of a large pub that looked hundreds of years old. Tom parked the Jaguar behind the Range Rover and got out, whistling to Dusty. His breath plumed and he wrapped his arms about himself.

"Bloody parky now," he said.

"Yep," agreed Peter. "It's going to snow tonight. But we should be snug in here."

Peter tried the pub door. It was locked.

"Wait here," he said. "I'll see if I can find a back entrance."

Tom waited, stamping his feet and bending occasionally to stroke Dusty when he bounded up to him before scampering away again, excited to be outdoors. Ceri had decided to leave the warmth of the Jaguar and join him when there came the sound of bolts being withdrawn and the pub door was thrown open.

"Welcome to *The Barrel and Bell*," Peter said with a grin.

They all went in, Tom calling Dusty to join them. Peter held a torch, which revealed tables of dark wood and red-cushioned benches. Overlying the faint smell of yeast was a smoky aroma that Ceri recognised before Tom did.

"They've got a fireplace," she said.

Peter's torch beam picked out the huge stone chimney breast and grate. Neatly stacked alongside it was a bundle of split logs.

"I reckon," said Peter, "that this place was closed up at the outbreak of the plague. I had a peek behind the bar. It's fully stocked. The beer in the pumps will have gone off, but there's loads of canned and bottled drinks. And a ton of crisps and other snacks." He flicked the light beam towards a door at one end of the bar. "I opened that—it leads to the living quarters. Best keep it closed. A little, er, aromatic."

Ceri grimaced, but Tom found that the thought of spending the night beneath a rotting corpse or two no longer filled him with distaste.

They hunted around. In the cellar, they found crates of soft drinks, cider and beer, boxes of crisps, pork scratchings and nuts. In the kitchen, they unearthed catering-sized jars and tins of food.

Peter exclaimed with delight when he opened a cupboard in the corner of the kitchen.

"Paraffin lamps! Six of them. Trimmed and filled. They must be used to power cuts around here 'cause they're well prepared."

Within the hour, the three people and one dog lounged on cushioned benches drawn up before a crackling log fire, coats and boots discarded, munching on flame-toasted hot dog sausages, crisps and pickled eggs. Dusty wolfed down a couple of sausages and a large tin of ham, lapping water from a giant ashtray they found behind the bar. Tom washed his food down with a bottle of Australian lager; he carried a few more bottles outside and left them to chill. Peter drank a can of cola. Ceri took a bottle of vodka from behind the bar and sloshed it into a glass with orange juice.

Tom watched her surreptitiously in the flickering light of the paraffin lamps. She gulped down the first few mouthfuls and coughed. Then she gulped down some more and refilled the glass. It was her business if she wanted to get drunk, but Tom wanted her to wait until he had tackled Peter in case he needed her support. He started to plan what he could say to her when he realised that he wouldn't need to say anything. Ceri only took small and occasional sips of the second drink as though some desire or need had been satisfied by the first.

He turned his attention instead to Peter and was about to embark on his opening gambit when Ceri beat him to it.

"Tell us about earlier," she said softly. "What you showed us. Tell us."

Peter glanced at Tom, who nodded emphatically.

Peter sighed heavily.

"Okay," he said. "What I showed you today was only an impression of the truth. An amalgamation of what happened. How do they say it in the movies? A montage? Yes. A montage."

"I knew it," said Tom. "It was something you made up."

"No," said Peter. "Part of what I showed you I did not witness, but is nevertheless an accurate representation of what took place." He was silent for a moment and the only sound was the settling of logs in the fireplace. "I guess the best way to do this is to tell you it all from the beginning. It's a long story, but I can make it manageable if you let me tell it without interrupting." He raised his eyebrows and looked at Ceri.

"So long as you men don't mind me smoking in here," she said. "And we can take an occasional pee break. I'm a good listener."

Peter looked at Tom.

"I can ask questions when you've finished?" said Tom.

"One or two. But it might be quite late by then and you'll have a lot to digest. You may find that you'd rather keep the bulk of your questions for tomorrow. And I'd prefer that, too."

"Okay."

Peter shifted his backside on the cushion, making himself more comfortable.

"Right then," he said. "Let me tell you a story…"

A long, long way from here—many systems away—exists a planet. It is similar in some respects to this one: oxygen-rich atmosphere, an abundance of water, plentiful ore and mineral resources, almost identical surface gravity, the dominant species bipedal mammalian creatures.

The main differences between that planet and this can largely be accounted for by the star around which that planet orbits. Billions of years older than Sol, the distant star has entered its early death throes. It has expanded, puffing up like an inflating balloon, on its way to becoming what astronomers call a red giant.

As the star expanded, so its outer edge drew closer to the planet in its orbit. The planet was buffeted by solar winds that increased in intensity while millennia passed. The planet's surface became ravaged—the winds dried up oceans and rivers, destroyed vegetation and decimated wildlife. With increasing frequency, solar flares added to the devastation of the surface. Very gradually, over many thousands of years, it became a barren wasteland.

The dominant species—let's call them 'people'—was eventually driven underground. That's where the water could be found. The people had plenty of time to plan, to develop new technologies and advance existing ones to enable subterranean life to flourish. Drilling and tunnelling, ventilation, pumping, glass and plastic manufacture, waste disposal, greenhouse horticulture, hydroponics, optics, thermodynamics… and many more that humans would not recognise, like aquapology and geogenics.

It began on a small scale, but rapidly expanded. Underground settlements the size of villages grew into towns, became cities. Great civilisations that had existed on the planet's surface were replicated beneath it. All the grand structures—the pyramids, the palaces, the minarets and monoliths—that had been lost were rebuilt beneath protective glass and plastic domes. Prisms and mirrors and light tubes carried sunlight to places not illuminated by the domes. Aqueducts carried water to places not accessible to the vast underground lakes. Subterranean jungles were cultivated to perform the photosynthesis that was slowly decreasing above ground.

But the people knew it was not enough. It may take many more millennia, billennia even, but eventually their sun would explode, sloughing off its outer shell like a snake shedding its skin. If their planet was able to withstand the blast of debris and still support life, it would not survive the cooling process that would follow while the star changed from a white dwarf to a dark one. Whether from the explosion of the sun or the ensuing cooling, the people knew their days were numbered.

They began to turn their attention outwards. They already possessed the knowledge and materials for space travel within their solar system, although they had only toyed with the technology, sending out the occasional localised probe more for fun and diversion, rather than for significant scientific pursuit. But now they had good reason to treat space exploration as something more than a hobby. The ultimate survival of their species would depend upon the ability to seek out another planet in another solar system to which they could decamp before their sun exploded.

They did not waste time on the three other planets in their system. Even if one of them would support their life forms, the problem would only be relocated, not solved. They needed to seek beyond their system.

Deep space travel involves distances that the human mind struggles to comprehend. It means crossing expanses so vast that reducing them to mathematical expression results in numbers so ridiculously long or ludicrously factored as to become meaningless. The only way to express such distances in vaguely comprehensible ways is to reduce them to absurd simile or metaphor. To travel from that planet to this at the speed of light would thus be like releasing a helium-filled balloon on a still day. Imagine the balloon continuing to rise at that same barely-moving velocity; up and up, on and on, into the atmosphere and beyond, until one day it passes the Moon. Imagine that it continues on through the Solar System until it reaches Mars; then on, until eventually it reaches Neptune. That journey would take the balloon centuries. So it is with interstellar space travel, even at the speed of light.

The people knew that they needed to discover the secret of travelling beyond—far beyond—light speed. Now the people of that distant planet are governed by the same laws of physics that pertain here: The Theory of Relativity and so on, that forbid the possibility of travelling faster than light. However, they are not limited by the inhibitions inherent in the human intellect. They knew that with their combined wisdom there was a chance that they could discover the answer and they bent their collective will to achieve a solution.

They failed.

Something eluded them. A vital piece of the puzzle remained hidden. And would remain hidden still if not for a remarkable piece of good fortune.

Life within the subterranean cities went on. At the edge of one of them, near the planet's equator, a small team of tunnelers was working on an expansion to the storage area of a food depot. They broke through into a vast network of caverns that nobody had hitherto suspected to exist. There, deep within the caverns' dark recesses, they made the discoveries that would change their people's future.

They found the remains of an ancient, unknown civilisation. If the civilisation had inhabited the planet in distant times before it became the home of the people, no other traces of its occupation had previously been discovered.

Many strange artefacts lay in the darkness of those caverns, untouched for millions of years. Amongst them were objects of wonder that are not pertinent to this tale. The purpose of some of them yet remains unclear.

A series of tablets formed from a black substance caused much scratching of heads. Upon the surfaces of the tablets, strange symbols and diagrams were marked. The people have no use for writing or other forms of record. It took them many years to understand that they were looking at recordings left by that dead civilisation. It took them many years more to begin to decipher them. The people viewed the markings much in the same way that Victorian explorers regarded Egyptian hieroglyphs: with awe and utter perplexity.

The first tentative translations were largely nonsensical and greeted with scorn. However, enough of a hint of what the tablets contained was soon revealed to ensure that the people pooled their resources, their intellects, to tackle the decryption. When at last the cypher was cracked and the tablets could be read in their entirety, the people rejoiced for here was a fine gift indeed from the ancients. The secret of faster-than-light travel, the missing link in their search, was revealed.

Not only that. The ancients had understood how to travel at speeds that made deep space exploration practicable, but it was more than mere theoretical knowledge. Much more. The ancients had built a craft.

The tablets contained a complete blueprint. Materials, propulsion, proportions, dimensions… The last one, dimensions, caused a great deal of consternation. The craft built by the ancients had been vast, as huge as a mountain range. The people doubted that they had sufficient of the materials listed in the tablets to replicate the craft on the same scale. In particular, they lacked sufficient of the ore of a radioactive element, one that doesn't exist here on Earth. The ancients must have nearly exhausted the reserves of ore in constructing their craft. The problem wasn't insurmountable—the ore most likely could be found on the other planets within the solar system—but extraction would be a lengthy process. One that happily turned out not to be necessary.

The tablets also contained something that caused further ripples of excitement among the people, and they are not a species readily given to excitement. A detailed account of the first and, so far as can be ascertained, only journey of the craft. The account is worthy of reading in its entirety, but a brief recount of the key points will suffice here.

It is not known in what numbers the ancients existed, though it is surmised that they must have extended into many hundreds of thousands, millions even, to necessitate such a large craft for, as has already been implied, a much smaller craft would have been as capable of safely conveying a living cargo the vast distances involved. However many they were, the vast majority of them made the journey, leaving a mere handful of volunteers behind. Those volunteers faithfully recorded the journey on the tablets from messages that their brethren sent back. What then became of those who remained behind is not known.

But why would an entire race travel many light years across the galaxy, leaving their home planet behind, at a time when the sun around which they orbited was much younger and millions of years from causing devastation to the planet's surface? The answer is not so clear from the markings of the tablets, but they contain sufficient hints and references that a satisfactory theory can be confidently propounded.

The ancients had enemies. Foes who hunted them and who the ancients were afraid might soon find them. They set off in their enormous craft not to escape the effects of a dying sun that would not occur for many more millennia, but to flee an imminent threat from a deadly and feared enemy. No clue could be found in the tablets as to who, or what, this enemy might be or where it might come from.

What is certain is that set off they did. Aiming at a promising solar system hundreds of light years away, the craft left the planet, never to return.

Months later, it arrived in the target solar system. *This* one. It made for the planet that the ancients identified as most likely to support them, the one with water and vegetation and oxygen. *This* one.

The craft plunged into and through the Earth's atmosphere. It was only then that the flaw in the craft's design became apparent. So intent had the ancients been upon constructing a vehicle that would handle the rigours of interstellar travel, they failed to pay sufficient attention to being able to manoeuvre it when it arrived at its destination. Although the craft contained systems designed to slow it down on descent, the systems lacked finesse. Without the ability to adequately control descent, the craft crashed into the Earth's surface.

More accurately, it came down into one of the oceans, the North Atlantic, near what is now eastern Mexico, but what then was probably just ocean. The impact of such an enormous body caused a vast tsunami that wiped out the dominant life form at the time and that subsequently allowed the mammal to evolve from the mouse-like creature it might otherwise have remained.

The bottom of the craft gouged out a crater in the shallow ocean bedrock. The bedrock, in turn, ripped the bottom out of the craft. While water rose to fill the interior, the ancients who had survived the crash used their last moments to submit messages back to their home planet, reporting their fatal design error.

Over the millennia that ensued, the craft was most likely crushed further by continental drift and submerged beneath rising seas. What is left must now lie beneath miles of silt and compacted sediment. The only evidence of the impact is the crater and the disappearance from the fossil record of the life form that the crash rendered extinct.

Peter took a long slug of cola. "That'll do for tonight. There's more, but it will have to wait."

"No," said Tom. "You said we could ask a couple of questions."

Peter nodded.

"Are you saying," said Tom, "that the dinosaurs were wiped out by a crash-landing spaceship?"

"Yes," said Peter. "The tablets on our home planet contained information that enabled us to roughly date when the ancients' craft set off. The geological evidence on Earth corroborates the date. Around sixty-six million years ago."

"Huh. Stupid us thinking it was a meteor when all along it was a flying saucer. I want to…" He tailed off as Peter glanced towards Ceri.

She was almost asleep.

"Sorry," she mumbled. "So tired…"

"It's okay," said Tom. "Go to sleep. The rest can wait till tomorrow. I'm going to have another beer."

When he returned, Ceri had curled onto her side on the bench, eyes tightly closed, breathing deeply. Peter, too, had lain down before the dying fire, his eyes shut.

"It's snowing," said Tom. "Heavily."

Peter gave a soft grunt, but there was no further reply.

In South Ruislip, around six miles by road from Hillingdon Hospital, lies the airbase RAF Northolt. Established three years before the RAF itself, the airbase was instrumental in the Battle of Britain and has since been in the public eye for occasions such as the repatriation of the body of the Princess of Wales after the fatal crash in Paris, and the return from exile of the train robber, Ronald Biggs, to be arrested the moment he stepped down from the plane.

The roads around the airbase lay deserted. If there had been any attempt at storming the base by disaffected and infected protestors during the first days of the Millennium Bug, no evidence remained.

A light snow had fallen overnight, barely enough to provide the roads and grass verges with a powdery coating. The air was crisp and clear under a pale winter sun.

Two cars pulled up to the base entrance and disgorged seven people. Out of the first car stepped Troy Bishop, Diane Heidler and George Wallace. Out of the second came three of the men and one woman who had worked as groundcrew in Hong Kong and had travelled to the U.K. from that island in the Airbus piloted by Bishop.

Industrial-strength bolt cutters made short work of the gates and they quickly entered the base.

Bishop had not expected to find what he was seeking and was prepared to travel further afield to other bases, but he was in luck. Sitting on the apron on the edge of the runway was a yellow RAF Sea King helicopter.

"Not my colour," he remarked. "But it'll do."

"Search and Rescue," said one of the groundcrew, a surly, thick-set man with oriental features. "Not normally based here. Must have been flown in during the crisis."

Bishop paced while the groundcrew went to work on the chopper. Wallace stood and watched them, saying nothing. Diane lowered the bag she was carrying—it made a dull clunk—and sat on it. Her expression said that she had been more comfortable.

The surly man walked over to them after about thirty minutes, wiping his hands on a rag.

"It's almost dry," he told Bishop. "We'll have to pump the juice by hand. Engine needs a bit of work. Nothing we can't handle."

"How long?" said Bishop.

"Three, four hours."

"Make it three."

The man shrugged and walked away. Bishop turned to Diane.

"We should be away by noon. Eat, piss, do whatever you got to do, but make sure you're ready to go as soon as they're done. Unless you've changed your mind about coming…?"

She stared at him for a moment, her face expressionless. If Bishop was the type to feel uncomfortable under such regard, he would have started to squirm. But the only emotion he felt was impatience.

"Well?" he demanded.

"I'm coming."

Bishop nodded towards the helicopter. "Those things aren't equipped with guns," he said. "So we'll need what you're sitting on."

"You want me to check them over?" asked Wallace. "Give me something to do."

Bishop shook his head. "I cleaned and oiled them last night." He glanced again at Diane. "You know how to use them, right?"

"The handgun, yep. The Uzi, nope."

"It's point and press, baby," said Wallace with a grin. "Point and press."

Diane's lips drew tight. Bishop had a feeling that she didn't much care for Wallace. Or for him, for that matter. It made no difference, so long as she was committed to their mission. But of that he was uncertain, too. He had almost turned her down, but saw the sense in taking someone with him and he wasn't exactly inundated with offers.

"I'll handle the Uzi," said Bishop. He pulled aside his jacket to reveal the worn grip of the pistol poking from the waistband of his trousers. "It'll nicely complement this little darling."

He turned back to Wallace. "If you want something to do, give them a hand pumping the fuel."

Wallace opened his mouth as if to protest. He probably wasn't used to taking orders from someone other than Milandra or one of the other Deputies, guessed Bishop. But then Wallace seemed to reconsider.

"Yeah. Good idea, man. I'm getting cold just standing around."

"Right," said Bishop to Diane, "I'm getting a little chilly, too." He nodded towards the main building. "I'm heading inside. See if I can find some chow. You should think about doing the same. You'll need all the energy you can get before this is done."

Diane leaned her head back, pointing her face to the sun. While the morning wore on, the temperature had nudged above freezing and the dusting of snow had almost melted. "I'm fine by here," she said.

"Suit yourself." Bishop turned and walked towards the airbase building.

One hundred and fifty miles north-west of RAF Northolt, the morning sun remained hidden behind thick cloud. A foot of snow lay on the ground, showing no signs of melting.

Dusty bounded through it like a leaping dolphin, burying his face in it and sneezing.

"May as well hole up for the day," said Tom, kicking at the snow. "Plenty of logs for the fire, plenty of food, plenty to drink."

"Nope," said Peter, buttoning his coat. "We have to keep moving. I want to reach the Lake District by nightfall."

"I won't get far in the Jag," said Tom. "Not unless we can find some tyre chains."

"Then we'll all go in the Range Rover. Or…"

"Or what?"

"I'll go on alone."

Ceri appeared in the pub doorway, tousle-haired and yawning.

"What?" she said. "What's this about you going on alone, Peter?"

Peter spread his hands. "Look," he said, "I've told you that they're coming after me. If you stick with me, you're bound to be in danger. If we separate…" He shrugged. He knew that he spoke the truth, but dreaded them following his advice. After years of being alone following Megan's death, Peter had discovered that he preferred not to be.

"There you go with the 'they're coming after me' routine," said Tom. "Who exactly are 'they'?"

"I need to finish my story. Then you'll understand." Peter knew that he was making it very difficult for them to refuse accompanying him, but did not chide himself for being sneaky. He had sat long into the night playing cards during long voyages in the merchant navy and had never bemoaned his luck with what he had been dealt, merely doing his best with the hand in front of him. He felt that he was doing the same now.

"I think we should stick together," said Ceri. "We've only just found each other." She glanced at Tom, and Peter thought he could read desperation in her eyes.

Tom sighed. "Yes, I guess so." He looked at Peter. "You're not giving us much choice. I *need* to hear the rest of what you've got to say, even if it is utter bollocks."

"I can only tell you what has happened," said Peter. "I cannot make you believe it. Okay, let's get on with it."

They transferred Tom's suitcase, Dusty's basket and the remaining provisions from the Jaguar to the Range Rover. They added as many tins, bottles and packets of food and drink from the pub that they could fit in. Peter also packed the paraffin lamps into an empty crisp box that he squeezed onto the back floor of the vehicle beneath Dusty's basket.

After a hurried breakfast, they left *The Barrel and Bell*, Tom giving the light-blue Jaguar a last regretful look when Peter drove off.

The Range Rover easily handled the snow; Peter didn't even need to switch to four-wheel drive.

He headed north.

Chapter Nineteen

Milandra, after taking the unusual step of grabbing a few hours' sleep, awoke refreshed and fully recovered from the rigours of the Commune.

The hours of mental inactivity while she completed her recovery had given her time for introspection. A certain notion had grown more insistent of late, nagging at her to allow it in so that she could examine it. Once it had gained a foothold, it would never go away, not unless, having prodded, weighed and given it full consideration, she dismissed it as something for which she was not ready.

She had not yet subjected the notion to a thorough examination. In truth, she was afraid to in case the outcome was not outright rejection. She suspected that, in fact, it might be the opposite: full-on embrace.

She probed, looking for Grant. She found him in the downstairs lobby.

Would you come see me when you have a minute? she sent.

A few minutes later, Grant entered the suite.

"You're feeling better, then," he said, taking a seat next to her. "Well enough to *send* for me as opposed to sending for me."

She smiled. "Fighting fit."

Grant looked at her closely, his eyes narrowing. "You're looking well. Not tired. But there's something different. You're looking a little…" He drew in a sharp breath. "A little older."

"Am I?" She was suddenly aware of how quickly her heart was beating. Racing, almost.

"What's going on? Have you decided to…?"

She shook her head. "Not fully, though I'd be lying if I said I hadn't been thinking about it. Not properly, mind. Only skirting around the edges."

"Why now, when we're so close?"

Milandra glanced down at her hands in her lap. Her fingers

clasped and released, fidgeting. "I am over the Commune." She spoke slowly, uncertain of exactly what to say. "But I'm still tired. Dog tired." She pointed to her head. "In here." She brought her hand down and laid it on her chest. "And in here, where it really counts." She sighed. "How long have I been Keeper?"

Grant didn't hesitate. "Two thousand, six hundred and forty-two years."

"That's three times longer than my predecessor. And I was the Chosen for almost a millennium. I took that station seriously, too. Unlike the present incumbent."

"We were fortunate when you were named Chosen. You have great strength, Milandra."

"Maybe once. It's nearly all used up." She leaned towards Grant and grabbed his hand. "Much of my strength has come from you, my good friend." She squeezed his hand before releasing it.

"That's not true, but nice of you to say so. When will you decide for sure?"

"Not yet. Not until the Great Coming. And if that succeeds, my mantle will pass anyway. It's a burden I'll be glad to shed."

"The incoming Keeper will take precedence?"

"I shall insist on it. The Chosen may also be out of a job. Hmm… I wonder if Simone has realised that yet. That girl keeps her true feelings carefully hidden. Maintain a close watch on her, Grant."

Tom sat in the front passenger seat of the Range Rover. Ceri sat in the back with Dusty. Peter drove back to the main road. The vehicle's weight and the thick tread of its tyres gained it purchase in the snow, even on inclines, and they made slow but steady progress.

"We'll stick to the A roads for now," Peter said. "They're as likely to be as clear of obstructions as the motorways. Perhaps more so. Maybe we can pick up the M6 north of Birmingham."

"Whatever," said Tom. "I want to hear the rest of your story."

"Me, too," said Ceri from the back.

"Okay," said Peter. "I'd got as far as the ancients' craft crashing into the ocean, right?"

Tom grunted.

"Well, then, I'll continue…"

The people of the distant planet with the dying sun determined to build their own craft, following the blueprint left behind by the ancients, but on a much smaller scale for which there were more than ample reserves of the ore. The craft would be manned by fifty people and would be large enough to hold one thousand drones.

And what of drones? The people had long been masters of genetics and had developed the ability to create simple life forms, manipulating DNA to produce whatever characteristics they required. They had already created simple drones to carry out manual labour: mining minerals on the planet's inhospitable surface, for example. Now they created more, imbuing them with strong survival instincts, and the ability and urge to reproduce. The drones were created broadly in the image of the people, but with sloping foreheads, hunched bodies covered in hair—for protection, until they learned how to clothe themselves—and with only the most basic organ to serve as a brain.

Fifty thousand years ago, the craft took off, carrying the hopes of the people with it. The journey was successful and the craft landed safely on Earth on the continent now known as Africa, in the region currently covered by sand and known as the Sahara Desert. It was not a desert then, though. Much wetter, it was covered by grassland and shrubs. It became a desert later following dramatic climate changes. The craft must still be there, buried beneath shifting sands.

The drones were sent out to begin to colonise the planet, while the fifty people who had journeyed with the drones sent back messages from the craft. Messages of joy, of how fertile and virgin and ripe the land was, of how perfect a new home it would make for the people. And the sun; they waxed lyrical about the sun—how bright and yellow and life-giving. They urged the construction of a new craft, one big enough to hold the entire population, and for them to follow without delay.

But the people prevaricated. While they rejoiced that a safe haven had been found to which they could flee when they needed to, many felt that the need had not yet arisen. Some were afraid of change; many were afraid of having to start over again in an alien landscape. Self-interest overruled the common good.

Then, within less than a year, the messages from Earth stopped. Whether the craft's systems had ceased functioning or whether some calamity had befallen the advance party of fifty, nobody knows. Their last message had contained no hint that they were facing some threat or menace. If they died, their experiences and memories were never absorbed into the collective—the distances were too great for them to pass. Naysayers amongst the people seized on the drying-up of the messages as an excuse to delay further, arguing that the haven may not be so safe after all.

Over forty millennia passed. It took an increased awareness of how much their sun had expanded, how red it had become, and a sharp increase in the devastating solar activity, for a sense of urgency to re-establish itself in the people's consciousness. Yet still they were divided and a consensus could not be reached for leaving en masse. Instead, a compromise was agreed. Another craft would be constructed, one large enough to hold ten thousand people—around one eighth of the total population. We are not talking about a large civilisation.

Around five thousand years ago, the new craft landed on Earth. Although the braking systems were effective, the ability to steer a large craft within a planet's gravity was rudimentary and the craft landed in the ocean. But it splashed down safely, creating a small wave that only affected the first few miles of coastland on the nearby land. The ocean was the North Atlantic and the nearest land turned out to be the British Isles.

From the reports of the topography of the planet transmitted by the first craft, the possibility of landing on water had been anticipated. The craft's interior fittings had been moulded to be waterproof if immersed in water and fitted with simple buoyancy aids. They could be used as basic boats, though with little by means of propulsion or directional systems. The ten thousand people ripped out these fittings and took to the seas. A message was first transmitted to the home planet that the craft would have to be abandoned and it was left to its own devices. Presumably, it sank to the bottom of the ocean for it was never seen again.

The majority of the ten thousand made landfall on the coasts of Cornwall, Devon, Dorset and South Wales. Some were swept into the Bay of Biscay and ended up in France. Some landed in southern Ireland. Around three hundred and fifty were lost and their psyches absorbed into the collective.

It quickly became apparent that during the intervening forty-five thousand years the drones had been busy. A sentient, bipedal species had already evolved on Earth before the first craft landed in Africa. That species had been completely eradicated by the drones, partly through interbreeding, mainly by conquest. The drones' instincts for survival and propagation had been firmly instilled at their creation. Those instincts had developed and branched into other areas, for now violence and a talent for destruction lay at the core of the drones' being.

As pre-arranged, the surviving people made for the spot where the majority had gathered. This is the area now known as Salisbury Plain. With the loss of the craft, the people had no way to send messages to their home planet. The distances were too vast and their numbers too few to be able to communicate through Commune. But they still had sufficient numbers to hold dominion over the drones. And the drones' brains, though greatly developed from the basic organ they had been created with, were still sufficiently primitive to permit coercion. Then, at least, though that would not be the case for much longer. The people held a Commune and called the drones of the British Isles to them.

The drones, a ragtag collection of warring tribes, came. The people used them to build a beacon that would transmit to the home planet and guide the remainder of the people to their new home.

That done, the people dispersed and waited for news to come that the rest of their civilisation was following. They knew it would not happen immediately—a new craft large enough to transport seventy thousand people would have to be constructed—but none anticipated that it would take another five thousand years before they received word.

During that time, the drones developed further, the rate of development increasing dramatically in the last three hundred years. The people's ability to influence the drones had been all but lost when the drones' brains grew bigger and more complex, and the drones' numbers increased and kept increasing, swelling until they crowded the surface of the planet like ants on a discarded apple.

While the drones multiplied, the people's numbers diminished. Less than half of the original party of ten thousand remained. The people watched what was happening in the world, dismayed at the violence, the cruelty, the pollution and casual destruction of rainforests, but powerless to intervene. However, they laid plans for the day that they received the message from home. Though they despaired about whether there would be anything left worthy of calling their new homeland, they never gave up hope. And, at last, around three weeks ago, the message came.

The people swung into action.

Peter stopped talking and, for a few moments, there was silence. Tom broke it.

"These drones… They're us, humans, right?"

"Yes," said Peter.

"And you're one of the 'people', right?"

"Yes."

"So you're saying that you came here five thousand years ago. You're claiming to be thousands of years old." Tom's voice was flat, without inflection.

"That's right," said Peter. "I know it's difficult to believe…"

"I believe you," said Ceri.

Tom turned around to look at her.

"How on earth can you say you believe him?" Tom realised that his voice was a little strident, but he could do nothing for now to moderate it. Dusty was looking at him, ears cocked. "He's obviously crazy."

"Then how do you explain what happened at my house?" said Ceri. "Dusty howling, that sense of something inside our heads, taking over our minds. Peter grabbed us and the sensation went away. He saved us from whatever it was."

"I can't explain that," Tom admitted. "But that doesn't prove he's from another planet or that he's ancient. How can that be possible?"

Ceri shrugged. "I don't know, but I still think he's telling the truth."

Tom made a dismissive noise, a 'pfft' sound, and faced front again. He was about to open his mouth to say something else when a movement the other side of the road caught his attention. Peter had obviously seen it, too. He was already slowing down.

Peter brought the car to a halt and got out. Tom and Ceri followed.

"Stay, Dusty," Tom called to the dog, who seemed happy to oblige.

On the other side of the road a man was walking, stumbling, through the snow. Blood poured from a large gash in his forehead, turning his face into a red mask and staining the front of his shirt. He wasn't wearing a coat. He seemed unaware of the three people approaching him until they were right up to him. He stopped and stared at them blankly. He was shivering.

"Hey," said Tom. "Where are you going?"

"Hnggh," said the man and Tom wondered for a moment

whether he had broken his jaw or bitten off his tongue, until he made a coherent sound. "London."

"London?" said Tom. "That's a long way to walk. Especially in this weather." Tom glanced down at the man's feet. They were shod in navy blue plimsolls that were already sodden. *His feet must be frozen*, Tom thought.

Tom glanced at his companions, waiting for them to say something. But Ceri was looking at the man with a twisted, horrified expression on her face. She didn't seem inclined to join in the conversation. Peter was regarding the man intently.

"No," said the man, though nobody had spoken. "Got to."

He wafted his hands in front of his bloody face as if swatting away a bothersome fly, then stumbled forward. Tom went to put his arms across him, afraid he was going to fall.

"NO!" the man screamed in his face and Tom took a step back. "London!"

The man continued stumbling forward, brushing Tom's shoulder as he passed.

"Let him go," said Peter. "There's nothing we can do to stop him."

Ceri started to cry, clutching her hands to her mouth and staring after the man while he shambled away.

"Look at the state of him," said Tom. "He's not going to last an hour out here dressed like that."

"Maybe that will be better," said Peter.

"What are you talking about?"

"I tried to persuade him, but I can't overcome the power of the Commune. He's been called. He has to go to London and there's nothing any of us can do to interfere. Come on, we need to be on our way."

Peter turned and started retracing their steps. Ceri followed him.

Tom looked at the man. He was now twenty yards away.

"Hey!" Tom called after him. "Everyone's dead in London. Why don't you come with us? You'll be warm. We've got food."

The man gave no indication that he had heard. Tom watched him for a few moments longer before, feeling sick, he returned to the Range Rover.

The engine of the Sea King sounded incredibly loud in the silence that had fallen on London. Birds in trees around the base took to the air in alarm.

Wallace spoke to them before they boarded the helicopter.

"They tell me this thing has a range of almost seven hundred miles," he said. "That should be enough to find them and get back here in it. Good luck."

"Thanks," said Bishop. "But luck won't come into it." He looked at Diane. "Still coming?"

She nodded. In one hand, she tightly clutched the bag containing the submachine gun and the pistol.

In a crouch that comes automatically when running towards a stationary helicopter with blades awhirl, Diane and Bishop reached the machine and climbed aboard. Bishop took the pilot's seat and Diane strapped herself into the seat next to him, though she would be no use as a co-pilot—she didn't know the first thing about flying a helicopter.

Bishop donned a pair of earphones with a microphone attached and motioned to her to do the same with the set that lay on the dashboard in front of her. When Bishop spoke, she could hear him clearly above the drone of the engine and clatter of rotors.

The helicopter lurched and jerked into the air. For a sickening moment, Diane was staring directly down at the runway.

"Oops," said Bishop. "I'm a little out of practice. But don't worry, I'll soon get the hang of it."

Diane was glad to hear it. She had only been in a helicopter once before, one that had flown over the Grand Canyon. That had been a completely different-looking machine, with a frontage like a glass bubble. This one had a flatter windshield, more like a car's, divided into five sections. She had been acutely aware that the helicopter in the States flew on only one engine. Although she'd been informed that this one possessed two engines, and they wouldn't be flying over a mile-deep gash in the ground during this flight, she nevertheless felt small and vulnerable.

The chopper smoothed out as it gained height and they began to fly north-west. Diane relaxed a little. The Sea King seemed more dependable to her than the smaller, but quicker machine she'd been in before; more cumbersome, maybe, but steady and reliable: a bumble bee to a dragon fly.

"It's equipped with radar," said Bishop, pointing at a circular screen. "But I don't think we'll need it."

"Why?" asked Diane, her voice sounding tinny to her ears.

"Look where we're headed."

Ahead of them a low bank of cloud was approaching that seemed to stretch away before Diane's eyes, covering the whole country to the north. She lowered her gaze and could see green fields beyond the edge of the city. The green did not extend far. It soon gave way to whiteness.

"The snow's melted in London," said Bishop. "But not further up by the look of it. That should slow them down. If we keep below the cloud, just high enough to avoid trees and pylons, we should even be able to make out tyre tracks."

"That doesn't explain why we won't need to use the radar," said Diane. "There'll be thousands of survivors on the move. How will we know which is Ronstadt?"

"For a start, darling, the radar won't tell us which one is Ronstadt either. But we'll know it's him the moment we spot him."

Diane bit her tongue to keep back the retort she wanted to shoot back at his term of address. Instead, she said, "How will we know it's him?"

"Easy. He'll be the only one going north."

The only sound that intruded above the purr of the Range Rover's engine was Ceri's gentle sobbing. A little under a mile further on, they passed a car on the opposite carriageway that appeared to have skidded off the road and struck a tree. Wisps of steam drifted into the air from the crumpled bonnet.

"He must have been driving that," said Tom.

"He wasn't the first, you know," said Peter quietly.

"Not the first what?"

"Not the first survivor we've passed who's been heading south to London."

"I haven't seen any others."

"I haven't seen them either," said Peter. "But I've sensed them. Since they were called, their minds have been open to me. Two or three passed nearby when we were in the pub. That man was the second we've passed today. The first was a mile or two to the east. That seems to be the limit at which I'm aware of them."

The sound of Ceri's sobbing stopped. Tom turned around to look at her. She had fallen asleep, half-lying across the back seat, her head next to Dusty's basket. The dog was asleep, too.

Tom kept his voice low.

"What did you mean earlier when we were with that man? You said words to the effect that he'd be better off dropping dead than reaching London."

Peter thought for a moment. He, too, kept his voice low.

"Remember the part of my story where we—the ones who'd survived the journey from the craft to land—held a Commune and called the inhabitants of Britain to Salisbury Plain?"

"Ye-es."

"Well, the same thing's happening now. The remaining people of my kind, almost five thousand of them, have held a Commune. That's when everyone's minds join together and can reach out to influence dro… er, humans. We haven't been able to do that for a long time. Too many humans, not enough of us. And the human mind has grown too powerful. The only reason that the Commune has worked now is that the survivors are weak and bewildered and alone. Even so, forcing them to go to London is about the limit of what the Commune could achieve. As the survivors arrive and start congregating, they will become stronger and the ability to influence will lessen further. And so the reason for my comment about that man—I suspect that they are doing something to the survivors when they arrive. Something that will give them complete control over them. Something like…"

"A lobotomy?" Tom's hands clenched in his lap.

"I fear so. They will need to destroy or disable a good portion of the frontal lobes, the areas of your brain that have most developed and that give you the ability to keep us out."

"Nice," said Tom, struggling to keep his voice down. He could feel the earlier stridency trying to return.

"No," said Peter. "It's barbaric. I'd clench my fists too if I were you. But most of my kind won't see it that way. They still regard you as drones."

"And you don't?" Tom forced his hands to relax.

"No," said Peter. "I married a human."

"Megan was human?"

"Yes. She died in my arms of old age. *I* still looked the same as the day we'd first met."

"Did, er, did you have children?"

Peter uttered a low laugh. "I couldn't have given Megan children even if I'd wanted to. She knew that and accepted it."

"You mean, you can't?"

"Not in the same way. My kind seldom reproduces." Peter's tone suggested that he wasn't keen on talking any more about that.

Tom didn't want to push him and make him clam up. He still had other questions.

"So, you can't influence us except during this communion thing?"

"Commune. No, not really. We can give a little nudge now and again. Force someone who's wavering down a particular path without them noticing. But that's about all."

"Have you given me a little nudge?"

"Maybe. A touch. To get you to agree to coming north with

me." Peter shifted a little in his seat.

"What about Ceri?"

Peter glanced over his shoulder to check she was still asleep. When he replied, it was in such a low voice that Tom had to strain to hear.

"Once or twice."

"That's why she so readily agreed to come with us. And earlier when she said she believed you—"

"Shh. Keep your voice down. Look, there's a reason I want Ceri to stick with us that has nothing to do with keeping us company." He glanced back at her again. "When I protected you from the calling at her house, I saw some things in your minds. I didn't look deliberately, you understand, but I couldn't help but see them."

"What sort of things?" Tom felt his hands clenching again and forced his fingers open.

"When we found Ceri, she was preparing to kill herself. She'd have done it that evening."

Tom felt his mouth gape and closed it. "Are you serious?" was all he could think of to say.

"Yes. And when you allowed me into your minds yesterday when we stopped for lunch, I took another peek. That time was on purpose, but I wanted to see if she had pulled back from despair."

"And?"

"The blackness has receded a little, but is still very much present. We need to keep a careful watch on her."

"What about me, Peter? What did you see in my mind?"

"I think you already know the answer to that one. She would have died anyway, you do know that?"

"Lisa, you mean?"

"Your mother."

This time Tom allowed his hands to ball into fists. "That's none of your fucking business."

"Tom, I'm sorry, but—"

"Drop it!"

Tom stared out of the window, at the white fields and glowering sky.

Peter cleared his throat. "There's a village signposted ahead and it's way past lunchtime. Let's go and find somewhere warm and dry to eat."

Tom realised that his stomach agreed with Peter.

"Okay," he said.

When Wallace returned from the airbase, he went to see Milandra in her hotel suite as she'd requested.

"Bishop's on his way," he told her, "in a bright yellow helicopter."

"Alone?"

"Nope. A woman named Diane something is with him."

"Diane Heidler?"

"Yep, that's it."

"Interesting," said Milandra. "I spoke with her at JFK. That woman is conflicted."

"Unless there's something else…?"

"No, George, that's all. Thank you."

She watched him leave and close the door behind him.

Diane Heidler, she mused. *Very interesting indeed.*

When she had spoken to the woman in New York and probed, Milandra had caught a glimpse of something before Diane had slammed the door closed on her. She couldn't be sure what she'd seen, it had been too brief a glimpse, but something told her that there were far worse companions Bishop could have chosen. All depending on your point of view, of course. But from Milandra's point of view, there were far worse companions, of that much she was certain.

Chapter Twenty

The cloud lifted and the temperature plunged. The snow began to form a frozen crust, making driving trickier, even for the Range Rover. It grew deeper as they progressed northwards and had drifted in places, making hedgerows resemble green-crusted meringue. Peter switched to four-wheel drive and found the going easier, though he remained cautious.

The village was only a mile or two off the main road. Peter pulled up in front of the first row of cottages they saw and turned off the engine.

"Where are we?" came a sleepy voice from the back.

Peter turned and smiled at Ceri. "We're stopping for lunch, sleepy head. You hungry?"

"Mm, could eat a horse."

"Might be able to rustle up a tin of ham. Maybe beans."

"Cold?" asked Tom.

Peter considered for a moment. "Well, the roads are getting quite treacherous and it'll be dark in a couple of hours. If they're already after us, the weather conditions will slow them down, too. Maybe we can safely stay here for the night. In which case there's no rush so, hell, why not, let's have hot food for a change."

"Now you're talking," said Tom.

They broke into the first cottage that didn't emit the sweet odour of spoiled pork. The interior smelled dank and unlived-in, but was free of the stench of death. There were no Christmas decorations, suggesting that the occupants had left before the Millennium Bug hit.

Peter brought the camping stove and paraffin lamps in. When Dusty had finished relieving himself in the icy snow, he followed them inside and spent the next thirty minutes exploring every nook and cranny of the cottage.

They found sufficient tinned food in the kitchen to avoid dipping into their own rations. There were even a couple of tins of dog food. In a tiny cupboard beneath the stairs, Ceri discovered a portable gas fire with enough gas in its bottle to keep them warm until morning. With that lit and the flickering glow of the paraffin lamps, the dampness was driven away and the cottage took on a homely, comfortable feel.

When they had finished the last of their tinned, but hot, meal, Peter readied himself for further interrogation. Tom had been shooting him glances while they ate and Peter did not need to read his mind to know that Tom was keen to learn more. He couldn't blame him; Peter would have wanted to know more if he had been in Tom's shoes. He probably would have been as sceptical as Tom, too.

Tom cleared his throat. *Here it comes* thought Peter.

"If you don't mind me asking, how old were you when you came to Earth, Peter?"

"I was one hundred and eighty-three. Little more than a boy."

"And that was five thousand years ago."

"Give or take a century."

Tom snorted.

"How can that be possible?" asked Ceri. "You look about fifty."

"Anatomically, we and humans are almost identical, now that you've lost your pelts, and your foreheads have expanded to house your developed brains, and your jawlines have receded a little. But there are two major differences between us. The first is that we can influence lesser creatures with the power of our minds and can combine with others to exert greater power. The second is that we have the ability to regenerate, using almost any source of energy to revitalise our cells. A sun—the Earth's sun in particular—is especially effective. We lived long lives on our home planet, but nothing as compared to here." Peter shrugged almost apologetically. "It was not considered prudent to impart either ability when we created humans. Instead, you were given the ability to reproduce at will and a keen instinct for survival. Too keen, I have come to believe."

"Can you be killed?" asked Tom.

"Oh yes," said Peter. "If both our heart and brain are destroyed at the same time—through oxygen deprivation, trauma, fire, extreme cold—we die. Thus we have lost over half our number. But if only our heart is damaged, or only our brain, provided we have a power source that can be readily accessed—sunlight, for instance—we can recover. I fought in both world wars. Countless civil wars and conquests. I've been stabbed with dagger, spear and sword. I've been shot six times. But I'm still here."

"What if your head was chopped off?"

Peter thought for a moment. "Yeah, that'd work."

"If what you say is true," said Tom, "how come we don't know about you? How could you keep such abilities hidden from us?"

"It is easy to hide less than five thousand amongst seven billion. Of course, it was not always thus. Humans numbered far less in centuries past. We have not always escaped notice."

"For example?"

"Well, like I said, almost any source of energy will suffice for us to regenerate. In times long past, during never-ending European winters when sunlight and food were in scarce supply, some of my compatriots grew sufficiently desperate for sustenance that they resorted to a ready supply of energy—human blood. Some were caught and killed. Quite effectively, too. Stake through heart and decapitation."

"What, you're bloody Dracula now?"

Peter smiled. "The cloves of garlic and fear of the crucifix are artistic inventions, but fresh human blood *is* remarkably rich in energy. Do not look like that, Tom. I have never indulged and have no intention of starting now."

"Glad to hear it." Tom jumped to his feet. "I'm going to the car to fetch a beer."

"Bring the vodka, too, please," said Ceri. "Listening to this stuff's enough to drive anyone to drink."

Peter watched Tom go, unruffled by his lack of belief. Before too long, Peter suspected that Tom would have every reason to believe everything Peter had told him. Better for Tom that it be delayed as long as possible.

Bishop steered the Sea King on a north-westerly bearing until they were clear of Greater London and passing to the north of Oxford. Then he turned to face west and the Welsh border. While they passed over Gloucester, Bishop's voice came over Diane's earphones.

"Keep your eyes peeled from here on, darling. That's Wales up ahead, where they were last seen. I'm going to meander up the border until we pick up their trail."

His term of address once again grated on Diane, but she kept her thoughts to herself. She stared down at the ground, looking for tracks in the snow. They had already seen a few vehicles driving steadily south; four-by-fours, Bishop informed her, from the easy way they handled the snow. Diane nodded and said nothing; she wasn't really sure what a four-by-four was—she had thought it was a cut of wood. They also saw one or two vehicles that didn't look so steady, weaving across lanes, progressing south in a series of jerking, sliding motions. The sight made Bishop laugh.

They flew low enough for Diane to be able to make out a man who had got out of a car and stood watching them as they flew by. Bishop ignored him: he had been driving south so didn't interest him.

They flew over a river—the Severn, Bishop told her—that didn't seem as wide here as the two motorways she could make out from her vantage point. White, deserted motorways, dotted with the occasional dark knot of abandoned vehicles.

Bishop turned the helicopter and followed a main road towards Hereford. He circled the deserted town and then seemed to choose another road to follow at random. But when Diane glanced at the compass, she saw they were heading due north.

She had almost forgotten the purpose of the journey, was

beginning to enjoy gazing down on the peaceful, white world, when she heard Bishop draw in breath sharply.

"There!" he said.

It took Diane a moment to spot it. Even when she did, it took her a moment longer to realise that it was what had excited her companion. A set of deep parallel lines in the road outside a small village.

"I can see tyre tracks," she said. "But how do you know they're theirs? The tracks could be leading south, *into* the village."

"No. They're on the right side of the road."

"No, they're not. They're on the left."

"I meant the *correct* side of the road. They drive on the left in Britain, darling, like in Australia. Ronstadt has lived here for at least sixty years. Even with the roads to himself, he'd instinctively drive on the left. No, those tracks are heading out of the village. North. But let's make doubly sure."

Diane gasped as the helicopter swooped around and down. Bishop brought it to hover what seemed to her like mere yards above the roofs of the buildings.

"There!" said Bishop, a note of triumph in his voice. "That pub. The tracks start there. From next to that blue car—a Jaguar, I think. Yep. They must have stayed the night in the pub, it snowed and they left this morning. We've got them, baby, we've got them!"

Before Diane had time to object to his latest form of address, her stomach dropped when Bishop brought the Sea King up sharply and turned it to face northwards once more. He set off in the direction of the tyre tracks.

Tom offered Peter a beer, but he refused, seeming content with soft drinks. Ceri once more downed a large slug of spirit, but only sipped at the refill. It was she who asked Peter the next question.

"What's ninety-three multiplied by six hundred and twelve?"

Peter blinked. "I haven't a clue," he said. "Why are you asking?"

"Oh, merely wondering if you're really that much more intelligent than us."

Peter smiled. "Ah, I see. Actually, we're not more intelligent than you, at least not individually. We certainly were once, long ago, but not for centuries. Collectively, however, that's a different matter. You see, we have no use for books or records or computers. Well, not for storing knowledge, in any case. All our knowledge and skills and experiences, and those of our ancestors, are pooled and held by one of our number who is known as the Keeper. If we die, our memories pass to the Keeper and are added to the pool."

"And if the Keeper dies?" asked Ceri.

"They will pass to another of our number who has been selected to succeed to the Keeper. She is called the Chosen." He shrugged. "The titles aren't important. What those holding them do is. They don't have to be female, but tend to be."

"What if the Keeper and this Chosen die at the same time?" asked Tom.

"It has never happened, but it is believed that the knowledge would pass to all who survive the Keeper and Chosen. You see, we are all connected to them by a psychic link. We would not be prepared to receive the weight of the knowledge—it would be of inestimable weight, all those millennia of experiences—and it would come as quite a shock. A debilitating one, I would imagine." He grimaced.

"If you were to drown tomorrow, all your memories would pass to the Keeper?"

"Yes. Her name is Milandra. I last saw her before the Second World War, in Florida. I like her." Peter smiled wryly. "Tom, I wish you'd stop asking questions that involve me dying in some horrible way."

Tom was struggling to keep his scepticism in check, but couldn't help returning Peter's smile.

"You mentioned a beacon," said Ceri. "You said you made the drones build one in Salisbury?"

"We felt it prudent," said Peter. "When we entered this solar system, there had been some debate about which planet was the right one. The ancients' records were a little vague on this point. We obviously chose correctly, but didn't want to run the risk of the rest of our people choosing incorrectly. Since we could no longer send messages home without our craft, a beacon was required. That's why we called the drones to us and set them to work."

"Ha!" said Tom. "I can guess what comes next. You're going to tell us that the beacon is Stonehenge, right?"

Peter nodded. There was no hint of playfulness in his expression. "And it will need to be reconfigured. I suspect that this will be one of the tasks to which your fellow countrymen will be put." Peter looked as though he was about to say more, but then changed his mind. He got up to refill his glass with orange juice.

Tom took the opportunity to relieve his bladder. When he returned to his seat, Peter was talking about his home planet.

"… underground cities and pyramids and domes. It's no coincidence that many of your own ancient civilisations erected similar buildings."

"How far away is this planet?" Tom asked.

"Four hundred and seventy-nine-point-four light years, to be exact."

"And the rest of your people set off, what, two or three weeks ago?"

"Yes. We expect them to arrive in around five months' time. May or June."

"Huh. Almost five hundred light years in six months. Not possible. It's why they're called light years."

"Not possible within the normal laws of physics, no. But such laws don't pertain outside the gravitational pulls of compact solar systems like this one and our home system. How can I explain? You've heard that the universe is expanding?"

"Ye-es," said Tom. "So what?"

"Well, it's true. Mankind has made huge strides in its scientific knowledge of late, though it has barely completed the first hundred yards of a marathon. But it has got this right: the universe *is* expanding and at a much faster rate than the speed of light. The ancients knew how to harness that expansion—to tag onto it. How best to imagine it? You've seen a leaf floating in a swollen stream, perhaps bobbing in slack water? When the current takes it, it's swept away like a swimmer in a riptide. In order to be that leaf we needed knowledge and materials. The knowledge was provided by the ancients in their black tablets; the materials we already possessed. Of course, it wasn't enough merely to know how to join the current; we had to know how to escape it again when we reached where we wanted to be. That knowledge the ancients provided, too."

"Dark energy," said Ceri. "You're harnessing dark energy."

Peter nodded. "Very good, Ceri. I'm impressed."

Tom looked at her and raised his eyebrows.

Ceri shrugged. "I read a lot of science-fiction."

Tom sighed. "Well, I'm no scientist and since we've not ventured further than the Moon, we're hardly in a position to argue. What do you call this planet of yours, anyway?"

"I was wondering when you'd ask. The closest English translation from our native tongue—again, no coincidence—is Earth."

Tom stared hard at Peter, waiting for some sign that he was joking. None came. He glanced at Ceri. She was also staring at Peter, a mixture of wonder and something else, maybe fear, in her expression.

"Okay," said Tom, turning back to face Peter. "That's enough hokum for one day. It's time for the answer to the million-pound question. We've skirted around this long enough. What I and Ceri…" He glanced at her again. She returned the look and nodded. "What I and Ceri want to know is how, and why, the Millennium Bug?"

~ ~ ~

The rate of arrivals at Hillingdon Hospital slowed. Those who had entered the hospital and come back out again joined in the clearance and burning of corpses, and the gathering of food. They moved slowly, but purposefully, pausing in their work only to shamble off to one side to eat or to defecate. They showed no interest in their surroundings or in each other. Though they had not lost the ability to talk, they did not speak except to mutter some guttural reply to a barked command from an overseer.

At night, they slept huddled together in their own filth in rows of houses cleared of the dead.

They had come in sufficient numbers to allow the non-humans to stop doing the dirty work themselves and leave it all to the drones.

"Over six thousand have come from outside the city," Grant informed Milandra upon his return from the short trip to Hillingdon. "Almost seven hundred from London itself. There are still some arriving from Scotland. One man came in from Yorkshire while I was there. He'd cycled all the way." He glanced at Milandra as though expecting a comment. She said nothing.

"Some have died from a disease they caught from corpses," Grant continued. "Kind of ironic, really. It's been contained and we're making them wear surgical masks. Oh, and one was killed when he was attacked by a pack of feral dogs. But they won't be a problem again. We don't want too many of the drones dying on us just yet."

"No," said Milandra. She was making a monumental effort at keeping her face expressionless and to hide any hint that Grant's words were sickening her. "We were able to get the hospital generators working?"

He nodded. "Just as well since we were fast running out of car batteries. The generators have enabled the, er, treatments to progress at pace. And, once treated, the drones work well. Quite single-mindedly, you could say." He laughed, but Milandra sensed that his heart wasn't fully in it.

"How about work on the Grid?"

"There's a team over at the electrical substation at North Hyde. They expect to get it ready to be operational by tomorrow. It's only needed replacement coils and fuses; maintenance stuff, really. Then they'll move on to the stations in the centre—Battersea and a few others. London should be ready to be reilluminated within a couple of weeks. Before we throw the switch, we need to get the drones turning off as many of the millions of appliances that were running when the power went down as we have time for. The more we can catch now, the fewer problems we'll get when the juice goes back on."

"Millions of appliances? Many people were probably dead or dying when the power went out."

"You're right. But many of them would have left the central heating switched on, TVs on standby, that sort of thing."

"Okay. But we can't allow the drones to spend too long on that. They've more important tasks to attend to."

"I know. The Beacon."

"Yes. The Beacon. Send word that a hundred drones are to be placed in confinement. They are to be kept clean and well-fed. Gentle exercise. The fitter they are, the more effective it will be."

"If it's all the same to you, I'll *send* word myself, from here."

Milandra smiled. "Of course. You know, we've lived among them for so long, that on occasions I forget who we are."

"No," said Grant, "you don't. But sometimes I get the feeling that you want to."

The helicopter flew from beneath the cloud cover and the world suddenly seemed sparklingly white to Diane in the pale afternoon sun. The tracks below could now be made out more clearly and Bishop could afford to take the chopper up a little.

"Bit more height up here, little less noise down there," he said. "We can't be far away. I suggest you ready the weapons."

Diane hesitated, trying to examine her feelings. She had not come on this trip expecting it to be a pleasant Sunday afternoon outing, but the finale had seemed distant, something that would involve others, not her. Now that it was close, she tried to see inside herself, seeking the woman who was capable of pointing a gun at another living creature and pulling the trigger. She could not find her, though that didn't mean she wasn't there. When the time arrived, Diane would yank her from the depths, kicking and screaming if needs be, and force her to the fore.

She unbuckled her shoulder straps and reached for the bag on the floor. She hefted it to her lap and rebuckled the straps.

Opening the bag, she withdrew the pistol. The not unpleasant smell of gun oil filled the cabin. Diane fitted a magazine into the handle of the pistol and slid it home with a click. She checked that the safety was on and placed the gun between her knees. Then she withdrew the submachine gun, checked that its safety was on and fitted a magazine. Bishop brought his attention from the tracks in the snow long enough to shoot appreciative, almost hungry, glances at what she was doing.

"Yeah, baby," he said in a breathy whisper. "That's what I like."

Diana held up the loaded Uzi for inspection and he grinned, baring his teeth like a dog. She returned the weapon to the bag, leaving it unzipped, and placed it in the narrow space between them, within his reach.

She picked up the pistol from between her knees and held it loosely in her lap, occasionally lifting it to test its weight, trying to imagine shooting it.

Bishop's voice came over her earphones, low and breathy.

"We are in business, baby. There they are. We're going in."

Diane followed Bishop's gaze and saw a small row of buildings on the edge of a village, surrounded by white fields. The tracks led to the buildings. Where they stopped, she could see the roof of a bronze-coloured vehicle.

Her breath left her in a rush as Bishop brought the helicopter swooping down towards the buildings.

~ ~ ~

Peter appeared lost in thought and Tom was about to repeat his question when at last he spoke.

"Why the Millennium Bug? In some ways, this is the easiest of your questions to answer. In other ways, the hardest. As I've already told you, we never suspected we would be here for so long without the rest of our people following. We did not think the rate at which humans multiply would be quite so rapid. We did not anticipate the degree of complexity and intelligence with which you would evolve. We did not anticipate the level of savagery you would display to other species and to each other."

"Hold on a minute—" started Tom.

"Hisht!" said Ceri. "Let him speak."

"Tell me," said Peter, looking at Tom, "how would humankind have reacted to the appearance in the skies of a vast, black craft? To it landing and seventy thousand aliens disgorging from it? They look like you, but aliens they are and as aliens they would be regarded by man. Would you—and by 'you' I mean humankind in general—would you have extended the hand of friendship? Attempted to communicate with them? To understand them? Or would you have reacted with fear and aggression, greeting my brethren with bullets and missiles? I'm not a betting man, but I know on which side the odds were stacked."

"I would hope with friendship," began Tom, but Ceri shushed him again.

"Nonsense. You know as well as I do that we would shoot first and ask questions later."

"Yes," said Peter. "That is precisely what we thought. We weren't prepared to risk being wrong. Don't forget, we're talking about the entire remnants of our species arriving on this planet. We would be too few, even seventy-five thousand of us, and you too many, to be able to influence your attitude towards us. And we are not a violent species—we would have stood no chance against an armed assault by any one of your major powers, let alone all of them combined. So we agreed on a plan that we would put into action as soon as we received word that the Great Coming was underway."

"A plan?" said Tom.

Peter reached into the bag by his feet, the one in which he had brought the camping stove into the cottage. He withdrew a shiny canister that looked to Tom like a vacuum flask.

"The plan was hatched at the end of the First World War when it became apparent that man's warlike nature would never be moderated. When the Second World War broke out, any doubters among us were silenced. We worked on developing a virus, one genetically programmed to kill all but a very small percentage of humanity. One that would be so virulent and so deadly as to make the great plagues of the past like the Black Death seem like the common cold in comparison. When each new version of the virus was perfected, we each received containers." He turned the canister over and over in his hands. "This was the most recent. This one has not been opened. All the others were and the contents—an organic powder—disseminated throughout the planet."

The room had grown so quiet and tense that the hissing of the paraffin lamps sounded loud to Tom's ears. He could feel his fists clenching once more, his finger nails biting into the flesh of his palms.

"The contents of that canister killed my mother. My girlfriend. My children from school. Ceri's husband. Her son. Everyone we know."

Tom could not tear his gaze away from Peter. For once, Ceri did not tell him to be quiet. Tom felt a rushing of blood in his ears and a white-hot rage surged through him, one he could not remember ever experiencing before. He stood and took a step towards Peter, his fists bunched and rising…

Peter's eyes widened, but they weren't fixed on Tom. As though from far away, Tom heard Ceri gasp and Dusty give a soft bark. He took another half-step towards Peter, but stopped in confusion when a noise intruded on his anger.

The others had already heard it and risen to their feet.

The clatter of an engine and the *whoomp-whoomp-whoomp* of rotors.

Chapter Twenty-One

The bronze vehicle was parked alongside a line of buildings, which looked to Bishop to be old stone cottages. Opposite stood a similar row. He scanned the surrounding area, looking for somewhere to land.

"That road's a little narrow," he said. "The rotor span is too wide. And there are overhead wires. Might have to land in that field behind the cottages."

"Okay," came Diane's voice, sounding a little breathless. "You're the boss."

"Better believe it, darling."

Bishop chuckled. Adrenaline coursed through his body, making him feel vital and invulnerable. If he'd been human, he reckoned he'd have a hard-on and the thought made him chuckle more. If there was one thing besides alcohol that Bishop envied the drones for, it was their sensuality—it looked kind of fun.

He brought the helicopter in lower until he could see the fronts of buildings, staying horizontal so as not to stray near the cables that were strung across the road from the end cottage. He carefully swung the machine around to face the row of cottages and hovered, watching. He daren't go any lower here: the road between the rows of cottages had probably been built in the days before the petrol engine had even been dreamed of, this was such an antiquated country, and there was no room for him to risk landing.

"Look for movement in one of the cottages," he told Diane. "If you see any, shoot."

Diane's voice came back in almost a squawk. "*Shoot*? How am I supposed to shoot from up here?"

"That small window next to you. It slides open."

A blast of icy air whooshed into the cabin when Diane slid the window open.

"Jiminy cricket!" she exclaimed. "It's freezing!"

"Concentrate on those— There! Third one from the left. The

front door's opening."

Bishop swung the Sea King a little to the right, bringing it more side-on to the cottages so that Diane could see them through the side window. The only problem was, his view was now obstructed.

"What's happening?" he demanded.

"Someone's looking out at us. A man. Oh! And a woman."

"Shoot them!"

"I can't—"

"Shoot, you stupid woman!"

He held the helicopter steady, ready for the report of the pistol. It sounded shockingly loud in such a confined space, even with headphones on, and he jumped, making the helicopter jerk. Diane shrieked.

"Did you get them?"

"No. I'm not sure…"

"Oh, for fuck's sake!" Bishop was almost shouting. "Unbuckle and take the controls."

Diane's mouth formed a perfect ring when she swung around to look at him. "Are you crazy? I can't fly this thing!"

"You only have to hold it steady."

"No! I can't—"

"Aaarggh!" Bishop put all of his frustration into the yell. His left hand, which had moved to the buckle of his shoulder straps, went back to the controls. "Fine! We'll have to land."

Peter ran to the front door and swung it open. He knew that he wasn't exercising caution, but had realised the moment he heard the engine that they were undone. He hadn't counted on the pursuit coming by air.

He felt Ceri rush to his side.

"Peter, what are you doing?" she hissed, as though she might be overheard. "They'll see you."

He glanced at her. It might have been the snow-glare spilling through the open doorway, but she looked as pale as milk.

"They know where we are," he said. "They've been following our tracks in the snow."

Ceri's hand clasped over her mouth and her eyes widened.

Peter leaned forward and squeezed her other hand. "Be brave. I need to see what sort of chopper they're in."

He peered out of the doorway. Ceri came and stood alongside him.

A bright, yellow helicopter was hovering about twenty yards in the air directly in front of them. It was turned slightly away and he could see an arm protruding from the open side window. Peter drew in a sharp breath; he hadn't expected it to be so close. They must have been too engrossed in their discussion to have heard it until it was upon them, or the snow had deadened the noise of its approach. Probably both.

Two noises sounded almost at the same time. A dull *thunk* as something thudded into the stonework above their heads, bringing down a light shower of snow and stone dust; a *pop!* like the sound of a champagne cork being drawn in an adjoining room.

Peter grabbed Ceri's arm. "Back inside!"

He pulled the door closed behind them and turned, meeting a dazed-looking Tom coming towards them.

Ceri grabbed Tom, about-turned him and gave him a shove in the back that sent him stumble-walking back from where he'd come. He seemed to shake himself and turned to face them, the stunned expression replaced by one of fear.

"What's happening?" he said. "Is it them?"

Peter nodded. "But they're in a search and rescue chopper." Ceri raised her eyebrows. "I was in the merchant navy," he said, as if that explained everything.

"Um," said Tom. "So…?"

"It's not armed," said Peter. "Though the people on board have guns. They shot at us."

Ceri uttered a low moan and would have fallen if Tom hadn't flung out an arm to steady her. Peter felt a little relieved; at least

Tom had come around enough to perhaps be of some use.

"H-how many people?" asked Tom, his voice as unsteady as Ceri's legs.

"Can't tell. At least two."

"Why don't you speak to them?" said Tom. "You know, inside your head?"

"Too risky," said Peter. "If I probe them, I'll leave myself open. They'll be able to see our plan."

Tom blinked. "We have a plan?" His eyes widened. "Do you have guns in the Range Rover?"

"No guns," said Peter. "Besides, I haven't fired one since 1945."

"But you have a plan?" said Ceri. She seemed to have recovered a little poise and shrugged off Tom's hand after giving it a squeeze.

"It's not much of a plan," said Peter. "For a start, we can't stay here. They'll simply land and walk in. We could barricade ourselves in, but we don't know what sort of firepower they have. A lot more than the popgun they just used, I'll bet. Our only chance lies in outrunning them in the Range Rover."

"We can't outrun a helicopter," said Tom.

"Actually, we probably are faster than a Sea King, but not in this snow, and we can't travel in straight lines like they can," said Peter. "But they must have come from London in that thing and it's unlikely they'll be carrying spare fuel since it would be sort of self-defeating: the more weight they carry, the worse the fuel efficiency. We topped the Range Rover up less than ten miles back so it's well over two-thirds full. So long as we avoid wide open spaces where it can fly alongside us and they can shoot at us from the windows, if we stick to country lanes and trees and steer clear of main roads, we might be able to avoid them for long enough that they have to go in search of more fuel."

There was a moment's pause.

"You're right," said Tom. "It's not much of a plan. They could have friends nearby who they're radioing as we speak to tell them our position. They could land near a car and come after us by road. They could drop hand grenades on us. They could—"

"They could do all that and more," said Peter. "But unless either of you can come up with something better, it's all we've got. And we need to get moving. Now. I can't hear the chopper."

In a whirlwind of activity, they flung on their shoes and coats, Dusty bounding between them and trying to lick Tom and Ceri. Peter extinguished the paraffin lamps and replaced them in the bag, together with the camping stove and the silvery canister. He didn't bother switching off the gas heater.

"Ready?" he said and received two answering nods. "Tom, keep Dusty close. No looking round when we get outside. Concentrate only on reaching the car and getting in."

Peter strode to the front door, the bag clutched tightly under one arm. He opened the door again and looked out. The sound of the helicopter was much fainter, coming from somewhere behind the cottage.

"It sounds like they're landing in the fields at the back," he said. "Come on, then. Let's do it."

In single file, Tom running in a half-crouch so he could keep a tight grip on Dusty's scruff, they hurried to the Range Rover.

Placing the pistol between her knees, Diane gripped the shoulder straps tightly with both hands while Bishop brought the helicopter in to land on a snow-shrouded field. At the last moment, she closed her eyes, then allowed her breath to escape in a deep sigh when he brought it safely to a halt. She drew it in again sharply when she felt the machine lurch a little, but it was merely settling on the grassy tummocks that must have lain beneath the snow.

Without switching off the engine, Bishop flung off the earphones, unbuckled his shoulder straps and grabbed the Uzi from the bag.

"Wait here!" he barked.

She watched him jump lightly to the ground and set off across the field towards the back of the cottages. The snow came over his ankles. He made for the end cottage, the one furthest away from where they'd seen the people, and climbed the wooden fence that bounded the field. She saw him stiffen and crouch, raising the Uzi to shoulder height. Diane tensed, her lips drawing tight.

A large, bronze car appeared beyond the end of the cottage and passed quickly out of sight. Bishop lowered the Uzi and fiddled with it, before turning and retracing his steps over the fence and across the field at a run. He climbed back into the helicopter, his cheeks flushed, dropped the Uzi on top of the bag and replaced his earphones.

"They're making a run for it." He sounded incredulous. "There's three of them. Ronstadt and two drones."

He fumbled at the buckle of the shoulder straps, forcing the clasps home with clicks loud enough for Diane to hear above the whirl and clatter of the helicopter.

"Did you shoot at them?" she asked. Her stomach had suddenly begun to churn.

Bishop glanced at her and she saw something that seemed quite out of place in his expression: embarrassment.

"Tried to, but nothing happened." Diane felt the blood drain from her face, but he didn't seem to notice. "I'd forgotten to remove the safety."

She turned away so he wouldn't see her puff out her cheeks. She felt her stomach lurch, but this time from motion, not anxiety, and watched the ground recede while Bishop took them back up.

It was easy to spot their quarry—it was the only thing moving in the landscape. The vehicle wasn't far away, appearing and disappearing momentarily as it passed between houses at the other end of the village.

Bishop flew towards the car and began to circle, keeping it in sight. But he could not get close to it. The village was too cramped, the houses too close together; too many power lines criss-crossed the air. Clearly, underground cabling was rare in this part of the world.

The vehicle did not move quickly, appearing to be crawling along. It skirted the edge of the village and then took a lane out of the village. The lane was bounded by skeletal trees to one side, and a row of electricity pylons to the other. The pylons stretched away to the horizon, following the line of the lane for as far as the eye could see.

Bishop continued to describe lazy circles with the helicopter, unable to drop lower due to the trees and pylons.

"Shit!" came Bishop's voice through the earphones. "The sly bastard!"

"What?"

"Can't you see what he's doing? He's taking a leisurely drive in the countryside, making sure he sticks to lanes like this one with trees and pylons stopping us getting too close. If he's got plenty of fuel in that four-wheeler then he can probably outlast us."

"How long can we keep this up?"

Bishop glanced at the array of dials in front of him. "Another hour or so, darling. Two and a half tops. We won't be travelling all the way back in this bird, either. We've already used up more than half our juice."

Diane let out a deep breath, hoping she sounded disappointed. She was still uncertain precisely how she felt, still not sure why she'd volunteered to accompany Bishop. Something like an inner voice, some instinct, had suggested it and she had obeyed. When she'd met Bishop, she had immediately noticed the ready sneer into which his mouth could twist and, without needing to probe, felt cruelty wafting off him like cheap aftershave. It had taken her back a little when he readily agreed to her going with him. Now she was starting to feel a certain reluctance to see him get his way.

"I guess we'd better turn back, then," she said. "Get as far as we can and then put her down. We should easily find a car to take us the rest of the way back to London."

"Hmm," said Bishop. "That would be a good idea if I was the sort of guy who gives up easily. But I'm not."

"But what we can do?"

"Well, I can get us close enough for you to blow out their tyres with the Uzi…"

"I told you—I have no idea how to use one of those."

"Yeah. Guessed you'd say that. That leaves only one thing."

"What's that?"

"I'm gonna force them off the road."

The Range Rover trundled along the lane, the snow crunching beneath its tyres as the frozen surface churned. The softer snow beneath presented little challenge to the vehicle's road-holding capabilities at this speed and with the four-wheel drive engaged. All Peter had to do was keep the vehicle in the centre of the narrow lane: at either side, snow had banked into low drifts against the drystone walls that ran both sides of the road.

In the passenger seat, Tom craned his head from this side to that, front to back, while he tracked the progress of the helicopter.

Ceri also kept glancing out. Her colour had returned, but she was very withdrawn. Only Dusty seemed unconcerned, napping happily in his basket.

Peter sensed the attempted probe and slammed the door to his mind closed, but not before he'd caught a glimpse of the invading intelligence.

"That was a mistake," he murmured.

"What's that?" said Tom sharply.

"The pilot of the chopper tried to enter my mind. I kept him out easily enough, but he inadvertently revealed himself, and his companion, to me. His name is Bishop and he hates me—all of us—with a rare passion. He won't stop coming until we're dead."

"We?"

Peter nodded. "I told you it would be dangerous coming with me. But he's also furious that he can't get to us. And furious people often make mistakes."

"Can he invade our minds? Mine and Ceri's?"

"I think he's tried, but the protection I gave you against the

Commune will last for many weeks yet. He won't stand a chance of getting past the barrier. Not on his own."

"You said 'companion'. Are there only two of them?"

"Yes. The other one's a woman. Bishop doesn't fully trust her. Seems she doesn't share his hatred."

If Tom was about to say something further, he was interrupted by a sound from the back seat. A low, rolling noise, like a distant idling motorbike.

Peter glanced in the rear-view mirror to see Ceri shrinking against the door.

"Tom? Peter?" Her voice was small, timid. Scared. "Why is Dusty growling at me?"

A black shape rose into view in the mirror; Peter slammed on the brakes. The Range Rover slewed a little to one side, but its speed had been pedestrian and the tyres found traction, bringing it to a halt.

"Shit," said Peter, twisting round in his seat. Dusty had stepped from his basket and approached Ceri, his hackles raised and the low growl turning into a snarl.

"What the—?" said Tom, also turning in his seat.

Ceri said nothing, but hunched her shoulders and brought her hands up to protect her face from the imminent attack.

Dusty lunged. Ceri screamed.

Bishop recoiled and his head thumped against the back of the seat. He glanced at Diane, who was watching him with concern, though whether he was the object of that concern he wasn't so sure.

"Damn! Damn! Damn!" he muttered.

"What happened?" Her eyes narrowed. "Did you try to probe Ronstadt?"

"He kept me out. I couldn't get anywhere near the drones."

"But you might have given us away!"

Bishop felt his mouth turn down into a sneer of contempt and didn't try to hide it. "Given us away? They know we're here, darling." He snorted. "There was a mind I could enter. They have a dog."

"And?"

"It almost worked, but Ronstadt drove me back out before I could inflict any real damage. Gave the female drone a fright, though."

Diane looked away. Then she shouted.

"They've stopped!"

Bishop glanced out of his side window, down at the lane. Sure enough, the vehicle had halted, skewed a little to one side.

"Now's our chance."

He yanked on the joystick, making the machine turn sharply and Diane scream.

The dog's lips were drawn back, exposing its teeth; teeth that looked long and sharp to Ceri in her heightened state of awareness. Wolf's teeth.

When Dusty lunged at her, Ceri shrieked and felt her bladder let go in a hot rush. Something hard struck her hands where they covered her face. Too late, she tried to bring her knees up to her chest, but the animal was in the way.

But it was no longer growling. It was… whining? And she could feel something warm and wet against her hands. She slowly lowered them. Dusty licked her face instead. She tentatively pushed him away and the animal shuffled backwards, its tail lowered, still whining.

"Are you all right?" It was Peter, peering at her with such a look of concern that she almost laughed.

"Um… yes. I'm fine. What just happened?"

Tom unbuckled his seat belt and knelt on the passenger seat so he could stroke the dog. Dusty licked his hands.

"He's trembling like a leaf," said Tom.

"It wasn't Dusty's fault," said Peter. "Bishop entered his mind and made him attack you, Ceri. I should have anticipated that. I'm sorry."

"You made him stop?" Ceri realised that she, too, was trembling.

Peter nodded. "He's further away. My closer proximity trumped him. I've given Dusty protection. It's not as strong as yours, but it's enough to stop that happening again."

"All the same," said Ceri, "I'd like to swap places with Tom." She looked at Tom, who nodded.

"No problem. I want to calm him down."

Tom squeezed himself through the gap between the front seats and helped Ceri to squeeze into the front.

"Mind where you're putting your hands," she said, unable to keep a note of shame from her voice. "I had a little, er, accident."

"Don't worry about it," said Tom. "Once we've shaken them off, we'll stop so you can change."

"Speaking of which…" said Peter, turning around to peer through the windscreen. "Ah, fuck!"

Ceri followed his gaze. The helicopter was lower, barely clearing the tops of the trees, and headed straight for them. The pylons to the other side prevented it from coming down the middle of the lane, but it was being flown as though the pilot didn't much care if the rotors hit wood or metal so long as it also hit the Range Rover.

"Fasten your seat belts!" yelled Peter, slamming the vehicle into second gear and gunning the accelerator.

The wheels spun, throwing up snow, but then gripped and Ceri was pressed back against the passenger seat. She fumbled for the belt and managed to do it up while the Range Rover shot forward.

The engine whined as Peter fought the steering wheel to control a slide. A drystone wall abruptly loomed in her vision, looking sturdy and way too close.

It disappeared when Peter corrected the slide and the Range Rover surged forwards again.

Ceri peered through the windscreen. The helicopter hadn't

come any lower, couldn't because of the trees, but it was still making directly for them. As it drew nearer, the front end dipped slightly, the top branches of the trees swaying in the turbulence. Ceri was certain that the pilot was going to fly it into the Range Rover and closed her eyes.

"Shit! That was close!" Tom's voice sounded high-pitched behind her.

She opened her eyes. The helicopter had gone. She craned her head back to look out of the rear window, past Tom's wide-eyed, pale face.

The helicopter looked like some giant yellow bug as it skimmed the trees, before lurching upwards again when it seemed its rotors must snarl in the branches.

Diane's fingers felt tingly, she had gripped her shoulder straps so tightly.

While the Sea King rose sluggishly, she turned on Bishop. He gripped the joystick in a white-knuckled grasp; his jaw was set firmly and he looked as though he was willing the machine to gain height.

"You freaking nutjob!" she yelled. "You almost killed us!"

"Shut up." Bishop's voice was low. She almost couldn't hear him above the clatter of the straining engines. He didn't look at her.

The helicopter had risen higher than the pylons and Bishop levelled it off. Immediately, he started to bring it back around to pursue Ronstadt.

Diane's inner thighs ached and she felt something hard clutched between her knees. She had forgotten about the pistol. With a shaking hand, she grabbed it and turned it on Bishop.

"Back off!" she said. "Bishop, goddamn it, back off! I'll use this."

Now he did look at her, his lips curled into a snarl. His left hand shot out and knocked the pistol from her grasp. In the same movement, his hand rose and struck her nose with the knuckles.

Pain flared hot and white.

Diane brought her hand to her face and felt the warm flow of blood. Hot, stinging tears flowed from her eyes to mix with it.

"Bastard!" she muttered.

Bishop returned both his hands to the controls and his attention to the vehicle. Having completed the chopper's turn, the bronze roof was visible below and directly in front of them once more.

"A bit of advice, darling," said Bishop. "*Never* tell me what to do again."

"Fuck you."

Bishop laughed. "In your dreams, darling. In your dreams."

The shooting pain in her nose slackened to a dull throbbing ache. She tentatively explored it with her fingers and winced when she felt something jiggle that she was sure hadn't moved before.

Bishop gave a low whistle. "They're approaching a bend."

She looked down. It was true. The lane turned sharply to the left about fifty yards ahead of the vehicle. The electricity pylons continued in a straight line, marching across fields towards a distant town. The line of trees on the left side of the lane continued, following the bend, but only the wall separated the lane from the fields on the opposite side.

"They're going too fast," Diane murmured.

"Yes," agreed Bishop. "They are."

Bishop turned the Sea King a little to the left, choosing a course that would take it ahead of Ronstadt, over the trees towards the open fields beyond the bend.

Diane held her breath as she watched the vehicle's brake lights flare. Too late. It spun in a half-circle and slammed into the snow piled in front of the wall, the driver's side of the vehicle taking the force of the impact. The wall toppled, dislodging puffs of snow, and the vehicle came to a halt.

"Whoo-hoo!" Bishop thumped the roof of the cabin with his left fist. "Got 'em." He thumped the roof again. And again.

In one swift movement that might have surprised Bishop had he been watching her, Diane unbuckled her shoulder straps and leaned into the gap left by Bishop's raised arm. With all her force, she brought her right elbow crashing down into his groin.

Uttering a high-pitched shriek, his face clenched in agony, Bishop brought both hands down to clutch at his groin. Diane swayed sharply out of his reach.

The helicopter spun out of control towards the trees.

He may have passed out, but only for a matter of seconds. Tom became aware of two things: a dull ache in his right shoulder and a wet tongue licking his face.

"Dusty? You okay? Good dog." He reached sideways to ruffle the dog's ears and drew in his breath at the pain in his shoulder.

Peter was shaking his head as if to clear it. Ceri was glancing desperately from one man to the other.

"Thank God you're all right," she said. "Yes? Tom?"

"I think so. Done something to my shoulder, but otherwise seem to be in one piece."

"Peter?"

"Hng…" muttered Peter and, for one horrible moment, Tom had a wild idea that Peter's brain had been knocked out by the impact. "Bashed my head a little, but I'll be okay."

The Range Rover had stalled in the crash, but the world was not as silent as it should have been. A high-pitched, straining scream enveloped them.

"Quick," said Ceri. "We need to get out. We're sitting ducks."

She opened the passenger door and icy air came in, waking Tom fully. He felt behind him with his non-injured arm and tried to open the door. It wouldn't budge. He half-turned and realised why. Immediately the other side of his window lay a mound of compacted snow and a leaning stone wall. They would all have to get out Ceri's side of the car.

He sidled across the rear seat, shooing Dusty out of the way.

The dog's basket had ended up on one end on the back seat. Tom flipped it into the rear compartment and opened the door. The scream of the helicopter sounded very near and Tom felt a strong urge to duck. He glanced wildly around.

Ceri had also got out and was crouching, staring behind Tom with a look of abject terror on her face. Tom turned to follow her gaze, also dropping instinctively into a crouch.

A life-jacket yellow, screaming helicopter came hurtling over their heads. As it passed, the engines cut out and it completed the short remainder of its journey in an eerie, near-silence, only broken by the faint whirr of its still-rotating blades.

In the field beyond the wall, in the corner formed by the sharp left turn of the lane, a bunch of trees formed a small copse. The leafless branches snapped and splintered when the stricken Sea King plummeted into them. It came to rest about twenty feet above the ground, lurching at a steep angle head-first towards the ground like a gigantic sick canary. The trees creaked and complained, but bore their burden.

Tom let out his breath in a rush and turned to Ceri. She looked back at him wild-eyed. They both turned at a sound from the front of the Range Rover and they stood, hurrying forward to help Peter from the vehicle.

He looked groggy and a lump was rising on the side of his head the size of half an orange, but he shook off their concern.

"Really, I'm fine," he said. "It'll take more than a bump to the head to keep me down."

Together, they turned towards the helicopter and, together, froze.

The side window of the helicopter that faced towards them had been slid open. The head and arms of a man poked out, but not far as though he was constrained somehow. Tom did not wonder twice about that. He was more concerned with what the man was holding in his hands.

A short, mean-looking gun, with a long hand grip and a large magazine. Some sort of machine gun, perhaps. The man pointed it directly at them and his mouth split into a wide grin. Even from the distance of thirty or so yards that separated them, Tom could clearly see the man's finger move as he pressed the trigger.

Without the shoulder straps hugging her to the seat, Diane was thrown about and buffeted during the helicopter's crazed fall from the sky. She ended up in the footwell, which probably saved her from serious injury when the descent abruptly ended in the trees.

A little shakily, dazed and bruised, she rose to her feet. An acrid smell hit her nostrils: some sort of gasoline. She clutched the back of the seat to avoid falling into the windshield due to the sharp angle at which the Sea King had come to rest. She looked at Bishop.

Apart from a cut to his head, which he didn't seem to be aware of, Bishop appeared unhurt and fully recovered from the blow she had administered to the groin. He had opened the side window and was leaning out as far as his shoulder straps allowed. Diane leaned back a little to see what he was doing. With a start, she saw that he had somehow retrieved the Uzi and was pointing it at the small group of people that stood outside the bronze car a little way off.

Still gripping the seat, Diane crouched and felt around for the pistol. Instead, her hands closed around the bag.

Inside, amongst the jumble of spare magazines, she found a small knife. She took it and squeezed around her seat, wanting to be near the rear door behind Bishop. She heard an empty click and Bishop started to curse. With a grunt of effort, she slid the door open and glanced down. Through splintered branches, she could see the snowy ground, perhaps twenty feet below her.

"Where are you, bitch?"

Diane turned back to Bishop and stepped to the far side of the drunken craft to stay out of his reach. She moved within his sight. He was fumbling with one hand at the clasp of his shoulder straps, but it was clearly refusing to release. In the other hand, he still clutched the Uzi.

When she moved into his line of sight, Bishop flung the gun at her. She ducked and it clattered to the floor.

"You did something to it, didn't you?" he spat. Not waiting for an answer, he tried to reach behind him, grunting with effort, but he was held too tightly by the shoulder straps. "Can't reach my pistol…" Using both hands, he scrabbled desperately at the clasp.

The smell of aviation fuel grew stronger.

"Well," Diane said, "I told you I didn't know anything about submachine guns and Uzis in particular. That might have been a teensy white lie. You see, I know enough about them to know what parts to remove to prevent them from firing."

"You're dead," Bishop said.

"Blame yourself, *darling*," said Diane. "After all, you would leave me in charge of the weapons while you went off to stuff your face."

"Dead. Dead. Dead." It sounded like a mantra.

"You have to free yourself from those straps first," said Diane. "Someone snapped them on too violently, methinks." She held up the knife for Bishop to see.

Bishop stopped struggling and a sly look came over his face. "Okay," he said. "Here's the deal. You cut me free and I won't kill you. I won't even mess you up. And, man, if you knew how much I want to slice you into little bits…"

"You're not very good at making deals, are you?" said Diane. "But…" She shrugged and stepped towards him.

Bishop's eyes lit up and a smug sneer appeared on his lips.

Diane stopped inches beyond his reach. She opened her fingers and let the knife fall to the floor.

In your dreams, darling. In your dreams she sent.

She turned and stepped to the open door. As she arrived at the opening, the leaking aviation fuel, dripping onto hot engine casing from a tank pierced by a snapped tree branch, reached its flash point. The fuel tanks, a quarter full, exploded with a dull *Hump!*

Diane was flung through the doorway and into the next tree.

The last thing she heard before her world went black was the sound of Bishop screaming.

In the penthouse suite of a hotel a mile or so outside Heathrow Airport, Milandra stopped talking in mid-sentence and clutched at her blouse. While Grant rushed to her side, she gave a short sigh.

"It's Troy Bishop," she said. "Dead."

She allowed the man's memories and experiences to flow through her. Some of them made her shudder. At one point, she cried out.

Grant knelt by her side and grasped her hand, offering such support as he could. When it was over, she sighed again, heavily, and patted his hand.

"Thank you," she said. "That wasn't pleasant."

"Ronstadt?" Grant asked.

She shook her head.

"Heidler?"

"Only Bishop."

Grant looked at her closely. "Shall we send someone else after Ronstadt?"

"I think that there's no need to waste any more of our people. Let's not let anything divert us from the real task. Preparing for the Great Coming."

Grant nodded slowly. "I think you're right. Maybe we should keep Bishop's passing to ourselves. For now."

"Good idea," said Milandra and smiled. It felt like the first genuine smile to touch her face in days. It felt good. "We've a trip to make ready for. A pilgrimage, of sorts. We're going to Salisbury."

A few days later, a battered, bronze Range Rover, a large dent running down the driver's side, crossed the border from England into Scotland.

In the front sat two men. In the back, two women with, between them, a black, sleeping dog.

One of the women slept, too. The cuts and bruises covering her face had faded and healed to faint purple blushes and pocked scars. Within a day or two more these, too, would fade. The broken bones had already started to knit together, even with only the most rudimentary splints to keep them in place. Her breathing had become more regular, the tortured wheezing of the punctured lung a memory of the day before. She had only woken twice, to eat painfully but extravagantly. She had not spoken, but expressed gratitude for the food with her eyes, before slipping back into unconsciousness.

The young man sitting in the front passenger seat was fiddling with his wristwatch. With a large grin that managed to appear both happy and tinged with sadness, he turned to the conscious woman behind him.

"If the date on my watch is correct," he said, "it's January first. Happy New Year, Ceri!"

The woman smiled, but her face, too, managed to convey gladness and sorrow in the same expression.

"Happy New Year, Tom," she said.

Tom turned to the man driving. All trace of the lump on the side of the man's head had gone.

"Happy New Year, Peter," said Tom.

The man smiled, but said nothing.

The Range Rover headed towards the Highlands, driving through an empty, silent land.

About the Author

Sam Kates lives in South Wales, UK, with a family, a computer and *way* too many books. To connect on social media:

Website: samkates.co.uk
Facebook: www.facebook.com/writersamkates
Twitter: @_Sam_Kates_
E-mail: samkates@samkates.co.uk

Note

Please consider leaving a review—reviews can be of immeasurable help to authors in gaining visibility and running promotions.

Thank you for purchasing and reading this book.

To sign up for news of releases and special offers, most of which are only available to subscribers (no spam, promise): http://www.samkates.co.uk/stay-in-touch/

– Sam Kates
December 2013

Printed in Great Britain
by Amazon

33550748R00177